Raised by parents with a passion for amateur dramatics, Cheshire-born Christopher Holliday was enthralled by theatre from an early age. His enjoyment in make-believe was furthered by a passion for exotic gardens in adulthood. He first discovered the Lake District as a place to live during a number of peculiar years in hotel management where he felt somewhat out of place.

His life changed when he settled permanently in Grange-over-Sands, where he was inspired to create a Mediterranean garden. Re-training as a garden designer, he also became a freelance garden writer. He once spent two days in the rain being filmed for five minutes of airtime on BBC's Gardeners' World. His love of borderline exotic plants was demonstrated in *Sharp Gardening* (Garden Media Guild Practical book of the year, 2005), and his enthusiasm for historic houses can be found in *Houses of the Lake District*, both published by Frances Lincoln.

He has since lived in Grange-over-Sands, six miles from the southern tip of Windermere, for most of his adult life, and shares similar interests as his characters.

Books by Christopher Holliday
Sharp Gardening
Houses of the Lake District

Wilde about Windermere

Christopher Morrison

Christopher Holliday

Wilde about Windermere

Vanguard Press

A CIP catalogue record for this title is available from the British Library.

ISBN 978-1-80016-527-4

Vanguard Press is an imprint of
Pegasus Elliot Mackenzie Publishers Ltd.
www.pegasuspublishers.com

First Published in 2024
Vanguard Press
Sheraton House Castle Park
Cambridge England

Printed & Bound in Great Britain

For R.A.H. with gratitude

I owe a particular debt to R.A.H. who has made so many valuable suggestions. I would like to take this opportunity to thank my editor Judy Heckstall-Smith, and Colin Shelbourn for creating the map.

"The general was essentially a man of peace, except in his domestic life."

Lady Bracknell
The Importance of Being Earnest
Oscar Wilde

The Persons of the Play

John Worthing, J.P.

Algernon Moncrieff

Rev. Canon Chasuble, D.D.

Merriman, Butler

Lane, manservant

Lady Bracknell

Hon. Gwendolen Fairfax

Cecily Cardew

Miss Prism, Governess

The Scenes of the Play

Act One Algernon Moncrieff's Flat in Half-Moon Street, W.

Act Two The Garden at the manor House, Woolton

Act Three Drawing-room at the Manor House, Woolton

Time: The Present.

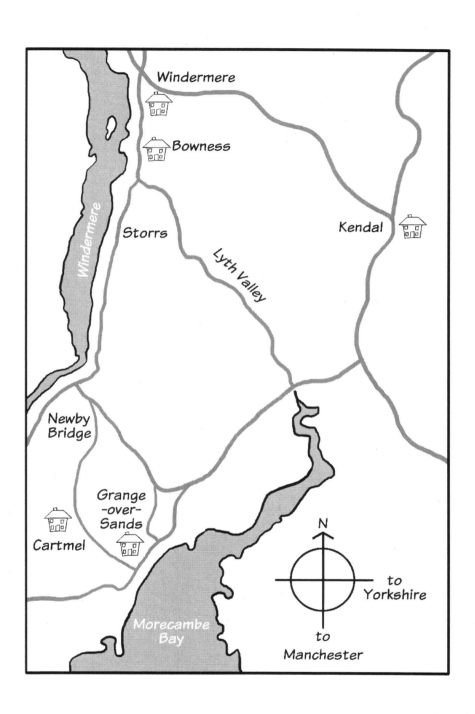

Act One

2010

Chapter One

The Westmorland Amateur Festival Theatre was not what it had been. Known locally as WAFT, its annual productions were unforgettable for all the wrong reasons, and while no one would have argued about its status as an amateur group, Westmorland was no longer on the map. In addition, the company had no access to a theatre, and the idea of a "festival" as a celebration had long lost its sparkle. Moreover, the unhappy few who witnessed a performance through to the end emerged with a fund of dinner-party stories. In short, it was an undistinguished company taking itself too seriously.

According to the membership, Matthew Hunter and Eleanor Vane had played the leading roles for far too long, having slid so seamlessly into the places of Eleanor's parents, the festival's founder members. Now regarded as a veteran player, Matthew had unwittingly placed himself in the position of wronged husband whenever he was on stage with Eleanor. This year, however, heralded some changes. They began with Eleanor's unsolicited phone call; even more unwelcome so early in the day one cold, barely light morning at the beginning of January. Tom had gone out on an errand, so Matthew was begrudgingly clearing up after breakfast and wanted to get on with his day. They always closed Langdales, the country house B and B they ran together, as soon as they could after the New Year had chimed in. After all, this was supposed to be a special time for them both.

'Something dreadful has happened,' she announced. No preliminaries, he noted, but she was often like that, especially after they had not been speaking for some time. He let her wait. 'You're very quiet?'

'Don't I have good reason to be? Come on, then. Out with it.' He pressed the phone closer to his ear.

'I won't be playing Lady Bracknell.' Eleanor spoke authoritatively – as if she was still addressing the board – although she had never done a stroke of work in her life.

'That's a pity,' said Matthew, smiling to himself because she was not getting her own way for once. The play that he had disassociated himself from selecting, because he had flounced off the committee, was Wilde's *The Importance of Being Earnest*. 'The role you've been waiting for all these years?'

'Less of the *"all these"* if you don't mind!'

'So you won't get to say *"A handbag?"* in stentorian tones?'

'Does it sound like it?'

Matthew sighed. Perhaps, because he had known her so long, she must have felt she could be off-hand; rude, even.

'What's going on, Eleanor?'

'Nothing is going on, as you put it.'

'Then what seems to be the problem?'

She needed no further invitation. 'You know how you and Tom kept telling me to take it easy after–'

'Let me stop you right there, Eleanor. What we actually said was for you *not* to give up control of the festival entirely–'

'Could *you* have gone on with it, had you been in my position?'

He hesitated. 'You mean if I'd had to go through–'

'Exactly.'

'No, I don't suppose I could have,' he agreed reluctantly, glancing at the empty cafetière in front of him.

Eleanor warmed to her theme with evident enjoyment. 'Once I'd informed her I was taking a back seat, I felt it was only fair that Felicity upped her sponsorship.'

'And? I'm on the edge of my seat,' said Matthew, although he was standing.

'I seem to have been double-crossed,' said Eleanor, sounding more than ready to take on Felicity. He formed a picture of her wide mouth, which she lost no opportunity to use to the full.

He moved over to the kitchen sink and frowned at the garden, looking as if it had been re-drawn in charcoal. 'Didn't I tell you not to make her Festival President? You've always blown hot and cold with Felicity, and now look what's happened.'

'I had hoped only to blow cold,' laughed Eleanor, mirthlessly. 'But she seems to think that just because she's agreed to sponsoring this year's festival...'

Dismayed by the unusually hard edge to her voice, he asked, 'Why are you being like this?'

'I'm sorry, Matthew. I'm tired. I didn't sleep well last night.'

'Surely there's more to it than that?'

'I'm still drained after the divorce.'

'Ah! Then in that case you need to take better care of yourself.'

'Don't worry about me. I'm *fine*, apart from finding out there's a hell of a lot wrong with the festival.'

'You know best. May I ask in what way?'

'Felicity thinking that she has *total* control over the new director, for a start.'

'Blake Benedict's replacement?'

Eleanor's tone could never be described as soft; this morning she was putting its harder qualities to good use. 'Yes, of course, the replacement. How was I to know that Blake would go and have an accident just when I'd handed over everything to Felicity?'

Trying to sound involved – or at least interested – because it was clear that she was set to launch into a long rigmarole, Matthew murmured, 'Do we know anything about this new man?'

'I'm just coming to that. The thing is, I can hardly bring myself to tell you...' Was that a suppressed sob that he could hear? 'My big news is that Felicity has seen fit to allow *him* to play Lady Bracknell.'

Visualising her arched eyebrow and tilted chin, he gasped. 'Sort of opposite to a "trouser role?" So, you really won't be playing Lady Bracknell? I thought you were joking.'

There was an even harder edge to her voice. 'Matthew, this is no laughing matter.'

'Sorry. But you've had your eye on that role for years. How could she?'

'Quite easily, it appears. You can imagine my thoughts,' she said, her tone dead-pan.

'Murderous? Still, it *is* rather funny, in a way.'

'I fail to see how.'

He turned round and glanced at the debris on the kitchen table. 'This is what comes of delegating.'

'Hardly. I just inform people what they ought to be doing.'

'More like abdication of responsibility, then?'

'Which, all things considered, *under the circumstances*, I think I had a right to do this year.'

He murmured something non-committal.

'Well, at least you see things from my point of view.'

'Would I dare step out of line?'

'Not if you know what's good for you.' She paused. 'Can you imagine the reviews?'

'*"What a drag!"*' Matthew chuckled, then became serious. 'But do they really need to alter the dynamics in *The Importance of Being Earnest* quite so dramatically? Can't you reverse the decision?'

'Not since I've given up being president and chairman.'

Matthew tutted, and sat down at the table. It was evidently not going to be a short call. 'Well, you must have something in mind, otherwise you wouldn't be phoning me.'

'Ah, Matthew – always the realist. Well, I can tell you what I *won't* be doing, and that's accommodating this new director when he comes to meet the stage manager and wardrobe.'

Realising her intentions, he swallowed. 'When?'

'We don't have much time. Next week.'

'So soon?' he asked, wondering how he could head her off.

'It will be a short visit, I can assure you,' she replied. 'He won't want to stay long up here in early January, that's for sure.'

'Can't you act nice for twenty-four hours before getting rid of him?' asked Matthew, although recognising this would be something of a stretch.

'After what he has been more than happy to go along with?' she scoffed. 'Certainly not. Anyway, I don't *act*. I merely play *me*, which could have serious consequences. There's no way I can look that man in the face without wanting to *hit* him.'

'I see,' said Matthew, placing the dishes nearest to him on a tray. 'You're asking us a favour, even though you have five bedrooms?'

'Good. You've cottoned on so quickly.'

He picked up his empty coffee cup, hoping that it might have been magically refilled for him, and then replaced it on its saucer. 'And now for the big question. Why us?'

'Because you and Tom are such good hosts, darling, and you're in the business.'

'Oh, really, Eleanor, you are the absolute limit. Just because we run a B and B. You know we close in January, so we can't even make up an excuse. I feel cornered.'

'Calm down, Matthew,' she purred. 'Not just any old B and B. Langdales is so wonderfully bijou.'

'You mean boutique?'

'What's the difference? You must tell me some time. He couldn't ask for a nicer place to stay than with you at Langdales. So can we say that it's settled?'

'Aren't you forgetting something?'

'What?'

'You realise I'll need to consult Tom? We *are* supposed to be closed, you know.'

'That won't take you long. You know how easy-going he is.'

'Implying I'm not?'

'Look, Matthew, I've known you far too long to start arguing with you. In spite of grabbing *my* role, this director does appear to be very nice, actually. You'll adore him! Quite the charmer and *very* handsome. For his age.'

Matthew felt a glimmer of curiosity. 'Really. You think that might make him a good guest? Well, if he's as decorative as you claim, how old is he?'

'About the same as you.'

'Oh,' said Matthew, losing interest. 'You know I prefer younger–'

'But he's not as distinguished-looking as you.'

'Don't think you can get round me so easily. He's well-established?'

'Sort of.'

'Will I have heard of him?'

'You might have done,' she replied, airily. 'He's been on television.'

He finished piling the dishes onto the tray. 'You know Tom and I are too busy to watch.'

'As you never tire of telling me. Does *Jubilee Way* mean anything to you?'

'Of course not.' This was not strictly true, but Matthew invariably shied away from anything when he realised that it was favoured by a mass audience.

'So you won't have heard of Rupert Hammond?'

Matthew held the phone away and put his hand to his mouth as if he had been struck. Rupert Hammond had been his first romance: Eleanor was reminding him of years that he had hoped were long behind him. Just the thought of him was enough to make his stomach tighten. If this was true, things were serious. He knew she would be waiting for some response, but when Matthew realised that his nails were cutting into his palms, he knew he needed time to think. Momentous news required quiet contemplation. Realising that he could only give Eleanor half his attention from now on, he must end the call.

'As a matter of fact, I haven't,' he lied. 'Listen, Eleanor, I'll have a word with Tom, and get back to you. If we can't accommodate, perhaps Felicity might help you out? After all, she's not exactly living in a cottage.' He paused. 'Tell me, how could this happen?'

'Felicity is always looking for ways to undermine me, as you well know. Apparently, when they got talking, she found out that Rupert Hammond has been appearing as a pantomime dame of late, on the back of *Jubilee Way*, and one thing has led to another.'

'But the pantomime season is still going at full throttle, surely?'

'It isn't fair of you to expect me to have every detail at my fingertips. Don't forget he's news to me, as well.' She paused, as if mulling things over. 'Clever tactics – I'll give Felicity that – but I'm seething. Lady Bracknell has two great opportunities for practically unrivalled scene-stealing, leaving this Hammond creature more than enough time to direct.' She paused for breath.

Matthew attempted a light-hearted approach. 'And the very idea of anyone stealing a scene from you would be insupportable?'

'You did, I seem to remember.'

'Once was enough.'

'Seriously, though, there's a possibility that I won't have a scene to be stolen.'

'Really?'

'Yes, because I intend to be conspicuously absent. I refuse to come trudging on as Miss Prism.'

'Perhaps you could come skipping on, then?' He paused. 'These grand protestations are all very well, but you'll be making an appearance somewhere, I have no doubt.'

'Possibly.' Then her final bombshell exploded. 'By the way, you won't get to play Jack, either.'

Matthew's throat dried instantly. '*What?* But I *always* play the leading roles. What the hell is going on?'

'Steady on. Hammond's asked for a broad overview of our membership. He thinks you're too old.'

'Of all the cheek! But I suppose he's right. The lead is supposed to be mid-thirties, wouldn't you say?'

'Late twenties, from memory. Don't forget you're knocking fifty, Matthew. Canon Chasuble is more in line with your increasing seniority.'

'I don't do supporting roles,' he snapped.

'Perhaps we should both take a back seat this festival?'

'There must be a way round this!'

She allowed herself a discreet chuckle. 'I always felt that any scheme involving you as the young lead was doomed.'

'How kind of you to have kept it to yourself.' This elicited no response. 'Perhaps Tom could play Jack?'

Eleanor appeared to jump at this. 'He'll not see thirty again, but he *is* more the right age. Why not make that the perfect opening when you broach the subject?'

'Put Hammond up for the night when we are closed, but persuade Tom that he can impress him with his eager charm and youthful good looks?'

'Another lightning observation.'

'A dangerous one.'

'You have nothing to fear with Tom.'

Matthew hesitated a moment before coming out with his next question. 'Is Hammond straight, do you think?'

'Having spoken to him on the phone,' she replied, 'Felicity says that there can be little anxiety on that score, which is why she felt he'd be perfect for Lady Bracknell.'

'More perfect than you? I don't think so!' Eleanor demurred, but he could tell she was pleased. 'That might just have a bearing on Tom influencing him. He's bound to like Tom.'

'As long as Tom doesn't make him feel his years. I've seen a photograph of him. He has the face of an ageing cherub and suspiciously blond curls for a man pushing fifty. And he couldn't be more camp in *Jubilee Way* if he tried.'

'Yes, but–'

'Don't leave it too long before you get back to me. Goodbye, darling.'

'You do realise we're closed?'

But she had already hung up. Matthew shook his head. Not only was he not going to play the lead, he had to face the prospect of being reunited with Rupert Hammond.

He had last seen Rupert when he was in his mid-twenties; things between them had not ended well. If Rupert really was coming up to the Lake District, Matthew did not want to fall for him again.

As a good-looking, not over-tall, nineteen-year-old who looked younger, Rupert had been cast in five or six children's films in quick succession. However, as the years went by, just when his future seemed secure, the film company registered that Rupert's private life was not as wholesome as the films in which he was appearing. They had no qualms about releasing him from his contract.

Rupert had been the most vivid attachment of Matthew's life. When they were both at school together, Rupert, at seventeen, and a year younger than Matthew, had been the most attractive boy in the school, with his elfin face and cheeky expression. What a life force he had been. God only knew what he had been up to. But for twenty-five years, Matthew had forced himself to shut out anything to do with Rupert. One question continued to haunt him, however: if things had been different, could they have been happy together? Neither had spoken to the other since that last morning. Realising that his emotional life since then had been a failure, Matthew had never recovered from it.

In fact, it was Matthew's handling of the unravelled affair with Rupert that he counted as his greatest misdemeanour. Years later, he felt he had not atoned for having lost control, and losing Rupert all on the same day. The memory of it still rankled. Recognising that Tom must never know about his relationship with Rupert, or how it had ended, Matthew made a decision.

Nothing of their history must be revealed to anyone; he must pretend to know nothing of Rupert and if anything did get out, he would have to make light of it, even if he had to lie. Priding himself on his acting skills – such as they were – he congratulated himself for not revealing anything to Eleanor. What a relief that she had phoned him; he hadn't found it necessary to adopt a fixed expression, for she would have been sure to have picked up on any facial irregularities instantly. Regarding Tom, Matthew had always given the impression that Tom was the love of his life.

He was left labouring under the impression that to declare anything about Rupert was unthinkable. Matthew also realised that if Tom found out about their affair, he might begin to question whether things might be rekindled between them. There were far too many imponderables; far too much at stake for Matthew to declare anything. Dreading the reappearance of Rupert in his life as festival director, Matthew realised that he needed to make a fresh decision not only about his approach to Rupert, but any involvement he himself had with the production. He would need to act quickly.

Soon after Tom had returned from his errand, Matthew was discussing Eleanor's favour with him in the sitting room. 'Do you know what really irritates me about her?'

Tom looked at him thoughtfully. 'I think I'm going to find out.'

'She thinks she can bludgeon us by sheer force of personality.'

'Yes, I've never liked that side of her,' he agreed. 'The trouble is, she is so often right!'

'You would say that, seeing as you'll end up playing the lead. She's misjudged Felicity, at any rate.'

Tom smiled. 'You say Hammond is supposed to be coming up next week?' Matthew nodded. 'Have you thought how this could work in our favour?'

'You mean in *your* favour?' asked Matthew. 'No, that was the last thing on my mind.'

'Wining and dining him, plus putting him up, might mean that we get him on our side for the auditions? After all, I *am* the right age to play Jack.'

'More or less. The problem for you is divided loyalties. At least, I hope that's the problem. You'd be a fool not to want to play Jack, but you don't want me to be left out.'

Tom brightened. 'I'm relieved that you can see it from my point of view, for once.'

Matthew folded his arms. 'Well, I've come to a decision.'

'What's that?'

'I'm not going to audition for Canon Chasuble, after all. It's an insult.' The thinking behind this was that he may as well disassociate himself from the production altogether, as a way of avoiding Rupert.

'You know best,' said Tom, 'but I feel I have a vested interest, so I'd still like to take a look at him, if only to see what the fuss is about.'

Matthew turned to look at him. 'Rupert Hammond? Seems a bit of a nobody to me. I just hope you won't be disappointed.'

'Shall I get the laptop, so we can look him up?'

'Do we have to?' groaned Matthew, yet secretly delighted with how this was developing. Tom took no time in finding Rupert Hammond. Not trusting himself to look at the photographs for long because he found them fascinating, Matthew pretended to glaze over. Tom, however, seemed mesmerised by the images of Rupert, and seemed particularly struck by the black and white studio portrait revealing a three-quarter profile of Rupert in his early thirties. Rupert was clearly as in love with himself as he always had been.

'I think I recognise him,' said Tom, when he must have had his fill. Matthew shifted his position. 'I'm sure he was in some films I watched as a child.'

'You are probably mistaking him for someone else, far more famous.'

'If I'm to impress him before auditioning for the lead,' said Tom, 'I need to have a plan. Why don't you check with Eleanor to see if that cottage of hers will be ready to holiday-let by the spring?'

There was a sudden shift in Matthew's feelings, especially as the cottage was less than ten minutes' drive away. Now that he had seen photographs of Rupert, Matthew's interest in him had been reawakened, and his mind was going off in several different directions. Naturally, Matthew would not want to jeopardise his relationship with Tom, supposing that he and Rupert actually spoke to each other again, but what would be the harm in a little light flirtation? Having Rupert living nearby would add an extra dimension to what was becoming a pretty monotonous existence. That cottage would make an ideal base for Matthew to visit Rupert without having to travel far. A round trip might be executed without Tom even knowing where he had gone. He jumped at Tom's suggestion.

'What shall I say?'

'Eleanor will no doubt want to get the place off to a good start in its first season, so why don't you press the point about a block booking of several weeks? I think she might buy into that.'

Matthew smiled. 'Not when she knows that it's for Rupert Hammond.'

Yet Tom would not leave the subject alone. 'It's sure to be tastefully furnished, and everything will be brand new.'

Matthew reached for his phone to explain the proposition to Eleanor.

She was in imperious mode. 'I hope you're not suggesting that I do that man a favour?'

'Let's get to the point, shall we? Will it be ready or not?'

'It's supposed to be,' she replied sulkily. 'By late March.'

'That would fit in then. Remember we're trying to help *you*.'

'Really, Matthew. What makes you think I need help all of a sudden?'

'Think about it. You could have a single gentleman—'

'That remains to be seen,' Eleanor interrupted.

'For a block booking of six weeks or so. The wear and tear will be minimal. Couldn't you at least show him around?'

She hesitated, as if thinking how to work things to her best advantage. 'Well, I'll go over the place with him if you *promise* to look after him at Langdales next week. I'll text you his number.'

Later that day found Matthew preparing dinner with Tom. Struggling to slice the tough ends off the asparagus, Matthew wondered why he invariably agreed to Eleanor's demands. Deep down, he was well aware of the reason, of course. There had been that slight fling with Eleanor, when he had come to live in Cumbria on the rebound from Rupert. He knew that he would always be in thrall to her, and although he counted her as his best friend, he was never sure whether he was hers. She was often high-handed and did not give him the respect he felt he deserved, and yet they were inextricably linked.

She was often maddening, often upset him, but they invariably had the same mind-set. And, more importantly, she was usually there for him, like he had been for her during her divorce. Not one to show too much affection, the fact remained that he still adored her.

After a few moments of unsatisfactory sawing, Matthew remarked, 'We shouldn't get asparagus out of season, you know. It's tough.'

'That may be because you've got that broken wooden coffee-grounds spoon mixed up with them. No wonder you weren't getting anywhere.'

Matthew laughed, but squirmed. 'So I have.'

'You've not been yourself since we looked at those pictures of Hammond.'

Hoping to make Tom uncomfortable, Matthew looked at him for longer than he needed to. 'Haven't I? Perhaps I feel the weight of responsibility on your behalf. Talking of which, do you still want me to get in touch with him?'

Tom glanced at the kitchen telephone. 'If we want to put in a good word about me playing Jack, surely it's best coming from you?'

'Good idea, but would you mind if I did it in the other room, so that I can concentrate? If you wouldn't mind carrying on with the dinner?' Matthew was now wondering how best to explain things, should Rupert hang up on him, as he had every right to do.

Tom was all smiles. 'Just get him here!'

Matthew glanced at the text from Eleanor, nodded and left Tom to prepare dinner. Drawing the curtains and lighting the wood-burning stove gave Matthew time to worry about that call. Heart thumping, he tried to get comfortable in his favourite armchair and finally rang the number. Sweeping thoughts of their last contact to one side, he found himself breathing hard until his call elicited a curt response.

'Hello? Hammond here.'

'Rupert? I don't suppose you remember me, but it's Matthew.' From the hesitation at the other end, he presumed he had been airbrushed out of Rupert's life long ago.

'Not Matthew Hunter, surely?' asked Rupert, at length. 'Impossible!' Impossible that he was on the line, thought Matthew, or impossible to forget? 'Didn't you ever think to get in touch?'

'You told me not to,' replied Matthew, sheepishly.

'Ah! Did I? That's as good a reason as any, I suppose.'

'Didn't you receive my letters?'

'Maybe the odd one.'

'But I posted so many. At least, to begin with.'

'I was probably touring,' said Rupert, unfeelingly, in the fruity, orotund voice that he must have honed over the years. 'Or have you forgotten? Most likely they were chucked away before I returned. You forced yourself out of my life, remember?'

From this Matthew assumed that he had not been forgiven. The call promised to be as difficult as he had anticipated, and he stammered his apologies.

Rupert remained steely. 'So, what have you to say for yourself? You can't just walk back into my life as if nothing had happened.'

'I wouldn't dream of it, but I was under the impression that you might be walking back into *my* life.'

'And what makes you think that?'

'We run a bed and breakfast called Langdales, in the Lake District.'

'Who's we? Or shouldn't I ask?'

Matthew cleared his throat. 'I suppose I ought to tell you that I have a partner. His name's Tom.'

Rupert sighed. 'That's allowed.'

'I've been very lucky.'

'They all say that.'

'It's funny but I found Tom standing on the front door step one day.'

'*Found?*' asked Rupert, in the manner of Lady Bracknell. 'And you had no qualms about taking him under your wing, being the good-hearted soul that you are?'

'I might have done better,' said Matthew, trying to gain the upper hand, 'but I have also done a lot worse in my time.'

'Oh, you have, have you?'

'Shall we move forward, Rupert? You'd like him. You see, he's a good bit younger than I am, and I know you always had an eye for– '

Rupert's interest seemed to quicken. 'How much younger?'

'Fifteen.'

'Steady on!'

'No, I meant he's thirty-five – fifteen years younger,' replied Matthew, unable to conceal a note of triumph.

'What's he like?'

Although he could not imagine Tom stooping to listen at the keyhole, Matthew lowered his voice. 'Good-looking.'

'Ah! But is he better looking?'

'Than?'

'Me, of course.'

Matthew thought it best to humour him. 'How could he be? Fair hair, small face, rather delicate features...' The line went quiet for a moment as if he was thinking this over, or knowing Rupert, checking for wrinkles in front of a mirror. Almost involuntarily, Matthew stood up to check his own reflection in the mirror over the fireplace, as if already under Rupert's scrutiny.

'How long have you been together, did you say?'

'What is this?' replied Matthew. 'An inquisition? I don't think that's relevant.'

'I think I should be the judge of that! So, the Lake District. Do you know anything about WAFT?'

'Actually, that's why I'm calling.'

'I'm already shuddering at the prospect of all those flat northern vowels.'

'We're mostly off-comers, except Eleanor, but in the unlikely event of there being any, I suppose you won't make them any flatter?'

'Ah! I'll do my level best to straighten things out.'

'That will be a first. Anyway, Tom and I get involved, and we've been asked to accommodate you by our former president, chairman and leading lady, Mrs Eleanor Vane.'

'Busy lady?'

'She was, until recent events forced–'

'Well, they're prepared to pay me to direct them. Imagine!'

'In addition to playing Lady Bracknell?'

'Which I shall do superbly. That's the part I'm really looking forward to. Where did you say you lived?'

'I didn't. *South* Lakes.'

'Sounds like a shopping mall. *"You are now at South Lakes exit."*' Rupert chuckled. 'Or, even worse perhaps, a theme park.'

'Depends what you make it. *We're* in the Lyth Valley, although you won't have heard of it so don't pretend you have. It's a quiet area between Windermere – the lake, that is – and Kendal. Known for its damsons –'

Rupert cut him off. 'How reassuring. Does one sprinkle them on one's muesli?'

'No, but they will be blossoming while you're here, and they make an exceedingly good damson gin in these parts.'

'Now you're speaking my language!' Rupert went quiet and he appeared to be thinking. 'I've just had an idea. Do you remember Bumps?'

Matthew stepped backwards into the past as if it had been yesterday, and found that he was smiling to himself. 'Do you still call her that?'

'Only when I want to annoy her.'

Bumps was Rupert's nickname for his elder sister by about ten years, Caroline. When Rupert had been a ten-year-old, her shapeliness had intrigued him. Caroline had always reminded Matthew of his mother's plain-speaking elder sister. Matthew's mother had cross-questioned him one day about the real nature of his friendship with Rupert. Caught off-guard, he had replied frankly. She put her hand to her mouth, fled the room and telephoned said sister. Only after a long conversation with her did his mother seek out Matthew and bring herself to discuss it with him. She must also have spoken to Matthew's father, although the only perceptible change here was that his father coughed and rustled *The Daily Telegraph* more than necessary whenever Matthew appeared in the sitting room.

'I'd like to know more about her,' said Matthew.

Rupert explained. 'She's early retired, and a luxurious night away would do her good.'

'It's not at its best here in January, I have to say, and I'm not sure we're equal to her high standards' said Matthew, fearing Tom's reaction. After all, he hadn't been planning to ingratiate himself with the elder sister. 'But if you're certain it would work, I'd love to renew our acquaintance. Although…'

'What?'

'Caroline must never let on about us, you realise that? I wouldn't like Tom to draw the wrong conclusion. Not that there's any chance of our rekindling what happened so long ago, of course.'

'Absolutely no chance whatsoever, after what you put me through.'

'You weren't exactly easy yourself.'

'Well, I suppose we all need to move forward. I'll tell her to keep stumm, although I can't imagine why it has to remain a secret.'

Matthew sighed. 'I don't want Tom to think that either of us is looking over our shoulder.'

'That's never going to happen,' grunted Rupert, and then softened. 'Tom, you say? Sounds delightfully uncomplicated. You must be a good match.'

'Thanks.'

'You have my word that you won't hear a squeak from me. Can I come back to you after I've spoken to Caroline?'

Matthew gave him his number and then decided to have a little joke. 'Would you prefer Benjamin Bunny or Squirrel Nutkin during your stay?'

Rupert took a moment to absorb this. 'What sort of establishment are you running up there? *Who*, or I hope, *what* are they?'

Matthew laughed. 'The names of our bedrooms.'

'Don't tell me you've gone twee, Matthew.'

'Tom's idea. Beatrix Potter is big business up here.'

'Naturally, I shall want the best room. So Tom's the twee one? I can't wait to meet him.'

'Listen, Rupert, I must insist that things remain private whenever you're with Tom. You used to be something of a loose cannon. I've not breathed a word about us to him, and I don't intend to.'

'I'll *try* and be on my best behaviour,' said Rupert in wheedling tones, 'although I can't promise anything.' He paused. 'You wouldn't have taken to living with me, you know.'

'Why not?'

'You're still obtuse! Because I was usually filming or on tour.'

'I wouldn't have been exactly living with you then.'

'Gradually,' said Rupert, becoming tight-lipped, 'I had to accept you couldn't have been that interested in me, otherwise you wouldn't have abandoned me as you did.'

'Let's get one thing straight, shall we? I never abandoned you.' He hesitated. 'You're sure that we're doing the right thing?'

'Listen, I need the work.'

'But you seemed destined for great things?'

'That "early promise" appears to have fizzled,' said Rupert, breezily. 'By the way, seeing as we simply *ooze* so much shared history, do you think you might be able to put me up during rehearsals?'

Matthew instinctively backed off. 'I'm not quite sure we could take out a room for single occupancy over that length of time.'

Rupert chuckled. 'Who said anything about it being single?'

'Still up to your old tricks?'

'Well, if there's no room, you might know of a flat to rent? It would save me a lot of leg work.'

Matthew indicated that they might do and agreed to look into it. 'But don't forget, I must swear both you and Caroline to secrecy.' He felt that he could not emphasise this too much. 'Tom must *never* know about us, so I'll need Caroline to be on her best behaviour, too.'

Rupert seemed in much higher spirits than when he had answered the phone. 'There's not much chance of that!' There was a slight hesitation. 'The funny thing is, I'm glad you got in touch.'

Rupert had sounded conspiratorial and Matthew swallowed. 'Honestly?'

'I was furious at the time, and who wouldn't have been? But after a while, I began to think of you more kindly. It's rare that a week – well, a month or two, I suppose – goes by when I can't help thinking about you.'

Heart thumping, Matthew said, 'Hardly a week goes by without you crossing my thoughts, either.'

'You still have that dimple?'

'Of course.'

'And the brown hair?'

'Greying a bit.'

'I've still got mine, too, although it's probably more golden than when you last saw me.'

Matthew chuckled, they proceeded to swap stories about mutual acquaintances who had not fulfilled their promise, and he soon lost track of the time. When he finally ended the call – far more amicably than he had anticipated – he smiled to himself. His mind raced. He seemed to have been accepted. Perhaps even forgiven. It was as if they had never lost touch.

He was about to share the good news with Tom when his phone rang. Thinking that it might be Rupert coming back to him with a date, he was surprised to hear that it was Eleanor's arch-enemy, Felicity Kilbride, from The Croft in nearby Grange-over-Sands. Felicity was both older and shorter than Eleanor, but still retained her pretty, kindly face. She was a wealthy widow with two daughters, Jane and Clare, who were also involved in the festival. In spite of being very stiff on-stage, Felicity was heavily involved in another am dram group.

However, she aspired to the kudos surrounding WAFT, although it was nothing like it had been in the early days. So far, she had had to be content with playing supporting roles. This had led her to resent the way that Eleanor dominated the proceedings as if she had a right to play the leading role. After Eleanor's climb-down, there was a possibility that she might play a larger role.

After the usual preliminaries, she was quick to come to the point.

'I suppose you've heard?'

Matthew felt his shoulders sag. 'I have no idea what you're talking about.'

'Don't be like that,' said Felicity. 'Operation Bracknell, of course.'

'What?'

'Eleanor's already making a move to undermine my decision about Mr Hammond.'

'How serious is she? Is this her usual sabre-rattling, or should we be worried?'

'I'm not leaving anything to chance. Not when I've come this far.'

'Because she still wants to play Lady Bracknell?'

'Wake up, Matthew! You know how underhand she can be. I'd like to put it on record that I have no intention of siding with that woman on some trumped-up sub-committee,' she told him. 'There is to be no going back. Not now; not tomorrow; not ever.'

He chuckled. 'Isn't that rather final?'

'I mean it, Matthew. This is my chance to stop that woman. I've even gone so far as to renounce playing the part myself.'

'It would have seemed somewhat Machiavellian otherwise, eh?'

'Quite. What luck to think of offering it to Hammond!'

'Genius,' said Matthew, 'as long as there's no backlash.'

Felicity snorted. 'No, I mean it. I'm not having any truck with Eleanor's manoeuvres, but I'm quite happy to audition for Miss Prism, as long as it's above board.'

'What happened, exactly?'

Felicity was happy to divulge. 'Eleanor offered me the position of president, feeling she wasn't up to it.'

'I can understand that.'

'But, and here's the inevitable catch, it was offered to me only if I upped my sponsorship. It was assumed that she would be playing Lady Bracknell and I was promised Miss Prism, but things altered dramatically when the new director appeared.'

'So I gather.' Matthew hesitated. 'Tell me, was it *you* who found him?'

'Keep that to yourself.'

'But you persuaded him to play Lady Bracknell?'

She laughed. 'I didn't have to work hard. Sorry, Matthew, but I have further calls to make. I know you invariably side with Eleanor, but I really *don't* want her to play Lady Bracknell. Just the thought of it makes me sick.'

'So you would rather have a stranger – and a man, to boot – playing that role?'

'Anything!' And with that, she hung up.

Matthew found himself bounding into the kitchen but slowed down just in time, and his broad smile disappeared when he saw Tom ostentatiously checking his watch. He had forgotten that Tom was enjoying a head start with a bottle of Shiraz.

Tom glanced up from stirring something that smelled delicious. 'You've heard his life story then?'

Wrong-footed, Matthew half-smiled. 'Just the abridged version, but he comes over as being very amenable, and you'll have nothing to worry about.'

'Funnily enough, I wasn't. More to the point, how am I going to resurrect this meal?'

'Sorry if I've been longer than I expected, but it's all sorted.'

Tom pushed a glass towards him in silence and refilled his own. Matthew looked longingly at his wine but refrained from touching it; he needed to keep a clear head.

'The chicken will no doubt be drier than I would have liked,' said Tom, stiffly, and then looked over the rim of his glass. 'So what kept you so long?'

'It's not as simple as I'd hoped.'

'But he *is* coming *here*?'

'He can't wait,' replied Matthew, dreading how best to indicate that Rupert's sister would in all likelihood be staying too. In the end, he just blurted it out. 'But, and this will be news to you, he will be bringing Bumps.'

A humourless smile crossed Tom's face. 'Who, or what, is Bumps?' Matthew explained. 'We're supposed to be closed. Now, suddenly, we have a full house!'

'Don't exaggerate.'

'Can't he come on his own?'

'Why don't you ring him yourself and find out?' Tom drained his glass. 'Don't frown, Tom.'

During the silence, Matthew could not resist making a start on his wine, but swallowed the wrong way and spluttered. Meanwhile, Tom lifted a second bottle out of the rack and unscrewed it.

'Please don't spoil the evening, Tom. You know what will happen if–'

Tom splashed some into his glass. 'I've not even begun. It was the simplest of calls you had to make, and now we have Buggles coming.'

'Bumps. And stop being so melodramatic.'

'That's good, coming from you. But – don't you realise? I was planning a one-to-one chat with him, and now the dynamics have altered.'

'There's no need to rule that out just yet.' Matthew began to rummage inside a cupboard for something to soak up the wine. 'Don't tell me we've run out of nibbles.' Feeling his stomach rumble, he wished that those pieces of chicken were not smelling quite so impressive, but his search was arrested when Tom came out with what proved to be a pivotal question.

'You're sure there isn't a Mrs Hammond who'll come creeping out of the woodwork to complete the party?'

Trying not to over-react, Matthew turned sharply. 'What made you say that?'

'We have his sister coming, so why not the wife?'

'If that black and white photograph is anything to go by,' chuckled Matthew, not entirely convincingly, 'Hammond looks as if he is too much in love with himself to get involved with more than his own reflection.'

Tom downed more wine. 'That sounds a little glib.'

'I am *convinced* there is no Mrs Hammond.'

Tom searched his face. 'How can you be so sure?'

Not being able to reveal the truth about Rupert was going to put Matthew under a lot of pressure, especially since he had done his best to destroy the relationship between Rupert and his fiancée. Matthew wondered if they had ever gone through with it.

'Are you feeling all right?' asked Tom, still staring at him. 'What is it about Mrs Hammond that seems to have hit a nerve?'

Because I wrecked her wedding-day, and Rupert's, for that matter, thought Matthew. He had never allowed himself to forget that they had vowed never to see each other again after what happened and Matthew had dreaded coming into contact with Rupert again. The rift had been total. His hands went clammy at the thought of Rupert in close proximity. Suddenly, there seemed no limit as to what might go horribly wrong.

'Why do you have to keep going on about it?' asked Matthew.

Tom regarded him coolly. 'Perhaps because you looked so radiant after what was supposed to be a routine call?'

Unable to meet Tom's gaze, Matthew's eyes shifted towards the everyday objects on the worktop, but he struggled to maintain the upper hand. 'Don't forget that I was putting myself out on your behalf.'

Tom looked away quickly. 'I shouldn't have been so cool with you. I've been having a caffeine-free day.'

'A new year resolution that clearly did not include being nicer to me?'

'I'm sorry, Matthew. I was starting with a headache and the wine didn't help.'

'How was I to know that he was going to be so entertaining? Who knows, he may even turn out to be what the festival needs.'

'It certainly needs an injection of something. It's suffered too long under the Vane shadow.'

Matthew tried to appear jovial. 'Exactly! So, let's not hear any more about it, eh?'

Tom gave him a sideways look. 'The problem is…'

'Yes?'

'It's going to take time to forget that look in your eyes, Matthew. You looked, er, positively *ecstatic* and so happy to be alive after talking to *that man*. Is there something you haven't told me?'

Matthew swallowed. 'Of course not. It's just that Rupert is a born raconteur. I see no reason why you won't take to him, as well.'

Tom stopped stirring. 'Really?'

Matthew hesitated. 'You know how full of themselves actors can be. It took so long because – very sensibly – he grilled me about the festival, and he may well be interested in Eleanor's cottage, so things might yet fall into place for you. To be honest, I feel we both might have a friend waiting in the wings, if you'd only give him a chance!'

There was a long pause, then: 'I have a confession to make.'

Matthew stared at him. 'And?'

'You were taking so long that I found myself outside the door.'

Matthew felt the back of his collar. 'Eavesdropping?'

'I had to rush back to the hob, remember? You were giggling away out of all proportion with a stranger, and it didn't ring true.'

Matthew took a moment to respond. 'He's very entertaining…'

Seeing that Tom still looked unconvinced, Matthew waited for things to calm down, as he knew they must. Even so, the conversation during dinner was strained. Needless to say, once Tom had cleared up and gone to bed, claiming that he needed an early night, Matthew thumbed through *The Complete Works of Oscar Wilde* in the study, and reconsidered himself in the supporting role of Canon Chasuble. A spring and early summer with Rupert in close proximity promised much dissembling on Matthew's part, and would require all his acting skills, limited though they were.

To keep their previous relationship a secret would involve a nest of nightmarish complications. One false move, or uttering something that did not ring true, threatened to wrong-foot him. If all was revealed, Tom would take a dim view not only of why it had to be kept secret, but further question his enthusiastic change of manner after that initial phone-call. And there would always remain a lingering suspicion as to whether Matthew was open to revitalising his once passionate relationship with Rupert.

Yet having recovered from the initial shock, and having spoken to Rupert, Matthew's attitude to the predicament was changing. In spite of Tom's reaction, he was warming to the possibility of Rupert resurfacing. The idea of Rupert living nearby as director – for weeks on end – was a powerful aphrodisiac, stirring thoughts that he had long suppressed. It was difficult to ignore the rush of adrenalin.

Leafing through the pages, totting up the number of times the character appeared, he then sat musing for a while. When he finally made his way up to bed, Tom was fast asleep and did not stir. His handsome face was looking even better in repose. Matthew, however, had a disturbed night. How could he miss out on so much drama, as anything involving Rupert almost always dictated? Upon consideration, (albeit brief), the role no longer seemed quite as inferior as it had done a few hours previously.

Chapter Two

Over breakfast next morning, Tom and he spoke tentatively, only becoming bolder if they had to discuss the nuts and bolts of the day ahead. When yet another silence was broken by Matthew's phone jangling, he jumped, and when he realised who it was, made a face and disappeared into the sitting room. Rupert's tone was clipped, almost as if he had had second thoughts about how familiar they should be to one an another. Striving to recapture the ecstatic tone – as he now thought of it – of their previous conversation, Matthew kept him on the line for an age, and finished by telling him he must expect a full morning meeting the stage manager, the sound and lighting man, and the wardrobe mistresses. At first, it felt good to have a firm date to work to. Rupert and his sister would be arriving within the week. On being informed, Tom merely smiled and nodded as if the matter was now out of his hands. They tried not to speak of it, unless they had to.

In the few days before "the visit" – which had become something of an event in Matthew's eyes – there were further sea changes and awkward moments of self-doubt. Memories of Rupert continued to jostle in his head, as did endless future possibilities. As the days disappeared, Matthew lost count of the times he picked up the phone to cancel Rupert's visit.

On the night prior to their arrival. Matthew did not sleep well, and spent a restless couple of hours trying to ignore the wind battering the roof. By mid-morning, dazed with tiredness, he was on the verge of calling the whole thing off when he realised there were only two hours to go. Rupert and Caroline would no doubt have set off from the Manchester area. When the clock struck one, it was clear that they were running late, and he began to fret. There was a discreet sign for Langdales in black and gold, but they could easily have missed it.

Hidden from the road, Langdales could be found via a dead-end lane, which threaded its way through fields and round the occasional copse. The house was firmly rooted in the valley floor, so the name of Langdales was wishful thinking – for the house lacked an astonishing view – although the surrounding countryside views were pleasant.

As the minutes seemed to speed up, Matthew peered out of the window. Although the sky threatened rain, he felt that a stroll would give him something to do, and Tom readily agreed. He always enjoyed an amble along the lane, but today, the branches of the oaks and the ash trees were swaying and creaking, and although the wind was behind them, it was wrenching every twig. They had walked some way when they heard raised voices, and shrugged at one another. Approaching cautiously, they turned a bend, and were surprised to see Caroline and Rupert standing by what must have been Rupert's old car.

Matthew caught Tom's eye, signalling that they should tip-toe towards the broad trunk of the nearest oak tree and hide. This was mainly because Matthew wanted to take stock of them, or rather Rupert, before they were noticed. He peered out from behind the tree. Rupert had his back to them, but the hair was suspiciously gilded. Matthew shifted his gaze to the sister, who was staring sideways at him. Taller than her brother, which was not difficult, Caroline was as sensibly dressed as Matthew might have expected, wearing a long coat with Inverness cape and a hat. She and Rupert were inspecting a hefty oak branch barring the way. Caroline appeared to be in charge.

'You'll never shift that on your own,' she told Rupert, folding her arms. The Hammonds were a good-looking family. Roughly sixty, she had retained some of the prettiness Matthew remembered, although as far as he was concerned, her attractiveness had always been eclipsed by her younger brother. Unlike Rupert, Caroline had shunned the stage, but she was still prone to theatricality. She kicked the branch with her boot and railed at the forbidding sky with her gloved hands.

'This is some welcome, I must say.'

'Must you?' retorted Rupert, raising his voice because of the wind.

'Are you sure it's down here?'

'Well, you told me to turn left!'

'I see Anthony's sudden departure has done nothing to improve your mood.'

'If you mention Anthony once more, I swear I'll...' His voice trailed off.

She smiled grimly. 'But then we would run out of things to argue about. I'd still like to know what possessed you to come this far north in January?'

As Rupert made no response, she retrieved a black umbrella from the car and stared at him meaningfully, as if this would be enough to coerce him to join her on foot.

'That won't last five seconds in this wind,' he remarked.

'Nonsense. There's nothing else for it but to walk. Unless it's some stately pile, which I doubt, it can't be far. Don't tell me you're nervous?'

'When was I ever nervous?' enquired Rupert.

'What about that rather too memorable occasion when you had stage-fright and I had to prop you up with whisky?'

When Caroline looked ready to abandon Rupert, Matthew and Tom ventured out, as if stepping from the wings. Turning towards them, Caroline studied their faces, perhaps trying to work out their motive for keeping out of sight until the last moment. The next few seconds passed quickly. Caroline was introduced – but not as Bumps – and was duly shaken by the hand, as if Matthew had never set eyes on her before. From that flinching look in her eyes, Matthew could tell that she remembered him. Tom, and then Matthew, shook hands with Rupert, who was still drenching himself in after-shave. The hand-shake, held a fraction too long, was familiar.

The seventeen-year-old face that Matthew had held in his mind's eye had, of course, vanished, and so had the features of the twenty-five-year-old. Rupert was neither the Rupert he remembered, nor the Rupert in that photograph. Yet if anything, he was more good-looking; his features had matured and the lines around his mouth suggested laughter rather than age and irritability.

'How'doo,' said Matthew.

'Good afternoon,' said Rupert, glancing at Tom. 'Is that a vernacular greeting?'

'Yes. I suppose it is.'

'Really, Rupert,' said Caroline, smiling, but sounding slightly superior. 'Should I have brought my passport?'

Tom and Matthew smiled uncertainly.

'I'm sorry about the branch. Must have come down in the night. It's a bit unwieldy for us, don't you think?' asked Matthew.

The four of them stared at it, as if trying to move it by concentrated mental effort alone.

'It needs someone young and beefy,' volunteered Rupert, feasting his eyes on Tom, whose skinny frame looked bigger in his thick coat.

'Nothing is going to budge that in a hurry,' said Tom.

Matthew agreed. 'I'll call the farmer when we get back to the house.'

It began to spit with rain. Caroline stamped her feet and harrumphed. 'If we don't get inside soon, we'll *freeze* to death.'

'Don't exaggerate,' said Rupert.

Matthew suggested that Rupert should reverse to the nearest passing place, and Tom decided he would go with him. Caroline shuddered as she watched Rupert reverse.

'You look anxious,' said Matthew. 'Rupert's not likely to pounce on Tom, is he?'

'I doubt it, although it's not unknown. Mind you, there's a young man he should be chasing, but – typically – he's stalling on that one.' Matthew was intrigued, but made no answer. Caroline turned to look him up and down. 'Rupert prefers them darker, as you're only too aware.'

'Not a word, please!'

'Don't worry, I've been primed. I know all my lines.' She winked. 'No, I'm not keen on seeing him reverse with stone walls on either side. With Tom in the car, he might lose concentration and go off on a diagonal slant.'

'Yes, he was never good at keeping to the straight and narrow.' Matthew grinned.

Caroline was now clutching her hat and holding her umbrella as low over her head as she could. Matthew could not see her eyes and he sensed that this would make conversation a strain. In the pause that followed, he recalled that Rupert had never really earned Caroline's respect, although she could be a staunch defender when she chose to be. His family had never approved of his acting career; it was not considered a proper job, especially for a man. In addition, Caroline had not seemed able to take his general gaiety seriously, in every sense of the word. This was something that Matthew partly shared with her:

he had often found it hard to cope with not only Rupert's desire to have a good time, rather than facing reality, but his too well-developed belief in himself. Like his slightly unbelievable good looks, Rupert was not of the real world.

'Did you have a good journey?' he asked, struggling to make conversation.

'Not particularly,' she replied, stamping her feet. 'He drove, and refused to let me take over halfway.' She raised the umbrella so that his face became visible, and eyed him curiously. Sensing she was about to take advantage of them being alone for a few moments, his mouth dried. 'Well, Matthew, I don't suppose we'll ever discover what prompted your singular behaviour?'

'The wedding-day?' he asked, hardly recognising his own voice. 'How has he been?'

'Why the sudden interest, when you saw fit to abandon him?'

Shifting his gaze, Matthew procrastinated.

'I'm waiting.'

'I didn't see fit. It was a difficult morning.'

She shuddered. 'You're telling me.'

'How has he been, er, after all these years?'

'Can't you guess?'

'Up and down?'

'More down, than up, I'm afraid.' She sighed. 'What one might call a chequered career, but you know how it is.'

'I'm sorry to hear that. He did mention that I have no wish for Tom to know anything about that time?'

She gave him a sharp look. 'Too ashamed to have kicked over the love of your life?'

'It's not as if I've anything to be ashamed of. His behaviour, the countdown to the wedding...it was becoming a problem.'

'And so you eliminated him? I see.'

Matthew cleared his throat. '*You* didn't have to put up with him. Moving on to the festival, it can be complicated enough as it is, without making it more so. I would hate Tom to think that we might rekindle things.'

She took a step closer. 'Rupert appears to have come with an open mind, but, after what I've just been through with him, watch out – '

When they saw Rupert and Tom approaching, enjoying what appeared to be a spirited conversation, the umbrella was gradually lowered. As the upper part of her face disappeared, Matthew could not help noticing that her lips were drawn into a thin line. Rupert and Tom joined them just as the wind ripped her umbrella inside out and hurled her hat into a puddle. A smiling Tom bent down to return it to her and brushed it on his sleeve. In return she handed him the umbrella. He pulled it back into shape and, looking into the offending puddle, tried – but failed – to admire his reflection in the opaque water.

'You men are all the same,' she remarked, with a nod in Rupert's direction. Tom grinned. They set off, hunching themselves against the wind with the hosts wheeling the overnight bags. The rain had eased and they walked in silence, mainly because it was too windy to talk comfortably, until they turned the last corner, and ran their eyes over Langdales. The sandstone mullions had never been able to diminish the sobriety of the dark slate walls, and the house appeared somewhat uninviting in the dismal January light, even though several lamps were doing their feeble best.

Rupert whistled through his teeth. 'Hans Christian Andersen meets the Tudors?'

'If you say so,' murmured Matthew, eyeing him.

'Sorry to correct you, but looking at the steeply pitched roof and those spheres, I'd say more "Jacobethan", or what's also known as Jacobean Gothic,' volunteered Caroline.

Rupert was holding Matthew in his gaze. 'You're sure it's not too cramped?'

'It's bigger than it looks,' replied Matthew, 'being one pile deep. The reception rooms are on the other, the south side; hall, staircase and utilities are on the north side.'

'A very sensible layout, if you ask me,' murmured Caroline.

'It seems longer when you're carting cases up and down the long landing,' said Tom.

'I can just see you as a cute bellhop.' Rupert grinned. 'I love a man in uniform.'

Tom smiled, but with a wary eye. 'With a bell-boy hat? If that's a compliment, I think I'm a bit old.'

'Nonsense,' said Rupert, 'and with your looks and figure...'

Matthew felt his stomach turning over and pretended to miss this. Caroline, standing slightly apart, and presumably also turning a deaf ear, was engrossed in looking for signs of life in the standard rose trees bordering the apron of gravel in front of the house. They gave every appearance of being stone-dead. Possibly satisfied that they were, she directed her attention back to Langdales. The climbers adorning the house were looking more dead than alive, and the highest, inaccessible shoots were either waving about or smothering the sandstone spheres and short runs of balustrade separating the attic dormers. Tangles of debris were caught among the bare stems. A few crows came flapping over the jagged roof line, and went off into the nearest oak trees, cawing and bickering over the best branches to perch on. To Matthew, they sounded like a WAFT committee meeting.

'I don't suppose you know anything about the architect?' asked Caroline, head tilted back, as if counting the number of chimneys. '*Solidly* Victorian, but in a way, I quite like it.'

'Sadly, the architect died young, so the house is unique,' explained Matthew.

Rupert blew on his fingers. 'Something of a relief, perhaps?'

'Many of our guests have likened it to a bank,' said Matthew. 'It may not be the prettiest house, but it gets a mention in an early edition of Pevsner.'

Tom laughed. 'Where it was described as *"having a fugue of chimneys."*'

'But that has musical connotations...' said Rupert, hugging himself.

Coming nearer, Caroline winked at Tom as she steepled her hands. 'How about aggressively gabled?'

Rupert nudged her boot with his shoe.

Tom nodded. 'It *is* cosier inside, I can assure you.'

Matthew wanted to shake his head. Not only were they making fun of Langdales, Tom was already getting on better with Caroline than he had ever done. In fact, not only the brother, but the sister seemed taken with Tom.

'What are we waiting for?' asked Rupert, with a nod in Matthew's direction.

He took the hint and directed them towards the front porch. Keen to take cover, Caroline was the first inside. Matthew stepped forward to relieve her of her coat. She placed her hat on the console table in front of the mirror, its gilt frame sprawling with cherubs, and grimaced slightly. Matthew examined the finely worked flowers on her silk jacket.

'So, who was responsible for all this... er, artistic endeavour?' she asked, her eyes coming to rest on the stencil above the plate rack.

'Tom stencilled every single one of those *fleur-de-lys*,' replied Matthew, grateful for a talking-point.

'You must have a lot of time on your hands,' observed Caroline, trying to show an interest.

Rupert's eyes lit up. 'It would have kept you out of mischief, at any rate.'

'Had there been any to keep him out of,' muttered Matthew.

Caroline – having prodded Rupert in the back – tidied her hair and once she had been directed by Matthew, disappeared into the cloakroom under the staircase. It was then that Matthew realised he had not removed the two paintings that Rupert had painted from the wall behind the door. (Rupert had planned to be an artist if the acting career had failed, although Matthew would have been surprised if it had come to anything.) Would she recognise his style and cross-question Matthew about them? She seemed oblivious of boundaries. Rupert handed his hat and coat to Tom with more smiling and touching than was necessary. While Tom was placing Rupert's coat on the nearest chair, Matthew and Rupert took stock of each other. Matthew was searching for blemishes, and hoped that Rupert was not doing the same, for he was under no illusion that he looked his age. Uneasy with this scrutiny, Matthew backed into the kitchen to leave a message for their tame farmer about the branch, returning to find that Tom was almost rubbing shoulders with Rupert.

Eyelids fluttering, Tom was on the charm offensive. 'Didn't I read that *Jubilee Way* has been a personal triumph?'

Intent on missing nothing, Matthew hovered.

Flashing his teeth, (*could they be his own*, wondered Matthew), Rupert replied, 'Even so, I've been left lying in a coma, while they chew over my contract, but I know who to blame.'

'Who?' asked Tom.

'The director, of course. He's had it in for me for some time.'

Noticing Matthew's look of intense concentration, Tom moved over. 'How odd, when I've read that you were brilliant.'

Throwing his hands up in mock disbelief, Rupert stepped back. 'You've never actually watched it?'

'We're so busy with the B and B, the house and garden, or the festival, that it's hard to find the time.' Tom looked as if he was floundering. 'What are the chances of you being revived?'

Rupert shrugged. 'Perhaps I'm kidding myself about my contract being renewed. Meanwhile, I'm going to make a name for myself as a director with your play. "Life upon the wicked stage" is not what it was when you're my age. In fact, it's never been harder.'

Caroline returned from the cloakroom. 'I hope I haven't missed anything?'

Rupert half-smiled. 'Just touching on the injustices of *Jubilee Way*, dear.'

She raised an eyebrow. Matthew felt the back of his collar while his former lover stared at him unashamedly.

'Where were we?' asked Rupert. 'Ah! The run-up to Christmas was–'

'Rather frantic, what with one thing and another, but let's not go into that now,' said Caroline, silencing him with a raised hand.

'Why not?' asked Tom.

'You don't have time,' she replied, looking heavenwards.

'Would you like a drink?' asked Matthew.

Caroline glanced at Rupert uncertainly. 'Isn't it rather early? Oh, you mean something warm and wet?' she replied. 'Not just yet, thanks all the same. Wouldn't we be better employed taking a look at where you're putting us?'

Matthew nodded and led the way up to their rooms. Tom brought up the rear, carrying their overnight bags, and proceeded towards the far end of the landing to show Caroline into the room they had named after Jemima Puddleduck. Matthew threw open the door of Squirrel Nutkin, their most spacious bedroom above the sitting room, with a three-windowed turret. He made sure he closed the door properly behind him, just in case. Taking in the room as an actor does on stage, Rupert glanced at the prancing squirrels in the Beatrix Potter prints above the bed, until his eyes came to rest on Matthew. Fully cognizant of Rupert's attitude towards tweeness, Matthew turned away, sat on the sofa in the turret, and removed the soft toy Squirrel Nutkin while trying not to look irritated.

'You've done very well for yourself,' said Rupert.

'Do you mean with Langdales, or with Tom?' drawled Matthew, secretly delighted.

'Both. He's very easy on the eye, and *such* a good listener, although do I detect a slight – '

'That's enough,' said Matthew. 'And why shouldn't I have done well? This house has a certain appeal and Tom has the advantage of youth.'

'You've seen he's balding on the crown, I take it?' Matthew did not reply. Rupert proceeded to stand behind him and look out. 'By the way, I never did get an explanation of your antics that morning, did I?'

His stomach knotted, for he had not expected this acidity to be thrust at him so quickly, and drummed his fingers on the sofa arm. 'You need to keep your mouth firmly shut about us, remember?'

'What a pity. I was hoping for a little chat over a large cognac, later.'

'With or without an audience?' asked Matthew, tight-lipped.

Rupert thought for a moment. 'Preferably without, so that I don't have to be polite. What beats me is how you could begin to afford this place?'

'You, of all people, should not be asking that.'

Rupert came closer so that he could look Matthew in the eye. 'Why not? You're the man I mistakenly believed would be my life-partner. It might be refreshing to hear about what I've missed.'

It was best not to rise to that, especially as Tom might burst into the room to check if they were ready to go downstairs. Matthew turned to glance at the door, clasped his hands behind his head and gazed out. 'It's really quite simple. Where should I begin? A place that needed some remedial work in a remote location was considered something of a white elephant when we were house-hunting. When it came to be auctioned, in heavy snow one March, it only just made the reserve. Even so, it was more than we could afford, but an inheritance came at the right moment.'

'How convenient. It must be worth a fortune now?'

'Hardly, compared to down south. Even now, there's a limited market for this type of house. It's a slow commute on winding lanes to a decent-sized town – and these minor roads don't get gritted...' He paused to think of more reasons. 'It's rather substantial for most retired couples, and the garden is generous to say the least. It really doesn't make sense as a second home, and we still sometimes struggle as a B and B. But, in spite of everything, Langdales has a hold over me. We're very comfortable here, and I'd like you to respect that.'

'I don't set out to break up relationships, unlike some I could mention.' Matthew said nothing, while Rupert began moving about the room, glancing at the antiques and the pictures as he did so. 'You've had to put up with a great deal, obviously.'

'I shall ignore that. We only need two wet summers on the trot, or an outbreak of foot and mouth and we're done for. There's still a mortgage. Happy now?'

Matthew turned his head only to see Rupert wiping the surface of the chest of drawers with his index finger. Thinking the longed-for reunion had been a mistake, Matthew looked away. It was raining again. Rupert glanced through the door into the en-suite and made a show of wringing his hands while approaching Matthew.

'Somebody *has* slipped up! Not a squirrel in sight.'

'So how long have you needed a minder?' asked Matthew.

'I wouldn't go that far, but...' Rupert sat down next to Matthew. 'I had a few problems some years back. She watches out for me.'

'She must have her work cut out. Drink?'

Rupert leaned towards him. 'Not now, surely?'

'No, because of drink, I meant.'

'Not that it's any of your business, but I am allowed to drink, although I can get a bit...'

'Excitable?' Rupert nodded, but avoided the look Matthew was treating him to. 'That's a pity. Well, we want a quiet life while you're under my roof, is that clear?' Matthew stood up.

'Shall we join the ladies?' asked Rupert. 'And just when we were having so much fun! Will little Tommy Tufty be getting jealous?'

Matthew frowned. 'Tom must *never* know about us, remember?'

'Are you so ashamed of me?'

'Of course not. I don't want Tom to think that there might be a resurgence in our affections,' replied Matthew. 'You know very well what I once felt for you.'

'Then why do you have to shroud it in secrecy?'

'Because I think it will complicate things. Personally, I'm not finding the age gap all that easy. Never have done. I don't want him to know about any blemishes in my past.'

'So, I'm a blemish?'

Matthew blushed. 'If you must know, I was surprised that you'd worn so well.'

Rupert laughed. 'You still fancy me?'

'You've kept your looks, but you don't need me to tell you that.' Matthew hesitated. 'Even so, a little of you still goes a long way, and *that* I find a trifle off-putting, so don't get your hopes up.'

'Thanks.'

'I gather you're on your own? Did I hear Caroline mention someone when you were standing by the car?'

'Yes, and good riddance to him!'

Matthew hurried Rupert out of the bedroom onto the landing to find Caroline and Tom looking as if they had been hovering there for some time.

'I love the themed room, Tom,' said Rupert. 'May I call you Squirrel from now on? Or perhaps Tufty? By the way, did you know your hair was standing up on the crown?'

Tom set his face as he smoothed it down. 'I've just had it cut.'

Rupert stroked his chin. 'In my honour? And where do you bed down? I suppose Squirrel would have his dray in the attic?'

'Yes, our flat takes up the entire roof-space. It really is a marvellous area, full of interesting angles and corners, isn't it, Matthew?'

Matthew nodded sullenly, but remembering the stove in the sitting room would need attending to, he urged them to return downstairs. Tom looked as if he could cheerfully push Rupert down them.

They entered the sitting room, or, much to Matthew's annoyance, what guests referred to as the residents' lounge. Rupert, with his propensity to position himself in the middle of a room, as if centre stage, stood under the crystal chandelier. 'Remarkable! It's like something out of Coward. *Hay Fever* comes to mind.' He coughed when he saw Matthew's face and added, 'In the nicest possible way, of course.'

So much for our attempt at definitive country-house style, thought Matthew. Meanwhile, Caroline was appraising their dark, heavy furniture, her eyes coming to rest on a glass-fronted cabinet, crammed with Beatrix Potter figurines. Matthew had realised for some time that the room was looking tired, although that feeling might have been reinforced since the Christmas decorations had been stowed away. However, it looked passable on the website with the foreground framed by lilies and what was left of their pink and gold "Royal Gardens" tea set. Matthew directed Caroline to the sofa.

Her gaze fell on the smouldering logs in the wood-burning stove and she smiled archly. 'Surely you must have one chimney that draws properly, out of so many?'

'You've forgotten to open the vents properly,' murmured Tom. Matthew fiddled with them. Rupert and Tom were standing as if unsure where to place themselves. Rupert had probably wanted to sit next to Tom on the sofa but Matthew had scotched that by seating Caroline there. When Matthew was satisfied with the growing flame, he turned round to see Rupert undressing Tom with his eyes, and promptly showed Rupert over to the sofa so that he could sit next to his sister. Matthew and Tom sat down in the armchairs.

'So, with all this to look after, Squirrel, how much time do you get for the festival?'

'One has to *make* time. Actually, I got very good reviews last year.'

'No one likes a show-off, Tom,' said Matthew.

Tom's eyes glazed, but he did not pick Matthew up on this. 'Sorry, Rupert. I'd hate to bore you.'

'Don't worry about that,' said Caroline. 'Another five minutes and you'll be lucky to get a word in edgeways.'

They had been discussing the previous festival for some time, when Rupert got to the point. 'Never mind last year, Squirrel, what have you set your heart on in *Importance*?'

Tom stared at Rupert as if he were simple. 'Isn't it obvious?'

Rupert laughed, knowingly. 'Does he always give this much trouble, Matthew?' Matthew ignored this, but noticed that Tom's eyes were shining. 'I'd like to see your face if you didn't land the role you'd set your heart on, but I never will of course.'

'Why's that?'

'Don't worry, Squirrel. From what I've heard, and, more to the point, *seen* of you, there seems no doubt that you'll be walking away with the role you richly deserve.'

The effect on Tom was instantaneous. Not for the first time did Matthew notice that blush appearing. Tom ran his hand through his hair; he was justly proud of it, in spite of the bald patch. 'You think I might be in with a chance?'

Rupert made an expansive gesture, brushing against Tom's arm as he did so, and lowering his voice. 'More than a chance. So, now that's settled, what else do I need to know?'

'Apart from Tom,' said Matthew, 'things were none too good last season.'

Tom smiled, as if gaining confidence. 'Poor crits, except for me. Disastrous box office receipts and as if that wasn't enough, a thoroughly unsettled wet week.'

'Perhaps I should explain,' said Matthew. 'May had been sweltering, but the rain reached biblical proportions for the one week in June when we were playing. We had an unparalleled deficit. And the play itself was not a comedy, of course, which never helps.'

Rupert opened his mouth, but Matthew and Tom were beginning their well-practised double-act.

'It wasn't that bad, Matthew,' said Tom. 'By Wednesday, there were enough people to stand up and be counted.'

Matthew threw back his head. 'And by the last night, it was almost half full!'

Rupert frowned as he looked from one to the other.

'Perhaps if Eleanor had not broken the director's spirit...' mused Matthew.

'Such a pity that he felt compelled to flee in the small hours. After all, why wouldn't he, after an eighteen-hour technical rehearsal?'

'Which left *me* in sole charge,' said Matthew.

They chuckled over this to unnerve Rupert a little; perhaps to make him less sure of himself. Matthew checked that Rupert had his attention.

'Remind me, Tom, if ever a director walks out on us again, never to oversee the dress rehearsals *and* play opposite Eleanor as her husband. I still have the battle scars.'

Feeling that Rupert had probably heard enough, and noticing that Caroline's eyes were resting on the sherry and whisky decanters on a side table – probably wondering whether Rupert had noticed them – Matthew realised they had still not had a drink, and suggested tea, which they agreed to. Matthew signalled to Tom. When he returned with the tray, Caroline was speaking.

'And with so much going on, the run-up to Christmas did not turn out as either of us had expected.' She finished with a shrill laugh.

'Thank you, dear, but we don't need to go into that now,' said Rupert. 'I intend making the most of the spring and early summer after the rigours of the winter.'

'A post-Christmas *pamper* perhaps?' she enquired.

'If you say so. Regarding my accommodation, I feel I deserve somewhere very comfortable, and preferably secluded.'

Matthew and Tom glanced at each other. 'You'll need a bolt-hole to escape to during the inevitable falling out with the cast,' said Tom.

'Which usually kicks in after three weeks of rehearsal, but it's usually blown itself out by the first night,' said Matthew.

Rupert grinned, but looked down at his shoes, which would have been improved with a polish.

'The cottage we have in mind may well suit you then,' said Tom. 'It's quite remote.'

'And there are no neighbours,' said Matthew. 'Tell me, Rupert, do you still get plagued with autograph hunters?'

'Not as much as I would like,' he replied, with a narcissistic pout worthy of Norma Desmond. 'But I do a certain amount of entertaining, if you see what I mean, and I don't want any net-curtain twitchers knowing my business.'

Tom winked. 'Privacy we can do in spades, but there *is* a catch.'

Matthew smiled. 'Even so, it's not insurmountable.' For the moment, the subject was closed.

It took Tom a moment to catch Rupert's eye and mention that he would like to perform a reading for him as Jack. Rupert agreed almost too readily and they disappeared into the study. Caroline took this as her cue to go upstairs and change. Shuffling about in the hall, with a duster at the ready, Matthew could hear Rupert overplaying Lady Bracknell, and he even caught a few words from Tom. Mindful of being caught eavesdropping, he gathered up the tea things and made his way into the kitchen, hoping that Tom would make a favourable impression. Tom had clearly set his heart on it, and the idea that he might not succeed was proving unthinkable. Remembering previous occasions when the normally easy-going Tom did not get his own way, Matthew trembled to think of the inevitable fall-out that would ensue if he did not.

Chapter Three

Once Rupert had finally emerged from the study, Matthew – who had continued hovering with the kitchen door ajar in a vain attempt not to miss anything – asked him to come down for seven o'clock. Rupert disappeared up to his bedroom to change, the hall, stairs and landing ringing with compliments regarding Tom. As soon as it was safe to do so, Matthew lost no time in asking Tom how he thought his reading had gone. He was cheerfully optimistic.

When Rupert and Caroline descended the staircase, looking – if anything – slightly over-dressed, it was clear they had made an effort. Brother and sister took up their positions on the sofa once more, while Matthew and Tom sat rather stiffly in the armchairs. Matthew was permanently on edge, ready to head Rupert off should he reveal anything about their shared past.

Caroline took one sip of her gin and tonic, and made a face. 'I'm sorry, Tom, but this is virtually neat! Could I trouble you for some more tonic?'

Tom smiled and rose to top up her glass, as if nothing could ever be too much trouble. Caroline took another sip, nodded, and as the gin gradually began to take hold, she leaned over the arm of the sofa towards Matthew who had sat down in the armchair next to her. Praying that she would make no mention of their having met previously, Matthew tensed.

She was watching him, as if thinking of a good opening gambit. 'I suppose you're wondering why Rupert has accepted this posting, should I call it, for want of a better word?'

'Working with amateurs?' asked Matthew.

Rupert chuckled. 'It's not every day I'll get to play Lady Bracknell. You see, we've been having a terrible time.'

'So you keep mentioning, although we never seem to get to the bottom of it,' said Tom.

'Since father had his stroke,' said Caroline.

'I'm sorry to hear that,' said Matthew.

'Not as much as we were...' said Rupert.

Gerald Hammond had been in his early sixties when he came to terms with Rupert's sexuality. Matthew had been invited to the villa for a father and son crisis meeting. He recalled an overdose of garden statuary, the dome of sky stretching above the umbrella pines, the dazzling limestone of the Alpes Maritimes and the winter wind stirring up the Mediterranean into foaming flecks. Matthew had never forgotten their tête-à-tête on that vast expanse of terrace, and felt imprisoned by the yards of white balustrade when Gerald had begged Matthew to take his "waster of a son" off his hands. Matthew had not risen to the challenge.

Still sipping her gin and tonic, Caroline eyed Tom, and then Matthew. 'It has become what you might call an unusual ménage.' She glanced at Rupert, as if to check how far she should go. 'I suppose now is as good a time as any to explain things? Naturally we didn't want father to go into a care home and as he *refuses* to return to England, he now has a live-in carer, and...' Here, she paused to search for a tissue.

'At eighty-nine, Dad's losing it, I'm afraid,' said Rupert. 'But there is enough money to keep him in his own home.'

'More than enough. Well, that's what we're hoping,' she added. 'But we feel so helpless.'

'What is it that's bothering you?' asked Matthew.

'Fortunately, or unfortunately, Dad has a nosy neighbour, and she's started phoning us because she's worried that Louis Philippe, the carer, may be exerting undue influence–'

'And trying to swing the will in his favour,' said Rupert. 'She saw papers lying about one day. Louis Philippe may well be a rogue.'

She pursed her lips. 'I do wish that you'd let me finish at least one sentence. We are the natural heirs, and therefore have every right to take what rightfully belongs to us.'

Rupert leaned away from her. 'I'm not stopping you.'

'I can't begin to describe how dreadful it's been. Considering what's at stake...'

'Do we have to? We've only just got here,' pleaded Rupert.

'The brewery had to be sold, of course,' said Caroline, meeting Matthew's gaze.

'Yes, I was wondering what had happened to that–' Recollecting that he was not supposed to have any previous knowledge of Hammonds Brewery in front of Tom, Matthew froze. While failing to imagine either Rupert or Caroline excelling in *"the purple of commerce"* as Lady Bracknell described it, he tried to ignore the sideways look of curiosity he was getting from Tom.

Rupert's eyes dulled. 'That was my fault, of course. It usually is.'

Matthew turned to her. 'Do go on.'

'After mother died, that was the time to do it.'

Rupert frowned. 'To do what?'

'Put him in a home.'

'But I didn't want that.'

'But you're never around when you're needed, are you?' She turned to Matthew once more. 'Father's clearly not been able to cope for some time. We could have done something about the villa earlier.'

Rupert half-smiled. 'And there's the Bentley, presumably rusting away.'

'I'm sure cars don't rust in the South of France,' she huffed.

'Those houses near St. Pancras, purchased in 1968 – '

'I think you'll find it was 1969.' Caroline shifted her eyes from Rupert to Matthew. 'Fine houses reduced to a honeycomb of bed-sitting rooms with almost indecent haste.' The words tripped off her tongue as if she had used the phrase before; she appeared jubilant that she had managed to recall it.

'Did you not get a power-of-attorney organised?' asked Matthew, somewhat incredulously.

It was time for a grimace and a roll of the eyes. 'You might well ask.'

Rupert looked up from his drink. 'What do I know about things like that? I'm just an actor.'

'And not a very good one at that,' she told him. 'The shock was so intense that we were frozen into inertia.'

'We could do with some money now,' said Rupert. 'Caroline's taken early retirement, against my advice, and I'm working hand to mouth. That's why I need this job with the festival.'

She rolled her eyes. 'Yes – no savings, despite my warnings, and as to the film money…' Here she paused, as if to relish the situation fully. 'He blew that long ago. Anyway, as far as we can gather, after that far-from-satisfactory phone call with the neighbour, it could be a disaster waiting to happen.'

'I have to agree that it does sound very dodgy,' said her brother.

Tom reluctantly excused himself to check on the dinner.

'Do you get on?' asked Matthew, tentatively.

Caroline put down her glass. 'There you have it. Father has never got on with Rupert, not helped by going down the acting route.'

'When there was a perfectly good brewery to run,' said Rupert, not looking either of them in the eye. 'I mean, what *was* I thinking of?'

'And he didn't take kindly to your lifestyle.'

'That's an understatement,' grinned Rupert.

'And although I've done my best, I've never been awfully keen on him, but that doesn't make it any the less worrying.'

'About him, or your inheritance?' asked Matthew.

'Both! With him being so far away, we haven't seen him since mother's funeral, and that must be four, no, five years ago now.'

'He's probably forgotten who we are,' said Rupert, 'which is why we're terrified he might change his will.'

'All this chit-chat is giving me a headache, but this festival thingy of yours might give Rupert a chance to prove his mettle as a director. I hear they pay well.' She knitted her brows. 'It's not too late to hope that he can make a success of something.'

Matthew turned to Rupert. 'You haven't directed before?'

'Of course not,' said Caroline, smiling, 'but he'll soon pick it up.'

'I'm looking forward to it enormously,' said Rupert, before raising his voice an octave as if already playing Lady Bracknell. '*Director*, and my name *above the title* in a key role.'

Matthew turned to see Tom framed in the doorway, looking so young compared to the rest of them, and almost provocative. Glancing at Matthew, Tom appeared to forget their guests for a moment and said, 'As a battle-axe in a third-rate production of a play that's been done to death?'

Matthew straightened his face and looked at Rupert. 'I'm afraid that you have already upset our most important member.'

Rupert threw up his hands in mock horror.

'*The* most important, I think you mean, but that's too good a story for now,' corrected Tom, raising a hand. 'It ought to be saved until dinner, which is ready, if you'd like to come through.'

Matthew showed Caroline the way into the half-panelled dining room, while Tom went to collect the pâté and toast. The chandelier had been dimmed and the reflections of the candle flames flickering in the mirrors created a romantic glow. Rupert and Caroline glanced around the room and then at each other, approvingly, while Matthew poured the wine.

'Perhaps now is the time to turn to the story of our leading lady and one of my oldest friends,' said Matthew, when they were all settled. 'Eleanor Vane was under the impression that she'd secured the role of Lady Bracknell until you came on the scene, Rupert.'

'She selects every play with an eye to playing the lead, so you can imagine how she greeted the news,' added Tom.

Rupert held up his glass against the light of the nearest candle. 'To the festival!' They raised their glasses. 'A woman with sharp elbows? I can't wait.'

Matthew agreed. 'She's been conniving with a view to this for some time. It's difficult to blame her. It *is* the role of a lifetime.'

'Such telling phrases,' said Caroline. 'So beautifully expressed.'

Tom nodded. 'And she's the right age, more or less.'

Matthew shook his head. 'I disagree, especially as she's always looked younger than she is.'

Tom laughed. 'Not that he's biased. Eleanor used to be Matthew's girlfriend.'

There was a quickening of interest in the room. This was the last thing that Matthew needed just now, and his lips tightened. He glared at Tom, but this was wasted as he was beaming at Rupert. 'A long time ago, and not for very long,' said Matthew, observing Rupert's expression, and not liking what he saw.

'But he's always had a soft spot for her.' Tom turned to Matthew. 'I was led to believe she's forty-five.'

'Who told you that?'

'She did.'

Rupert piped up with, 'As Lady Bracknell has it: "*...no woman should ever be quite accurate about her age. It looks so calculating...*"'

'However old she is,' said Matthew, 'it didn't stop her from being incandescent.'

Tom nodded. 'You see, Rupert, the decision took place without the president and the chairman feeling they were under any obligation to tell Eleanor.'

His sister frowned. 'They are trying to squeeze her out?'

'Ah! An inside job,' said Rupert, entering into the spirit of it. 'By your very *own* members?'

'Perhaps this Eleanor has burned too many bridges?' asked Caroline.

Relieved that their attention was diverted by Eleanor's shortcomings, Matthew glanced in Tom's direction to signify that their dinner party was going well, while the others were concentrating on their plates. 'But she tends to over-commit and then flakes out with exhaustion.'

'I have to confess,' Rupert told them, 'that the idea of playing Lady Bracknell had never crossed my mind until it was suggested to me. And when I'd trailed the idea that my name above the title would increase ticket sales, I was home and dry.'

'If only Blake Benedict had not slipped so badly,' said Tom.

Rupert started. 'What do you mean by that?'

'Well, that role has been considered Eleanor's for as long as anyone can remember.'

'So he's the one who dropped out?' Rupert frowned. 'Rumour has it that he missed his footing coming out of his favourite watering-hole...'

Tom leaned forward as if he could not get enough of Rupert. 'So you read the gossip columns, too?'

'His friends, those who are still in touch, inform him.' Caroline shrugged. 'He's just upset that he's no longer in the inner circle.'

'It's lucky you were available, then,' said Matthew.

'Something happened before Christmas, otherwise–'

'Not now, Caroline dearest.'

'Still, this production is taking you a long way from home, Rupert, and that's never a good idea,' she told him.

'Away from your watchful eye?' he asked.

Caroline turned to Matthew, pointedly. 'Tell me, do you have trouble finding the right sort of person to direct?'

Matthew looked at Tom to help him out. 'Sometimes, but we do pay above the going rate.'

'No, Matthew, you mean that up until now, Eleanor's company, Vane Construction, has always paid,' grinned Tom.

'She's in charge of a construction company?' asked Rupert, sounding bewildered.

'Not exactly,' replied Matthew. 'She was divorced last autumn from her husband Julian Vane, and we have been discouraged from talking about it. But because of that, she has asked Felicity to be the main sponsor. She *claims* she won't have as much spare income as she's used to, or so we have been led to believe.'

'Even though she's managed to keep hold of that sprawling house on Windermere,' said Tom.

Matthew nodded. 'Spinnakers. Vulgar beyond belief, but there's no getting away from its location in Storrs Park.'

'With oodles of lake frontage,' added Tom.

'The divorce is also the reason why she's stepped down, and also why this play was selected. If only I could have had more of a say in it.'

'Why didn't you?' asked Caroline, peering at him through the candles.

'He flounced off the already minuscule committee in a huff,' said Tom.

'The role of Lady Bracknell needs no introduction,' said Matthew, becoming expansive in the hope that he would not be questioned about his petulant exit. 'She dominates two big scenes, and she felt she could manage that.'

'And,' said Tom, rising to clear the plates, 'everyone felt that, under the circumstances, we needed a comedy.'

'So there is a great deal of discontent already,' observed Caroline.

'For me, as well, as I normally play the lead, and there's *nothing* for me in this.'

Matthew rose to help Tom, leaving Rupert and Caroline staring bleakly at each other. Once in the kitchen, Matthew carved the lamb, and he and Tom fetched everything in together. Once they had helped themselves to vegetables, Rupert held the floor. Matthew had hoped for some key insights regarding his favourite plays, but Rupert was far more interested in telling them funny stories, which they duly chuckled through, including Caroline, who had surely heard them before.

By the time they had rounded off the meal with a much-applauded chocolate mousse, one of Tom's specialities, Rupert was rubbing his eyes. This must have been his cue to Caroline, as she refused coffee, pleaded exhaustion and made as if to retire early for the night. Profuse in her thanks, she was gone in a matter of moments. When Rupert also declined coffee, Matthew feared that he might miss the opportunity to have that tête-à-tête, however uncomfortable it might prove to be. They had pushed back their chairs and stood up before she left, were following her into the hall when Matthew congratulated himself on the dinner had gone better than he had dared hope. Now was the chance to get Rupert on his own, if only Tom would fade into the background. They were standing awkwardly in the hall when Tom announced that he must tidy up in the kitchen. Rupert readily agreed to a night-cap in the sitting room. Even so, it appeared difficult to shake Tom off, for he followed them.

The oak-panelled sitting room, all lamp-light and shadows. Having realised that they both needed a kindly light, Matthew kept the chandelier dimmed, and soon had the stove built up. Tom unlocked the corner cupboard and selected a single malt, a phenomenon not witnessed by their paying guests. He poured them a couple of measures, replaced the bottle, but left the key on the side. Smiling, Tom closed the sitting room door like a model butler.

Relaxed, Matthew and Rupert were both looking younger in the subdued lighting. Having joined Rupert on the sofa, Matthew sipped in contented silence, enjoying the smoky, peaty flavour on his tongue and the warmth of it in his chest until he felt his eyes grow heavy. He came to with a start, leaning on Rupert's shoulder, only after a nudge from Rupert, who was rubbing a finger around the rim of his glass and smiling to himself.

'I suppose you're disappointed in how things have turned out for me?' asked Rupert.

There was no answer to this, so Matthew, still befuddled, said, 'I suppose we all find our own level.'

Judging from the way Rupert stiffened next to him, this was clearly not the correct response, for Rupert's voice took on a brittle quality Matthew instinctively shied away from. 'By the way, what will you do when Squirrel's no longer so good-looking?'

Matthew felt his stomach contract. 'I'm not sure what game you're playing, Rupert, but I don't like it. I will not allow you to come between us, is that clear? I don't care if he's as bald as a coot and gets to look like W.H. Auden because I'll be looking at our shared history, mutual passions, rather than what he looks like.'

Eyes bulging, Rupert clasped his hand. 'How worthy you make it all sound. Well, if you and Tom ever do drift apart, I don't intend making the same mistake twice.'

'Who said anything about drifting?' asked Matthew, leaning away from him. 'You've only just got here.'

'You shouldn't have leaned against me and fallen asleep,' said Rupert, squeezing his hand. 'Surely that signifies your true feelings, even if they're subliminal?'

Matthew snatched his hand away as if it had been scalded. 'What makes you think that?'

'Am I that toxic?' asked Rupert. 'Have you ever wondered why we didn't try harder?'

'You know very well why not. For a start, no one could have said that you didn't have a roving eye. Besides, you were never around.' Matthew eyed Rupert. 'I don't want to spoil this nostalgic furrow you're ploughing, but you need to put all that *firmly* behind you. Tom and I have been together for roughly ten years.'

'You're uncertain? That's not a good sign. We almost managed seven,' muttered Rupert, sipping his whisky.

'Not really. You can't count school, or when you were filming. And we never really lived together, did we?' He paused for a moment, wondering how far he should go for Rupert was looking as if he had been struck. 'Most of the time it was more off than on, or had you forgotten?'

'Well, if you want my opinion, Tom's too young for you,' Rupert replied. 'The strain is written all over his face.'

Matthew blinked. '*Strain?* What strain? You have the audacity to stay under my roof and start–'

'But didn't I just get the impression that you had other ideas?'

'Because I dozed off? Never,' said Matthew, rising and moving towards the fireplace. 'We can't go back. The idea is grotesque.'

'Yet, I have to say, it was *you* who hinted in the bedroom that you still find me attractive?'

Matthew looked him in the face. 'What?'

'Perhaps I still have a hold over you?'

'More likely I couldn't help smiling at your absurd presumption that everyone falls at your feet.'

Rupert chuckled. 'Ha! That's not how I read it.'

'You're living under a delusion, and all because there's a faint indication of your former good looks.'

Rupert shot Matthew his most melting expression. 'I want you back again.'

Matthew closed his eyes and shook his head. 'What's that out of?'

Rupert grinned. 'Coward, of course. *Private Lives.*'

'I might have known.' Matthew glanced in the mirror over the fireplace. There were shadows under his eyes. Composing several imaginary responses, but knowing that he could never utter them and retain Rupert as his guest, he turned round to face him. 'If you seriously think that I would fall for you again, and jeopardise my life here with Tom, you've got another think coming.'

'Say it often enough and you might come to believe it.'

'You disgust me.'

'Then why are you looking at me like that?' asked Rupert.

Matthew took himself off into the darkest corner of the room and perched on an occasional chair. 'If you think you're going to drive a wedge between Tom and me, you're living in a fantasy.'

'I wouldn't dream of it.'

Matthew's head was thumping. He would have given anything to be rid of Rupert. Should he drag Tom in from the kitchen? No, that would only make things worse. There was a long silence. Matthew made as if to leave the room, and then sat down again.

'I see now that I've been away from you for too long, and it's done you nothing but harm.' Rupert's self-satisfied grin was hard to bear. 'But tell me, when did you become so dull, Matthew?'

This took Matthew by surprise. 'Not dull: just monogamous, and that goes for both of us, so no more flirting, either with him, or with me.'

'But you've known me for most of my life,' said Rupert. 'Doesn't that count for anything?'

'You mean known *of* you,' Matthew countered. 'Do you really believe that I feel anything for you now?'

'You were very insistent at one time.'

Matthew laughed, but it was dry and brittle, and hung around in the room like the stale air he felt he was breathing in. 'That was my first mistake.'

'Perhaps you never understood that I couldn't afford to let you stand in the way of my career?'

Matthew stood up once more. He wanted to splutter. Had he misheard? 'Was that really at the forefront of your mind?' Looking back on this first evening of being reunited with Rupert, he never knew whether he was more shocked that his voice seemed to fill the room, or by the silence that followed. Fortunately, the kitchen was some way away across the hall, and Tom was unlikely to have heard him.

Matthew returned to the sofa this time, folding his arms, and they sat next to each other in silence for a few moments until Rupert offered him a rambling reconstruction of events, finishing with, 'You have no idea what it was like for me back then, being in the public eye.'

'Meaning?' asked Matthew, tensing his arms more tightly against his chest.

'For one thing, I wasn't as discreet as I might have been.'

'Why doesn't that surprise me?'

'I then became anxious about my career.'

Matthew caught Rupert's eye. 'Shouldn't you have thought of that before sleeping with every young actor or technician you could lay your hands on?'

'Not *every* single one,' said Rupert. 'Only those who were ready and willing.'

'Well, there were enough of them,' said Matthew. 'If you'd been capable of keeping things between ourselves, it would have been far more low-key.'

'You appear to have a very short memory,' retorted Rupert, somewhat pompously. 'Remember how the press tackled AIDS in the mid-eighties? Rock Hudson? I still had my contract for those children's films, and I couldn't afford to lose it. That, dear boy, would have been career suicide.'

'Yes, they were so incredibly wholesome, weren't they?'

Rupert half-smiled. 'That's why I had to manipulate things to show that I was settling down and getting married. Otherwise, it would have been career suicide. I couldn't be seen to have a live-in male partner back then, as well you know. Unfortunately, I couldn't shake you off without–'

'Shake me off?'

'I'm sorry. Perhaps that was the wrong expression. Without doing something drastic. Like giving marriage a go.'

Matthew stared at him and shook his head. 'You do realise I would have done anything for you back then?'

'That was part of the problem. You were too keen.'

Matthew wanted to scream. 'Hadn't I a right to be? I was in love with you.'

'Well of course, if I'd known how public opinion would alter, I might have taken the risk and carried on with my lifestyle, but by the time public opinion *had* changed, it seemed too late for us. All rather tragic, don't you think?'

'I don't do tragic, Rupert. Although, clearly, you still do.' Rupert sat there, head dipped, eyes fixed on the floor. The long pause that followed was in danger of gathering too much weight. 'Seriously, Rupert, I'm not sure I'd go so far as to say tragic, but it was deeply upsetting at the time. For me, at any rate, if not for you.' Matthew glanced at him, but he appeared strangely mute for once. 'If you really had cared for me, we could have found a way round it, somehow.'

'I guess you're right,' Rupert yawned and stretched. 'I suppose it was all my fault, as usual. I should never have allowed things to drift.'

'*Drift?* Wasn't it a case of you cutting the ropes and casting me off?'

'You were the one who abandoned me that morning.'

'Oh, we're back to that, are we?'

'Yes, and with good reason.'

They glared at each other in silence.

'Let it go, Matthew,' urged Rupert, after a while. 'You know I've never been one to hold grudges...'

This was more than Matthew could cope with. '*Grudges?* I've heard everything now. You were the one who wanted to get married.' Rupert's expression turned ugly, and realising he had been raising his voice, Matthew lowered it. 'Hadn't we better start again?'

'What did you have in mind? Rewind to our late teens?'

Ready to escape as soon as he could, Matthew decided that it was not worth throwing another log into the burner, but he raised an eyebrow when Rupert jumped up from the sofa to unlock the French windows, stepped outside and allowed the cold air to rush in.

'Now what are you up to?' asked Matthew.

'We should be enjoying the night sky, not arguing. Come and share it with me. It's such a clear night after the rain...' The back of Matthew's neck prickled. He could not help himself from inwardly reminiscing about their relationship when it was at its height: they had enjoyed working out the most obvious constellations.

'Please come back inside,' Matthew implored him. 'I'm sorry, but it shouldn't have to be like this.'

'Like what?' asked Rupert, returning and closing the doors behind him.

'So much unpleasantness.'

'I'm trying to be nice, even if you can't be,' said Rupert. Matthew did not respond. 'You must feel something for me, even if you're not prepared to admit it.

'How did you reach that startling conclusion?'

'You've kept my paintings, even if they are relegated to the cloakroom.'

'I don't know how you work that out. Don't breathe a word about them to Tom, either, or I'm finished.'

Rupert sighed. 'I've often wondered what it would be like if our paths crossed again, and now I know. How sad that you've never been able to move on.'

He did have a point. When Rupert sat down next to him, Matthew experienced a surge of affection, for on their good days together everything had been pointing in their favour.

'Do you remember the time we spent your birthday together?' asked Matthew, looking into his eyes. 'I felt sure that it would stay in my memory at the time, and so it has proved. It was one of the few occasions when I thought I was living the high life.'

'When I got us those tickets for the Haymarket, and we went on to the Dorchester?'

'No, it was an early lunch at the Dorchester followed by a matinee,' insisted Matthew.

'I could have sworn it was the other way round.'

'You were performing in the evening, so it couldn't have been,' argued Matthew. 'I've thought about it a lot. I still live in hope of something happening again with every detail as perfect.'

'Difficult, but perhaps not impossible,' said Rupert, grasping Matthew's hand once more. 'Anyway, once the film work finished, and I got on to the touring treadmill, it became hard finding anyone who could stay the course with me. You'll never be able to comprehend how lonely you made me.'

'Why didn't you do something about it while you still could?' asked Matthew, hardly believing what Rupert was telling him.

'I suppose I was crazy with rage for too long.' Rupert averted his gaze. 'Why were you in such a hurry to make contact and get me up here, if you had no intention of–'

'I didn't.'

'That's not what it looks like.'

'It was Tom's idea.'

'Oh, my fan club wanted to meet me in person, is that it?'

'Not exactly,' replied Matthew. 'If you must know – but please don't tell a soul – Tom wanted to get to know you, twist your arm perhaps, so that he could be sure of playing the lead.'

'In that case,' said Rupert, his tone menacing, 'he needs to be careful what he wishes for, because there is no way I will–'

The door flew open. Caroline stood framed in her silk dressing-gown. Realising that Tom was standing behind her, Matthew snatched his hand away, but probably not soon enough.

Her eyes fell on the empty glasses. 'What *on earth* is going on? I suppose *you've* been at the whisky?'

'Yes, what's going on?' asked Tom, although lacking Caroline's dramatic inflection.

Rupert, for once, remained silent. Clutching her dressing-gown to her throat, Caroline looked her brother up and down. 'I don't mind telling you I'm very disappointed, when you *promised* to be on your best behaviour.' Silence. 'You have nothing to say for yourself? Well, you can count me out of coming to stay with you during rehearsals. I have better things to do with my time than look after the likes of you.'

Rupert muttered, 'Some good news at last.'

Caroline's unyielding tone continued. 'I would have thought you'd know how to behave as a guest under someone else's roof –

especially when you swore to make a good impression – but obviously not.'

His colour heightening, he glanced up at her for a second and looked away just as quickly. 'You've made your point, dear.'

'I tried to ignore the racket you were making until I could bear it no longer.' Her eyes looked as if she was searching for the right phrase. 'Not only am I thoroughly ashamed of you, once again I find your behaviour perfectly idiotic.'

'Nothing new there,' said Rupert insolently.

Caroline took a step forward as if to strike him. Unable to bear any more, for fear of what might come out, Matthew fled to the kitchen and slammed the door behind him. Their voices became instantly muffled. Blinking at the brightness, he pressed himself against the back of the door. Not for the first time, he told himself that Rupert was nothing to him.

Unable to cope with someone repeatedly knocking on the door, he opened it to find Tom, with Rupert standing behind him. Caroline was calling down the last of her glacial good nights from the top of the staircase.

Rupert smiled at him fiendishly. 'You see what you've done now?' Without waiting for an answer, he excused himself and made his way up to bed.

'What was all that about?' asked Tom, joining him in the kitchen, while Matthew closed the door and threw up his hands.

'Didn't I tell you that this festival was doomed? There's no dealing with that man.'

Tom turned to face him and spoke slowly and deliberately. 'Yet only a moment ago you were holding hands. Would you mind telling me what's going on, or would you rather I didn't know?'

Matthew tried to improve on Tom's hard look. 'Well, you practically threw yourself at him when he got here.'

'I'm surprised you noticed, you were so busy eyeing him up. You do know there's a connection between you two?'

Matthew threw back his head and laughed. 'Really? I've heard everything now.' His mind and body were suddenly weary, and he ached for bed. 'Well, connection or not, I want him out of here first thing.'

'I can't see that happening, with all that you've planned, but you know best,' said Tom. He paused while he searched Matthew's face, slightly more sympathetically. 'You're sure you haven't run into him before, by any chance?'

'Don't you think I'd have told you?' spluttered Matthew.

'Can you explain, then, why you said you wondered what had happened to the brewery, if you hadn't set eyes on him before?'

Matthew turned this over in his mind, desperately trying to think of a way out. 'There can't be that many Hammonds Breweries and I had a hunch that they might have been connected with the one I had heard of. They were taken over some years ago. You won't remember it, seeing as you were probably ten at the time.'

Tom did not look convinced. 'Well, you *looked* as if you knew them, that's all. And you're obviously quite taken with him.'

'Most amusing,' said Matthew. 'I know you want to gossip, but it doesn't seem right to talk about him while he's still here, so shall we go up?'

Flicking off the kitchen lights, Matthew pretended not to notice that Tom was shaking his head, as if the situation was far from being resolved. While following him upstairs, Matthew paused when he passed Rupert's door, and wondered whether or not they ought to remove that Squirrel Nutkin name plate. After all, there was something infantile about it that he had never come to terms with, and the last thing they needed was Rupert making fun of Tom. Dire thoughts of tomorrow morning soon overpowered any trifling concerns about name plates, however, as Matthew groaned at the prospect of another restless night.

Chapter Four

Rupert and Caroline emerged for breakfast later than had been agreed, but were well-dressed enough to pass muster with Eleanor for the viewing of her cottage. Rupert reeked of something divine out of a bottle. There was no mention of the night before, but from the black looks passing between brother and sister, it was clear that their departure could not come soon enough. Even so, everything pointed to it being a full morning: after Rupert had seen Eleanor in her cottage, he was to have meetings with the wardrobe mistresses and later with the stage manager and the sound and lighting expert. Anxious that Rupert might get lost, Matthew offered to drive them over, especially as it was a murky day. Caroline had to be included in the trip as Matthew could not possibly leave her alone with Tom, for fear of what might come out. Tom had reluctantly agreed to stay behind and clear up.

The journey was indeed only ten minutes or so along minor roads margined with dry-stone walls or tightly clipped hawthorn hedges. It remained misty and was very much a monochrome day; grey, still, lifeless, as if the country was resting before the onslaught of spring. Matthew pulled up outside Eleanor's cottage. She had arrived already, and had parked her huge black vehicle – the tinted windows making it appear vaguely presidential – at an awkward angle. He parked alongside and noticed her staring out of the window with her arms folded. She had scraped back her hair into a pony-tail which made her look more severe than usual, and was wearing a Hermès scarf and a Barbour jacket. She was a handsome woman, who carried herself well, but the small lines around her mouth revealed more historic disappointment than happiness. Having been introduced, with much hollow laughter, and after a few generalisations about the weather, they moved into the living room. Caroline distanced herself immediately to view the garden through the window, while Eleanor got down to business.

'Although it's hard to believe on a day like today,' she began, 'this room is south-facing.' She then invited Rupert and Caroline to view the upstairs by themselves. 'There's no need for *you* to go upstairs, too,' she whispered, once they had reached the landing. Matthew took his foot off the bottom tread and turned towards her. 'I get the impression that Felicity doesn't want me to oust him with Operation Bracknell.'

Matthew laughed, but it was more a release of tension than anything else. Eleanor had not given up, and probably wouldn't until the first night. Was it time to speak out? He moistened his lips. 'Let me explain,' he replied, lowering his voice and leading her away from the staircase towards the window. 'Felicity never fancied the idea of your Lady Bracknell towering over her Miss Prism.' Eleanor fixed him with a similar insolent look he had witnessed so often on stage. 'But you seem to think that since you're not playing Lady Bracknell, you can play Miss Prism, and she's furious as it's the role she was expecting to audition for.'

As she turned away to glance out of the window, and felt her pony-tail, her face hardened. 'That's absurd.'

'And have you considered that you might be miscast as Miss Prism?'

She turned sharply. '*Miscast?*'

'You didn't shine as brightly as usual last year, and you wouldn't want two duds in a row.'

Eleanor was still looking ill at ease and Matthew hoped he might have the upper hand for once: retaliation on his side was long overdue. 'Duds?' She took a step back. 'Who said anything about duds?'

'Let's not dwell on that now.' Matthew felt his skin prickling; he indicated that she should lower her voice. 'Put yourself in Rupert's place for a moment. He won't want you anywhere near the festival, knowing how much you loathe him, so I doubt you'll get to play Miss Prism.'

She shook her head. 'How much have you told him about me?'

Studying the floor, he murmured, 'He prised it out of me.'

'So, I can't even trust *you*?' Her mouth became little more than a thin line. 'I'm to be left out of my own festival – the festival inaugurated by my parents. Is that it?'

Unable to look her in the eye, Matthew felt the back of his collar. 'Haven't Tom and I indicated that it would do you good to take some time off?'

'Well, let me tell *you*, Matthew, that I've been doing some thinking of my own,' said Eleanor, waving a finger at him. 'I never wanted to be steam-rolled into this rental agreement with Rupert in the first place, and having set eyes on him, I'm not sure I want to go through with it. I can't accept that man's money.' They could hear animated voices from above. 'I don't suppose you stood up to him for me?'

'In what way?'

'Persuade him to relinquish Lady Bracknell and stick to directing?'

Matthew swallowed. 'I did try, Eleanor.'

She clutched his arm. 'You do realise how much I still want Bracknell?'

As her grip tightened, he pulled away; in spite of Eleanor's continued plotting, Matthew regarded Rupert playing Lady Bracknell as a foregone conclusion. Glancing towards the ceiling, Matthew lowered his voice. 'Of course, but we're in too deep with Rupert now. I don't think you'll budge him. We, that is Tom and I, both think you need a complete rest. And so must you, if truth be told, otherwise you wouldn't have stepped down as president and chairman.'

'That's nonsense.'

'Why not have a complete rest and don't act this year? You say you're exhausted. You've never had to run Spinnakers on your own before, and the garden will need tackling in spring. I mean, how much energy have you got at fifty?'

Her face turned steely. 'I'm nowhere near fifty.' He tried not to splutter. 'You really don't have any conception as to how much I'm relying on you, do you? You're my man on the inside, as it were.'

Had Tom already mentioned to her that he suspected some sort of connection between him and Rupert, *perhaps while I was driving over,* he wondered. 'I'm not sure what you mean by that. Rupert has been my guest for one night, at *your* bidding. I know very little more than you, and I certainly have no influence over him, or anyone else for that matter.' He drew closer to her and with his voice just above a whisper, he told her, 'But Felicity, and the others, want *his* face on the posters to sell tickets.'

She tossed her head. 'I'd like his head on a block.'

'Do you enjoy being so acid?'

'I'm exhausted, I tell you!'

'Make up your mind...'

When they heard Rupert's enthusiastic cries at the top of the staircase, Eleanor rolled her eyes, but by the time Rupert and Caroline had come downstairs, she and Matthew were smiling, albeit rather tightly.

Rupert said, 'It's not quite what I was looking for, but–'

'It's exactly what you were looking for,' said Matthew.

Rupert glared at him. 'I wonder if we might come to some sort of arrangement?' He reached for his wallet. 'I find it so much easier *not* to be troubled with deposits, and in the unlikely event of any damage, I will take care of whatever may be owed.' He shot her a look. 'Now, seeing that I'm paying cash, what do you say to a ten per cent discount?' A shadow crossed Eleanor's face. 'As it happens, I've already worked it out. Here's two whole months commencing in April, up front. Now you can't say fairer than that.' Counting out the crisp notes on the work-top, Rupert pushed them towards her as if they were her roulette table winnings. Unusually, Eleanor's face suggested that there was no point in arguing; she simply nodded and slid the cash into a zipped pocket in the recesses of her purse. There were no smiles.

'Thank you. It shouldn't take long to send you a receipt and organise the contract,' she told him. Rupert handed her his card and they shook hands. Matthew stared at her, not quite believing she had done the opposite to what she had told him less than five minutes before.

Caroline was gazing out of the window once more. 'You *will* arrange to have something done about the garden, won't you? I feel that will help to sustain Rupert while he's here, although I'm sure I don't need to tell you that.'

Eleanor's eyes flickered, and Matthew realised that she was showing great self-control. 'I've got plenty of perennials that need splitting. I'll send Dorian round with some divisions.' She paused, and a thin smile appeared. 'Well, Rupert, I should add that if you like a bit of eye-candy, you're sure to like him.'

Rupert blinked. 'Dorian? Do we have another Oscar fan in our midst?'

'It's not a name one encounters every day of the week, I admit,' said Eleanor. 'Dorian is...well, let's say a friend of the family.' This was news to Matthew, especially as Eleanor didn't have any family.

Matthew was more than ready to be gone when Eleanor traced a pattern on the dusty work-top with her fingertips. She tilted her chin before glancing at Rupert. 'I presume you've been informed that the auditions are presided over by *me*?'

Rupert looked quickly at Matthew for help, and then back to her. 'What a pity. I normally conduct private auditions.'

Eleanor looked askance at him. '*Private auditions*? But that's unprecedented.'

Rupert sidled up to her. 'Perhaps things are changing.'

Eleanor snatched up her keys from the work-top and turned them over in her hand. 'But not for the better.'

'The role of Miss Prism has so much *hidden* potential,' said Rupert.

She lifted her chin further, which couldn't be doing her neck any good, pondered Matthew. 'Really? I'm not convinced it's the role for me, especially as Lady Bracknell describes her as *"a woman of repellent aspect"*. I have been described as many things, in my time, but repellent has not been one of them.' Matthew cleared his throat and winked at Rupert. 'You're probably not aware,' she continued, in a lofty tone that made Matthew wince, 'and how could you be, but Matthew and I have had such fun playing husband and wife over the years, that – naturally – we expect to play the leading roles. Sadly, for this festival, at any rate, that no longer seems to be the case.' She nodded in Matthew's direction, as if this was his cue to help her out.

It wasn't much fun when the double doors had stuck on stage and she kicked her foot through one of them in a fit of temper to shrieks of laughter from the audience, but he did not say anything.

Rupert was rounding off the proceedings with some disingenuous thanks when Eleanor interrupted him with further key rattling. They were looking each other in the face as if both were wary of a standoff.

'Well, you can rest assured that I'll be double-checking with the committee about those private auditions,' she told Rupert, as a parting-shot. 'I do need to be kept in the loop.'

There was very little that Rupert could do but half-smile as he and Caroline brushed past her on their way out. Seeing them pause momentarily on the garden path, Matthew turned back from the doorway to face Eleanor and hissed, 'By the way, who's Dorian?'

'A surprise! I think you'll like him,' she beamed. 'Not quite as tall as you, and not really your type. He's dark-haired and very good-looking.'

'Well, don't be so secretive!'

'And he's very articulate,' she said in a rush.

'He talks too much?'

'Self-confidence is not a problem.'

'Very pleased with himself, then? I obviously need to look him over at the first possible opportunity. Why haven't we been introduced?'

She inclined her head on one side, a gesture guaranteed to irritate him. 'Perhaps because I didn't want you to be your usual judgemental self, and spoil it for me.'

Noticing Rupert and Caroline shivering by his car, Matthew clicked the remote, and turned up his coat collar. Once Rupert had opened the rear door for Caroline and had jumped back in the front, Matthew turned to him while fastening his seat-belt.

'Perhaps I should add that I have been assisting with the auditions for some time...' he told Rupert.

'I'm sure that won't be necessary on this occasion,' came Rupert's terse reply.

'Well, someone has to show them in, and tick off the names, or had you forgotten?'

Matthew still had to deliver Rupert to his meetings, first with the ladies in charge of wardrobe and props, Eileen and Janet, followed by one with Mike, the stage-manager and Steve, the man in charge of sound and lighting.

WAFT performed in the Hotel Majestic, mainly because of its prime location; no one passing through the busy resort of Bowness-on-Windermere could be unaware of its presence. It was no secret that WAFT could collect a few more unwary play-goers through appearing in an hotel with a high profile. Although the stage was shallow, they used the band's stage in the old ballroom.

Once Matthew had parked the car, they left Caroline in the residents' lounge so that she could find fault with morning coffee. They then made their way to the back of the hotel where the company hired a storeroom.

The wardrobe mistresses, Eileen and Janet, had very little idea about costumes, but enjoyed working together. They also provided props. The storeroom was windowless but dry, if a little airless, with a musty odour as if it had not been opened for some time. Most festival members were interested in being the first to give the new director the once-over, and Eileen and Jane were no exception. Eileen, the stouter of the pair, was wearing a different wig from her usual one, and this morning was looking resplendent in an unlikely shade of red, no doubt selected for Rupert's benefit. It suited her kindly face. On the other hand, Janet's white bob accentuated her severe features and angular figure.

Once the introductions were over, Rupert mentioned that he required some old, long black skirts for the women to rehearse in so they could get accustomed to wearing them.

'Now, I'm looking for the most flamboyant outfits that you can find for Lady Bracknell and Gwendolen.' Rupert's eyes rested on a sumptuous burgundy dress. 'How about this one?'

'You can't wear that,' said Janet, glancing at Eileen to help her out.

'Why not?' asked Rupert.

'It was worn three years ago.'

'No – two, I think you'll find,' said Janet, winking at Rupert. 'It'll be recognised.'

Rupert threw her a peevish look, shrugged and turned to an ice blue dress with black piping. He lifted it down and passed it to Eileen, who, while unzipping the bag, said, 'This was a favourite of Eleanor's in– what was it?'

'Don't you mean it was her mother's favourite?' asked Janet. The two women stared at each other, while they pondered this. 'Her mother wore something similar, but not this one, I think you'll find.'

'Ah! Eleanor's mother, the wonderful Millamant,' murmured Eileen.

'Surely she wasn't christened that?' enquired Rupert, his tone challenging.

'Of course not,' said Janet. 'But it was her best role. Eleanor's mum started out as plain old Maureen Blodgett.'

Eileen smiled. 'Before she married and not only changed her maiden name, but her Christian name as well, to become Amelia Young.'

'And Eleanor changed from being Young to Vane. It's one of our little jokes,' said Janet, looking Rupert up and down. 'What a pity that you're so much shorter than Eleanor.'

He frowned. 'Not *so* much, surely...'

'As if we haven't got enough to do,' said Eileen, as she handed him the dress.

'You do both enjoy sewing, I take it?' enquired Rupert, holding the blue against himself. It suited his fair hair and pale colouring so he disappeared behind a beautifully worked cloak pressed into service as a curtain.

'When you've appeared in panto, it's nice to wear something less gaudy,' he enthused. The transformation was remarkable.

'Eleanor won't like hearing about that,' said Janet, looking more than ready to start pulling and tweaking the dress so that it sat more comfortably on him.

'Does she need to be told?' asked Rupert, wriggling his smooth, pale shoulders. 'Can it be our little secret?'

'She probably knows already. It will need shortening.' Eileen turned to Janet.

'I'm sick of altering hems,' grumbled Janet.

Rupert was admiring himself in the mirror. 'I think it will do very well.'

Feeling a draught and sensing the door fly open, Matthew turned round to see Mike and Steve framed in the doorway, looking stony-faced. Realising that they had been noticed, they cleared their throats. When Rupert saw them, he tittered (long enough to embarrass Matthew), and went to undress. Matthew could not fail to notice that Mike and Steve were smirking at each other. Meanwhile, Eileen caught Janet's eye. While Rupert was changing, the conversation was strained, but when he emerged and handed over the dress, the men took a step closer to see what Rupert would choose next. His eyes fell upon a cream travelling coat and matching cape with dark piping.

'Don't you simply adore this?' asked Rupert, clearly for the men's benefit. Matthew felt his insides shrivel. 'This would be perfect for Act Three, if you have a suitable hat to go with it?' Eileen made a note. 'Now run along, ladies, and see if you can find me a coat as stunning for the first act, perhaps in dove grey. That set is going to be purple, you see.'

Matthew shuddered while Eileen made another note. Having thanked them, Rupert gave them a coy wave, then made his way with Matthew towards the ballroom where the discussion about the set was to take place.

Matthew was over-familiar with the director's routine at the beginning of a production, and Rupert was no exception. He glanced despairingly at the shallow stage and shrugged at Mike, as if to suggest that he had had to face many problems in his time, but nothing on the scale of this. Mike, practical and experienced, was in his mid-sixties, retired, and well known for thriving on conflict, voiced the same concerns with each new director, but usually calmed down after the initial meeting. Yet he never seemed to mind working full-time building the set for a few weeks, although he would have hated anyone to know it. He always showed great flair, in spite of often muddled leadership. As Matthew had anticipated, he made the usual grumbles and was quick to point out that, 'They usually choose a one-set play. I'll have to design the set for the first act to twin with the last act.' He scratched his head. 'As for that second act...that garden scene's going to be very tricky.'

Rupert rummaged in his bag for his pencil sketches. 'Please remember that I had nothing to do with the choice of play.' Mike shuffled his feet. 'However, you may find these helpful, as I've been thinking along the same lines.' Matthew recognised Rupert's "put-out, but graciously hoping not to show it look" of old. 'As it happens, I'd like both sets placed on the diagonal for the first and third acts. And, whatever you may think to the contrary, the second act must give every indication of being an actual garden.'

Matthew watched keenly while Mike stroked his chin. 'Never like doing outdoor sets.' There was some sucking-in of breath, but as the conversation developed, Rupert seemed to win them over and the meeting closed with firm hand-shakes, from Mike and Steve at any rate. By then, it was almost midday.

'I have no wish to fall out with you, Rupert,' said Matthew, as they made their way to collect Caroline, 'but I don't want a repeat of last night's raised voices when you come to stay up here in April.'

'Surely Tom isn't jealous of a decrepit old thing like me?'

'Stop fishing for compliments.'

Rupert stopped walking and blinked, while Matthew hoped that the receptionist at the desk would not look up. 'Why so much fuss?'

'I can't afford to have Tom knowing that you and I go way back.'

'No one could accuse you of holding back and being secretive, could they?' Rupert looked him in the eye. 'By the way, I've got the message that we can never patch things up loud and clear.'

'That's a relief, especially as I don't want him wondering more than will be good for him.'

Rupert set off again. 'Do I detect the classic overprotective father figure?'

'I wouldn't want to encourage lots of awkward questions.'

'Because you won't come out of it well?'

Matthew sighed. 'I'm not sure that this is going to work, after all.'

'What?'

'You working in close proximity to me for weeks on end.'

Rupert stopped and stared. 'So, you're really expecting Tom to play Jack, and you to play Chasuble, are you? Well, we'll see about that. Besides, it's too late for me to even think about not going through with this project. You're probably sick of hearing it, but I need the work.'

Once Caroline was installed in the rear seat of the car, Matthew relaxed; his business with Rupert was pretty much over, and brother and sister would soon be making their way home. But then further disagreeable thoughts began to crowd in: it crossed his mind that he ought to invite them to lunch – even if only for sandwiches – but he kept this to himself. Doubtless, Rupert would be in full flow until mid-afternoon, and there was always the threat that his careless talk would reveal their joint past to Tom, who would inevitably start asking questions.

He invited them for coffee instead, which was just as well as Tom had thought to prepare a tray, although something in Tom had altered.

He was still polite to Rupert and Caroline, but Matthew sensed that Tom was not himself. The farewells were almost sincere, but any protestations of meeting up before the beginning of April rang hollow. Relieved to have Langdales to themselves at last, they returned to the sitting room.

Tom's forehead crinkled and the tiny lines around his mouth deepened as he joined Matthew on the sofa. 'So, now that they've finally left us in peace, is there anything you'd like to share with me?'

'I'm not sure that there is, apart from thanking you for being a wonderful host.'

'So would you mind telling me what all that was about?' asked Tom in a monotone.

'All what?'

'I couldn't help noticing the way he looked at you throughout his visit.'

'You astonish me,' said Matthew, smiling, anxious to deflect the focus from himself, and perhaps get the better of Tom. 'I'm surprised that you noticed, seeing as you spent the entire time trying to catch his eye.'

'He would hardly have been staring so intently at you if he didn't feel there was something coming from your side.'

Matthew, although unprepared for this confrontation, saw that this was a fair assessment of the situation but attempted to laugh it off. 'Nothing could be further–'

'Did I *really* see you two holding hands?'

Avoiding Tom's stare, he cleared his throat. 'It's not looking good, I admit.'

'That's an understatement.' Matthew swallowed but said nothing. 'It seems to me that you've come across him before, so why didn't you let on?' Matthew rose from the sofa and moved over to the window. 'You never thought to mention it?'

Matthew fixed his gaze on the grey, skeletal garden, and without turning to look over his shoulder, said, 'It's not what you think.'

'That old get-out clause.'

'You coined it.'

'Now I get treated to the hangdog expression, I suppose?'

Matthew turned to face him at last. 'Let's leave it right there, shall we? There's a simple explanation.'

Tom folded his arms. 'You don't say.'

'Rupert was in the year below me at school.'

Tom threw back his head. 'At school? Really? Is that an explanation or a confession?'

'It was all on his side.'

'That's not how it came over last night when you were practically–'

'It was not the kind of school-boy crush that one forgets in a hurry.'

'Especially if your name is Rupert Hammond, it seems. You don't appear to have erased it from your memory, either.'

Matthew shook his head in the pause that followed, but filled the silence by gabbling. 'You've got all this wrong. He had a crush on *me*, Tom. But he was just some wayward, insignificant little sprog. Once I'd done my "A" levels, I couldn't get away from school, or him, fast enough.'

'You make it sound quite intense.'

'Perhaps on his side, it was. You see, he was a spoiled, rich kid who was used to having own way. He wouldn't take no for an answer, so I was quite relieved when my schooldays were over.'

'So if he never meant much to you, why were you being so secretive? And please tell me the truth, Matthew.'

Matthew struggled to think quickly and set out a convincing case, while returning to sit next to Tom. 'It's just that I didn't want you to read more into it than you may have done. If you must know, he really did have a crush on me, but we're talking over thirty years ago. You know, dating from when he first noticed me.'

'That doesn't explain why you two were looking at each other in a particularly intimate way. Am I right to have a hunch things go deeper than you're admitting?'

'I'm not sure how you work that out,' said Matthew, trying to sound as if all this was beneath him. 'I only went along with this because you wanted to play the lead.'

Tom's eyelids flickered. 'I hope you're not suggesting it's my fault?'

'I'm not saying anything of the kind!'

'There's no need to be so touchy.' He looked Matthew in the eye. 'Tell me about last night.'

'What about it?' asked Matthew, feeling a pit forming in his stomach. 'Well, when you burst in like that with Caroline, I was warning him off.'

'That's funny, because it didn't look like that,' said Tom, 'although you pulled your hand away quickly enough.'

'Do you really think that I'd jeopardise what we have together in our own home?'

'You're not indicating that you'd jeopardise things *outside* our own home?'

'Why do you have to twist everything?'

'I can't help what I see.' Tom shrugged. 'If he's gone as far as holding hands with you, on this very sofa, he must still think there's a connection.'

'Only on his side, I can assure you.'

'So you keep insisting. Why didn't you just leave him to it?'

'I didn't want to upset him. After all, he was our guest.'

'It still doesn't ring true. If he'd tried anything on like that with me, I would have shown him the door without a moment's hesitation.'

Matthew smirked. '*After* you'd secured the role of Jack, I presume?'

'I shall ignore that. To me, it looked as though you were sitting there so comfortably together – how can I put it – as if you couldn't *wait* to pick up where you left off.' Eyes widening, Tom finished triumphantly so that Matthew felt that he had to respond.

'How can I get through to you? This belongs to the realms of ancient history as far as I'm concerned.'

'We can come back to that, when you've had time to perfect your story,' said Tom, as if growing weary, 'although I'm not expecting a direct explanation for one minute. Until then, can we get one thing straight?'

Matthew felt his throat tighten. 'Fire away.'

'When he comes here to direct, I refuse to live in his shadow.'

'Nobody's asking you to. And if Rupert damages what we have, I'll have him thrown – no, frog-marched – out of the festival.'

Tom stared at him in disbelief. 'Oh, yes? With Eleanor as the henchman?'

'I've given you an explanation, but if that's not enough–'

'It isn't even true, is it? If you could see yourself when he's nearby. Anyone can see it's more than a school-boy crush.'

'What's that supposed to mean?' Matthew shook his head as he stood up. 'I don't know what's come over you.'

'What's come over *me*?'

'There's no need to shout.'

'Listen, Matthew, you have no idea how I feel about this, do you?'

'You're clearly jealous – of *nothing* – but can we just keep things in proportion?' Matthew sensed he was breathing hard, becoming louder, and paused. Tom was biting his lip. 'Look, we *both* agreed to try and find him some accommodation, or have I got that wrong, too? He doesn't know a soul up here, remember, and we offered some help. It's not as if I've been boring you to tears about him.'

Tom rolled his eyes. 'He's quite capable of doing that by himself.'

'I thought it was the other way round.'

'What was?'

'You were flirting so convincingly from the moment he arrived, I took it that you were falling under his spell.'

'You know that's not true. I merely wanted to get him on my side, so that he thinks well of me, and then – hopefully – I'll get to play Jack.'

'Put him under an obligation by playing "Mr. Nice Guy"? Now do you see how easy it is for things to be misconstrued?'

Tom shook his head. 'Aren't you forgetting something?'

'What?'

'I wasn't gazing into his eyes and holding hands.'

'Have it your own way, Tom. I've done my best to explain the situation.'

'Is that really your best?' Tom waited. Matthew stared back at him. 'You're telling me that I'll have to put up with whatever connection you two have?'

'There is no connection.'

'I'm upset that you didn't explain the background before he arrived.'

'This is all in your imagination!' Matthew laughed, but it was unconvincing.

'It just shows...'

'What?'

'Well, Matthew, I never imagined that something that happened so long ago could be that important to you.' Matthew looked at Tom more closely but did not like what he saw. 'You must have been worried before Rupert arrived?' What remained of Matthew's attempt at a smile vanished. 'So where do we go from here?' asked Tom. 'Up until now, I thought we could trust each other.'

Speaking slowly and deliberately, as if to a child, Matthew said, 'I'm sorry, but you're forgetting that *I* had to stand by and say *nothing* while you were so obviously flirting with him, whatever you might say in your defence.'

Tom's lips were drawn into a snarl, something Matthew had never witnessed before. 'It was the *other* way round, I tell you. I couldn't shake him off.'

'You're saying you weren't cosying up to him, after all?'

Tom gave him a sideways look. 'I was being polite. He was our guest. But I hated the way he looked at me as if I was fair game.'

'You're certainly not that.'

'So you're back on my side?' asked Tom, glancing at him.

'This is not about sides.'

'You could have fooled me. You know I've not so much as glanced at anyone else, never mind thought of...'

Sighing, Matthew returned to the sofa. 'I know you haven't, and for that I've always been grateful.'

'Then why don't you show it?' asked Tom, his mood seeming to lift for a moment. 'I want to stay here with you for as long as we can.'

Matthew looked into his eyes. 'Until I snuff it, I suppose?'

'If you want to put it like that, yes, and I thought you felt the same, until now.' Matthew was deeply touched, but resentment over what he regarded as an inquisition, held him back from hugging Tom. 'My problem...' began Tom. Matthew nodded at him in encouragement. 'My problem is that I could tell when you were thinking about him. And you did change while he was here, no matter what you say.' Tom hesitated, looked around him, and started speaking again, but this time more slowly. 'I'm not sure that I can stand it if he's going to be staying in that cottage. I mean, it's less than ten minutes away. How often am I going to be abandoned here while you're enjoying a cosy supper *à deux*?'

'You're way ahead of me,' said Matthew, feeling his world closing in on him.

'You may thrive on emotional conflict, but I don't,' said Tom, his words coming out in a rush. 'I don't want to be sitting here on my own worried about what you're up to at Rupert's. And don't tell me he won't be inviting you over, because I can assure you he will be. That much I have picked up.' Matthew shifted his position. 'However much you deny it, there's a connection between you two, and we face weeks of kow-towing to Rupert in rehearsal. From what we've seen of him, I imagine you realise how exhausting *that* is going to be.'

'Neither of us are even in it yet, remember?' Matthew reminded him. Then he altered his tone . 'I really cannot emphasise how very sorry I am, Tom...'

There was a change in the atmosphere as Tom pressed himself against the back of the sofa. 'Are you? I'm so glad. Honestly?'

'...that you're not the man I thought you were,' finished Matthew, sounding grave.

Tom sat up with a start. 'What's that supposed to mean?'

'So jealous, in spite of no proof, no unreliable track record on my part, nothing which deserves what I find myself on the receiving end of...'

'Yes, all right.' Shoulders drooping, Tom seemed to diminish for a few moments before he looked Matthew in the eye. 'You have no idea how you came over while he was here, have you? You walked taller. You smiled more. It was quite scary.' Matthew was about to defend himself, thought better of it and remained silent. 'So, enough of that. What was Rupert really like?'

There was no real answer to this. 'I'm not sure I can remember that far back.' Matthew tried to prepare his thoughts, wanted to become expansive, but dared not overdo it. 'Mischievous, primarily. He hasn't changed there. And he was always terribly enthusiastic about everything, only...'

'What?' asked Tom, sounding genuinely interested and more his usual self.

'Well, you always got the impression that whatever he had to say was more interesting than what you were saying.'

'Didn't that grate?'

Matthew smiled to himself as his mind rushed back through the corridor of years. 'Frequently, but he could be such a charmer, and so intensely *lovable* with it.' He stopped abruptly. 'I mean, everybody adored him.'

'I've heard enough,' said Tom. 'No point in digging yourself deeper. Besides, what does it matter?'

'I'm glad you're feeling less unsettled about it now, and I hope that I have finally put your mind at rest.'

'You can't be serious. All I meant was that when Rupert's staying up here it won't take me long to prise it out of him.'

'Ah! But what if there's nothing to tell?'

Tom gave him a knowing look. 'I'll be proved wrong, won't I? But if there's one area where Rupert excels, it's his ability to express himself freely.'

Chapter Five

Although Matthew had squirmed enough for a lifetime, he could not help feeling that they needed to have that conversation. Tom had been unexpectedly firm with him, yet his heart warmed when he reflected on Tom's trenchant devotion; this was a strong basis on which to build, given the change in dynamics since they had first seen Rupert. After all, ten years was a reasonably long time, and they had established a reliable working routine. Given his loyalty, how could Matthew think of making eyes at Rupert, even in jest?

Quite easily, as it happened. Contemplating Rupert's forthcoming arrival and living in their midst Matthew was not above thinking foolish thoughts. In spite of the jealous streak in Tom, he was forced to admit to himself that he quite liked the idea of flirting with Rupert, perhaps for old time's sake. Naturally, it would be a scene that neither of them would dare to overplay, and what could be the harm in that? He had been lacking a bit of fun in his life for some time.

Even so, his fear of being exposed cast a long shadow. After all, it could happen at any time during the run-up to the festival, and that was going to involve several weeks forced to live a lie. Matthew remained uneasy at the prospect of Tom discovering more than he need know, especially as he was still ashamed of the events leading up to Rupert's wedding day. He still quivered at the thought of that threatened one-to-one with Rupert.

His stomach contracted not only over the embarrassment the truth would cause, if it ever got out, but over the possibility that Tom would become so jealous that their relationship splintered. Matthew would have to be on his best behaviour; it was clear that he could not allow himself a single wistful look at Rupert – in public – in case it was misconstrued. Nothing further was mentioned between Matthew and Tom, especially as Matthew was determined not to raise the subject.

Meanwhile, Tom seemed only partially reassured by their conversation, and this created an atmosphere, so Matthew spent the rest of the day wishing he had never heard of Rupert Hammond.

Over the next few weeks, his stomach turned over more than it had done in his life before; waiting for Rupert to appear in April became excruciating. Whenever he went shopping in Windermere, he thought he saw Rupert in any middle-aged, fair-haired man coming towards him, or walking ahead of him, for that matter.

Tom's silence on the situation perhaps indicated that he had resigned himself to having Rupert nearby. Meanwhile, they had plenty to occupy them before reopening Langdales to guests in mid-February. The only thing of note at this time was a heavy, overnight snowfall early that month, a rare event in such close proximity to Morecambe Bay. Felicity's house, The Croft, was located just outside the resort of Grange-over-Sands. Inspired by Grange's south-east location and Gulf Stream influence, Felicity had filled her sloping garden with borderline-hardy, exotic-looking evergreens. In February, however, she was sitting on a terrace in Spain.

'We must do what we can to get the snow off the more brittle foliage,' said Matthew, looking out at the eerie expanse of their own garden.

'Yes, especially if it fails to thaw properly and then freezes hard overnight,' agreed Tom.

When they arrived at Felicity's place, the garden looked magical, and had the tranquillity and the silence that snow brings with it. It seemed a pity to get to work with the brushes they had brought with them, but so many sub-tropical leaves were bent over that they had little choice. They did what they could, and then reluctantly came away. Unfortunately, that week saw night after night of temperatures below freezing. Matthew knew that many of the plants could survive the odd night of discomfort, but not several, consecutively, and there were sure to be many casualties. Yet by the time Felicity returned, ten days later, the snow had melted, and the landscape had gone back to its usual dull buff winter monotones. Trying to be helpful, Matthew suggested that Eleanor's garden design guru, Dorian, might be able to help her.

As the date for Rupert's arrival and the auditions approached, Matthew lost no time in making sure that he was on the list for Canon

Chasuble. As indicated to Rupert, he had always helped on the day, and as usual he received the revised and final lists of names in March. This was in good time for auditions on Saturday, the second of April, the day after Rupert was due to arrive. The festival operated a time-honoured scheme in which only five members could sign up to audition for each individual role, but anyone could audition for more than one role, not that anyone usually did. They were usually a formality anyway; Matthew and Eleanor always played the leading roles and the supporting roles were lightly sprinkled among the ever-dwindling membership, mostly because WAFT had a reputation for being awkward and cliquey.

When Matthew saw that Eleanor had requested the final audition for Miss Prism, which would also be the final one of the day, he smiled; she was clearly intent on leaving a lasting impression. To simplify two walk-on parts, Rupert had suggested that the roles of Lane, the manservant, and Merriman, the butler, should be played by one actor. Matthew had his friend Archie in mind for that. Archie had been his only employee at Langdales before Tom arrived, and could usually be called upon in an emergency, although much of his time was spoken for as night-porter at the Queens Hotel.

Matthew was double-checking the audition list while sitting at the kitchen table after breakfast, possibly in the hope that the more he looked at it, the more his dream for Tom might materialise. Running his eyes down the cast list, he noticed the name of James Longstaff beside that of Jack, and shivered involuntarily. As promising new talent was not encouraged, he could not quite understand what had happened, until he remembered that as the new president, Felicity would be working behind the scenes with Martin, their new chairman.

Normally, new members were tested out in a minor supporting role before being allowed near any role considered remotely demanding. But things were changing, often suddenly and without warning. Any threat to Tom playing Jack must be squashed, thought Matthew, so he telephoned Felicity, who also acted as (under-used) membership secretary, to find that James Longstaff was in his late twenties, dark and good-looking with plenty of charm and more than enough sex appeal to make a perfect leading man. Thanking her, Matthew tried to make light of it, but feared for Tom.

Knowing Rupert's roving eye and proselytising attitude to his own sex, Matthew feared for James, too. Dreading Tom's reaction should he *not* be offered Jack, Matthew waited until Tom was in a good mood before referring to James, but had difficulty in calming him down.

'Unbelievable!' Tom was pacing up and down the kitchen, biting his hand. 'This guy sounds as if he could be a real threat. I loathe him already. After all we've done to help Eleanor over the years – you especially – and the moment she chooses to take a back seat, the whole thing starts to unravel. What happened to our tried and tested audition system?'

'You mean rigged? Look, do you want me to have a word with Eleanor and make sure that Rupert realises he must not give the role to James? Don't forget that she's not above over-ruling the director's decision.'

'Not any longer, now that Felicity's sponsoring more of the festival than she's done before.' Tom turned to look at him. 'I'm not averse to the rules being bent once in a while, but I'm sure the new chairman wouldn't agree.'

'I hadn't thought of that,' said Matthew, lamely.

What neither of them took into account was Rupert's unpredictability, and his refusal to kow-tow to Eleanor. Moreover, not wishing to goad Tom about Rupert, Matthew had decided that it would be prudent to avoid laying on a big welcome for him, much as he felt under some obligation to invite him over for lunch or dinner to celebrate his arrival. There was another reason: Matthew had been in denial, never quite believing that Rupert would become part of his life again. This feeling had been strengthened by phantom notions that *Jubilee Way* might have Rupert back for a second series, and his involvement in the festival be called off.

Yet Matthew never lost sight of the fun that Rupert's presence would add to his life, not only in rehearsal, but because he would be living nearby, albeit temporarily. This was taking a gradual hold of Matthew, not only because they had shared something special but because he felt that he was in dire need of a good friend. Eleanor had distanced herself (by way of a change) now that she was free to pursue an unencumbered single life. Inevitably, she was bound to be taking more care of her house and her garden. Meanwhile, Tom was standing up to him more, which perturbed him slightly.

There were no preliminaries, or frantic messages, before Rupert arrived on Friday, the first of April,. The damson trees were beginning to bloom, with their pretty clusters of small white flowers on bare stems, and Matthew had hoped to take him for a scenic drive. Having heard nothing, Matthew felt curiously disassociated from WAFT until Rupert telephoned towards the end of the afternoon to announce that he was ensconced safely. Eager to indulge him, Matthew sat down to listen to a set of instructions regarding the auditions on the following day, but his conversation could not have been more different. Rupert appeared to have relented regarding "private auditions", but it was what he went on to say that intrigued Matthew more.

'I've just met Dorian. Dorian Manners. Can you believe it?'

'His name? I know nothing except that he is Eleanor's gardening guru, and she seems quite thick with him. She appears to be keeping him to herself, but I have gleaned a few bits and pieces from what she's let slip.'

'Well, you've missed a treat! I'm smitten.' Rupert sounded as if he could not get the words out fast enough.

'I think Eleanor has the prior claim.'

Matthew could tell that Rupert was smiling. 'More than that, I think you'll find. Still, it's never stopped me before.'

'You've only just got here. Be careful.'

Matthew was now compelled to hear all about Dorian, a seemingly inexhaustible topic of conversation. He was, of course, charming, but surely Rupert was exaggerating his description of swarthy masculinity? When he had finished, Matthew arranged a time to meet up next morning and then got rid of him.

That first Saturday in April began with a cold blue and white sky, setting off the damson blossom. Spring was the season of optimism, and helped to give Matthew high hopes for Tom's audition as well as his own. Matthew and Tom duly set off together for the Hotel Majestic. His name, thanks to Matthew, was now at the top of Rupert's list.

As usual, the day would be spent on the ballroom stage. The plan was to devote the morning to hearing Jack and Algernon, Gwendolen and Cecily, so as to match the young female leads to the young male leads in terms of appearance, height and voice.

Tom seemed unusually animated, but Matthew put this down to nerves, and the feeling of spring in the air. As Matthew would be required all day, Tom had said that he would do some shopping for their dinner once he was no longer required, and then drive home on his own. They agreed that Matthew would phone him as soon as he was free to be collected.

The ballroom had a lofty ceiling and a line of tall windows running the length of one wall. Rectangles of sunlight flooded across the parquet. Matthew was looking through one of these, enjoying the sunshine behind the glass, when he saw Rupert pull up. Unpacking his bag while sitting behind the table allocated, roughly five rows back, Rupert grimaced at the hardness of the chair, and glanced despairingly at the apology for a stage. Having enquired whether Rupert was comfortable in Eleanor's cottage, and hearing that he was, Matthew pulled up a chair, only to be treated to Rupert firing off his instructions so quickly that he had trouble following them. These included checking whether everyone showed up, handing out the acting editions at the relevant pages if necessary, showing each member in, and finally, making sure that ample supplies of complimentary tea, coffee and chocolate biscuits came Rupert's way.

'You mentioned private auditions when you first appeared, although we've heard nothing since,' said Matthew, 'but how private? After I've shown each hopeful onto the stage, I normally get to look in from time to time.'

'It will be a one-to-one session as I will be reading the cues. All decisions will be mine, and mine alone.' Rupert opened the text, transferred to a large folder, and arranged his pad and pen neatly to one side of it as if the subject was closed. 'Now your job is to make sure that I don't lag behind, so run along.'

'Surely it's up to you to make sure that they keep time?' enquired Matthew. 'By the way, Tom is ready whenever you're ready.'

Matthew's meet-and-greet station was in the adjacent foyer. In between auditions, the plan was for Matthew to look in through the curtains framing the ballroom double doors and get the go-ahead from Rupert so that the next one could enter. On no account was Matthew to allow the next victim in before Rupert had finished making his notes. As well as organising that first pot of coffee for Rupert, Matthew had plenty to do, so when Tom stood up, there was only just time to remind him to smile before ushering him in.

While Tom was auditioning, Matthew – unable to concentrate – was gazing through the glass double doors which led to the main body of the hotel when he saw the dark head and tall figure of the next individual approaching. This could only be James Longstaff, the new member who had come to audition for Jack. He was even more good-looking than Felicity had indicated, but there was a problem, or to Matthew's way of thinking, an asset, which might help Tom. James had a beard, and although it was neatly trimmed, Rupert hated beards.

Matthew looked him over while they shook hands for rather longer than was necessary. There was a quickening of interest on both sides, and James's eyes stayed on Matthew's for longer than they should have done. A born flirt! Somebody in the cast, somewhere along the line, was going to find this young man irresistible, thought Matthew, hoping that it would not be him. But for now, Matthew could think of nothing more delightful than having a good-looking younger guy a few feet away.

From his accent, James was evidently a Yorkshireman and Matthew wondered if his vowels were too northern for the milieu of Wilde's characters, although he knew that Rupert could make him lose his accent for the play, and demand that he shave off that beard, should he decide to give him the role of Jack. Hopefully, Rupert would honour his agreement with Tom (which was looking vaguer by the minute) and if James was any good, consider him for the role of Algernon. Rarely was everybody happy in WAFT, however.

When James settled himself in the nearest chair and opened his play-copy, Matthew returned to his table, his heart fluttering slightly. He could not help glancing occasionally at James's admirable profile with its straight nose, good cheek-bones and strong chin. Recognising that James would be anxious, Matthew knew better than to engage him in conversation, but Matthew's face fell when he saw Jane Kilbride, Felicity's daughter, approaching in a tight blouse and skirt. She was to audition for the female lead of Gwendolen, and had arrived far earlier than required. Jane, with her flaming hair and pale complexion, was widely regarded by everyone, except Eleanor, as being Eleanor's rightful successor.

Matthew had known her since she was a girl and was well acquainted with her technique: it was clear that she had come to check not only on her female rivals but the male talent, for Jane's boyfriends came and went with alarming regularity. Greeting him as she always did, as "Uncle Matthew", which made him feel ancient in front of James, she kissed him as he rose from behind his table. Matthew introduced James, who also stood up, and observed her taking him in.

'You'll have to endure a long wait, I'm afraid. What were you thinking of?' muttered Matthew, when she had finished staring into James's eyes and shaking his hand.

Jane let go of James's hand reluctantly, shrugged, sat down and cosied up to James, who edged his leg sideways away from her.

Matthew cringed as she leaned over to peer at his play-copy. 'You've no idea how I adore this play,' she remarked, playing with her hair. Using his forefinger and thumb to remove a stray hair of Jane's from his trousers, James murmured something non-committal before engrossing himself in his copy of the play once more. Jane was still staring at him. 'Is this your first time?'

'How do you mean?' asked James, edging his thigh a little further away from hers. Her skirt seemed to be rising up of its own accord.

'I meant have you appeared in it before? You see, I played Gwendolen when I was seventeen.'

James did not look up. 'You don't say?'

'Actually, I won the school Drama cup.'

'Really?'

During the silence that followed, Tom, emerging from his audition, caught Matthew's eye, gave nothing away as to how it had gone, and ran his eyes over James while Matthew introduced them to each other. Inconsequentialities soon followed, and there seemed almost too much to talk about nothing in particular until Rupert called out, 'Do I need to drag the next one in by myself?'

Matthew jumped to attention and pushed James into the ballroom. James ascended the set of steps leading up to the stage as if to the gallows. Seeing that James was under intense scrutiny from Rupert while he got into position, Matthew stood in a patch of shadow between the windows, and pressed himself against the wall. Rupert gave James his cues, never failing to overplay with his delivery of Lady Bracknell's lines.

Tom had left by the time Matthew crept out, soon to be followed by James, grinning. He thanked Matthew for showing him in, said goodbye to Jane, but there was no opportunity to ask him how it had gone. After he had left, Jane adjusted her blouse and skirt to show herself off to best advantage and proceeded to busy herself with her hand-mirror, reapplying her lipstick until settling down to read her play-copy in dreary silence.

Three other, rather plain men auditioned for Jack, and while they were seated in a row, Matthew could not help overhearing that Rupert's appearances in *Jubilee Way* had lent him minor celebrity status. Once Rupert had seen the last of the possibilities for Jack, he auditioned the Algernons.

In due course, Matthew ushered Jane in for her audition. Feeling that Rupert had grown more relaxed about his intrusions, Matthew continued to lurk in the shadows whenever possible. Rupert must have noticed him but made no comment. Jane benefited from having played the role and she read well, although any feeling for comedy appeared to have eluded her. Towards the end of the Gwendolen auditions, Jane's younger sister Clare arrived to read for Cecily. Clare was prettier than her sister and had already proved herself in eager, ingénue roles. Matthew looked on as Rupert fell under her spell. Once she had finished, it was time for their sandwiches and hopefully a post-mortem. Matthew went over to sit with Rupert, and after his initial hunger had been satisfied, Matthew asked, 'Has anyone mentioned that new members rarely get a leading role?'

"Be radical", was Felicity's parting shot.' Rupert took a bite out of his sandwich as if the subject was closed.

'Well, then – is it too soon to hear your thoughts on Tom?'

Dabbing his mouth with his paper napkin, Rupert frowned but revealed nothing, and Matthew thought better of raising the subject again. As Eleanor's audition was the final one, so that she would hopefully be freshest in the director's memory, Matthew was quick to point out that as the daughter of the founder members and usual leading lady, she expected special treatment.

Rupert chuckled as he glanced over the names. 'And you say that Eleanor and Felicity Kilbride don't get on?'

'That's an understatement. There was a slight thaw in January, but they only speak when they have to. That's why Felicity will be the first to audition and Eleanor the last. They *have* to be kept apart. And don't forget that Eleanor must not be kept waiting.'

Rupert rolled his eyes and grinned. The afternoon was also to be spent on the auditions for the supporting roles of Canon Chasuble, Merriman the butler and Lane the manservant, and Miss Prism, the role for which Eleanor and Felicity were both auditioning. Matthew's own audition went off without incident, and he responded well to Rupert reading his cues. The auditions for Merriman and Lane came and went, and were mostly unremarkable, mainly because they were such small roles.

When it was Felicity's turn to audition Matthew took her by the arm and ushered her in, squeezing her arm encouragingly when he realised how stiff and tense she had become. Retreating to his favourite bit of wall, he listened in. She threw herself into it, but, unusually for her, she read too quickly and stumbled over her words, to the accompaniment of uninhibited sighing from Rupert. Matthew sucked in his breath when Rupert told her that he had heard enough, and picked up his pencil.

'I'm sorry, Rupert, but that's the shortest audition I've ever had,' she remarked, stooping to retrieve the book she had let slip out of her hand. Dusting it off and slapping the cover with the back of her hand, she asked, 'How about picking it up from *"Prism, where is that baby?"'*

Matthew, unable to bear any more, hurried off to the gents, but by the time he had returned, Felicity had vanished. He sidled up to Rupert's table.

'I hope you witnessed that sorry little scene?' asked Rupert.

'How could I, when you stressed that the auditions had to be private?'

'Well, I noticed you sneaking about from time to time.'

'But you insulted her,' said Matthew, sitting down next to him.

'I did not mean to, but it's been a long day and I'm tired.'

'You must be aware of the seething discontent about to be unleashed if you choose the wrong person?'

Silence. Rupert put his hands behind his head and stretched out his legs, as if mulling over the day. 'You may have a point, Matthew. I don't want to make any more enemies than I have to!'

When he noticed the fourth, rather faded woman to audition for Miss Prism emerging, he knew it was time for Eleanor's audition. She arrived with her head held high, and acknowledged Matthew with a curt frown. Fleeing her audition, the woman glanced at Eleanor as if their paths had crossed unhappily, and scuttled off.

'I didn't expect that he would be keeping to time for one minute,' said Eleanor. 'So it has come to this? *Miss Prism*. It's not what I signed up for.'

'We've been well and truly hobbled this time,' said Matthew, forcing a grin. 'Did I hear you ask how my audition went?' She smiled back – coolly – in return. 'My audition for Chasuble went well, thank you. Don't forget that if you get to play Miss Prism we might echo some of our former glories?'

'I can't imagine how you work that out with just a few lines together, and rather poor ones at that.'

He liked it when they fell back into their familiar, abrasive groove.

'Eleanor, there is nothing you can fix this time.'

'Don't be too sure of that!'

He watched Eleanor's audition from start to finish, not that he needed to, for he was fully conversant with her delivery and posture. She read – of course – superbly, even managing to rise above the choppy waters of Rupert's overplaying her cue lines. It was an impressive display, and she even contrived to appear rather humble, as if in unspoken admission of Rupert's superior position as director. Not having witnessed what would no doubt be Rupert's telling characterisation, Matthew privately mourned that she had had to forsake any hope of playing Lady Bracknell. She wafted out, wreathed in smiles.

At length, eyebrow only slightly raised by her imposing presence, Rupert turned towards him again and invited him over to the cottage for dinner that evening, ostensibly to discuss the final outcome.

'But I didn't see all the auditions,' remonstrated Matthew.

'You saw enough, creeping about in the shadows, that's for sure.' Rupert looked heavenwards. 'Come on Matthew, you know very well what I'm looking for.' Matthew could feel the festival, as he knew it, swimming out of control. 'I'm not sure I want to get involved to that extent, thanks all the same.'

'What do you think this is?' asked Rupert. 'A nativity play? They can't all come rushing on as angels or shepherds.' He threw him a disingenuous smile. 'Don't worry. It shouldn't take us long, then we can have one of those nice, late-night chats you're so fond of.'

Matthew tried to moisten his dry mouth. 'You don't need me at all. This is just a ploy to entice me over. Tom's not going to like it one bit.'

Rupert yawned. 'The perpetual refrain.' In the silence that followed, Matthew discovered that he was wringing his hands. Rupert turned to look at him sharply. 'Not frightened of Squirrel, are you?'

This was only Rupert's second night, and Matthew already felt bowed by the weight of his presence and the awkwardness of trying to please both him and Tom. He would probably upset them both before too long. How was Matthew going to square Rupert's invitation with Tom, and avoid the impression that he would often be dining at Rupert's? But Matthew could not help smiling to himself at the prospect of spending an evening on his own with Rupert, so he accepted without bothering to phone Tom for a lift. Rupert dropped Matthew off at Langdales so that he could freshen up. Knowing that Tom would hate the idea of him going to see Rupert, Matthew tried to look nonchalant as he walked into the kitchen. He could only hope that Tom might be appeased when Matthew told him he had accepted Rupert's invitation in order to break down any possibility of James playing Jack.

'I'm afraid there's going to have to be a post-mortem,' he announced, as soon as he saw Tom.

Tom was in the middle of chopping vegetables, and chuckled as he glanced up. 'Who is it? Don't tell me Felicity and Eleanor have come to blows?'

Matthew grinned. 'Apparently, Rupert needs a few pointers, so I thought it would be a good opportunity to press your case.'

Tom stopped chopping, held the knife in mid-air, but did not look up. 'You really think that will be necessary?'

'You've no idea how much I tried to get out of agreeing to it.' Eyes ranging the room, Matthew moved a little closer to Tom. 'It's like this–'

'Don't tell me he's asked you over for dinner?'

He studied the floor. 'I'm afraid so, but he needs me.'

'That's obvious, but it's not what I need to hear right now.' Tom's face tightened as he wiped his hands on his apron. 'Didn't take him long, did it?'

Matthew could not look him in the eye. 'I'm not with you.'

'To entice you over to his cosy little den,' said Tom. 'I was wondering if you would have remembered, but I don't know why I bother.'

'What have I done wrong now?' wailed Matthew.

'You'll understand now why I was secretive about the shopping. Still, there's nothing here that won't keep.' Tom lifted out a plastic container from a cupboard and edged the chopped vegetables into it with his knife.

It had been a full day and Matthew's head was pulsating with the auditions. Needing to take the weight of his feet, he sat down at the table, cupped his head in his hands and tried to remember what important event had slipped his mind.

Having thought for a moment he struck his forehead as the dull realisation came thudding into his brain. 'It couldn't be?'

It was a relief when Tom spoke. 'Yes. Today is the anniversary of when I met you.'

'You're implying I've forgotten?'

'Come on Matthew.'

Matthew bit his lip. 'But we normally celebrate the date when you moved in, don't we?'

'We have done, from time to time, but I was getting edgy about us, and wanted to bring it forward. Give you a surprise. Didn't do me much good, did it?'

Matthew was still wondering how best to apologise when Tom sat down next to him and put his arm around him. 'I don't want to fall out with you over this, but I'm no fool. At last, I'm beginning to understand why you were so keen for Rupert to rent a cottage in the middle of nowhere, with no prying eyes watching your car come and go.'

Matthew had to think quickly. 'But wasn't the cottage *your* idea?'

'You jumped at it too, I seem to remember.'

Matthew sighed. 'Why are you making everything so difficult? The purpose of this evening is to help *you*.'

'That's the first I've heard of it.'

'I've been given a wonderful opportunity to help Rupert make up his mind. Not make too many enemies.'

Tom shrugged. 'Some hope! Sorry, but did you *see* that new guy? I haven't a hope...'

'Couldn't take my eyes off him! Neither could Jane!'

'That doesn't mean to say he can act.'

'I nearly fainted when he stalked in,' said Matthew.

'Yes. I noticed the lolling tongue. And Jane's.' There was a pause. 'So can he act or not?'

Matthew hedged. 'No idea, but his flat vowels are against him.'

'And then there's that beard to contend with.' Tom shook his head. 'Quite wrong for the play.'

'I know! And Rupert hates beards.'

'Does he? You seem to have established a remarkably in-depth knowledge on such slight acquaintance! I'm not saying that it doesn't suit him, but it certainly doesn't fit in with the role of Jack, as I see it. He clearly fancies himself, and that puts me right off him as a person.'

Matthew stole a look at him. 'It's been a long day. Can't we at least have a drink?'

'Don't you need to stay trim?'

'How do you mean?'

'If you're seeing your ex over the next few months, you don't want to start piling on the calories.'

'Rupert is not my ex!'

Tom turned away slightly. '*"The lady doth protest too much, methinks."*'

Matthew wanted to strike him, but stood up and gazed out of the window, trying not to clench his fists.

Tom broke the silence. 'I'm sorry, but I can't possibly drink and then drive you over to Rupert's.'

'The last thing I want is to spoil your evening, Tom…'

Tom raised an eyebrow. 'Any more than you have done already?'

Matthew felt as if he was dealing with Eleanor at her most exasperating. Knowing that Tom was getting the upper hand, he closed his eyes for a few moments, then tried to sound patient. 'Listen, why don't I call for a taxi?'

Tom assumed a mask-like expression, placed his arms against his chest, and glared at him. 'You're quite sure you won't be staying over?'

Matthew pretended he had not seen the look in Tom's eyes. 'I shall ignore that. You don't want to come out if it's frosty, and it looks like being a clear night.'

'You've misjudged everything.'

'Not quite everything.' Matthew advanced towards Tom, took him by the shoulders and began to unbutton the younger man's shirt. 'Are all the guests in their rooms?'

Tom pressed himself against Matthew. 'Why don't we be sensible about this? There's nothing to stop us from celebrating tomorrow night, especially if you can swing Jack for me.'

Matthew murmured, 'Of course I will do my best, but first let me…'

Before they became too engrossed, Matthew pulled away by mutual consent and they left the kitchen together before things got out of control. He glanced at the fresh flowers and new candles in the dining room on his way past, but told himself that he was still doing the right thing in going to Rupert's. If he did nothing else, he had to secure the role of Jack for Tom. Following him, Tom practically ran up the stairs, pulling off his shirt as he did so. Matthew prayed no guest emerged from their room.

Later, still lying in bed together, Tom propped himself up on his elbow. His eyes moved around the room, as if he was about to say something portentous but could not quite figure how. 'I was trying to hurt you before – I see that now – and I'm not proud if it. I apologise. But can I be deadly serious for a moment?' Matthew moistened his lips and nodded. 'You *will* be coming back tonight?'

'What do you take me for?'

Tom cleared his throat. 'It's just that we haven't experienced anything like this before, and I can't help wondering whether we're going to survive it.'

'Not if you continue to come out with jealous barbs about my past at every opportunity.'

Tom opened his mouth and then shook his head. 'It's more the present I'm interested in. You're my future, Matthew.'

'And I, yours, I hope.' He threw his arm around Tom's shoulder.

'Never mind that now, things might improve if you *promise* to bring me back some good news.'

Matthew nodded, leapt out of bed and phoned Rupert to say that the boiler had broken down and he was running late. He prayed that Rupert would be in a good mood when he arrived.

It was not easy leaving Tom on his own, Matthew reflected as he seated himself in the taxi. Used to passions running high during rehearsals, Matthew had rarely felt so strongly about a production in its early stages. Having to face up to a supporting role was not without its drawbacks, but he had to remind himself that he had never fancied the idea of being left at home while Tom was out rehearsing, and then having to listen to the gossip afterwards. He was now fully committed to playing Canon Chasuble.

During the ride he anticipated his next move if Tom did not play Jack, but quickly swept that thought aside. He *had* to make sure that Tom played Jack, otherwise their relationship might not stand the strain of Rupert's presence.

Another nagging thought refused to go away: Eleanor *must* play Miss Prism. She had never missed a festival yet. Eleanor, too, could not survive without it, and he could not bear the idea of being in a festival without her. He must fight her corner, too.

When the taxi pulled up outside the cottage, Matthew handed over the fare and told the driver that he would telephone when he was ready. Rupert – brimming with cordiality – threw open the front door, and launched into one of his chirpy monologues. Usually dilatory in such matters, he had laid out the glasses, wine and some olives in readiness, had even laid the table. Matthew lost count of the number of vases filled with tulips. Once they were settled on the sofas in the living room (both, it seemed, mindful of staking out their own territory) Rupert poured him a glass of white burgundy in silence, and the atmosphere darkened. Waiting until they raised their glasses to the success of the production, Matthew gave Rupert a sideways look.

'Tom says hello,' he began, 'and asked me to remind you that he is looking forward to playing Jack.'

This did not come out quite as he had hoped, so it was no surprise when Rupert eyed him steadily over the top of his glass and said coldly, 'Is he, indeed?'

Things were splintering already, so Matthew concentrated on Rupert's face. 'You said earlier you didn't want to tread on too many toes.'

'Well, we might as well get it over with,' said Rupert. 'Let's start with Tom, since you clearly want to get that out of the way. I know what you're both angling for – and I'm also well aware that you're not

106

going to like this – but I feel Tom's lightness of touch would be better suited to Algernon.'

Matthew exploded. 'I know you didn't see him perform last year, but Jack is well within Tom's range!'

Rupert raised a hand. 'Remember both the leading roles are excellent, and having played Algy myself, I can assure you that Wilde has given him some of the best lines.'

'But not always the best scenes.' In the pause that followed, Matthew stared at Rupert in the hope of unnerving him, but it would take more than a baleful look. 'You do realise, Rupert, that Tom is going to be livid?'

'Then let him be livid,' said Rupert. 'This is like kindergarten. You've quite spoiled him.'

Matthew closed his eyes for a moment. 'So it's a foregone conclusion? James will be playing Jack. Well, I hope you're going to make him lose that beard.'

'Of course. You don't need a second look to realise that he'd be much better off without it. He's a good-looking kid. I fell for the cheekbones straight away.'

'For me, it was those long, dark lashes...' said Matthew, warming to the theme. 'And as for the wavy hair–'

'Yes, I know; it's just not fair!'

'Just keep your hands off him, that's all.'

Rupert threw up his hands in mock horror. 'Moi?'

'I don't know what I'm going to say to Tom. He's a long-standing member and has set his heart on playing Jack.' One look at Rupert's face and Matthew felt the temperature plummeting. 'You haven't offered it to James already? Because if you have, that's strictly against festival etiquette.'

' *"Festival etiquette"* indeed...'

'Things are supposed to be run past the committee first.'

Rupert sighed. 'One casts a play by intuition and hard-won experience, not by committee.'

'Why can't James play Algernon?' asked Matthew. 'It's the usual practice for new members to work their way up.'

'Aren't you forgetting something?'

'What?'

'James hasn't *actually* auditioned for Algernon.'

'Neither has Tom!' Matthew heard his stomach rumble; he had to press Tom's case before Rupert served dinner. 'He'll kill me when he hears this.'

Rupert's eyes widened. 'Isn't that a bit strong?'

He went back to searching Rupert's face. 'Well, we've not been seeing eye to eye lately.'

'That's hardly my fault. Or is it?' Rupert laid a hand on Matthew's arm, but he pulled away. 'Squirrel being awkward? But he comes over as so easy-going.'

'He is, but he really proved himself as the young lead last year. I wish you could have seen him. If he doesn't play the lead this year, he'll be so disappointed. We don't know anything about this James Longstaff except that he's handsome. We don't know where he's from, what he's done...'

'Perhaps you don't, but he certainly looks as if he deserves to play the lead.'

'Yes,' grumbled Matthew, 'but how well? The trouble with you is that you are so swiftly taken in by a pretty face.'

'And you're not?' Rupert stood up. 'How many times do I have to tell you that Algernon's the better role?' He turned on his heel and went into the kitchen. 'The ones I saw this morning were more than unusually plain, and rather dull.'

Matthew moved over to the table, sat down heavily, ignored the cold, white roll sitting on his side-plate and stared blankly around him, only glancing up when Rupert emerged from the kitchen with the soup. He decided to play the only card he had left.

'I don't want to spoil this evening, but you can imagine my horror when Tom reminded me – quite forcibly – that today is the anniversary of the day we first met.'

Sitting down opposite him, Rupert spluttered in an exaggerated way. 'Forcible? I don't believe it.'

'He was preparing a gala dinner, when–'

'Gala dinner? When did you get to be so pretentious, Matthew? You never used to be like that.'

Matthew realised the soup was cooling, just as his lips were drying. 'So, I am here under duress. I've not only missed an important dinner, but I've left him on his own. If I return with bad news, things could turn nasty.'

Rupert shook his head. 'Fortunately for you, I don't believe Tom has a nasty bone in his body.'

'But he can have a very sharp tongue at times.'

'I'm sorry, but my decision is final. I believe that Tom has just the right lightness of touch to play Algernon.'

Matthew stared. 'So you're dismissing the fact that he did not audition for the role?'

'From what I've seen of his audition for Jack, I feel he is more than capable of capturing the same luminous quality as I did when playing the part.' Before Matthew could get a word in, Rupert held up a hand in warning and continued. 'Moving on to Gwendolen, Jane Kilbride is the only real contender as far as I can see.'

The mental turmoil for Matthew was more than he could bear, and he was going quietly frantic, wondering how he could possibly break the dreadful news to Tom. 'Oh, is that it? Have we finished discussing Tom? I hadn't realised.' He breathed in the French onion soup. 'This smells delicious, by the way.'

'We'll come back to Tom later, if you're good.'

'Jane is everyone's favourite to take over from Eleanor, in due course.'

Rupert smirked. 'Except Eleanor's?'

'Exactly. But moving on, what about little Cecily?'

'I feel that Cecily has to be played by Clare Kilbride. She has such an exquisite profile.'

'Yes, she's delightful,' murmured Matthew, relieved. 'And looks incredibly young.'

Rupert reached for an audition confirmation slip, filled it in and placed it in an envelope. 'This is turning out to be *so* much easier than I'd expected.' His eyes gleamed. 'Now as for Miss Prism, Felicity has a pleasing voice and manner, but I felt she was woefully under-prepared.'

Matthew sucked in his breath. 'Not to say acutely nervous. You've chosen Jane and Clare Kilbride already, and Felicity can be rather stilted, not to say wooden.'

Rupert was looking pleased with himself. 'Yes, but I've been informed that Felicity has raised her sponsorship money for the festival and that it's pay-back time.'

'She told you that?'

'Of course.'

Matthew thought quickly. 'You do realise how much of the budget goes on your wages?'

'Casting shouldn't depend on who pays most,' said Rupert. 'Although I realise with this festival that it's "pay and display".'

The mood lifted when Matthew winked. 'We have our artistic integrity to consider.'

Rupert grinned. 'Funny, but nobody has mentioned that until now.'

'Felicity is our main sponsor this year, but Eleanor was a founder member and is therefore entitled–'

'And has always shelled out for it previously. Yes, you've already mentioned Vane Construction. But magnificently experienced as she no doubt is, I don't want her anywhere near this production.'

'You're going to *have* to include her, I'm afraid.'

'Impossible! Eleanor's never going to forgive me for swiping Lady Bracknell from under her nose, and she'll be only too anxious to undermine me.' He paused. 'You see, Matthew, Eleanor is a type I've rubbed up against on more occasions than I care to remember.'

'She's bossy I grant you.'

'And far too domineering for her own good. That type needs taking down a peg –'

'You'll live to regret it, Rupert.'

'Nonsense. I'm the director. Besides, WAFT – from what I have seen so far – has become too self-satisfied, lazy, not to say fat. The entire operation is in dire need of shaking up.'

'Hence James?'

'Sparkling new talent, pure and simple.'

Matthew grinned. 'Probably not very pure, and certainly not simple! And all because you want to slide into bed with him?'

'We all have our fantasies, dear. More importantly, no more type-casting.' Here he glanced at Matthew. 'A clarion-call for a fresh approach!'

'That's all very well, but she has broken previous directors. Tom and I weren't joking.'

'I realise that, but I think you'll find she has met her – '

'Please, don't develop this line of thought further than you have to– '

Rupert began to raise his voice. 'I refuse to be cudgelled– '

'You're not listening, are you? She really does have it in her power to make life very unpleasant for you.'

'And yet if I do include her in the production she'll spend all her time undermining me.'

'Best have her on the inside, rather than the outside, I've found.' Matthew paused. 'Look, Rupert, now you're beholden to her for this place, she can use it as a lever and will think nothing of snapping you in half.' He relished Rupert's reaction over the top of his glass.

Rupert held his spoon in mid-air. 'How you both must have howled once I'd accepted her terms.'

'It was never like that, I can assure you.' He eyed Rupert for a moment, and then returned to the business of the soup. He may have failed with Tom, but he dare not let Eleanor down; he quivered at the thought. 'She could make life very difficult in all sorts of ways. For instance, be very slow on mending anything that needs it. There's bound to be snagging. You're the first occupant in here.'

'And that wilderness outside will have to be sorted, without a doubt.'

'Quite, but what would you say to having your electricity disconnected?'

Rupert almost choked on his last mouthful. 'You're joking?'

'I wouldn't put it past her.'

'If you're half as convincing on stage as off–' murmured Rupert, shaking his head.

'You grasped that Eleanor and I usually play opposite each other, I take it? I have to watch out for her.'

'What is it between you two?' demanded Rupert. Matthew said nothing. 'I'm surprised Tom doesn't get jealous.'

Matthew looked up quickly. 'What do you mean by that?'

'I wonder why you bother with her. She seems to be nothing but trouble, yet you keep trotting back for more.'

Neither of them spoke, until Matthew said, 'I can't help still being half in love with her.'

Rupert threw him an interrogatory look. 'Ah! Now we're getting somewhere. Tom mentioned something of the kind when we stayed with you that night, didn't he? At first I took it that you were simply in league together, but this goes somewhat deeper, I think?'

Matthew hesitated. 'I was so happy when I thought things were going to work out with her, but they fell through. That's a long time ago, of course.'

Rupert looked as if he was enjoying himself. 'Hardly surprising, given your propensity for younger men. But in spite of that, don't you feel that you're taking the festival too seriously?'

'The simple answer to that is that we all take it too seriously,' said Matthew. 'That's the point, although it's clearly not registered with you. We'd be nothing if we didn't have the festival to look forward to. WAFT means everything to her; her belief in it filters down to the rest of us, and that's why she never allows anything to get in her way.'

'You're too much in thrall to her and overburdened by ritual, if you ask me,' said Rupert, dismissively. 'Now, let me see – I don't seem to have much choice, do I? I'm a puppet in all this, a mere cypher...'

'You know what's right, and I can only trust you to do the decent thing,' said Matthew, meaningfully, hoping that Rupert would be naive enough to be taken in by the story about the threat to his electricity.

'I don't know what's fair about favouring Eleanor above the others, but the thought of having no electricity is enough to put the frighteners on me,' said Rupert, reaching for an audition slip and writing Eleanor's name next to that of Miss Prism. 'Have it your own way, you and your festival mafia! How I loathe this little set-up!'

'Seeing that her daughters have excellent roles, I think Felicity will be happy with that, all things considered.'

'Do you? I wish I could be so sure.'

Satisfied that he had stifled Felicity's involvement, Matthew's next priority was to show that he was serious about being included in the production, but before he began, Rupert came out with, 'Oh, by the way, before you start begging, Chasuble is yours, if you want it.'

Of course Matthew wanted it. The last few minutes had confirmed that he also *had* to be in this production. His eyes lit up. 'Are you sure?'

'Well, I couldn't separate you from the clique, could I? But I reserve the right to have you *totally* on my side, should there be any awkwardness ahead.'

'What kind of awkwardness? I may not be able to agree to that entirely, but I'm grateful all the same.'

'Reliability never was your strong point,' said Rupert, handing him his confirmation slip.

'That wasn't so difficult, was it?' asked Matthew, looking it over greedily as if it were a large cheque. 'So remind me, what did we decide about Tom?' Rupert did not meet his eye. 'Can't you at least call James back to audition for Algernon?'

'Don't be absurd.'

'All because you fancy him?'

'I can't argue with that, but doesn't everyone – you included and probably Tom – for that matter?' asked Rupert. 'That's why I need him to play Jack, don't you see? I want him to turn everybody's heads, including the audience.'

Matthew set his face. 'So your decision is final?' They sat in silence for a full minute. Rupert clearly was not going to budge. 'I'm not sure I can tell Tom that he won't be playing Jack.'

Rupert shook his head and laughed. 'You really are frightened of Squirrel, aren't you? Don't tell me I should do it for you?'

'Not frightened, I just want the best for him. How can I get through to you? He's the love of my life, Rupert, can't you understand that?'

'Thanks. I feel suitably upstaged.'

A shadow crossed Matthew's face. 'This isn't just about your crush on James, is it? You're jealous of Tom and you're prepared to go to any lengths to hurt him.'

Rupert's eyelids flickered for a moment. 'You've got that wrong for a start. I'm jealous of you both.'

Matthew forced a smile. 'I think you're making a big mistake, but if you're determined to go through with it, Tom *must* play Algernon. You won't renege? Promise me this at least.'

Rupert's eyes were blazing. '*Must* play Algernon?'

'Why did you invite me over if you're not prepared to listen?'

Rupert shrugged. 'I couldn't face being on my own again this evening, like I was on my first night here. That was beyond cruel, Matthew.'

'You told me that you needed this job, didn't you?' Rupert averted his gaze. 'I suspect that Eleanor is still going to cause trouble, and you're going to need me on your side at some point. So, let me tell you, I'm not prepared to help you if you leave Tom out of this.'

'Oh, for God's sake, Matthew—'

'You couldn't wait to pay Eleanor up front, could you? And that was *your* idea, not mine. If, or rather *when*, you have to leave this production in a hurry – like other directors before you – you'll never recover that money. You're aware of that?'

Rupert coughed. 'Well, I'm sure Tom will do Algernon justice, and that is as far as I am prepared to go.'

He scribbled Tom's name on the slip with all the coolness of an autocratic monarch signing a death-warrant, and Matthew made a great deal of business out of placing it in an envelope in case Rupert changed his mind. He did not.

Rupert then thrust back his chair, collected the soup bowls huffily and disappeared into the kitchen to serve the main course. The smell from the kitchen was making Matthew ravenous. He splashed half the bottle of red into the large glasses, but far from enjoying taking in the aroma of the wine, he quailed at the thought of Tom tearing open that envelope. Rupert reappeared in due course with two steaming plates of lasagne and this time they toasted the cast, if rather half-heartedly.

Rupert frowned. 'I knew I'd forgotten something.'

'Black pepper?'

'It's behind you, on the sideboard, but you won't need it. Now, where was I up to?'

'Lane and Merriman? One actor for both parts, wasn't it?' Rupert nodded. 'If I were you...' Matthew went on to outline the virtues of Archie, his friend and helper at Langdales, and an occasional bit-part actor in the festival.

'Oh, yes, he seemed competent enough,' said Rupert, writing down his name, in his flowing flamboyant script. 'The others were a bit too doddery. Tell me, how long will it take before they can drop their books?'

'Three weeks, hopefully. Have you finished the rehearsal schedule yet?'

'Mondays, Tuesdays and Thursdays, although being amateurs they will probably need more!'

A feeling of modified relief allowed Matthew to relax a little. Rupert seemed to have put the past behind them, for their conversation from now on concentrated on the future. There was no trouble finding things to talk about and for the most part all Matthew had to do was field Rupert's enquiries about the festival, remaining careful not to reveal more about its more distasteful machinations than he had to. Once they had finished the business of the evening, Matthew found himself warming to this agreeable little set-up with Rupert; they were so easy in each other's company and felt so right together, more than he could have imagined. Old friends really were the best, and they possessed that shared history of when things were good.

Meanwhile, Rupert had soon finished his lasagne and was quick to drain the red into their glasses. Refusing the offer of pudding – which was merely fruit – Matthew rose to clear the plates and make coffee.

Yet once he was in the kitchen, and recognising that their reignited friendship had more than a whiff of becoming domesticated, Matthew found himself yearning for the cosy but probably acerbic meals he might have shared with Rupert, had they settled down together. His mind wandering, he had to bring himself up sharp, recalling that Rupert would have soon got the better of him. Matthew returned with the coffee and they sat at the furthest ends of each sofa, as if wary of a straying hand or arm, and Rupert soon had him howling over his tale of a recent dire production he had been involved with. Consequently, he stayed much later than he had intended.

It was a chilly, cloudless night, and once he was sitting in the taxi on his way home, and thinking about breaking the news to Tom, Matthew found himself shivering. And yet his hands were warm and moist.

Chapter Six

Illuminated by the taxi head-lights, Matthew smiled when he saw that Langdales was in darkness except for the rather under-powered light in the porch; he could defer what threatened to become a big scene with Tom until the morning. Once inside, however, having fumbled for the hall light switch, and having thrown his coat over the back of a chair, Matthew put his head round the sitting room door, and snapped on the lights, just in case.

He swallowed when he saw that Tom had waited up. There were dark shadows under his eyes. Dazzled by the brightness, Matthew dimmed the chandelier and flicked on a couple of lamps.

Tom not only looked directly at him, but through him. 'What kept you?'

'I thought he would never let me get away!' Lowering his eyes, Matthew passed Tom the envelope. 'Sorry it's taken so long, but I thought you might want to see this,' he said, sounding hoarse from too much talking and laughing.

The seconds passed slowly as Matthew examined a miniature still-life he had hardly glanced at in years, while listening to Tom rip open the envelope. Although not in the same league as Matthew or Eleanor, Tom knew the value of a dramatic gesture. Rising slowly, a stifled mournful baying erupted from within. The bedroom above was occupied and Matthew could not help glance at the ceiling. Meanwhile, Tom would not look at him.

'If it's any consolation,' said Matthew, 'you have no idea how hard I had to work to get you that. And please keep the noise down.'

'So, I'm that good? I've only played– oh, what's the point?'

Matthew tried to sound as consoling as possible. 'Please let me explain.'

'How's that going to help?'

'If you must know, Rupert–'

'Please don't remind me of that man.' Tom came over to stand next to him, and seemed about to put his arm around Matthew's shoulder, unless Matthew was misreading the situation entirely. 'How could you let this happen?'

'Let's tackle this tomorrow, shall we?' Matthew took a step back. 'It's unfair of you to be lying in wait like this when we're both exhausted.'

'I was *not* lying in wait,' said Tom, 'but I *had been* under the impression that Rupert had promised me Jack.'

Matthew lost no time in trying to make a convincing defence. 'He appears to have changed his mind.'

'You're not wrong there.'

Stepping forward, Matthew rested his hands on Tom's shoulders. 'It's not been easy.'

Tom pulled away. 'No need to ask who's playing Jack?'

'You'll make a striking pair, one dark, one fair.' He then realised how ludicrous this sounded. 'It's not my fault that James is good-looking.'

Thin lines scored the sides of Tom's mouth, and his eyes were moist. 'I shall never forgive him for this.'

'Who?'

'James, of course. Rupert is beneath consideration.'

'From what I've seen,' said Matthew, thinking hard, 'James seems a pleasant young man, the sort of new member we should be encouraging. Please don't spoil the festival with petty jealousies and rivalries.'

'But that's what we *do*, Matthew.'

'Look, Algernon is the better role. Take my word for it.'

Tom set his face. 'That,' he said, 'is a matter of opinion. And it's not the lead.'

Matthew's eyes followed Tom while he paced up and down. 'But you've not asked about *me*.'

'What about *you*?' asked Tom, sounding not the least bit interested. 'Isn't it obvious you've got the role that you wanted?' He glanced at Matthew. 'I just hope you didn't have to go down on him.'

Matthew reeled back in horror. 'How dare you! It certainly is *not* the role I wanted. It's not even the play I wanted. But I wanted to be involved so that I could be with you. Although that seems laughable given your present mood.' Realising that he had been raising his voice, Matthew glanced at the ceiling again.

Tom started to lose control. 'Is it any wonder Rupert wanted sole control? *Egomaniac!*'

'Lower your voice, can't you?' Not having anticipated a backlash on this scale, he turned his back on Tom, and helped himself to some whisky. Everything was out of kilter. Retreating to the sofa, he leaned forward and buried his face in his hands. It was as if Rupert had jinxed them.

Tom had stopped in the middle of the room and was standing with his thumbs in his belt. 'So, can we all safely assume that Rupert fancies him? Because, if so, rehearsals will be a hoot. The unmentionable chasing the unattainable?'

'Yes, flirting with Rupert didn't do you any good, after all.' Matthew looked through his fingers at him. Tom seemed to have metamorphosed into narrow strips. 'Of course he does. I fancy James, too. And if you could be honest with yourself, so do you.'

Tom, eyes wild by this time, opened his mouth to remonstrate and then shut it again. Matthew thought it prudent to remain silent. 'Look, you can leave me off that long list you've no doubt been totting up with Rupert. I loathe James as much as Eleanor detests Rupert.'

'Finished?' asked Matthew, flippantly.

'Not even begun. Look what he's done to me. James has not even had to work for it.'

'You don't know that, although I guess Rupert can be quite persuasive when he wants to be.'

'That's a horrible thought,' said Tom. 'A lovely guy like him, probably having to do something he doesn't want to.'

'Don't even go there. But I think you *do* fancy James, if you'd be prepared to admit it. That's why you're so jealous of him. According to Rupert, everybody in the audience is going to fancy James. Isn't that why he's playing Jack?'

Tom shrugged. 'Rupert seems to have everything worked out, doesn't he? This festival isn't about acting, it's about sex. James comes stalking in as a new member, untried, untested, oozing sex appeal, and I don't know what else.'

Matthew offered a tentative smile. 'You've only just cottoned on?'

'I doubt if I'll get the chance to play that part again.' Tom paused. 'I'll be too old.'

'Well, you're on the cusp as it is, and you *are* going a little thin on top.'

Tom's hand jerked up to his crown. 'I could always wear a hairpiece!' He then flopped into the nearest armchair, pulled out a cushion from behind his back and hurled it at the sofa. Dust particles caught in the light of the table-lamps.

Matthew bit his lip. 'Have you ever considered–'

'What?'

'That James might *actually* be better suited to the role than you?'

'As it happens, no – I have not,' replied Tom. 'If this James had any decency he wouldn't have pitched for Jack in the first place.'

Matthew stared at him for some time, wondering how far he dared go with Tom in his present state. 'You really can't think of a way out of this?' Tom shook his head. 'Then throw yourself at Rupert, for all I care, if it means so much to you. It might not be too late.'

Tom clutched the chair arms, as if about to rise. 'That's grotesque.'

'What's the difference?'

Tom eyed him. 'What are you implying?'

'Compared to when you were cosying up to him when he appeared?'

'That was just a game,' he scoffed.

Matthew's face hardened. 'It doesn't sound like a game now.'

'Calling his bluff might backfire on me.'

'Stop behaving like a child.'

'I thought I *was* your child in what's fast becoming an ugly *ménage à trois*,' shouted Tom.

'That's rubbish, as well you know, but if it's that ugly, you may as well go. Go on, *get out*, and be quick about it.'

He put his hand to his mouth, and as the silence gathered weight, Matthew realised that those words could never be unsaid. Unwittingly, he had erected a barrier, which they were both aware of, but dare not refer to.

'I might just take you up on that,' said Tom, gleefully. 'You have no idea how insufferable you've become since you met *him*, looking him over at every opportunity–'

Matthew was about to deny this, when they heard a rap on the door and froze. He pulled himself together and ushered in a bulky middle-aged figure in a white dressing gown and offered him a chair.

Smiling thinly, the guest looked from one to the other. 'So sorry to intrude, and I hope I'm not interrupting anything, but – how can I put it – you woke us up.'

Tom stood up but did not meet their guest's eyes.

Matthew thought quickly. 'Mr Bainbridge, we owe you–'

'Beresford.'

Matthew kicked himself and tried to memorise his name. 'I do apologise, Mr Beresford. It won't happen again.'

'My wife and I have both had a particularly trying week,' continued their guest. Matthew groaned inwardly: it was the sort of thing he was used to hearing. 'We didn't expect to queue on the M6, to pay whatever it is we're paying, to be kept up half the night.'

'I've said I'm sorry, Mr Beresford,' said Matthew, standing a little taller. 'Would you care for a nightcap?'

Mr Beresford glanced at the decanter. 'I don't suppose you've changed it since this afternoon?' Matthew shook his head. 'Better not then, thanks all the same.' Catching Matthew's eye, his tone lightened. 'In some ways, you have my sympathies.'

Matthew stepped back. 'Really?'

'My wife and I have been having trouble with *our* eldest boy. I generally find that my wife is better at dealing with them.' He looked from one to the other more closely this time. 'She's turned in then?'

Matthew, catching on but trying not to sound strained, squeaked, 'Who?'

'Mrs Hunter, of course. Your wife? Although, I haven't had the pleasure yet.'

Matthew, mustering all the meaningless charm of a minor hotelier, could not help smiling as he patted his guest on the back. 'I'm not married, but I take your point.'

Mr Beresford looked askance at him. 'So who is this? And why the raised voices?'

'My assistant manager, Tom. Tom Bunting.'

Tom murmured how pleased he was as he shook Mr Beresford's hand. But after Matthew had shown him out, they both doubled up with stifled laughter, only piping down to avoid a repetition of the interruption.

'Let's hope that little interlude doesn't appear on Trip Advisor.' Matthew wagged a finger at Tom. 'It's way past your bed-time, son.'

Tom pulled Matthew towards him. 'This can't go on. It might affect the business. Ever since Eleanor told us about Rupert's impending arrival, there has been nothing but trouble.' Their eyes met. 'I almost forgot. Don't you think it's time you filled me in on the others?'

Matthew rubbed the bridge of his nose with his thumb and forefinger. This was all he needed. 'There haven't been any others. You know that. Not since you came to live here.'

'No, you fool – the auditions.'

'Why don't you explain yourself, then? Jane will be playing Gwendolen, and Clare is to play Cecily.'

Tom nodded as if he had anticipated this. 'And Miss Prism?'

'Felicity's out of the running, although she's still president, of course.'

'I thought as much. Eleanor will continue to be on military alert, but I suppose he had no choice.'

'Unless he wanted his electricity cut off.'

Tom stared. 'She wouldn't?'

'Probably not, but that was the best I could do.'

'To keep her in the show?'

Matthew nodded, while Tom clasped his hands together, thrilled. 'Archie will be playing Lane and Merriman no doubt. So you'll accept?'

'I can see nothing but trouble if I do.'

'And I see nothing but trouble if you don't.'

'Even so, I hope Rupert isn't expecting me to work with someone I detest,' said Tom, 'because I'm determined to go on loathing James, and I shall do my utmost to make rehearsals hell.'

'Don't take it so seriously,' said Matthew.

Tom chuckled. 'That's rich, coming from you.'

'Well, you'll have to learn to like James if you're going to work with him. That's all I can say.'

Tom crossed his arms. 'I can't wait for the reviews, when the leads aren't speaking.'

Matthew grinned. 'It sounds as if we're in for a black comedy.'

Tom smiled back. 'Just spare me the bedroom farce in between.'

'By the way,' whispered Matthew, as he held the door open for Tom and switched off the lights. 'Thank you for remembering our anniversary. Have I been forgiven?'

Tom nodded – somewhat half-heartedly – and they tiptoed upstairs; Matthew was in shock, however. Did he really look old enough to be Tom's father?

The next morning, having spent longer in front of the bathroom mirror than usual, Matthew felt an urge to phone Rupert and tell him Tom's reaction, but was soon dithering and putting the thought to one side. Tom was pleasant enough to Matthew, but remained subdued for the whole of Sunday. However, by Monday morning he seemed to be coming to terms with having lost out to James. It was a wet morning, but it was Matthew's turn to deposit a couple of cheques at their nearest bank, and – having run to the car – he set off for Windermere in a heavy downpour.

Once he was on his own, Matthew could not stop smiling to himself. It felt good to take stock while he had some time alone. Rupert had restored his spirits and the idea of being able to nip out and see him whenever he wanted was an uplifting one, for there were things he might be able to laugh about with Rupert that he could with no one else.

His errand complete, Matthew noticed Rupert approaching along the puddled pavement. Windermere, its blue-grey slate buildings looking darker when wet, was brightened by Rupert's presence. He wondered what his next move should be. Regardless of a sky bruised with purple, Rupert was wearing dark glasses, as if constantly badgered by autograph hunters. Matthew ignored the urge to ask him what he thought he looked like, but was determined to find out what he was doing.

Rupert seemed more than unusually pleased with himself. 'I'm popping in on James. He doesn't know it yet but he's about to become my new best friend.'

Matthew stared. 'Not *the* James?'

Rupert nodded. 'They have a branch office here.'

'What are you talking about?'

'You do realise that James is a practising solicitor? It's too good an opportunity to miss–'

'What is?'

'Caroline's been pestering.'

'What is it this time?'

'I've never had time for making a will, and she is rightly anxious.'

There was a quickening of interest from Matthew; he might just be included. 'Can you blame her?'

'As she has been quick to point out, I'm worth more dead than alive. Or might be one day.'

Turning up his collar, Matthew considered this. 'But as you've no children, wouldn't she be next of kin?'

'It's slightly more complicated.' Uneasy, Matthew put on the best bewildered expression he could muster. 'Caroline wants to make sure my will is drawn up correctly so that there can be no future arguments.' Shrugging, Matthew muttered something about being perplexed. 'Look, Matthew, I've never been able to get my head around the legal jargon. You couldn't join me, I suppose? Thistlethwaite and Penge. Only a few doors down.'

'I know exactly where they are, but surely this is just a routine appointment. How difficult can it be?'

'You never know where a thing like this might lead,' replied Rupert. 'Besides, my other aim is to ask him over for dinner.'

Curiosity now aroused by Rupert's real motive, Matthew glanced at his watch. His car was parked on the street but he had plenty of time left, and there was nothing to rush back for. Rupert used to have a gift for making prosaic activities entertaining, so Matthew went along – almost too readily – with the suggestion. If Rupert was about to make a move on James, Matthew convinced himself that he, Rupert, needed a chaperone and left a message on Tom's phone. He turned to Rupert. 'Your intentions are honourable?'

'Of course not,' smiled Rupert, 'but we're both strangers to the area. James may be lonely.'

'Nobody's that lonely. Don't forget he's young enough to be your son.'

Rupert curled his lip. 'And Tom isn't, I suppose?'

'Well, I'd have had to make a start pretty early.'

'If you had it in you in the first place.'

'I'm not a eunuch.'

'That much I do remember,' grinned Rupert, as he flung open the entrance door to the solicitors' office.

The bored-looking receptionist looked up from typing, managed a smile and took their coats. They did not have to wait long before being ushered in. James came round his desk, shook hands and invited them to sit down before returning to his chair. He looked very handsome in his crisp white shirt and dark-blue suit, but remained slightly obscured from Matthew by a multi-stemmed white orchid on one corner of the desk.

After the preliminaries, Rupert got down to business. 'I have a son, you see, and I have to make provision for him. That's really why I'm here.'

The addition of an heir put a new slant on Rupert's intriguing past and was the last thing he had expected. Matthew shifted his position; butterflies were flapping in his insides. As he turned things over in his mind, it raised several awkward questions, for there was something he had long regretted doing behind Rupert's back. He had not dared ask Rupert if he had gone through with the wedding, but whether he had or had not, it appeared that the union had led to a son. Matthew's head was crowded with questions that he dare not ask.

James smiled. 'So, can we assume that you'd like your son to be the main beneficiary?'

'If that means leaving the bulk of my estate to him, yes,' said Rupert. 'But put in a reasonable legacy to Caroline, would you, there's a dear? What would be appropriate?'

With a flicker of eyelashes, James asked, 'For your wife?'

'"Mr Worthing, I am unmarried!"'

James's fixed professional expression faltered for a moment. He ran his eyes over Matthew and Rupert, until Rupert explained his relationship to Caroline.

'May I ask your son's name?'

'Seth,' replied Rupert. 'Hammond. We decided he would grow up with my surname, you see.'

James asked further questions and made notes. Trying to look at ease, Matthew listened intently when James began asking Rupert about his son's whereabouts.

'I'll need an address, obviously,' said James, a note of irritation creeping in. Not for the first time, Matthew realised that he would need to have that accent drummed out of him.

Rupert raised his arms in the air. 'I suppose I could ask his mother, although I've not clapped eyes on her for years. We're no longer in touch, you see. I could try and get my sister to find out, if that's any use?'

'It's essential.'

When it was time to wind up the interview, James told Rupert to make a second appointment on his way out, so that the will could be signed and witnessed.

Rupert stood up. 'Thank you. Did you follow all that, Matthew?' Matthew nodded as he rose. 'There is one other thing,' said Rupert. James smiled apprehensively. 'Have you ever seen the film of *Importance,* starring Edith Evans?'

'A long time ago,' replied James, also rising. 'Why? Did you ever work with her?'

Rupert looked at a loss for words. 'Dame Edith? We were from different generations.' While he hesitated as if thinking, a sense of expectancy arose. 'Are you free next Friday or Saturday? Dinner followed by the film?'

James glanced at the orchid and thrust his hands in his pockets. 'How about Saturday?'

'You shouldn't be kicking your heels on a Saturday night at your age! Shall we say six o'clock?' Rupert gave him the address. 'The satnav runs out just before you get there so don't miss the third turning on the left after the lay-by.' He turned to Matthew. 'You and Tom must join us, too.' Making a lot of eye contact, and shaking hands for longer than necessary, Rupert was in no hurry to leave.

'Well!' said Matthew, as they stood on the soaking pavement and buttoned their coats. Shafts of sun were making interesting patterns through the clouds.

Rupert frowned. 'Well what?'

'What are you up to?'

'My little *soirée* is to find out whether he'd be ready to help out in a fire.'

'I'm not with you.'

'My dear boy,' said Rupert, airily, 'find out on which side he's batting, of course.'

'Because he's a Yorkshireman?'

'I give up! How does Tom cope with you? Without that little nugget of information, I'm stuck.'

'Ah! I'm convinced he's straight, if that's what you're referring to,' said Matthew, really wanting to talk about Rupert's will. 'You're in danger of making a big mistake.'

'I doubt it.'

'You haven't changed, have you? More's the pity. This production looks set to be complicated enough as it is. We don't want James storming out, because you've stroked his knee.'

'It's not his knee I'm interested in, but I'm sure that Tom would be only too delighted to step in and take over!'

'I wish you hadn't said that.' They waited for a gap in the cars and once they had crossed, Matthew could not help over-sharing. 'While we're on the subject, guess who I've fallen for?'

Rupert stopped and turned towards him. 'You too? I could tell you were staring at him. Probably nothing more than a crush, and at your age, you should know better. I expected this, seeing as you were so quiet.'

'You didn't think your invitation was a bit obvious?'

'There was nothing to stop him turning me down,' said Rupert. 'Besides, perhaps he's heard.'

Matthew blinked. 'I don't think he can be in any possible doubt about you.' Then he thought for a moment. 'Heard what?'

'My roast lamb is to die for,' said Rupert. 'And where better to sample lamb than around here? Will you both join us next Saturday? *Please?* Build some bridges between the boys?'

Deciding to risk it, Matthew agreed without consulting Tom. 'Sorry to harp on, but I can't help feeling that this latest development of yours leaves so many unanswered questions.'

'About James?'

'No, the son you've just dredged up from nowhere. I wonder, did you choose the name?' Rupert shook his head. 'And do you really not know where he is?'

Dark clouds were gathering once more. They did not have long before the next downpour. 'To be honest, no, but that doesn't mean to say I wouldn't mind finding out,' he replied. 'I think he may be still travelling. But we really haven't time to go into that now. Don't you need to scurry back to Squirrel?'

'Tom does have a name, you know. I should be going, but can you tell me a little bit more about Seth first?'

'Why is it so important to you, of all people?'

Matthew thought quickly; his hour was almost up and Tom would no doubt becoming fidgety. 'As you know, I've not had children of my own, and I like to show an interest. I hope you find him.'

'Thank you – sounds as if I need to – and I would like to keep on the right side of James. Not that I'm thinking of dying just yet. I suppose there's been so much going on in my life that it's easy to lose track of two or three years.'

'He'll be in his early twenties now, I guess.'

'More like mid, I think you'll find,' said Rupert, counting on his fingers. 'I must have been almost twenty-five myself.'

'What's he like?'

Rupert thought for a moment. 'Taller than me. Not difficult, I know, and, sadly, not as good-looking as I was then. He's nice enough, of course, but I haven't seen as much of him as I should have done, thanks to *her*, and with being away so much. When the film company dropped me so cruelly, my options were narrowed down overnight. Too many dreary, over-long tours, dear boy.'

This sounded over-familiar, so in order to change the subject, Matthew enquired after the health of Rupert's father.

'Not good, the last I heard. The mistral really got to him this last winter. I do hope he's not sinking.' Ruminating on this, he paused. 'Which goes to show there can always be trouble in paradise.' He glanced at Matthew. 'But then, I don't need to tell *you* that, do I?'

Feeling heavy spots of rain, they parted company before becoming saturated. Upon his return, Tom made no mention that he had been gone for well over an hour. Matthew had to tell him about the invitation which – inevitably – meant revealing that he had bumped into Rupert, but he stopped short of mentioning the meeting with James.

'Oh, by the way, Rupert has already invited James. That's why I accepted. We – that is, Rupert and I–'

'So, it's *"we"* now, is it?'

Matthew grimaced. 'We were thinking that you might like to put all this behind you, and shake hands?'

Tom scowled back. 'You have no idea how I feel about this.'

Matthew felt the back of his collar. 'And how do you think *I* felt when I couldn't play the lead in *Importance*?'

'The idea was laughable in the first place, but there was no point in telling you. Anyway, when you were agreeing to this with Rupert, couldn't you have phoned me to check?'

'I left you a message. Aren't you curious?'

Tom shrugged. 'I couldn't care less.'

'You have to go if I'm going.'

'I don't have to do anything of the kind.'

'You realise that I agreed to this because of you?'

A thin smile appeared on Tom's face. 'So it's my fault?'

'You're twisting my words. It's for the good of the festival.'

'That sounds like one of Eleanor's slogans.'

'Well, don't you think you should at least give it a chance, Tom? Personally, I think you should come.'

'You mean, you *both* think I should come, although I can't imagine why, unless you're calling my bluff in the hope that I won't come.' Tom made a show of widening his eyes, as if struck by a revelation. 'You weren't really intending to go without me?'

'Not unless you force me to.'

'If you think I'm letting you loose for an evening with Rupert and that – that creature – you can think again.'

'Actually, Rupert believes every good-looking man is fair game. Mull it over. You might enjoy it.'

Tom looked at Matthew as if he had taken leave of his senses. 'No pressure, then?'

The following day it came as no surprise to Matthew when Tom confirmed that he would be attending Rupert's dinner party, and when Saturday evening finally arrived, they went into the usual elaborate discussions over what to wear. Discarding several outfits in crumpled heaps on the bed, they left later than intended, and not in the best of moods. Their paying guests came and went as they pleased and had already gone out for dinner.

On a wet, pitch-dark evening, the glimmering windows in Rupert's cottage were a welcoming diversion from the anxiety Matthew was experiencing. He frowned at the thought of Tom cold-shouldering James. However, Matthew's spirits lifted when he saw James pull up behind them, for this would mean less time with Rupert on his own. Their radiant host, reeking of after-shave, gave them a warm welcome as he took their coats. In the subdued lighting, Rupert looked five years younger and had gelled his hair into a quiff at the front. Matthew tried not to blink, but there was worse to come.

They made an ill-matched group in front of the wood-burning stove. The living room central light-fitting had been dimmed so he could barely make out the face in front of him, and the wattage of the lamps was so low as to be not worth bothering with. Matthew surreptitiously turned up the dimmer while Rupert hung the coats.

Being as familiar as he was with the voice of Maria Callas, Matthew was disappointed to hear that Rupert had relegated her to providing background music; they had played Callas together often when they were young, and cried in each others' arms when her death had been announced. Matthew took Rupert's music choice as a not very subtle reminder of their shared history; but not only was it inappropriate, it was too loud. When the track changed, Matthew realised that it was a "highlights" disc. He turned the volume down discreetly while Rupert removed a bottle of champagne from the ice bucket, and began to fill his guests' glasses. Standing slightly apart, the four of them grinned at each other foolishly and toasted the festival. Tom was glancing round the room to avoid looking at James, and it was left to Matthew and Rupert to make small talk. Feeling the strain, Matthew sank onto the sofa, to be joined instantly by Tom with a proprietorial expression. Rupert threw his arm over James's shoulder and steered him to the other sofa.

'Where did you say you lived, James?' asked Rupert, sitting so close that James was forced to lean against the arm.

'I didn't. I'm only renting 'til I can find a house to buy.'

'That probably means a one-bedroom flat?' asked Rupert, to which James nodded. Rupert smirked. 'That's all you need, as a man about town.'

'Hardly that,' said James. 'Windermere feels like a village, after what I've been used to.'

Matthew, eyeing them both, settled himself deeper into the sofa, and sipped his champagne. After further mindless chatter, Rupert rose to top up their glasses. 'More champagne, Jamie?' he asked, resting a hand on James's shoulder. 'This will only go flat, if–'

'No more, thank you,' said James, removing the hand ostentatiously from his shoulder. 'Half a glass is my limit. I have to drive. And do you mind if we stick to James?'

'I'll stick to you any day.'

Tom rolled his eyes. 'Oh, *please*.'

'He'll be calling you Jack, if you're not careful,' said Matthew.

'Don't remind me of the play,' said Tom. 'It should be a taboo subject.'

Rupert arched an eyebrow, while he placed his hand on James's shoulder once more. 'Now, Jamie, don't be such a killjoy. Are you sure you won't indulge?'

James leaned so far to one side that Rupert was forced to withdraw his hand. 'Can we keep joy out of it? I don't want to mow someone down, or suffer a driving ban, or kill *myself* for that matter. This is my limit, and that's final.'

'Yes, stop being a bloody fool, Rupert,' said Matthew.

'That reminds me, Rupey, baby,' asked James. 'How did you stumble on WAFT? Small beer, after what you've been used to?'

'It wasn't small enough to prevent *you* from taking the lead,' muttered Tom.

James looked at him as if for the first time. 'Sorry, but I couldn't resist joining after I'd heard that one of my favourite plays was going to be produced. Do you have a problem with that?'

Tom folded his arms and glanced at the floor in silence, while Callas continued to make her presence felt.

'No one has produced anything yet, sweetie,' said Rupert, rising to put the final touches to the first course.

'I'd have preferred a serious drama,' said James. 'Easier to make a big impact in some histrionic role.'

'Angst-ridden young man versus the world?' said Matthew, glancing at Tom to see how he was taking it.

Tom was staring at James in disbelief. 'Yet you sauntered into our auditions without having carried so much as a spear, while I, with many years' membership behind me–'

'That's enough,' said Matthew, feeling a sense of responsibility towards a new member.

James glanced at Tom. 'Have I made a *faux pas*?'

'Of course not,' chuckled Matthew. 'Our festival's a bit top-heavy with prima donnas, that's all. Eleanor's the obvious example, and now Tom seems to be joining the ranks!'

'I didn't mean to upset anyone.' James stole another look at his audition rival. 'Least of all you. I'd hate to fall out over something so trifling.'

Tom bit his lip. 'But it isn't trifling, is it?'

James's face fell. 'Oh. Do I take it that you'd set your sights on playing Jack?' Tom nodded. 'And then I breezed in? I'm sorry.'

Matthew admired the way James was handling this.

'I'm *more* than sorry, but there's nothing I can do,' said Tom, rolling his eyes and tilting his head in the direction of the kitchen.

'Even if you wanted to,' said Matthew, nudging him.

Tom also seemed to register that James was handling this in a mature fashion, not something they were used to in the petulant, hysterical atmosphere they appeared to thrive on. Tom smiled tentatively at James. 'Look, James, I suppose I have to agree. It's stupid to fall out, when we could be getting to know each other.'

They drained their glasses and the conversation fizzled out at about the same time that Callas was soaring in another show-piece aria. Matthew glanced at his watch, hoping to kickstart the conversation, when James placed his hands to his ears.

'Who's responsible for all that shrieking?' he asked, as if conscious that the silence needed breaking.

Matthew replied haughtily, 'Maria Callas does *not* shriek.'

There was a change of track, but within a few seconds Callas launched into Puccini's aria, which was much more gentle: *"O mio babbino caro..."*

' *"Oh, my beloved father," '* said Matthew, trying to be helpful.

James sat up and grinned. 'Don't tell me! Janice Screechy?'

Tom smiled back, but Matthew pursed his lips. 'You mean *Gianni Schicchi*?'

James laughed. 'We should call *her* Janice Screechy.'

Tom was sharing the joke now, and this determined the fate of the evening. 'Janice Screechy,' he repeated.

Matthew was affronted, but was relieved that the tension had been broken. 'I have no quarrels with her singing,' he told them. 'Her phrasing is nothing short of miraculous.'

The conversation had died again when Rupert came crashing back in with a tray of coupe dishes. He misjudged the distance for the tray, probably due to the champagne – and whatever else he was slurping backstage – and it fell on the sideboard with a clatter. Fortunately, nothing was damaged.

Matthew was glancing at the horse brasses hanging on the wall – the only jarring notes in Eleanor's cottage – when Rupert cried, 'Those horse brasses have *nothing* to do with me!' The following aria had a slow introduction, and turning to address his audience, he talked over it. 'I regard prawn cocktail as one of my signature dishes. It never fails me.'

James made a face when Rupert was not looking. Tom smirked back.

'A retro-starter, eh?' asked Matthew, pausing the next screaming track as they made their way to the table. Rupert, rather pointedly glancing in Matthew's direction, dimmed the lights. Talking incessantly, he lit the candles and sat down. With a flick of the wrist, he shook out the linen napkin that had taken him more than one attempt to contort into a bishop's mitre.

Watching James out of the corner of his eye, Matthew imagined the dozens of solitary meals in his rented flat. James made another face as he peered at Tom through the vase crowded with tulips that obscured them from one another, and placed it on the sideboard. James and Tom seemed to be finding the most incidental things amusing, and Rupert deserved full credit for bringing "the boys" together. Although it was a relief to see Tom enjoying himself, Matthew wondered at the shared immaturity.

It was evident that something had clicked inside Tom regarding James. He was not sure where this was heading, but forced himself into believing that it might benefit the production.

The prawn cocktail contained a great deal of prawn and hardly any lettuce, and the white burgundy was crisp and well-chilled. Rupert stood up to clear the plates. 'Now, just wait for the leg of lamb. Half an hour in a really hot oven with rosemary and garlic and the result is absolute bliss.' His eye-lids fluttered. 'Handed down to me by the mother of a gorgeous young creature I spent a few days, or rather nights with, in Italy.'

When they heard Rupert singing "Life upon the Wicked Stage" from *Show Boat* in the kitchen, James smirked at Tom, clearly trying to make him giggle.

When he could tolerate it no longer, Matthew broke the silence. 'So, James, I believe you are in good company at the Queens?'

James turned sharply. 'I'm sorry?'

'The hotel. What did you think I meant?'

It was not the most prestigious hotel in the area, but it had a cosy bar and was within walking distance of James's flat. 'But surely you two never set foot in that place?'

'I used to work there, *actually*,' said Tom. James shifted his position. 'You're quite right, though. Matthew prefers to stay at home in his old cardigan and carpet-slippers and crack open a bottle of red.'

James narrowed his eyes. His manner altered, and not for the better. 'How do you know so much about me?' he asked in a cool voice that they had not previously witnessed.

'A mutual friend...' said Matthew.

He was smiling now. 'The famous Archie?'

'He and I go back a long way,' Matthew told him, while Tom raised an eyebrow as if Archie was beneath his notice.

James was staring at Matthew as if he was trying to work out the relationship. 'So, who *is* Archie, exactly?'

Matthew explained. 'He used to help me out at Langdales, but purely as paid help, prior to Tom.'

'I do not help out, as you put it,' said Tom. 'And I'm not very well paid.'

'As I was saying,' continued Matthew, startled by Tom's tone. 'Archie would think nothing of working the night-porter shift at the Queens and then helping me with breakfast for a couple of hours.'

'Not just helping,' said Tom. 'You mean doing the entire thing from grilling to serving it, and as if that wasn't enough, then washing up afterwards? Talk about abdicating responsibility. But that's enough about Archie. I– I mean *we* were wondering if you could join us for lunch one weekend, James?'

This was news to Matthew.

'I'd love to.'

The boys were still checking when they were available, on their phones, when Matthew was asked to take the vegetable dishes into the dining room, while Rupert sliced the lamb. It was galling to watch him slicing the pinkest, moistest middle slices for James and Tom.

'So, is he or isn't he?' hissed Rupert, once Matthew was by his side.

'Is he or isn't he what?'

'Do you work at being obtuse, Matthew?'

He shrugged. 'How should I know? It makes no odds to me. I'm fixed up with Tom, remember?'

Rupert chuckled. 'You can't have seen the looks that Tom is giving him, then?'

'How could I miss that? And as for the constant giggling, I fail to share the joke.'

'Oh, lighten up, Matthew. It's Saturday night, and the air is heavy with young men.' Rupert pointed to the plates. 'Now those two plates are for the boys. Put a bit of fat on them. Don't they look handsome together?'

Matthew promptly lost his appetite. He scrutinised the two of them while hurrying in with the plates, and was disappointed to see Tom spluttering over some private joke. Not for the first time, Matthew felt excluded. Tom was usually a model of restraint, dedicating himself to their guests' whims and being – if anything – a tad too noble about it. It flashed through Matthew's mind that pandering to guests almost twice his age or above may well be neither fun nor fulfilling. Was Tom establishing a rapport with someone nearer his age at long last? Once they were all sitting down, and helping themselves to vegetables, Rupert waved his glass insolently at James.

'Jamie, please, could you possibly... the *vin rouge*? Quite a heady little number, if I may say so.' James caught Tom's eye, made him snigger, and reached for the bottle of *Gran Reserva*. 'Thank you,' said Rupert, as James poured without dripping. 'Well, you can audition for the role of house-boy here!' Rupert took his first sip, and nodded appreciatively. 'Now, what were we discussing?'

Tom, forsaking any hope of keeping a straight face, winked at James. 'Yourself, by any chance?'

James seemed just as keen to egg him on. 'So, tell us, when did your inevitable sell-by date kick in?'

Three pairs of knives and forks hovered while Rupert studied his plate. 'Well, Jamie, since you're kind enough to ask, everything dimmed after *Hamlet*.'

A stupefied silence was about the only thing that could follow such a remark.

'*You played Hamlet?*' squeaked Tom, looking askance at him.

'Not exactly, although nothing was ever the same after that. Sir Miles Napier was very wicked to me.'

'You did actually take part?' asked Matthew, nonchalantly playing with his food.

'Not only that, I stole the show.'

'Really?' asked Tom. 'And how *exactly* does one do that in *Hamlet*?'

'I played Osric.'

'Which one is that?' asked James, almost choking with giggles.

'The courtier at the end,' said Tom. 'Has about three lines.'

James and Tom were wiping away the tears by now.

'Was it really *that* funny?' asked Rupert, the lines around his eyes looking deeper. 'That's enough about me, don't you think?' He drummed his fingers on the cloth before fixing his eyes on Matthew. 'Did you finish telling me how you met Squirrel?'

Tom opened his mouth in protest, but seemed to think better of it.

'*Squirrel?*' asked James, leaning forwards.

'A private joke,' smiled Rupert, taking in Tom's downturned mouth. 'Sometimes it's Tufty.'

'I don't believe I did,' replied Matthew. 'Curiously, it started with a notice in the post office.'

Rupert, rallying, put on his *grande dame* Lady Bracknell voice. 'A post office? *"Forming an alliance with a parcel"*, perhaps?'

'Archie and I were having one of our ongoing rows about pulling on king-size duvet covers,' replied Matthew.

'As you do,' sniggered James.

Matthew shot him a look. 'If you'll let me finish? I was left on my own by him turning on his heel and telling me to find a replacement. Still, when one door closes, or rather slams... After his flounce, I placed an advert in the post office, and that was the cue for the assistant manager at the Queens–'

Rupert, who had been listening keenly, turned to Tom. 'To come tripping on like Buttons, no doubt? It's time we heard your side of the story.'

'But I haven't finished,' said Matthew. Making sure he had their full attention, he took a sip of wine. 'I think it was meant to be, don't you?' Matthew was warming to the story, in spite of Tom discreetly nudging his shoe. 'As if redecorating Langdales wasn't enough, you went on to tackle the garden, didn't you?'

Tom stopped looking self-deprecating. 'Once I had ingratiated myself with the gardening society, we were inundated with plants.'

Rupert's cheeks were red and shiny. 'Doting on your charm and good looks?'

'That's enough about me.' Tom had no difficulty in getting James's attention. 'We're all *dying* to know what you've appeared in?'

'Really?' Shadows created by the candlelight enhanced his strong features; they enjoyed staring at him. 'Most recently, we revived *Witness for the Prosecution.*'

'Is that *still* doing the rounds?' asked Rupert.

James ran a hand through his hair and a stray lock tumbled over his forehead. 'It was the last thing I did before moving.'

Tom held James in his gaze. 'Leeds wasn't it? If you don't mind me asking, why?'

'That's simple. I needed to think about myself.'

Matthew raised an eyebrow. 'Surely, that didn't take you too long?'

'Putting oneself first is a primary duty of life,' said Rupert.

James half-smiled. 'I didn't have a choice.'

Tom eyed him. 'Surely this corner is too sleepy for you to make your mark?'

'Nonsense,' said Matthew.

'You're both right, but I decided to put quality of life first.'

Rupert began humming "Climb Ev'ry Mountain" from *The Sound of Music*. 'Not wishing to press the point, dear, but we still haven't heard *why*?'

He glanced at the flickering candles. 'That's easy. I'd become everybody's favourite uncle. They were joshing me for not having settled down.'

James's pale skin framed by dark hair and beard reminded Matthew of a religious painting; he had no inkling that he would come to loathe that face.

Rupert grinned and leaned forward. 'Who's *they*?'

'I've got three elder brothers, all married with children. But that wasn't what I had in mind for my own life.'

'Don't talk to me about *marriage*,' said Rupert, lifting his eyes to the ceiling.

Disregarding Matthew's set face, Tom exhibited similar astonishment as he had over *Hamlet*. '*Married*?'

'There's no need to look quite so shocked, Squirrel,' said Rupert.

Matthew's stomach tightened, but he found himself declaring, 'You should never have been allowed near an altar.'

Tom had become far too inquisitive for Matthew's liking. 'Now, this is something that really does have to be explained!'

Glaring at Matthew, Rupert replied hoarsely, 'A mix-up on the day, nothing more.'

Matthew tensed. 'There's no need to go into it now.'

'No point listening to Matthew stick to his story.'

The candles wobbled when Matthew struck the table. 'This is intolerable.'

Pursing his lips, Rupert tackled the wax with his fingernail.

'If I'd known you were going to be so oversensitive, I'd never have come,' said James, tears welling up. 'Are your sort – does it have to be like this?'

Matthew struggled not to put his arms around him, but it was Tom who methodically took out a clean, pressed handkerchief from his pocket and handed it to James in one seamless, mannered movement as if on stage.

'I didn't mean you, James,' said Matthew.

'Some of us wonder about the daily treadmill, but you've started a new life,' said Tom. 'I hope you will be happy, and I mean that.'

James glanced at Tom. 'But my looks seem to work against me.'

'I would have said the opposite,' chortled Rupert.

'It's personality,' said Tom, smiling encouragingly.

Matthew stopped chewing.

'That's one reason why I grew this beard,' said James.

'Well, it didn't work,' said Rupert. 'Because you're a very attractive young man, not that you need telling. Hard to believe now, but *I* used to be quite good-looking.'

'You still are. *Very*, in fact, considering...' said James.

Rupert could not take his eyes off James. '...How ancient I am, compared to you?' He hesitated. 'You must never be as lonely in a new place as I've been.'

'You're not lonely now, I hope?' enquired Matthew.

'Not something weighing on your mind too much, I suppose?'

'But I'm still single, and that grates,' said James.

'To alter Lady Bracknell's legendary observation on parents,' said Rupert, 'I think that you should *"make a definite effort to produce at any rate one..."* partner, *"of either sex, before..."* the production is quite over.'

This landed with a thud. James grinned nervously at Matthew while Tom inspected his lap. 'You must have noticed how Jane was trying to captivate me?'

Rupert chuckled. 'Matthew was probably watching *you*, too.'

Tom struck the table and the candles flicked yet more wax. Rupert shook his head.

Tom's pupils dilated. 'Can't you leave James alone, Rupert?'

'Tom...' said Matthew.

'Sorry, but I think we've got the message,' said Tom, curtly.

'What message would that be?' asked Rupert.

'That James is highly decorative.'

'It's my fault: I shouldn't have started it,' said James.

'You didn't,' said Matthew. 'Tom did.'

Tom's jaw tightened. Rupert sat back, drained his glass in a satisfied manner, as if he delighted in making his guests uneasy. Matthew gave Tom the nod. 'I've no appetite for dessert, Rupert, but thank you for a most– shall we say – interesting evening. Come on, Tom.'

No longer looking as fresh, Rupert took a second to register this. 'But you can't go yet. The wine won't have worn off. And what about the film of *Importance* I've got lined up?'

Matthew hesitated; Eleanor's dining chairs were proving uncomfortable. Even so, he was not really ready to leave. 'How about watching the first half now, and tackling the pud during the interval, if you think we can keep the peace?'

They agreed to remain. James and Rupert sat next to each other on a two-seater sofa, which Matthew thought unwise, but wishing to be diverted by the film, he said nothing, began to relax and temporarily forgot Rupert. James soon dozed off and leaned on Rupert's shoulder. Although James was capable of looking after himself, it crossed Matthew's mind that they should offer him a lift home. Having roused James, Rupert paused the DVD for their interval, and they discussed the performance over the chocolate mousse (not as good as Tom's). After coffee, they resumed watching, but James's eyes closed swiftly, and his head fell forward. When the film finished, they refused their host's offer of a nightcap, so Rupert found himself drinking his whisky alone.

'You did notice that he was flirting with me earlier, didn't you, Matthew?' asked Rupert, glancing at the still comatose James.

'You think he's interested in anyone our age?'

Turning to Tom, Rupert asked in a low voice, 'Do I detect a thaw?'

'I was only trying to be civil,' replied Tom. 'Please don't try anything foolish. We don't need any added complications.'

Musing, Rupert ran a finger around the rim of his glass.

Matthew struggled to his feet. 'Can we trust you with him?'

As Rupert did not reply, Matthew whispered in Tom's ear, 'Should we take James home with us?'

'It's rude to whisper,' said Rupert.

Tom roused James, and after a lot of blinking, he was rewarded with a smile. Appearing disorientated, he felt for Tom's hand. 'Thanks for coming. I've enjoyed it.'

Tom pulled his hand away gently.

'Bad news for you, James,' said Matthew, pretending that he had not noticed. 'You're too sleepy to drive home.'

'You could always stay here,' said Rupert, ignoring Matthew's frown. 'In the spare room, of course.'

Tom took control. 'I don't think that's your best idea yet, but driving is not an option. These roads are pitch-black, and it's a filthy night. Why don't we look after you tonight?'

Rupert rolled his eyes. 'How sweet. Both ugly sisters coming to your rescue.'

'You can stay in our spare bedroom, and *I* can drive you back here to collect your car in the morning,' said Matthew, ignoring Rupert.

James seemed reassured by the warmth of Tom's smile. 'But I haven't got anything with me.'

'Well, no doubt Squirrel can lay his hands on a toothbrush, and you can always squeeze yourself into a pair of his underpants tomorrow.'

'You need some fresh air,' said Tom, so forcefully that he could hardly refuse. Without waiting for a response, Tom made for the door.

James yawned and trailed behind him sheepishly. 'I'll do anything to keep the peace.'

That was touch and go, thought Matthew, glancing at Rupert's clenched teeth while he handed out coats and threw open the front door. The porch felt bitter after the over-heated living room. Subdued, they murmured thanks and fled, but Rupert looked singularly unimpressed as he waved them goodbye.

Having reflected that Rupert had always been a poor loser, Matthew disapproved of the way the evening had developed, and said little on the journey home. Once back at Langdales, they showed James into the spare bedroom. Strictly speaking, they could only operate with three bedrooms owing to fire regulations, but they had squeezed a three-quarter-size bed in, and used it for the occasional overbooking. Not used since last autumn, it smelled musty. Closing the door behind them, Matthew searched for the fan-heater in the bottom of the wardrobe.

'Can I get you a pair of my pyjamas?' asked Tom, in what Matthew felt was a simpering tone.

James shivered. 'I normally don't bother, but it does feel a bit cool in here, so if you're sure...'

As their eyes locked, Matthew picked up the connection. 'This bedroom is really for when we have a problem.'

James touched his ear between finger and thumb. 'Isn't that what I've become?'

Tom grinned. 'Not at all. You're more than welcome here at any time. Oh, I'd better find you a toothbrush.'

While Tom scampered off to bring one, Matthew drew the curtains, while James undressed. Matthew turned and ran his eyes over James's torso a fraction too long, and when Tom returned, he did the

140

same. From the few seconds' glimpse that Matthew had, he was muscular without an ounce of fat. They withdrew reluctantly, but unable to stop thinking about that burgeoning charge between James and Tom, Matthew tossed and turned in bed for some time.

The morning dawned clear and bright, and as soon as they had served their guests breakfast, Tom hurried upstairs to wake James, and although there was a kettle in the room, he took him a pot of tea. He was gone a long time, and Matthew had not only cleared the dining room but re-laid the table for their own breakfast by the time he returned.

'What kept you so long?' asked Matthew, wiping away his frown and trying to sound neutral.

Tom was all smiles, his tone light. 'James is somebody who commands you to spoil him without you realising it.'

'It was known as sex appeal in my day,' observed Matthew, drily.

'Can you imagine me running his bath with those prohibitively expensive lime and mandarin bubbles you've been raving about?'

'Only too clearly.'

'Oh – and I've lent him one of my T-shirts – though it's probably a bit tight across the chest – and some pants and socks. And he demanded a hair-dryer for when he got out. Knowing how impatient you are, I told him we'd probably have to make a start.'

This did not make for easy listening, especially as Matthew had something of a crush on James. He grunted and sat down at the head of the table. They had almost finished by the time James came down, looking none the worse for wear after a night in a strange bed.

'Good morning, and thank you for coming to my rescue,' he said, scooping up what was left of the assorted berries (considerable) and unsweetened yoghurt while Tom could not help rattling his cup and saucer while pouring coffee for him.

The conversation was a little hard-going to begin with, especially when all Matthew and Tom wanted was to clear the table. They put on a good face, however and sat back to watch James eat. Things picked up when James glanced out of the window. 'Quite a place.'

'We love it,' said Tom, while Matthew waited for developments.

'I'm quite happy to go for the quiet life,' said James, 'and I like being outdoors.'

'So do I,' said Tom.

'To be honest, I'm not keen on city life.'

'Neither am I,' said Tom.

Matthew, who was listening keenly, but mistrustful of so many echoes, said, 'A word of advice, James, if I may. You must watch out for Jane. She gets through boyfriends like nobody I know.'

'More than Rupert?' asked Tom, head on one side.

Matthew frowned. 'I couldn't comment.'

'She's already invited me to practise our lines at her mother's house, and meet her mother and sister,' said James. 'That's Felicity and Clare, right?'

'That's almost equal to a proposal of marriage with Jane,' laughed Tom, but the light in his eyes dimmed.

'You've accepted?' enquired Matthew.

James nodded. 'There was no way I could get out of it, or so it seemed. Funnily enough, I've already met Felicity fleetingly, when she signed me up as a member. She gave me the once-over.'

Matthew laughed. 'Felicity is famous for what novelists call a penetrating gaze.'

'So what happened to the father?' asked James.

'Heart attack,' replied Matthew. 'Jane and Clare were still at school, and Felicity had to appoint a chief executive.'

'So why doesn't Jane work in the family business?'

Matthew pondered this. 'It bored them. Jane and Clare are both directors, but they opened a shop and café called La Boutique Fantasque instead.'

'A little on the whimsical side?' suggested James.

'They named it after the Rossini-Respighi ballet. Fanciful or not, it's a real money-spinner.'

'We have had an idea' said Tom, as if he was not in the same conversation.

'You're not dating Jane, are you?' asked Matthew, ignoring this. 'Going over lines together sounds far too conscientious for WAFT.'

'No, there's nothing between us, although it will help our characterisations.' There was a sense of relief in the air, and James broke the silence with: 'Why? Should there be?'

'She's obviously keen,' observed Matthew.

'Who wouldn't be?' asked Tom.

James did not look either of them in the eye but smiled half-heartedly, while stirring his coffee zealously.

'As Rupert obviously has a crush on you,' said Tom, 'could you pretend to have a soft spot for Jane, without getting involved?'

James put down his spoon. 'Why would I even want to do that? Surely Rupert is harmless?'

Matthew declined to comment, but Tom looked heavenwards and said, 'Show us how good an actor you are?'

'She's certainly attractive.' James took a sip of his coffee. 'Although, I wouldn't want to let her down, or would she also be in on the joke?'

Tom leaned forward. 'Why? Don't you fancy her?'

'Wouldn't it be simpler if James told Rupert he's just not interested?' asked Matthew, so they never came to hear the answer, if any.

'He's been nice enough to me, from what little I've seen of him,' replied James, 'and he does make me laugh.'

'What a pity it's for all the wrong reasons,' smiled Tom.

James turned his attention to Matthew. 'What have you got against him, if you don't mind my asking?'

Matthew began fiddling with his table-mat. 'It's a long story.'

'It appears that they went to the same school,' explained Tom, and then hinted, darkly, in a stage whisper designed to be heard by Matthew, 'but there may be more to it than that.'

'We were never in the same class,' added Matthew, hastily, anxious to clarify the situation. 'Hardly came across each other, in fact.'

'Rupert was seventeen and had a crush on him,' said Tom, grinning. 'Or so I've been told.'

James looked at Matthew with a baffled expression.

'He's placed us both in a difficult position,' said Tom. James looked back at Tom as if eager to hear more. 'He's even had the cheek to suggest that he still has a soft spot for Matthew.'

James shook his head. 'How do you feel about that?'

'It's very one-sided, I can assure you,' said Matthew, watching James slowly finish his breakfast and sip his coffee rather delicately in silence. Seeing there was a convenient break in the conversation, Matthew volunteered to give James a lift back before Tom did.

Tom stood up. 'I could do with a bit of fresh air, actually. There's very little point in all three of us going.'

Feeling isolated and rebuked, Matthew saw that it would not do to appear over-keen, so he decided not to press the point.

Sensing the change in atmosphere, James said, 'Hey, I'm sorry, it's still a bit early. I should not have asked that, it was intrusive. And I am in no position to comment on Rupert. Maybe a little flirting never did anybody any harm, but I wouldn't dream of coming between you two.'

'If you'll excuse me, there are always plenty of jobs to be done in a place like this,' said Matthew, rising to clear the dishes.

'To sum up,' said James, 'although I did find Jane a bit forward at my audition, she is very attractive. I'll see if I can get anywhere with her, but I can't promise doing any role-playing that might antagonise Rupert.'

Tom bit his lip and seemed reluctant to add anything further.

Matthew tried not to look thrilled. 'Does that mean you're attracted to her?'

James finished his breakfast with a wink and a shrug.

Later, while Tom was chauffeuring James, Matthew turned the situation over in his mind. He had not taken to the way James had been transformed overnight from being a despised arch-rival to amicable friend.

But before he had too long to brood, Rupert phoned. 'How about combining watching the film's highlights with an initial read-through one evening to show the others how to move and speak?'

'Banish James's flat vowels?'

'I'll soon knock him into shape.'

'That's what I'm afraid of.'

'Had I better arrange it early evening,' asked Rupert, 'so we don't run out of time?'

The more he thought about it, the more he liked Rupert's idea of an initial play-reading; most directors went to inordinate lengths ironing out bad habits and mannerisms once it was too late.

Act Two

Chapter Seven

On the evening of the play-reading, they had been waiting for Eleanor in one of the conference rooms at the Hotel Majestic for what seemed like forever: white walls, laminate flooring, and an abandoned upright piano that had seen better days.

Rupert turned to Matthew. 'Perhaps I should have made myself clearer.'

'What is it this time?' asked Matthew, glancing at his watch.

'I expected the whole cast to be here, regardless of whether they were in the first scene or not.'

Matthew surveyed those present. 'So who hasn't shown up?'

Rupert threw up his arms in disbelief. 'Need you ask?'

'Miss Prism doesn't appear until the second act,' ventured Matthew.

Rupert sat down at his director's table. 'But the point of this meeting is to get an overview of the play.'

Matthew glanced heavenwards. 'Eleanor's only interested in not missing her cues. You'll have to get used to that. No way will she sit through the first act if she doesn't have to.'

Making it very apparent that he was put out, Rupert rearranged the folder and pens on his table. While pretending to ignore him, Matthew could not help overhearing what sounded like ribald laughter and noticed that James's and Tom's heads were practically touching.

'And that's why I hope we don't have too many seven o'clock starts,' James was telling him. 'I've really had to rush to make it here. I'd like to get to the Queens before ten.'

Tom cupped his hand against James's ear. 'Rule number one. Don't complain if you're playing the lead.'

Rupert invited them to gather round and sit down before asking them what the play was about.

James was the first to fill the silence. 'Cucumber sandwiches and muffins?'

Rupert's mouth tightened. 'Perhaps we might dig a little deeper? Why did I want to direct this play? Apart from the money, of course.' (Ripple of laughter.) 'Well, I adore the chameleon-like changes from serious moments to high comedy; I love the propriety and the hypocrisy, the double standards, the reversal of priorities.' He paused to check he had their attention. 'The reason I've called you here is not to deny you the pleasure of a fine spring evening, but because I would like you to understand the play, your role and how you interrelate with each other. Remember, I've picked you because you're each capable of sterling work.' He smiled graciously.

'What makes your character tick? What are your motives? Will anything prevent Algernon from being one step ahead of Jack? Will Lady Bracknell marry off her daughter Gwendolen? How will Jack discover who he really is?' He paused to look at James. 'Now, how many of you have concentrated just on your own lines?' No one looked him in the eye. He chuckled. 'Don't forget it's vital to know what's happening when you're not on stage. The play *does* carry on while you're lurking in the dressing room, or so I've been told.' (Polite titter.)

'Are you suggesting,' asked James, eyeing Rupert, 'that we have to play the character with your preconceived ideas, rather than our own?'

Rupert looked at him as if for the first time. 'Of course not, but we have to start somewhere. Think about spontaneity. To get the effect I would like to achieve, the lines should sound newly minted. So to start with, I'd like you all to sit in couples with another character, and work on how you think the dialogue should be delivered.' He glanced around. 'First the men: how about Jack and Chasuble? That's James and Matthew. Algernon and Lane: that's Tom and Archie. Now run along and find somewhere to sit.' His eyes swept over whoever was left. 'As for Gwendolen, Cecily and Lady Bracknell – that's Jane, Clare and myself – this evening is different, but normally you will be called for a rehearsal only for the act in which you appear.' Rupert glanced at them in turn. 'This will give you a chance of getting that overview, pacing your performance, separating the busy passages from the quiet ones. Can I suggest you turn to a scene where two or more of you appear and get a feeling for interacting with each other? Shall we spend five or ten minutes on it?' Everyone began examining their shoes, or the coloured tape on the floor. 'Please sit far apart so that we don't interfere with each other's conversations, and could someone please put the kettle on?'

Matthew could not help overhearing grumbles along the lines of 'We're only amateurs, so what does he expect?' 'We're doing it for fun, aren't we?' 'There seem to be so many instructions, *already*.' 'I hope this isn't a taste of things to come.' Matthew smiled uneasily at James, grabbed a chair and found a corner to sit with him.

Because his head was too full of what might be happening between James and Tom, Matthew found it difficult to concentrate, so to reduce the burden of actually thinking, he and James promptly joined Tom and Archie, which was not quite what Rupert had requested. Without any preliminaries, Matthew signalled to Archie that he did not want to discuss the play yet, and noticing how Tom and James had set their faces, he knew that there was little hope of progressing with the task Rupert had given them. What was worse, he did not care. Feeling in need of some gossip, Matthew leaned forward.

Glancing at James, Tom lowered his voice. 'I forgot to ask you if he's been in touch?'

James rolled his eyes in the direction of their director. 'Not a peep, but I managed to text him my thanks.'

Tom smiled. 'He won't want any awkwardness during rehearsals, if he's got any sense.'

Rupert was approaching and seemed intent on singling out Matthew. 'Where the hell is she?' he hissed. 'I must speak to her about her behaviour afterwards, so if she does show up, don't let her escape without me seeing her.'

After a few minutes left on their own, Rupert rapped on the piano. 'I need every actor not just to know their own scenes but to have an overview of the play. They also have to be familiar with those scenes that prepare the ground for their own. In addition, I want us to understand why the play is amusing. I want us to think about why Wilde wrote this play; why so many characters say the opposite to what you expect – especially Lady Bracknell – and go on to analyse what makes it funny. In addition, we need to achieve a sense of period. I want you to think of deportment; how these characters stand, sit, hold a cane, a fan, a lorgnette. In order to do this, I will be playing the first act of the 1952 film after our read-through. I'm sure many of you are familiar with it, but I hope it will be a useful exercise, nonetheless.'

Rupert called on James and Matthew to contribute first. They stood looking at each other and were still fumbling over where to sit, when Rupert stepped in. 'I don't want you checking where to sit down beforehand. Feel where the chair is and make a seamless movement, but never check your position. No, not like that, Matthew. Just sit down *there*, no, not there. *There*, for heaven's sake.' Matthew tried to stay calm. They read out some dialogue with little regard for timing or phrasing, always at the mercy of Rupert's suggestions along the lines of, 'Do you think you could come over as a tiny bit less northern, James? And you both need to be faster on picking up those cues, especially as you're reading it. Don't forget we require a sense of pace throughout, otherwise the whole thing will sink without trace,' said Rupert.

Eleanor arrived without warning, theatrically widening her eyes because they had had the temerity to start without her. Confident that all eyes were upon her, she slowly removed her coat. Matthew sat back and waited for her to make a thorough nuisance of herself.

'Late! *Late!*' cried Rupert, unable to bring himself to look at her.

She turned to face him as if he had just walked in off the streets. 'I wasn't late. You know I'm not required until Act Two, and no one ever turns up until a few lines before they're needed. Quite frankly, there's no need. Besides, I've been doing my exercises.'

Then, clutching the back of the nearest chair – it had been standard practice for a previous festival director to position players behind a sofa or an armchair for key speeches and since she had latched onto it, it had become one of her default moves – she began one of Gertrude's speeches from *Hamlet*.

' *"O Hamlet! speak no more!*
Thou turn'st mine eyes into my very soul;
And there I see such black and grained spots,
As will not leave their tinct." '

Her style, unfortunately far more laboured than usual, was high camp Gothic and by the time she had finished, Matthew's palms were dripping.

'Not bad, eh?' she enquired. 'That's one of the warm-ups I do at home.'

'Perhaps it should have stayed there,' observed Rupert.

'Was that from *Hamlet*, or was it Madama Arkadina quoting from the play in *The Seagull*?' asked Tom.

Before she could reply, Matthew leapt up, took her to one side and whispered in her ear. 'Nobody wants to be reminded of *The Seagull*. Can't you see that we've made a start?'

Rupert was lolling nonchalantly against the piano, as if he was used to witnessing this kind of behaviour. 'Tell me, since you've introduced the subject, and as we seem to have so much spare time on our hands, why is *The Seagull* best forgotten?'

'Hardly anybody came,' said Matthew.

Eleanor pulled away from him. 'We had performed *The Wild Duck* the previous year...'

'*Tried* to perform it,' corrected Matthew, wearily.

She glared at him, and enunciating the line perfectly, as if she had practised it, remarked, 'I don't think that audiences were quite ready for another play about birds!'

Here, James burst out laughing.

'But The Westmorland Gazette said,' she continued, 'and I quote: *"It was a production that had to be seen to be believed."*'

James was practically buckled up with stifled laughter, and even Rupert smiled. 'Nicely put! Now, Eleanor, as you've missed my mention of deportment, I'd like you to cross the room and visualise yourself making your first entrance as Lady Bracknell.'

'Don't think you can taunt me just because I'm not playing her,' she told him.

Without looking at her, Rupert moved over and held out a stick at arm's length so that she was forced to take it from him. Straightening her back and looking suitably self-important, she began a slow, measured walk.

'Now, Eleanor, keep your chin tilted, as if you are wearing a hat. The audience has to see your face at all times. Now glide into that chair, lean the stick at an angle and clutch the top of it.'

Rupert turned to pick up a fan he had left on the piano. 'I was told once that you must never use one of these to fan yourself with. Can you guess why?'

Eleanor seemed intent on playing the model student. 'Because it distracts the audience?'

'Thank you. You can use a fan to gesticulate, but nothing more.'

Rupert then played some extracts from the film, and fast-forwarded so that each person could get a feel of their role, but when they started the reading in earnest it unnerved Matthew to see Rupert making so many notes.

It was after ten o'clock when they finished, but Rupert must have been under the impression that there was still time to round off the evening.

'You'll see from the rehearsal schedule when I'd like you to put your books down. I can't emphasise too much that the real work can begin only when we don't have our books.' James pushed back his chair. 'And, getting the nuts and bolts right – as I call it – in the early stages is vital. Gauging how much time one has to eat before having to speak again will have to be practised. Eating and drinking on stage requires that you do it without thinking about it, so I'll be asking you to pour tea, eat sandwiches, cake and muffins as soon as we start.' He paused. 'There is one other thing. I would like the women to wear long skirts from the outset, which Eileen and Janet will provide. You also need to wear hats, when appropriate.' Rupert turned to the men. 'I'll need most of you to wear tailcoats some of the time. And we'll use as many props as we can early on, such as the cigarette case, books and so on. You may also find it easier if you practise eating and saying your lines before the rehearsal. Finally, and above all, I want you to enjoy yourselves.' His eyes came to rest on Eleanor. 'Most importantly, can I please ask you *all* to make rehearsals on time?'

When the scraping of chairs indicated that it was all over, Matthew went to join Tom and James.

'Can we tempt you over for that lunch this Saturday?' asked Tom.

'I'd love to. Will it just be me?' James nodded in Rupert's direction.

'You have our word,' Matthew assured him. 'Shall we say one o'clock?'

Thanking them and moving away, James almost collided with Jane, and Matthew could not help noticing the set of Tom's face as he watched them leaving together. Matthew turned to Eleanor, and whispered, 'Rupert will be here in a second. He would appreciate a word. Try and be nice.'

'What does *he* want?'

'It's about the play.'

'Well, of course, it's about the bloody play!' Frowning at her watch, she contorted her face into an insincere smile when she noticed Rupert approaching. Then everything proceeded to fall apart. 'How dare you put me through my paces like that?'

'Don't you like having an audience?' he asked. 'Listen, Eleanor – I cannot have you undermining me. And I will not tolerate lateness, or rudeness. I've been warned that you broke the last director, but I can assure you that similar behaviour won't have the slightest effect on me. You cannot blame me for having been offered the part of Lady Bracknell.'

She thrust out her chin and took a step forward but Matthew restrained her.

'Don't make a scene,' said Rupert, quietly. 'Just accept what's happened with good grace and become part of the team.'

'I've never been able to do that,' she retorted, 'but I'll bring you down before this show's over, if it's the last thing I do.'

Rupert stood his ground. 'I wonder what the committee will make of it when they get to hear that you've been threatening me?' Embarrassed, Matthew glanced to one side and could not help noticing that Tom was texting; contacting James no doubt, he thought to himself. 'And I have witnesses, haven't I, Matthew?'

Matthew, blinking, once he had registered that he was being addressed, nodded, although his thoughts moved swiftly on to what might be going on between Tom and James.

'You're only allowed so many gaffes,' said Eleanor. 'And then you'll be out.'

Matthew felt sick. 'Eleanor, let's have no more talk of bringing anyone down.'

Eleanor smiled glacially. 'When he seems more than capable of doing it by himself?' And with that, she turned on her heel and left.

'What does she mean by that?' asked Rupert, looking genuinely concerned.

'On behalf of WAFT, I owe you an apology.'

'Don't worry. I've come across far worse than her in my time.'

With that, Matthew and Tom bade Rupert good night, and drove home.

'I hope Eleanor isn't going to keep this up,' said Tom, after a silence that had lasted a couple of miles, but seemed longer.

'Funnily enough,' Matthew heard himself saying, 'I was thinking the same about you and James.'

'I don't know what you may be implying, but I don't like it,' said Tom, with a sharp turn of the head.

'You seemed very close. Is that the new normal?'

'I'm only doing whatever it is I'm not supposed to be doing for the good of the festival,' murmured Tom. 'I thought you wanted a thaw between him and me?'

Matthew said nothing. He was still troubled that a revelation about his side of the affair with Rupert could prove his undoing. Moreover, he felt that he could not enquire too deeply about Tom's fast-developing friendship with James, and he regretted that he had no one with whom to share his anxieties.

During the next few days, Matthew had taken to pondering how he could manipulate time alone with Rupert without upsetting Tom, so when Rupert phoned one wet morning to invite him for lunch at La Boutique Fantasque, he accepted with alacrity.

'Jane thinks that I ought to spend some money in their emporium, and I feel direct confrontation always works better in these circumstances,' explained Rupert, good-humouredly. 'Would you care to join me? My treat.' Once Matthew had agreed, Rupert added, 'But we'll need to go mid-morning so that I can have a good look round.'

Although he had jumped readily at the thought of being with Rupert, Matthew groaned inwardly both at the sacrifice of his morning and the choice of venue. He and Tom had never felt comfortable in that shop, mainly because they would invariably meet Jane, and she would persuade them to buy something – usually over-priced – that they neither needed nor wanted.

'Does this include Tom?' asked Matthew.

Rupert laughed. 'Does Squirrel always have to be there to hold your hand?'

'Of course not. Even so, I'd better check with him.'

'You know best.'

Remembering Rupert liked a glass of wine at lunch-time, Matthew told him to leave his car at Langdales so that he could drive. When they had hung up, he went off to prepare the ground with Tom and found him pressing sheets in the utility room (not a favourite occupation for either of them).

Tom looked up when Matthew told him about the planned lunch out with Rupert. 'I don't suppose the invitation was extended– '

'You were mentioned. That goes without saying. I assumed– '

'Assumed? You mean that you want some time together?'

Something had to be said to stop this line of thought once and for all, but it was difficult for Matthew to know how to pitch things without revealing more about his past with Rupert. 'Why would we choose somewhere so public, where we're bound to run into Jane or Clare? Besides, you've never been keen on La Boutique Fantasque.'

'Neither have you,' said Tom, eyes back to his work, 'but it depends what I might be missing out on.'

Trying to humour him, Matthew asked, 'Shall I tell him that I've overlooked something in the diary?'

'I wouldn't bother. He'll never believe you, for one thing.'

'Very well, if that's how you want to play it...'

Tom shook his head. 'Hold on. You're allowed to make insinuations, and I'm not, is that it?'

'Before I say something I regret, it's an appalling morning and this will provide a minor diversion. So if it's all right with you, I'm going upstairs to change.' Without looking round to gauge Tom's reaction, Matthew left him to it.

Guiltily mulling it over in the bedroom, Matthew almost cancelled the lunch, but as the forecast was unsettled for the remainder of the morning, he decided he may as well go.

'I've been a bit naughty with the layout of the theatre programme,' Rupert told Matthew in the car, a few minutes later. Matthew braced himself. 'Let me explain. I've cut the section on the history of the festival to insert a double-page spread all about *me*.'

'That's going to make you very popular.'

'I hope so. I felt that it was the least the festival could do for me.'

'Really? Has it been approved by the committee?'

'Of course not.'

'Which photograph are you planning to use?'

'That old black and white one, naturally. And before you say anything I'm well aware that it's out of date, but there's never been time for a proper sitting.'

Matthew asked something that had been on his lips for some time. 'So how serious are you about James?'

'He's adorable, isn't he? You don't get many like him in a lifetime.' *I should think not,* thought Matthew. 'But,' continued Rupert, 'I am beginning to think – to use your phrase – that Tom may have the prior claim.'

This was so unsettling that Matthew drove on in silence. On arrival, and having parked the car, they were uncertain as to which area to head first, so they hovered in the entrance, gawping at signs only to find themselves all but trampled by a select group of well-coiffed women. They spent over an hour wandering around aimlessly, until Matthew's feet ached enough to make him insist on having a coffee, while Rupert remained intent on finding something – *anything* – at a reasonable price. When Matthew caught up with him again, he was pulling a face over some over-priced notebooks and looked as if he was just about to say something derogatory, when Jane popped up at the end of the aisle.

She had been extolling the virtues of various new lines to one of her fresh-faced employees, but came to an abrupt halt when she saw them. The age of the staff seemed to be in inverse proportion to that of the clientele. This handsome young fawn looked as if he was in his late teens, but the moment Rupert leered at him, he cowered behind Jane, who despatched him on what sounded like a bogus errand.

'What beautiful things you have here,' remarked Rupert, while his eyes followed the retreating assistant down the aisle.

Jane seemed preoccupied. 'Kind of you to say so, Rupert. We are constantly sourcing products that are rarely found outside the fine food halls and exclusive shops in London.' Matthew shuddered at her hard-sell. 'In fact, we are currently spearheading a fresh campaign to extend our ranges.' It was a relief when she took a break from quoting the website. 'Take this Cortona leather-bound journal with acid-free paper. We source directly. At forty-nine pounds ninety-nine, it's an absolute steal.' She then waved the A4 size book at Rupert. 'Which colour do you prefer?' His expression indicated that he was hoping for a gift, but her face spoke otherwise.

'This reminds me of that young friend I made on an Italian holiday. Go on, I'll take the blue one.' He smiled. 'I wonder if they'll let me claim it on my expenses?' He placed it under his arm. When they turned the corner at the end of the aisle, he peered at the entrance to the Christmas grotto and looked at Jane as if she could not be serious.

Jane shrugged. 'I know! That's our year-round Christmas grotto. Not my idea, but the children love it.'

'Yes, but what about the parents?' asked Rupert.

She glanced at her watch. 'While you're here, can I tempt you with a bite to eat, on me?'

Rupert thanked her, and requiring no further pressing, asked the assistant behind the counter for a bit of everything, as if intent on setting it against the cost of his notebook. Matthew smiled because Rupert had allowed Jane to cover the cost with such ease. Ever mindful of his figure – and sharp reprimands coming from Tom whenever he gained an extra pound or two – he requested tiny portions of the healthier options.

Eyeing Rupert's pyramidal plate as she directed them to a table, Jane asked, 'You don't mind if I join you?' The window was almost obscured by a cellophane-wrapped Christmas hamper of Lakeland delicacies, with an urgent reminder to place orders in good time. (It was April.) Matthew sat down opposite Rupert, facing the entrance.

'This is my usual perch,' said Jane, coming to join them. She caught the dead-looking eyes of a waitress hunched over a nearby table. 'But you don't have a drink. Glass of wine, Rupert? I can't, of course.'

Rupert grinned, while the girl wandered over and stood to attention. 'White burgundy, please. Large, if I may?'

Jane nodded, and was just ordering a glass of the house Chardonnay when Matthew noticed James heading towards them. He resisted the temptation to nudge Rupert with his foot. Was James actually dating Jane, or pretending to, as suggested?

While shaking James's hand, Rupert observed, 'We'll soon have enough people to call an impromptu rehearsal.'

'Is that a problem?' enquired Jane. 'James finds it more congenial to come here than eat his sandwiches on his own.'

Rupert gave James a look out of the corner of his eye. 'Can't he speak for himself?'

Watching James peck Jane on the cheek, and seeing that she melted against him, Matthew realised that these lunches must have become a daily occurrence. The conversation was strained to begin with, while they waited for James's lunch and Rupert's wine, but Rupert brightened once he had a glass in his hand. Jane informed them – with more detail than they required – how hard James and she had been working together.

Having taken his first sip, Rupert caught James's eye. 'You don't feel that the play is taking over your lives?'

'Far from it. It's helped me to settle in.' James smiled at Jane. 'I've made so many new friends.'

'And I've realised that there's more to life than listening to the till ringing,' purred Jane.

'So do I hear wedding-bells?' While James reddened, Rupert winked at Matthew over the top of his glass, and became unbearably coy. 'Shouldn't we think about going as soon as we've finished, Matthew? I know you two young love-birds will want to spend some time together. Naughty Jane! You should never have kept this to yourself.'

Jane appeared sublimely indifferent to this, and without pressing them, half-heartedly suggested they stay for coffee.

'That's a kind offer, but we have other plans,' said Matthew, fully aware that Rupert would be thinking the opposite. Consequently, the conversation became perfunctory during the rest of their lunch.

When they could outstay their welcome no longer and it was time to round things off and thank Jane, Rupert asked, 'Now, you're quite sure we don't owe you anything for this?' She nodded. He turned to James and smiled thinly. 'Don't practise together *too* often. You need to leave some space for spontaneity.' They kissed Jane goodbye and shook James's hand. Rupert paid for his notebook at the exit.

Matthew drove in silence until Rupert asked, 'So what possible future do they have?'

'You seem to know the answer.'

Rupert was only too keen to expound on his theory. 'I suppose he'll get bored, start having dalliances with other men, and she will either have to put up with it, or face divorce.'

'Some men really are straight, Rupert.'

'I'm not convinced,' muttered Rupert. 'Certainly not in my experience.'

'You never will be. You've always held the belief that most men want to throw themselves at you, but you're no longer twenty-five years old and gorgeous. Talking of gorgeous, I know you think I'm too old, but I've rather fallen under his spell, too.'

'If only he knew how many poor souls were queuing up for him!'

'By the way, did you ever follow up the signing of your will?'

'Yes, I was hoping for a long session, but it was over so quickly, I might as well not have bothered.'

Matthew hesitated. 'I hope you don't mind me asking, but has there been any development tracing Seth?'

Rupert sighed. 'Well, you have become very insistent, but if you must know – there was a falling out some time ago – and he covered his tracks well. Since she's got more time on her hands, Caroline's agreed to look into it.'

Matthew glanced sideways. 'Is it your intention to meet up, if you do locate him?'

'Of course. It wasn't my fault that he disappeared in the first place!'

No, you're never to blame, thought Matthew. 'And has there been any news of your poor father?'

'He's not exactly poor, dear, but I know what you mean. He seems to have rallied in the warm, spring sunshine of the Côte d'Azur.'

'How marvellous,' enthused Matthew.

'I wish I could say the same,' said Rupert, his mood obviously darkening.

They drew up outside Langdales at last. To Matthew's surprise, Tom invited Rupert to stay for coffee and even went so far as to sit next to him while Matthew made it.

Having studied Rupert's face while they chatted desultorily, Tom came out with: 'So what are *you* looking so sore about?'

'You might well ask. In addition to being reminded of things that I would rather forget, I've just had to witness James and Jane making an exhibition of themselves.'

'Hardly,' protested Matthew, turning slightly to observe Tom's reaction to this key information about James, but his face revealed nothing.

'And as if that wasn't enough, witnessing ambition chasing greed has cost me fifty quid for a notebook,' said Rupert.

Tom's eyes flickered for a moment or two, but his expression was not easy to read. He turned to Rupert once more. 'You're very hard on those two all of a sudden, aren't you? What's happened? Only the other night, you gave us all the impression that they were wonderful in rehearsal together.'

Rupert leered at Tom. 'You mark my words, Tom – if there's going to be any chemistry on that stage, it'll be between you boys.'

Trying not to look round, Matthew struggled to listen over the noise made by the coffee machine. 'Wishful thinking on your part,' Tom retorted. 'Apart from what you've just told me about him and Jane, James is not interested in creating any chemistry with me, either on-stage or off-stage. Isn't that right, Matthew?'

Matthew, regretting that he was otherwise occupied, agreed.

'Well, you were getting on so well at my place that evening,' said Rupert, 'that I hardly knew where to look.'

Tom stiffened. 'Come off it, Rupert. You're the one who fancies him. Pity he's so wrapped up in Jane, isn't it?'

Rupert ignored this and went on to ask Matthew if it might be possible for Mike, the stage-manager, to have a frame made with some double doors for the cast to practise entering and exiting. Matthew, passing him his steaming cup, could imagine the head-scratching behind the scenes, but assured Rupert that Mike would no doubt say that he "can't promise anything in a hurry", but come up with whatever was required in record time.

Chapter Eight

The first rehearsal was concerned with blocking the moves for Act One. James and Tom, as Jack and Algernon, Rupert as Lady Bracknell, Jane as Gwendolen, plus Archie as the manservant Lane, were called. Matthew's character, Canon Chasuble, did not appear until the second act, but as he was never keen on being on his own at Langdales, he persuaded himself that watching how Rupert worked might be time well spent.

From the outset, Rupert had made it clear that they would start at half-past seven prompt, and finish at ten o'clock, rather than half past nine. When Matthew and Tom arrived, Rupert was wearing a wide-brimmed straw hat and a long black skirt, so they did not dare look at each other. Jane was already in her long skirt and Archie his tail coat. Mike had made the frame for the set of double doors so that they could get used to entering via either the drawing room doors or French windows. Impressed, Matthew watched them pencilling in their moves, but was surprised to see that James came over as inexperienced, and whenever Rupert took him on one side to show him how to move, he grew defensive. Not for the first time Matthew was struck that James had been given the part for his looks, but at least you could hear him. He had something of a penetrating voice, and his flat vowels thudding across the rehearsal room were missed by no one, least of all Rupert.

'James, dear boy, *try* and get some *flow* into it. And *do* something with your hands. Stop clutching at your clothes like a little boy needing a pee, and *try* and play to beyond the front row,' Rupert pleaded on more than one occasion.

Matthew had no experience of witnessing an actor directing the play in which he was reappearing. Rupert's technique was somewhat dizzying; no sooner had he made his first entrance as Lady Bracknell than he slowed the action by bobbing back and forward from "the stage" to "the auditorium", in order to see if he was gaining the right effect from his groupings, until it reached a point when he was spending so much time wandering to and fro, that he agreed to let Matthew stand in for him.

James's scenes with Jane crackled, largely owing to Jane; their practising had paid off. Having won the Drama cup at seventeen, and repeated this triumph to anyone who would listen, Jane already knew how to stand and sit as if she had grown up in that era, and she pitched every line correctly. Yet Matthew could not help feeling that she had no ear for comedy.

Once they had reached the end of the act, Rupert allowed them a break. Matthew stood up to talk to Tom, but stepped aside for James when he saw him approaching.

'I found that excruciating,' grumbled James.

'Why?' asked Tom. 'You and Jane were so good together.'

'Is he picking on me?'

Tom peered into James's face. 'Why don't you ask him?'

'I refuse to give him the satisfaction that he's getting to me.'

Tom shrugged, but said nothing.

Matthew, thinking that it was safe to leave them to it, went over to join Archie and Jane, who were comparing notes on how best to keep stock dusted. Such was Archie's enthusiasm that Matthew wondered if Jane might offer him a day-time job, but his suggestions ended abruptly when they started again, Matthew again standing in for Rupert. For Matthew, the novelty of standing in for Rupert was wearing off by this time, but he tried not to show it. Meanwhile, he was enjoying being a keen observer when he was not required, although it was difficult trying not to read too much into every nuance between Tom and James.

Inevitably, the first rehearsal proved difficult because people were reading from their books and trying to remember their moves; Rupert soon grew impatient. He was a stickler for making them adhere to the moves that they had been given, and pounced on anyone who was not keeping to their allotted place. He also demanded the highest standards regarding posture and audibility.

'For the last time: deportment, deportment, deportment!' he cried. 'Can't you people remember anything?'

Gradually, but it was a slow burn, everyone began to improve. Rupert sensed the change, and there were fewer interruptions. At the end of the act, Rupert asked them to gather round.

'Thank you, that was very much better,' he told them, 'but as you're tired we'll begin with the notes next time.'

James, standing by the door next to Tom, was reaching for his coat when Rupert sauntered over from the opposite side of the room.

'I don't want to see either of you in jeans again.'

James raised his eyes to the ceiling while Tom studied the floor. 'Perhaps you might prefer to see us both naked?'

'Very droll. No, but denims make you walk in a slouchy way that is *quite* wrong for the period. Can you please both wear trousers tomorrow? I am sure you'll feel the benefit.'

'You're sure you don't want us to wear skirts?' asked James. Rupert merely narrowed his eyes. 'But why do we have to move around so stiffly?'

'Who said anything about stiffly? You need to understand that this is *not* the sort of play that requires the actors to *loll* about the place, and the sooner you realise that the better.'

They stacked the chairs and fled. On leaving, Matthew's last glimpse was of Rupert stepping out of his black skirt.

For the second-act rehearsal the following evening, Rupert required the whole cast, and he could concentrate on directing without Matthew standing in, as Lady Bracknell is not called upon again until the final act. This involved James, Tom and Jane, and would introduce Eleanor as Miss Prism, Clare as Cecily Cardew, Matthew, and Archie who was also playing the small role of the butler, Merriman. The evening promised to be similar to the previous night's rehearsal, with countless repetitions to crystallise moves.

Everyone, except Eleanor, had assembled by half-past seven. 'Just to recap,' Rupert was telling them to fill in the time, 'don't forget how to move properly.'

Having waited until the last moment for Eleanor to show up – as Miss Prism, crucially, opens the second act – Rupert was forced to begin, and by the time she arrived, looking immaculate, she was fifteen minutes late. She had made up her face with more care than usual, must have had a late afternoon appointment at the hairdressers and was wearing her leather jacket and skinny jeans. Rupert raised a hand to stop the rehearsal and give her time to apologise.

She launched into some insincere protestations. 'And there I was thinking I was *early* for an eight-o'clock rehearsal. Oh, Rupert, I *am so* sorry. How can I put things right?'

Rupert merely scowled and handed her a black skirt, at arm's length, again without looking at her. 'Not to worry. I'm sure those who managed to get here on time don't mind you holding up the proceedings.'

Forced to take it from him, Eleanor's face never moved a muscle, although Matthew noted an almost imperceptible amused twitch of the lips when she turned her back on him. To her credit, she was word-perfect and her deportment was good enough for Rupert to ask the others to study her. She only used the book to pencil in Rupert's moves and pitched every line correctly, but after about five minutes of this studied perfection, she stopped, surveying the room to check that she had everyone's attention.

Rupert sighed as he rested his thumb and forefinger on the bridge of his nose. 'What seems to be the problem *this time*?'

'I'm sorry, but could you explain the motivation behind this move? It doesn't feel right somehow.'

Much to Matthew's surprise, Rupert took her arm, walked her up and down, all the while talking in subdued tones while she nodded gratefully. Smiling to herself, Eleanor returned to the stage area and picked up where she had left off. Matthew watched her closely, unable to believe that she and Rupert had become so cordial.

However, they would have all got on a great deal faster had Eleanor not kept up a continuous line of questioning as to why Rupert had chosen certain moves and she was always keen to fall back on irrelevant queries about motivation. Her suggestions were endless. Occasionally, those rehearsing lost concentration because of the slow progress. As far as the festival players were concerned, the point was to block the moves at this stage, as Eleanor well knew, and not to dwell on psychological motivation yet (if ever, for that was not something in their orbit). Having rehearsed with her so frequently, Matthew recognised that she was being deliberately pedantic. Often defensive, she would not only override a particular move but insist that Rupert listened to a lengthy explanation for her reasons in doing so. They continued briefly until Eleanor paused in mid-sentence again.

'I don't wish to be a nuisance,' she smiled, 'but I usually find that if a move is really good, I will remember it and if not I can usually think of a better one, so would you mind if I *don't* pencil in every single move?'

While the others stared, Rupert gritted his teeth. 'Are you suggesting that I am to be made redundant?'

'Of course not, but if I can't see the motivation the move doesn't sit easily with me, so I'm inclined to forget it. And where does that leave the others?' She stood helplessly and opened her eyes wider.

'Are you indicating that you have a poor memory?'

Eleanor opened her mouth, but Matthew got in first. 'Don't you think it would be more appropriate to discuss this another time?'

'Not when Eleanor is deliberately attempting to undermine me,' said Rupert, pulling himself up to his full height; he was still the shortest in the room.

'Surely you realise that, like you, I only want what's best for the production,' said Eleanor, hands on hips. 'Remind me, how many plays have you directed?'

'I'm not sure what you're driving at,' he replied, beginning to show signs of being ruffled, 'but you do realise that you are wasting not only my time, but everybody else's?'

'Rupert, please can we carry on where we left off and forget this for now?' suggested Matthew; it was best to stay on the right side of Eleanor as most of his scenes involved her.

Rupert gestured to him to sit down. 'I trust that any further queries can be dealt with in private?'

Head held high, Eleanor rolled her eyes and made her way towards Matthew.

'Why provoke him?' asked Matthew, under his breath, once she was sitting next to him.

Eleanor's face remained set, only interrupted by condescending and wry flashes of amusement as she watched the proceedings; she must have been delighted to have disrupted the rehearsal – in her small-minded way – for it failed to run as smoothly again.

The pattern for rehearsals was the same every week, and required attendance on Monday, Tuesday and Thursday evenings, exactly as

Rupert had set out. Accordingly, the cast met again on Thursday to block the moves for the third and final act. Matthew was relieved of the task of standing in as Lady Bracknell when Rupert returned to the role. Not a squeak out of Eleanor. Perhaps feeling that she had made her point the other evening, she had quietened down and the rehearsal was the better for it. Once they had finished, Rupert reminded them that they would have to start becoming familiar with stand-in props from next Monday onwards – in spite of continuing with their books – and he urged them to drop them as soon as they could. Relieved over the forward planning, Matthew sensed that by getting them used to those nuts and bolts – costumes, doors, food and props – Rupert was leaving nothing to chance.

The schedule for the following Monday's rehearsal set out to rehearse the first two acts. Trying to be model members, Matthew and Tom were the first to arrive. They watched in silence while Rupert pulled out a large teapot, cups and saucers, muffins, sandwiches, canes, parasols, hats, bread and butter from the assortment of bags at his feet.

Rupert winked. 'We mustn't have Eleanor confused about eating and drinking, must we?'

'Or not understanding her motivation?' smiled Matthew.

When the others had assembled, Rupert called on them to gather round. 'The first two acts involve quite a number of refreshments, so I want to make sure that all of you can handle the practicalities in your sleep. Any questions?'

None came, but those required to eat on stage began making appreciative noises. Archie was put in charge of the temporary props and had to remind the others of what they needed on stage, which would prove as ramshackle a scheme as it always did, until Eileen and Janet helped out nearer the dress rehearsals.

'I appreciate that there's a lot of detail at this stage,' explained Rupert, 'but it will help you by the time we get to the dress rehearsal, when there will be so much else to consider.'

These bits of stage business deserved the attention they were getting; the cast had to anticipate the tea's temperature and perhaps cope with melting butter. Inevitably, there were frayed tempers when things did not go right, but Rupert insisted they keep going over it, until it became automatic. No one knew what to do with their hands, and resented being taken to task. Inevitably, remembering lines was always a problem. Throughout rehearsals, Rupert was respected, but not admired.

After almost four weeks of steady rehearsal, everybody had to live with James being Rupert's favourite – and the one he had to work on most – which did not go down well. However, once he had been trained to move properly and stop sounding like a northern voice-over for a television advert, James had the makings of a strong leading man. Like the character of Algernon, he certainly looked everything, even if he had not quite honed his technique.

In addition, as Rupert had prophesied, there was more than a spark between James and Tom, and this gave their scenes together an added dimension; it was easy to see why Rupert encouraged and praised them at every opportunity. There was more to it than that, however. They were getting on so well, both on and off stage, that Matthew convinced himself that an underlying tenderness was developing between them.

Matthew was never exuberant about his own portrayals or performances, and this rehearsal period proved no exception. Over the years, he had come to believe that there was no danger of him copying the same mannered style favoured by Eleanor, but seeing Tom and James working together with such ease, he knew that whatever style he possessed was not only mannered but archaic.

Although she rarely failed to deliver, Eleanor was clearly bored, and – although nothing like on the scale of her first rehearsal – she seldom missed an opportunity to offer suggestions, no matter how irrelevant and unwelcome. Indeed, she and Matthew were both guilty of doing far too much with too little, another charge that Matthew had believed would never be levelled at him. Furthermore, she could not resist the temptation for a long sigh whenever Rupert was rehearsing, and loved nothing more than interrupting the middle of one of his key speeches.

Jane was, indeed, a competent player, if a trifle over-confident; as always, she would have improved in Matthew's eyes if she had possessed the slightest inkling for comedy.

Clare was pretty and beguiling and made the most of what was for her, an undemanding role.

Archie rattled Rupert's nerves a good deal. Sometimes, he appeared to be making as many unnecessary suggestions as Eleanor.

Nobody could ever be inveigled to perform the thankless task of prompt, and Matthew was not surprised when Archie was cornered into agreeing to it, if only to staunch the flow of questions emerging from his over-curious mind.

However, if James was the favourite, Eleanor had become the member of the cast who Rupert seemed to enjoy undermining, in spite of her (eventual) careful consideration of the role. This not only fuelled Eleanor's grievances, but reignited the desire to play Lady Bracknell that had never really left her. With only a couple of weeks to go before the first night, she had had more than enough, and was all set to incite a rebellion.

But to achieve her ambition – and gather the cast together, without breaking into their work or leisure-time – she had to engineer a rehearsal to finish early so as to give them all enough time to slope off to the pub. As far as making excuses, she herself had been too obvious a mischief-maker not to be above suspicion. It took only moments to persuade the easy targets of Jane and Clare to come up with an excuse that would be difficult for Rupert to check, rather than tackle any of the men. Doubtless, the men would side with Rupert and protest at her underhand methods. The trumped-up excuse involved a meeting that Jane and Clare were supposed to be having with their accountant the following morning.

Jane struck without any preliminaries while Eleanor was chatting uneasily to Rupert during the break. She sidled up between the two, and adopted a wheedling tone that was quite out of character. 'Excuse me, Rupert, but do you think we could finish at nine thirty this evening, so that we can have an early night before our meeting with our accountant tomorrow?'

'Couldn't you have asked me earlier?' enquired Rupert, turning to face her. Everybody stopped chattering.

'Something urgent has come up – that we don't quite understand – but we need to look into without delay.' Rupert was eyeing her so fixedly that Jane lowered her eyes, as if struggling with the lie. 'Sorry, but we've never requested anything before, and he does need to see us urgently. It's the only time he could fit us in. You know how busy these people are.'

There was a pause, during which he glanced at each in turn, perhaps trying to gauge the mood. To a man, or woman, for that matter, no one was prepared to meet his gaze, and Matthew wondered whether he was the only one who picked up on the unspoken air of conspiracy. 'Just this once, but please make sure that this never happens again,' said Rupert, glancing at his watch. 'I need hardly remind you that we open in *two weeks*.'

Eleanor turned away from him and muttered to no one in particular, 'Why mention it then?'

Rupert did not bother to register this, and called everyone to order so as to continue in the time they had left. As half-past nine approached, several members of the cast grew restless, and when Eleanor had checked her watch for the fourth or fifth time, Rupert snapped his notebook shut.

'Sorry, everyone. I seem to be under a misapprehension,' he announced. 'Silly of me, but I thought it was only Jane and Clare who wished to go early.'

No one would look him in the eye, so Eleanor acted as spokesperson. 'Take it easy, Rupert. Before you appeared, rehearsals used to finish around now, and previous festival directors delivered the play on time without difficulty.'

'That's not what I've heard, but you seem to be forgetting how little time we have left,' he replied, looking at their downcast faces collectively. 'I'm not happy, but as you seem in such a rush to escape, you had better disappear. I'll finish my notes tomorrow, but I take a very dim view of this.'

Jane stood up. 'Thank you, Rupert. I can assure you it won't occur again.'

They were all in such a rush to leave that they left Rupert to stack the chairs and turn out the lights. Matthew's last glimpse was of Rupert looking so sad that he was tempted to turn round and comfort him, but he had to keep moving, especially as Tom had accepted a lift from James. Becoming increasingly suspicious of James's growing interest in Tom, Matthew did not want to miss any subtleties of eye contact or small talk when they regrouped in the pub.

Their rendezvous was a short drive away on narrow country lanes and Eleanor must have chosen it because it was usually half-empty. When he saw the cars lined up in the car-park, he anticipated that James and Tom would be sitting together. Having hit his head in the low doorway, he felt wrong-footed when he saw that they were all cosily settled at a corner table. James and Tom were – of course – sitting very close to each other having what was clearly a spirited, side-splitting conversation. The others looked on, tongue-tied and avoiding Eleanor's penetrating gaze. Tom did not even glance up and acknowledge him. Feeling disassociated from the group, he noticed Archie standing at the bar, so he did an about-turn and asked for a pot of tea. Much against his better judgement, Matthew sat down with deep misgivings. It seemed inevitable that he would be allying himself with Eleanor because she would no doubt get the better of them all.

Once Archie had returned with the tray of drinks and given Eleanor her change, she glanced at each one in turn and said, 'That it should come to this.' She hesitated, as if being unkind about Rupert was against her better nature.

Matthew frowned. 'Can we get to the point, Eleanor?'

'Surely you've realised that he's too fond of upstaging us?'

'What's upstaging?' asked Archie.

'Oh, Archie, I could hug you,' said Eleanor, with that winsome expression that left Matthew wanting to fracture her skull. 'Allow me to explain. The offending actor keeps moving upstage towards the rear of the set, so that the actor who is at the front, by which I mean downstage, is forced to look in his direction. The audience ends up seeing more of the back of his head and he may become inaudible. I have tried so hard not to mention this, but I can't keep quiet any longer.'

'Never your strongest suit,' said Matthew.

'Don't worry, you'll find that I have called this meeting for a very good reason. Am I the only one here who feels that Rupert is not making any connection with us when playing Lady Bracknell?' No one responded, as her eyes passed from one to the next. 'I'm sorry, but I have never witnessed such self-indulgence before.'

'You couldn't be more thrilled,' said Matthew.

Eleanor's chill stare slightly unnerved him. 'We all know why *you're* rushing to his defence, so I'd keep quiet if I were you.' Stirring his tea, Matthew felt Tom's eyes on him. 'Cheap tricks and mannerisms are about the size of it,' she continued. 'And as for his mincing about in that long skirt, it makes me want to throw up.'

'Eleanor, we've got the message,' said Matthew, registering that the four people sitting adjacent had gone quiet. 'Whatever your misgivings about his acting, you must give Rupert his due as a director. He's very thorough.'

'Possibly, but don't you think that I have a shrewd idea of how Lady Bracknell should be played?'

'Might I venture to suggest you're being a trifle unreasonable, or is that not allowed?' asked Matthew, feeling pleased with himself.

Eleanor gave him another long look. 'At least I am the right gender.'

'You've always insisted that you could do it better,' said Tom.

'More to the point, you can't deny that you've always had it in for him,' said Matthew, watching her eyes glow like coals. 'You don't get to be something of a phenomenon in *Jubilee Way* without having some talent.'

She threw back her head and laughed. 'If you'd actually taken the trouble to sit down and watch it, you'd know that's debatable. So why was he sacked?'

'He wasn't,' replied Matthew. 'As far as I know his character is on a life-support machine, and is returning in the autumn to do a further series.'

'You seem remarkably well-informed,' observed Eleanor drily.

'Meanwhile you're planning to oust him and give the performance of your life?' asked James.

'Shame on you, Eleanor,' said Tom.

'It's getting to you that his name will be above the title, isn't it?' asked Matthew, noting her head dipping in embarrassment.

Bombarded, Eleanor collected her thoughts before glancing up. 'I can't deny it. If anyone's name belongs up there,' she replied, 'it should be mine.'

'Can we fast-forward to whatever trap you have in mind?' asked Matthew.

Eleanor continued to hold him in her gaze. 'Rupert may not be the pretty boy he once was but it's painfully obvious why you're sticking up for him.'

Tom leaned forward. 'What are you implying?'

'Perhaps you should ask Matthew.'

'Careful, Eleanor,' said Matthew, downing a mouthful of tea.

'As James pointed out,' said Tom, 'we're only here because you're craving to play Lady Bracknell.'

Matthew glanced at the others. 'What do the rest of us think?'

'I wonder who will take over if the committee thinks him unfit to proceed?' asked James.

Eleanor finished her drink. 'You'll soon find out.'

'Will there be another audition?' asked James.

'You have to be joking!' she cried.

'Can't the committee members who aren't in the play at least watch him in action?' asked Tom. This was greeted by murmurs of agreement. 'Why not let them attend the next rehearsal and see for themselves?'

Clare spoke for the first time. 'Do you really think that we should be setting him up behind his back? It's so underhand, and he's put a great deal into it.'

'That's my point,' said Eleanor, beginning to look flushed. 'He's putting *too* much into it. If we're not careful, any weaknesses in *our* acting will be revealed because he's a professional, and we are not.' The others began muttering until Eleanor struck the table, and the foursome smirked in silence. 'So, *friends*, I repeat, I cannot allow Rupert to compromise the production.'

'You mean, show us up?' enquired Matthew.

'I'm sorry, Eleanor, but don't you think that this could shatter Rupert's confidence? He's quite highly strung,' said Tom.

Matthew looked at him. 'What's the point, Tom? You know she's deadly serious?'

'I've tried to give him the benefit of the doubt,' said Eleanor, 'but it's getting worse.'

Archie turned to her. 'Rather than bother the committee, why don't we vote here and now as to whether we think Rupert should carry on as Lady Bracknell?'

Eleanor, not daring to look at him, traced a pattern on the table with her finger. 'I'm not sure that's one of your better ideas.'

'Yes, let's do that,' urged Matthew, raising a hand, soon to be followed by the rest.

'This is defeating the object,' said Eleanor.

'*Your* object,' Tom reminded her.

'You mean my mistake,' said Eleanor. She smiled as she glanced them. 'I realise now that you're all too closely involved to see reason, but I'd like you to consider this.' She put on her glasses and took her iPad from her bag. 'I only heard about this after I arrived home yesterday and it's given me a sleepless night. I quote: *"As part of the latest ground-breaking initiative we have come to expect from WAFT, the new director ranks with some of the nation's best-loved actors."*'

'Is this a press release?' asked Tom.

She nodded but raised a hand to silence any further enquiries. '*"He will not only be directing, but starring in WAFT's forthcoming summer production."*'

She regarded them over the top of her glasses. 'It gets worse. *"We are promised high-wire acting of a calibre previously unwitnessed by festival play-goers."*' Removing her glasses, she pressed the bridge of her nose, and stole a look at them to see how they had taken it.

'Who spews up all this drivel?' enquired Tom.

Eleanor laughed. '*He* did, obviously. More to the point, where does this leave us? He's so high-handed and we don't get a mention.'

They began to mutter among themselves, until James made them go quiet by asking, 'Does he mention the new members by any chance?'

She laughed even more, but without mirth. 'No, he does not. By the way, you might also be interested to learn that he was sacked from playing in panto.'

'That doesn't compromise his position,' said Matthew.

'How can you be so sure?' Eleanor shook her head. 'What sort of travesty will he make of Lady Bracknell when he's let loose in front of an audience?'

Tom spoke up. 'I'm sorry, but I don't think you have a strong enough case. Just because Rupert was in pantomime–'

She snorted. 'Not only in it, but sacked from it, playing Mother Goose.'

'Surely the role is irrelevant?' Matthew looked her in the eye. 'Will you let him finish?'

Tom continued, 'That doesn't mean to say that he's not capable of turning in a creditable performance as Lady Bracknell.'

'The whole point of a pantomime dame is that she is clearly a man, and I have a feeling that once Rupert gets in front of an audience, he'll play up to it. What if he can't adapt?' She considered her own question while the others murmured. 'However much you want to stick by him, there's no getting away from the fact that he never completed the run in the panto he was in last Christmas.' She turned to Matthew. 'Too much of a maverick; would think nothing of skipping matinees.'

'But we don't do matinees.'

'You're missing the point, Matthew,' said Eleanor, speaking slowly and deliberately, while he rubbed his chin. 'He frightened them all to death entering at the last minute; incapable of working as part of a team; kept falling out with people...'

'Sounds like you, dear, in a typical festival week,' said Tom. The others grinned at each other.

'Who is your source?' asked Matthew.

Eleanor became tight-lipped, and said in a voice they did not recognise, 'I'm not at liberty to say.'

Matthew held her in his gaze, but she did not appear to be unnerved. 'Perhaps we can talk to him about upstaging us, and get this press release revised, but do you honestly believe that he's going to revert to acting like a pantomime dame? I can't see it myself.'

'There are a lot of things you choose to ignore.'

He gritted his teeth. 'And just what is that supposed to mean?'

She scoffed. 'If you had any insight, you'd know.'

'We all know you're staging this little coup so you can play Lady Bracknell.'

'And why shouldn't I? He doesn't have a good track record, and could well alter the whole balance of the play, the way he's going about it.'

'Your mind is clearly made up, and we don't have much time,' muttered Matthew, 'so why don't you do what you've been intending to all along?'

'Nothing's stopping me, but I wanted to run it by you all first. You know I am democratic to a fault.' She half-smiled.

Those around the table who got the joke grinned at each other.

'Well, you need to bear in mind that I'm going to fight you all the way,' said Matthew.

'I don't see how, when you're no longer on the committee,' she said, rising. 'So if you'll excuse me, I need to get home, but before I bid you good night, thanks so much for coming.'

Matthew shook his head. 'I'm afraid Rupert will always make a better job of playing Lady Bracknell than you ever could.'

Her shoulders sagged and a shadow crossed her face as she sat down. Matthew groaned inwardly. Trying to rally, she said, 'You're not going to like this, but you might be interested to know why Rupert abandoned the panto before Christmas.' Matthew shifted his position while he watched Tom and James exchanging glances. The expectant hush gathered weight as Eleanor scrutinised their faces. 'Apparently, he had instigated a high-voltage affair with one of the stage-hands.'

'Nothing new there,' said Matthew involuntarily. From their suppressed mirth, he could tell that Tom and James were nudging each other under the table.

'If you'll let me finish, Matthew. Sadly, I have to disagree. It was an inappropriate affair of the worst kind.'

Scratching the back of his head, Matthew found himself asking hoarsely, 'You're sure you're not coming over a bit strong?'

'Far from it.' She glanced at the four – who had not spoken for some time – which galvanised them into some low murmuring, and continued in conspiratorial mode. 'I refuse to say anything further on the matter except that Rupert could not cope when it turned sour.' Hoping that this was nothing more than a nightmare and that he would soon wake up, Matthew swallowed. The others stared, open-mouthed. 'The theatre management got sweaty palms and to be on the safe side booted Rupert out in case things turned nasty.'

'And did they?'

'Who? What?'

'Turn nasty?'

'I take no pleasure in this, Matthew, I can assure you. You must draw your own conclusions, but I do feel that this is yet another reason for clawing Lady Bracknell from him. As far as I am concerned he can stay somewhat below the parapet as director, and that is it.'

Matthew leapt to his feet. Quoting Lady Bracknell, he found himself murmuring, ' *"The idea is grotesque."* '

'But not irreligious.' Eleanor paused to make sure she still had their full attention. 'In case you weren't already convinced, may I confirm that this man is not worthy to be given such a prominent role in our production?' Even Tom and James had ceased to find this revelation amusing; there was a hesitant show of hands. She collected her things together and rose from the table. 'I'm sorry it has to be like this, but I have it on excellent authority.'

Normally, Matthew would have risen to this, but he said nothing. Presuming the stage-hand must have been Anthony, he could understand why Caroline had been tetchy with Rupert at their first meeting. Seeing his old friend in a different light, *possibly*, for he refused to believe anything trumped up by Eleanor – now reduced to being his *former* best friend – Matthew had plenty to ruminate on. This time, Eleanor had seized and shaken them by the neck, although no one would ever know if Rupert had done what she claimed. Nonetheless, Matthew was disposed to consider the situation kindly, and regard it as the usual Rupert muddle; he determined not to shame him by mentioning it.

'That,' said Matthew, watching her sweep out, 'in case you were wondering, was Lady Windermere.'

Nervous laughs all round eased the tension somewhat, but without her dynamic presence they soon broke up.

Back in the sitting room at Langdales, Matthew poured out a large whisky for himself and a smaller one for Tom before settling down on the sofa with him.

'Did I miss something?' asked Tom, as he took the glass offered him.

Matthew smiled questioningly as he raised his glass. 'Depends what you had in mind.'

'What did Eleanor mean by your rushing to Rupert's defence?'

'Oh, *that*.' Matthew's smile vanished. 'A lot of rubbish. You know she'll stop at nothing, even if it means slanderous gossip.'

Tom took a sip of his whisky and then stared at Matthew for so long that he felt his throat tightening. 'You'd do anything for him, wouldn't you?'

'I *have* to do my best for him, if that's what you mean.'

'Yet you couldn't prevent him from giving James the lead?' Tom paused. 'Interesting, isn't it?'

'*You* seem to have taken to James in a big way.'

Tom looked up from sipping his whisky. 'We couldn't just sit there as if at a wake, like the rest of them.'

Matthew was determined to enjoy this. 'It's something of a turnaround from when you could hardly bear to hear his name mentioned so *comparatively* recently, isn't it?'

'What happened to working as a team?' asked Tom. 'Don't tell me that, after all these years, you're getting jealous?'

'Of course not,' replied Matthew. It was a relief to hear his phone ring, but not to hear Eleanor's voice.

'I've been thinking,' she said. This was all he needed. 'You've witnessed every rehearsal, and Felicity hasn't.'

'Your point being?'

'You didn't exactly see eye to eye with me earlier, but I'm asking you to back me up.' He said nothing. 'You're the only other older member in the cast with any gravitas.' She sounded desperate, so he remained silent. 'Can't you be objective for the sake of the festival, Matthew? *Please.*'

'What about your credibility, Eleanor? I'll never support you on this, and I will not have Rupert—'

'So that's how you're going to play it, is it? Very well. In that case, I'm going to hold a preliminary meeting, and get Felicity on my side.'

He laughed. 'Best if you don't see each other on your own then.'

'Why don't you join us, as that's clearly what you're angling for?' She was speaking in an unnaturally bright and cheerful voice.

'I am *not* angling for anything – '

'You're draining the life-blood out of me with this, Matthew. Let's talk it over tomorrow. In the summer house.'

'You do realise that the beauty of the location won't wash away your horrible intent?'

'You're becoming quite poetic when you get vindictive. Shall we say eleven o'clock sharp? Please don't be late.'

'You're not listening, are you?' asked Matthew, enjoying the conflict. 'You can hold a meeting when and wherever you like, but it won't make any difference to what I say.'

She laughed. 'We'll see about that. Don't breathe a word of this to Tom, will you?'

'You think we'll pair up as a rival faction? I'll be there, if only to shout you down in front of Felicity.'

There was a pause.

'I know I can always count on you for the *bon mot*, Matthew,' she said at last.

Time for what he considered his master stroke. 'Haven't you forgotten something?'

'What now?'

'I'm no longer on the committee.'

'But you are the only one I can trust as a reliable witness, so I'm prepared to overlook that.'

'And you are no longer chairman or president.'

'But I kept a foothold on the committee.'

'Really?'

'You're beginning to get on my nerves with this line of questioning. I can't imagine Felicity has anything lined up for tomorrow morning, but if she has, I'll let you know. You see, I'd like her to make notes, so that it comes over as impartial.'

He spluttered at this. 'You don't know the meaning of the word.' Finishing the call more abruptly than he had intended, Matthew turned to Tom. 'That, in case you hadn't worked it out, was Cruella. She's demanding that I attend a meeting with her and Felicity tomorrow.'

'Would it help if I came with you? I don't want to see Rupert's head spiked on the railings any more than you do.'

'Thank you for offering but it's just me she requires,' said Matthew, uncertain whether to tip off Rupert before he saw Eleanor, or wait to see how things developed.

Setting off for Spinnakers alone the following morning later than he had intended, without having murmured a thing to Rupert as to Eleanor's manoeuvres, Matthew arrived after eleven as he had sat fuming behind a tractor until it pulled into a field. He pulled up alongside Felicity's drop-head coupé. Matthew made his way to the sombre house with its Gothic-style windows and overbearing gingerbread gables. Today, more than ever, they appeared to be suspended like pincers over the triangles of black and white mock-Tudor detailing. Slate walls jostled uncomfortably with sandstone mullions. Not for the first time, did he catch a whiff of (minor) Edwardian country house turned nursing home.

One corner of this unlikely structure had been bitten out to accommodate the front porch, its roof and ceiling suspended by a heavy faux-Norman pillar. A twitching blind attracted his attention; he could not help noticing Eleanor's and Felicity's heads pulling back behind it. *So, they must be speaking to one another at long last,* he thought as he waved a fraction too late. The morning sun seemed very bright and he was grateful for the shade offered by the porch.

After what seemed an age, Eleanor finally opened the front door; her face told him more than he needed to know. Meanwhile, his eyes became accustomed to the gloomy panelled interior. He shivered slightly as he made his way past the antlers with frivolous hats artfully arranged on them. The entrance hall was eerily silent; it dawned on Matthew that Julian must have been allowed to remove the deafening long-case clock he had inherited. Julian had bought the place cheap some years ago as it had been in need of a thorough overhaul. Unlike Matthew, who could never have too many flowery Chintzes, Julian and Eleanor had plumped for a contemporary style; the furnishings looked curiously at odds with interiors more redolent of a gentlemen's club than a domestic home.

Felicity was standing stiffly in the study doorway, as if she was there under duress. Registering that his hands were damp, he was reluctant to shake hands, so he threw her a half-smile, but declined to air-kiss or shake hands with Eleanor, who was standing expectantly in the middle of the hall. They clattered across the parquet floor into the sitting room and sank their feet into the white drift of satisfyingly deep carpet. Further oppressive panelling and a pair of chilly white sofas. Glancing at the magisterial portrait of Eleanor curling her lip at him, he was again struck by the enormity of the tomb-like fireplace. Drawn to the light like a trapped insect, he fought his way past the fluttering voiles blowing in the French windows and paused on the terrace. Its panoramic view of the western fells across Windermere invariably made him catch his breath, but noticing the two women beetling across the terrace he did his best to catch up. Puffing slightly, he crossed the lawn and descended the steps leading down to the lake; Spinnakers was blessed with plenty of lake frontage.

In the revolving summer house overlooking Windermere Eleanor busied herself pouring out water. Matthew enjoyed the painterly reflection of white sails enhancing a couple of becalmed sailing dinghies, until it disappeared in the wake of a passing lake steamer. Yet again, he felt that the summer house – although elevated to take account of rising water levels – had been poorly sited; it was too exposed to the public gaze.

Once she had sat down opposite him, Eleanor offered a brisk and rather vindictive summing up of the current state of affairs for Felicity's benefit. Matthew watched with interest while Felicity wrote down the salient points in her neat hand. But by the time they had discussed the situation at length, she was struggling to keep up, and once Eleanor had started to repeat herself, Matthew became restless. He turned to Felicity.

'What do you hope to get out of this?' He chuckled sarcastically. 'You know you won't be playing Lady Bracknell?'

'Take no notice, Felicity. You *will* be involved, I promise,' said Eleanor.

'That's a good point, Matthew.' Felicity looked at Eleanor. 'What did you have in mind?'

'As you can imagine, I've been giving this a lot of thought. How about if you take over as Miss Prism?'

Felicity half-smiled, as if taken by surprise, but seemed to arch her back slightly. 'But what if I would prefer to play Lady Bracknell?'

'Well,' said Eleanor, glancing at Matthew for help, but he promptly looked away. 'My plans don't really include that possibility.'

'But you asked me to increase my sponsorship money, and I'm not at all sure what the benefits are.'

Eleanor sat up straight. 'Jane and Clare are playing the two young female leads, aren't they? Is that not enough?'

'I can't dispute that,' replied Felicity, 'but I haven't quite grasped why it always has to be you at the centre of everything.'

'You know why,' said Eleanor. 'Because, even if I say it myself, I am rather good at what I do.'

'To a limited extent. You always play yourself.'

'I don't think she's going to budge on this one,' Matthew told Felicity.

She nodded as if Eleanor was not present, and then turned to face her.

'If I do agree to take over Miss Prism, I expect there will be no audition, given this late stage?'

'That goes without saying and I know you'll do the role justice.'

'So Eleanor will be playing Lady Bracknell, after all, and everybody will be happy,' muttered Matthew. 'But Rupert's my friend.'

Eleanor smirked as she caught his eye. 'Rather more than that, I think.'

'I'm beginning to grow weary of your insinuations,' said Matthew, struggling with insides intent on forming a hard knot. 'How can you do this to me, or have you forgotten what friendship means?'

'Do I write all this down?' asked Felicity, looking from one to the other.

'By all means,' smiled Eleanor, drumming her fingertips on the table, while glancing sideways at what Felicity was writing. 'What you really mean is that you're still in love with him?'

Trying not to show any emotion, Matthew reached out for some water, hoping he would get the use of his legs back in due course. 'You're never to say that again, do you hear? Especially if Tom's around.'

'So it's true?'

'Of course not,' replied Matthew, glancing at Felicity – who was focussing on this new development too conscientiously – his forehead beading with perspiration, 'but I don't want Tom reading more into it than he might do.'

She pounced. 'Or than he has already!' Not for the first time, she demonstrated her hard stare. 'So there *is* something between you two, isn't there?' She waited, while he sweated it out.

'Not any longer, there isn't. Besides, it was all on his side, and a very long time ago. We were at school!'

'I've been sure of it for a while, particularly as you keep rushing to his defence.'

He ran a finger around the edge of his collar. Although they were outside, he felt stifled. 'I like him well enough – most of the time – and as we happen to go back a long way, I feel it's only right that I stick up for him.'

'You know best,' said Eleanor, dismissively. She turned to Felicity. 'Don't forget to write down that I am familiar with Lady Bracknell's moves. Well, not in Act One, but certainly Act Three.'

Once Felicity had written this down, she mimicked a comic voice, as if she were performing a voice-over for a cartoon. 'So what do you desire of me now, wicked Queen?'

Eleanor gripped the table. 'You'll be attending the next rehearsal with Martin. Do you think you can manage that?'

Felicity narrowed her eyes at Eleanor and resumed her normal voice. 'I can't say that I'm happy about betraying Rupert, but I would like to take part, even in a limited capacity as Prism.' She paused. 'Perhaps this is the moment to point out that by allowing you to play Lady Bracknell, I have something over you.'

Eleanor shifted her position, and attempted to laugh it off. 'That's something I shall just have to live with, isn't it?'

'Yes, just as I've had to live trying to help *you* with the festival in the hope of taking the leading role, but constantly being overlooked. I think you should regard playing Lady Bracknell as something of a Pyrrhic victory.'

Eleanor looked down her nose at her and shrugged. 'Do you indeed? And why is that?'

Felicity caught the look and glanced at her nails. 'Because I've almost succeeded in exposing someone with whom, let's say, you've grown attached.'

'How likely is that!' laughed Eleanor, but she looked troubled. 'Now to conclude, I don't want a discussion of this with anyone in the cast. We present them with a fait accompli, you understand? Rupert will be asked to stand down from playing Lady Bracknell. We just have to go through the proper channels, so that it looks above board.'

'As the committee is down to *three* – because you're impossible to work with – that shouldn't prove too difficult.' Matthew waited for her to challenge this. She did not. 'Tell me, Eleanor, will you let Rupert know of his fate immediately after the rehearsal, or have the grace to leave it to the following day?'

'I haven't had time to think about that yet. What do *you* think, you who have so many of his interests at heart? Naturally I'm anxious to bring things to a head soon–'

'Whatever you decide, please tell him in private, and not in front of the others.' He paused. 'I'd like you to bear in mind that once you have stopped Rupert from playing Lady Bracknell, our friendship will be at an end.'

Eleanor rolled her eyes and – in jest – mimed trembling hands. 'How often have I heard that before?'

'This time I mean it.' Hoping to emphasise the gravity of the situation, Matthew lowered his voice and delivered what he had to say

180

in measured tones. 'You've not heard the end of this; not by a long way. You know how much you need me if anything goes wrong?'

Eleanor looked slightly on edge, but half-smiled. 'I'm quivering, Matthew.'

He rose from the table and leaned towards her. 'All right! If that's how you want to play it, perhaps you could clear up something that's been bothering me? I thought you resigned as chairman and president?' Avoiding his stare, she bowed her head. 'Would you mind clarifying something?' She did not reply but set her face. 'You see, I don't quite understand how you still have so much clout?'

'It's called pop-up deus ex machina, in case you were wondering,' she told him. 'Climbing down was a mistake, I grant you. As you know, my parents were founder members, and I can't stand by and watch my festival dissolve into a pantomime. The whole thing is becoming a farce.'

(Felicity was scribbling frantically, her handwriting illegible.)

'Panto or farce? Make up your mind. And where is the chairman, might I ask?'

Looking straight ahead, she replied, 'No, you may not.'

Matthew's legs were shaking involuntarily. He tried hard to stop his voice from sounding wobbly. Pressing his hands on the table, he eyed her. 'I can't quite put my finger on it, although *sham* comes to mind, but there's something toxic going on here. Still, I've said what I came to say. so there's no point wasting any more time. I'm sorry it has to be like this, Eleanor.'

Eleanor snorted. 'Like *what*? How *dare* you leave like that! *Matthew, come back here this instant!*' she called after him in a tone worthy of Lady Bracknell. He walked briskly back up the steps towards the house, and was grateful to be out of earshot. He hoped they heard him slam his car-door.

Back at Langdales, Matthew spilled the story to Tom, although he was careful to omit Eleanor's insinuations. Eyes widening with every sentence, Tom was suitably outraged.

Wrestling with his conscience, Matthew decided not to disclose anything to Rupert about Eleanor's determination to oust him. Primarily, he did not want to be the bearer of bad news. Not only would it not be doing him any favours, but Rupert would blame him for not standing up to Eleanor, and it would lodge forever in his memory along with Matthew's other misdemeanours. Besides, that morning's meeting had taken it out of him, and he could not face the prospect of Rupert exploding in a temper. Matthew consoled himself with the thought that, as Rupert was a professional actor, he might be able to ride it out and leave Eleanor looking foolish.

By the time Matthew and Tom arrived at the rehearsal, Felicity and Martin were already mingling with the cast but, knowing what was to come, he found the cheerful hubbub unsettling. Martin was new to Matthew, and presumably his replacement. He had the cowed look of a man who knew his place.

Judging from Rupert's face, he remained sublimely ignorant of the committee's sudden appearance. He was still bringing them to order when Eleanor showed up, looking laid-back and casual, just as Matthew might have guessed.

'Good news, everyone,' said Rupert, when the chattering had died down. 'Your committee is here to watch Act Three, so give it everything you've got. I certainly intend to. And don't forget, enjoy yourselves and relax!'

The first few minutes could be regarded as a success, and Martin and Felicity gave each other encouraging glances, but things began to go awry when Rupert appeared. First of all, he was clearly overplaying for the benefit of a committee of two. Then, during Lady Bracknell's long sentence about *"... a more than usually lengthy lecture by the University Extension Scheme on the Influence of a permanent income on Thought"*, he dried. Repeating it over and over again, and over-compensating by playing it for all it was worth, he became louder. Trying not to look flustered, he then went on to miss cues and fluffed or forgot his lines. Archie, acting as prompt, lost his place once or twice. Rupert would snap his fingers impatiently, or chastise Archie for coming in too quickly with the line. Perhaps slowly realising that he had been set up, he stopped the action and shot Eleanor a beseeching look of incomprehension. She merely beamed at him and averted her gaze. After a pause, in which everyone began fidgeting or whispering, he thundered, 'So what's going on?'

There was not a murmur from anyone until Martin cleared his throat.

'Good question. The reason Felicity and I are here this evening is because we want to talk to you about your role in the play, Rupert.' The hush intensified. 'In retrospect, we find that – let's say it grieves us to tell you that we feel – that a man playing Lady Bracknell is not perhaps going to work, after all.' Itching to take over, and showing little restraint, Eleanor was scowling and sighing through this. Listening intently, Rupert was studying the floor and hid his hands behind his back. Matthew was convinced that he was about to explode. 'And although we have felt honoured to have a professional in our midst, there's no getting away from this being an amateur festival with amateur actors.'

'Well, you knew that before you started,' said Rupert, glancing at Matthew to help him out.

Martin referred back to his notes. 'It has been observed that you are upstaging the others.'

Rupert turned to Eleanor. 'May I ask who has been kind enough to make this observation?'

'And we believe that you have a habit of standing centre stage. In fact, you always place yourself to best advantage...' continued Martin.

Rupert laughed. 'I wouldn't place myself at a disadvantage!'

'And you're performing as if the others are there to feed you your cues.'

'I think what you're trying to say is that I'm treating it as if the audience has come just to see *me*? Well, it's not the first time that a similar charge has been levelled. And why wouldn't they?' Rupert, nostrils flaring, raised his arms in an expansive gesture, and looked Martin up and down as if he were a child, diminishing by the second. 'Can I make something clear to you bone-heads? Lady Bracknell is one of the most imposing characters in English theatre. I am still creating a character during rehearsals. One is constantly discounting ideas that don't work, and trying out new ones, right up to the last minute. And during the run, you continue to learn.' His face relaxed. The tension in the room eased, especially when Rupert began to weave among them, as if thinking up some masterclass for their benefit. 'Actually, it comes together during a long run, but you, as amateurs, will never know the thrill of that, or the tedium for that matter. I'm not saying that I won't continue to alter a bit of business wherever I can, because the honing and polishing is an ongoing process, but as far as

I'm concerned this production will be developing until the last minute of the final performance.' His eyes came to rest on Martin. 'You *are* familiar with the creative process, I take it?'

Martin crossed his legs. 'We feel it has gone beyond that.'

Glancing at Matthew once more, as if seeking help, Rupert edged towards Martin. 'Look, I'd be more than happy to re-think certain points if you think it needs it.'

'This may come as something of a shock, Rupert–'

'Hold on a minute! You've not given me the chance to respond to your comments or adapt my performance in rehearsal yet. Are you indicating that you want me to tone down my performance? I am well aware that the others have had no theatrical training, and I probably come over as something of a...' He struggled for the right word. 'Colossus.'

Martin widened his small eyes. 'We don't want you to jeopardise your talents as director by spreading yourself too thinly.'

'This has gone far enough,' said Eleanor, rising serenely from her chair. 'Listen, Rupert – we don't just want you to tone down your performance but to *step* down, so that you can channel all your energy into directing.'

Martin gasped, and shook his head. 'Eleanor, you promised...'

It was as if she had never spoken, for Rupert merely continued treating Martin to a long stare. 'How about I alter the way I am playing it and you return to see if you approve next week?'

'Time is not on our side,' said Martin.

'We open in less than *two* weeks!' Eleanor reminded him, gleefully.

Matthew groaned. 'If you say that again, I swear I'll–'

'You'll do what?'

'Forget it.'

Rupert moved so that he was face to face with Eleanor. Their noses were practically touching, when he demanded, 'With so little time, who can you possibly find to replace me?'

'Eleanor has *kindly* offered to step in on your behalf,' said Martin.

The cast began a slow hand-clap, which Martin struggled to talk over. 'Surely the best thing is for us to put any petty grievances to one side?'

'Petty?' cried Rupert, throwing Martin a look aimed at shrivelling him to dust.

'Anyone involved in the theatre expects to get his fair share of knocks. You, of all people, know that,' grinned Eleanor.

Rupert placed his hands on his hips. 'And who is to take over as Miss Prism?'

Felicity turned red from the neck upwards. 'We have all given this a great deal of thought...'

Rupert sidled up to her. 'Oh, you have, have you? Well, I hope you are word-perfect by next Monday. Now, as to my contract–'

'With regard to remuneration,' said Martin, 'we will honour your full salary, in spite of the diminution of your responsibilities.'

'Diminution? Is that what you call it? But I have a signed contract.' Rupert was breathing hard and his cheeks were glowing. 'I'm going to hold you to it, if it's the last thing I do!'

'Please calm down, Rupert,' said Martin. 'The committee had hoped not to resort to this, but if you care to refer to page sixteen...' He handed Rupert the members' handbook, open at the page.

Rupert threw back his shoulders and read out the relevant section which had been highlighted for his benefit, while the others fidgeted. ' "*Under such circumstances, the committee retains the right to intercede, if and when they feel that it is appropriate to do so, should the director, or actor, not be achieving the targets within the margins as laid down in Section Two, paragraph seven, and in such cases they retain the right to amend or cancel the agreement as indicated by the signed contract.* "'

Rupert threw the festival manual across the floor with such force that it landed at Eleanor's feet. 'Why isn't it written in proper English?'

'Shouldn't we look at this in more detail tomorrow?' pleaded Matthew, surprised at how small his voice sounded.

'Oh, you've piped up, have you? *What difference will tomorrow make?*' shouted Rupert. He then smiled and brought himself up to his full height. 'But, tell me, how would you like *The Westmorland Gazette* to get hold of this story?'

Martin glanced at Eleanor, but she was studying the floor with rigid intent.

'Would you accept one thousand, Rupert?' asked Martin, adding in a trembling falsetto. 'Cash?'

Rupert chuckled. 'What's to stop me resigning as director, which is really what you deserve, and leave you to it?'

Martin, Felicity and Eleanor shrugged and made faces at each other while Rupert paced the room. He was clearly making them wait.

'Two thousand and not a penny less, if I surrender Lady Bracknell. You can well afford it. But I continue as director on the same fee as agreed, without you returning to cast your eyes over any future rehearsals. Is that understood?' He stared at Martin until he forced him to look away, like a whipped dog. 'You have my bank details, I believe?'

Seeing Martin and Felicity leaping to their feet, Matthew took Rupert to one side.

'Are you sure about this?' he asked, his voice barely a whisper.

Rupert lowered his voice too, which had the effect of a strangulated hiss. 'What choice do I have? Besides, I'm getting rather tired of Eleanor's scheming, so I'll be doing my best to make her feel very contrite about what she's done.' He paused. 'It's strange, but no one explained that contract to me before I signed it.'

'Well, who would have thought that things would turn out like this?' asked Matthew, without expecting an answer. 'But whichever way you look at it, you have to take some responsibility for your own actions. Didn't you read it through properly?'

Rupert sighed. 'I glazed over very quickly, I'm afraid. Still, what difference would it have made?' He brightened. 'What a pity I didn't know James then. He could have come running to my assistance.'

Matthew noticed Martin stumbling out with Felicity in something of a hurry. Although it was difficult to concentrate, they ran through the act once again, and when it was over, Matthew left the rehearsal without saying goodbye to Eleanor. This was a first in twenty-five years.

When Rupert phoned Langdales next morning, Matthew offered him all his sympathy. Torn between Eleanor – who had always been there for him – and Rupert – who had not – he had been labouring with divided loyalties. Now the decision over who to side with had been made for him, and he resolved not to speak to Eleanor for the rest of the production, maybe even forever. They chewed the whole thing over endlessly until Rupert announced, 'I've discussed it with Caroline, who says that if that's the way they feel, I should take some time off.'

'Does she indeed?'

'She suggests I visit my father. With her.'

'So she's the one who's put you up to it?' Matthew could hardly speak. 'You realise she needs a chaperone?'

'Needs revenge on you lot, you mean? She warned me not to have anything further to do with you. Having seen far more of you *all* than is good for me, I feel as though I deserve a complete break.' He paused. 'You will put about the story as follows. My father has had a relapse, and I'm urgently needed by his bedside. Don't tell them he's sinking.' He winked. 'I may need to keep that in reserve for another time!'

'You can't just swan off.'

'I can do whatever I like.'

'But, you're putting the festival at stake.'

'I'm devastated.' Rupert went into coy mode. 'And now for a word of warning. Just keep your eye on James and Tom.'

'What do you mean by that?' asked Matthew sharply, hoping his voice did not betray him. Presumably, Rupert must have some proof – above and beyond the whispers – to appear so indiscreet.

'Come off it, Matthew,' said Rupert. 'You've seen how they look into each other's eyes when they're rehearsing together.'

'I've witnessed nothing of the kind!' Matthew did not choose to pursue this. Knowing how quickly Rupert could shoot down the motorway to Manchester airport and be flying off to Nice with Caroline, he merely asked when he might be returning.

Rupert replied, 'I couldn't care less whether I came back or not.' He rang off abruptly, even for him.

Matthew phoned Eleanor to warn her that the production was in danger of disintegrating; she was spiky in the extreme.

'His father should stop shilly-shallying.'

'You sound like Lady Bracknell.'

'You're referring to Bunbury? How convenient to have a permanent invalid with the power to drag him away when the going gets tough.'

Matthew murmured, 'Especially when it involves a mercy dash to the Riviera.'

'Can he seriously be abandoning the production? If so, we are well rid of him.'

There was no doubt now that the festival was in jeopardy. Somehow they all barked and ranted their way through two rehearsals on their own, but Matthew found himself wishing that they had not been left to their own devices. They were rudderless. Watching his fellow actors flailing about reminded him of panic-stricken ants running in all directions. It was felt that Eleanor was the natural successor, and she did attempt to take command, but soon grew weary of trying to act and direct. Agonising over whether he should volunteer, Matthew had a couple of disturbed nights. Gradually, information from on high filtered through. The committee had shrugged off any thoughts that Rupert might not return. Much to his relief, there were no plans to check if Blake Benedict might suddenly have become available. Meanwhile, Rupert refused to reply to any texts or emails.

In addition, he remained concerned by Rupert's warning about James and Tom, and hoped that it did not mean what he took it to signify.

Chapter Nine

Not a squeak out of Rupert until he burst through the door – late – for the following Thursday's rehearsal, looking tanned, relaxed and a little heavier around the middle. His fixed smile revealed little. When the cast had gathered round him, he looked Eleanor up and down, as if he had been waiting for this moment, and asked, 'I suppose it was only a matter of time before you got your own way?'

'Actually, several of us had to make what was, may I say, a supremely difficult decision.' She was able to look him in the eye, but her voice was unsteady.

'You just happened to be the prime mover?'

Her eyes were the coldest Matthew had seen them. 'If you must know, it didn't take a huge effort on my part. Your failed pantomime days clinched it.'

Rupert looked as if he was about to hit her. 'You don't even have *two* weeks left so we'd better make a start.'

Everyone seemed so keen to make the rehearsal work and the changes were seamlessly absorbed. Hoping that the Rupert-Eleanor conflict might be diminishing, Matthew turned his attention to James. Wishing to observe Tom and James together without the distraction of a rehearsal, he suggested inviting him back for a drink afterwards. Tom agreed too readily for someone who usually liked to get to bed early when they had guests, and James seemed only too happy to accept.

The sitting room at Langdales was deserted as their guests had already gone to bed, and Matthew found himself opening a bottle of Shiraz while Tom went to fetch a glass of water for James.

'So, how are things developing with Jane?' asked Matthew, once they were settled – but isolated – on the armchairs flanking the sofa on which James was sprawling luxuriously.

James drank a mouthful of water and ran it round his teeth, while considering this. 'I'm afraid there has been a misunderstanding.'

Tom raised an eyebrow. 'What happened to the fine romance?'

James glanced from one to the other. 'I'm not seeing much of her now.'

'Any particular reason, or shouldn't I ask?' asked Matthew, slightly on edge.

'I had enjoyed running through our lines together; liked her as a friend and all that, but didn't want to lead her on too much.'

'So, when you had fallen for her, was that genuine?' asked Matthew. 'Or did you go back to the little plan we were hatching to lead Rupert on and make him jealous?'

'At first, I had hoped that there might be a spark –' James hesitated. 'Until I realised it was hopeless.'

'I'd like to have seen her face,' said Tom.

James grinned. 'No, you wouldn't.'

Matthew sipped his wine, and as it began to relax him, stretched out his legs. 'Hopeless because you found you weren't attracted to her, after all? You must have known that she was looking for more than friendship?'

James's colour heightened. 'Not really. I never bought into your idea of making Rupert jealous.'

'No,' said Tom. 'That wasn't your finest moment, Matthew.'

Matthew gaped, but before he could close his mouth, James had gone off at a tangent. 'I suppose I was looking more for a walking companion.'

Tom swallowed some of his wine the wrong way and only just managed to stop himself from choking. He grabbed James's glass and threw some water down his throat. When he had recovered, he said, 'I'd have thought she was more interested in you on a horizontal plane.'

Matthew tutted. 'Really, Tom.'

'In the end, I told her I wasn't looking for a girlfriend just at present.' James shrugged. 'But hopefully there'll be somebody special in my life one day.'

'You'll soon get snapped up,' said Tom. 'You're the best-looking guy we've had in the festival.'

Matthew coughed. 'Calm down, dear. So you brought things to a close quickly, James? That was for the best, I feel.'

James drank some more water. 'Although it is *very* hard letting somebody down. You can imagine how I felt afterwards.'

'You seem to have kept it well hidden,' said Tom.

'And what would Jane be going through, I wonder?' asked Matthew. James looked down. 'It must have been hard for her to cope with?'

'I had hoped the beard might make me look less...'

'You don't need us to tell you what you look like,' said Tom. 'You look like a film star! So what have you been up to after what sounds like something of a subdued parting of the ways with Jane?'

'That first weekend I needed to clear my head, so I found a B and B in Keswick and went walking.'

Matthew, feeling a yawn coming on, covered his mouth.

'That sounds like my ideal sort of weekend, but weekends are our busiest times,' said Tom, 'and you're working during the week.'

James glanced first at Matthew and then at Tom. 'We could have gone camping together.'

This was all Matthew needed to hear. Tom rolled his eyes in jest. 'What? All boys together?'

'If Matthew wouldn't mind, that is? I want to try out a new tent before I use it in the summer, check that it's not too cramped for two. I mean, there's cosy and intimate – '

Matthew was trying hard not to frown. 'And, as you say, there's cramped.'

Tom smirked; he was on the edge of his chair. 'What a pity we never get the chance to do a big walk like Helvellyn or the Fairfield Horseshoe.'

'I've always thought they sounded rather epic, and I am a wee bit older than you,' said Matthew, feeling he was losing ground.

'Don't I know it!' cried Tom, turning to James. 'If ever you want to scale some heights, let me know. I'm sure we could come to some arrangement.'

Matthew tried to stay included in the conversation. 'Weekends *are* very busy here, but if you need a change, please feel free to ring us. Why not join us for lunch or dinner?'

'Yes, don't hold back from contacting either one of us,' added Tom, with a meaningful look.

'If you're looking for companionship, don't forget that Rupert's still a huge fan,' Matthew found himself saying. He looked forward to monitoring James's reaction.

'You treat him as a figure of fun, but he does have several redeeming features,' said James. 'He can be a little overpowering, I agree, but he means well. And he knows so much! Mind you, I can just see *him* in a tent with his candelabra and linen napkins. By the way, is it normal for the director to be treated like that?'

'Certainly not. No director has played a role before,' said Matthew, 'but we think it's very bad form.'

'Especially as you two used to be such good pals,' said James.

Matthew felt his mouth go dry and his palms moisten, but nodded and pretended he had not seen the surreptitious grin that James gave Tom. 'You see what can happen when somebody is thwarted in their pursuit of a role? As you know, Tom wanted to play Jack, but we think you're making an excellent job of it. And we do need new blood.'

Tom smiled thinly.

'Well, let's hope it's a defining role for me, and I must thank you for making me feel welcome.' James hesitated. 'People sometimes get a bit soft on each other in a play, due to the close proximity in a concentrated span of time, and...'

'Yes?'

'I hope you don't mind me mentioning it, but I've noticed you giving Tom and me odd looks. I'd hate you to think there was anything in it.'

Matthew leaned further forward. 'What are you implying?'

'Nothing, just what I regard as innocent fooling.'

'But why, when you should be concentrating on the rehearsal?'

'To relieve the boredom?' James shrugged, and treated them to his puppy look; not difficult with those lashes. 'I don't know why I fool around. I can't vouch for how Tom feels about finding a new friend, but doesn't it feel good to have struck up a rapport?'

Matthew hoped that the false bonhomie in his laughter did not sound forced. 'Perhaps you could only become such great pals after something as momentous as Tom's ill-feeling about losing Jack to you?'

'Not *so* momentous, surely?' laughed Tom, looking heavenwards. 'I *meant*, oh what does it matter?'

They continued to talk about the play for some time until Matthew could bear it no longer, stretched and stood up. 'I'm afraid you'll have to excuse me, James. It's been a *very* long day.' This was James's cue to go, but as he made no move, Matthew eyed Tom. 'You won't be long I hope?'

Tom nodded, but turned to look at James too quickly. Having said good night to James, Matthew rested his hand on Tom's shoulder; it was a risk, leaving these two together, but he felt he had to do it. By the time Tom came up, which must have been well over half an hour later, Matthew was pretending to be asleep, but his mind was working like a set of pistons.

Matthew's friendship with Eleanor was also giving him cause for concern, yet he still felt that his loyalties lay more with Rupert. He was still seething about how she had treated Rupert and he blamed himself for allowing things to have gone so far. (To some extent.) Perhaps he should have made things up with her before waiting for her to establish a rapprochement. He realised that he had to break his resolve to cut her, mainly because rehearsals threw them into such close contact. For the present, they had taken to only speaking when they had to (at rehearsal), and he missed their usual close contact away from rehearsals. Deep down, he could not bear the fact that they were growing remote from each other, but could not think how to make light of the situation without losing face, especially as he refused to make the first move.

Eleanor thrived on conflict, and her talent for giving him the cold shoulder was well-honed. He reflected that she had not telephoned him for days, and was soon piling the blame on her. Still, he was adamant he would not crumble before she did. After all, he recognised that things would get back to normal in due course, like they always had done, but there was usually an unspoken procedure to be followed: mutual silence, gradual thaw, return to normal, with their disagreement – seemingly – but not quite forgotten, until the next time. The mutual telephone silence was perhaps an expected and a required order of these events, dictated by the eruptions of strong feelings. He likened it to necessary rests found in music. Only after the desired rest could the music continue.

Even so, after a few more days of this, he remained scared of breaking his resolve and making the first move, when – much to his surprise – Eleanor telephoned. Evidently, the big thaw was on its way. It was one of those sublime, warm, sunny mornings and apart from the long shadow that she was casting, he had been feeling at peace with the world. She left him no alternative but to listen as if nothing had happened. Nothing was mentioned about the "Rupert incident" and she sounded determined to chatter away about nothing in particular. Of course, she excelled at that: her voice and manner as hard and bright as a well-polished diamond. Faced with her on the charm offensive, he would have sounded very mean-spirited had he decided to rake over old ground and berate her.

There were various reasons. To begin with, he wanted her to know that he was still feeling bruised, so he enjoyed sounding touchy and withdrawn, but he gradually mellowed, especially when it became apparent – so mixed were his feelings about her and so confused his thoughts meant he was only half-listening – that Eleanor required an answer.

'I was saying can you come or not, or did you not hear me?'

'I didn't quite catch– '

'As I thought, you've not been listening. I would like you and Tom to come for tea.'

'When?'

'Today if possible, as it's so fine.'

He chuckled. 'Shall I tell Tom that we have to admire your garden?'

'That goes without saying!'

'Will it be just us?'

'Naturally, Dorian will be here.'

Never mind the garden! Matthew had agreed of course, if only to look Dorian up and down. She was clearly proud of the developments – new plantings, and so forth – she had made with Dorian, and wanted to show either them or him off. Both, probably. So, she had deemed him privileged enough to be introduced to the famous Dorian! Matthew was intrigued.

The invitation boded well, and was a welcome first step to what would hopefully become a complete rapprochement. The dull ache within, that he had been trying to shrug off for some time, lifted in moments. He told Tom to be on his best behaviour and made him swear not to refer to the cloud hanging over the production.

Turning into Eleanor's drive later that afternoon gave him more pleasure than it had done last time; the prospect of an introduction to Dorian had been charged with anticipation. Spinnakers, although it could never be described as pretty, enjoyed one of the finest views of Windermere and the fells, in addition to boasting a well-planted mature garden, cascading via terraces down to the water's edge. Not for the first time, Matthew felt a pang of envy.

He frowned when he saw another vehicle, but brightened when he noticed a hunk clad in shorts stop wheeling his barrow. Tanned, and looking sickeningly healthy, he was clearly pleased with himself. After the face – Eleanor had done very well for herself – the long, dark hair was the next thing you noticed; thick, luxuriant, and glossy. Almost a mane, for it did need cutting. From the car, he looked about twenty-eight, maybe thirty. Rupert had not exaggerated and Matthew tried to stop salivating. Further envious thoughts, the likes of which he had not anticipated, began to permeate his brain.

There was no sign of Eleanor, not even twitching a blind or curtain. Once Matthew had parked the car in the shade, the stranger whisked open the car door and – thrusting his face a little too close in the door opening – greeted him. Slightly unnerved by the close proximity, he smiled; hopefully not too regally. Unable to keep his eyes off the hirsute chest as he slid off the car-seat, it struck Matthew more forcibly that Eleanor had invited them to show off this delectable creature, rather than the garden itself. He could also sense that Tom fancied Dorian just as much as he did.

As he had suspected – rather mean-spiritedly – the hunk was older than he looked. Close up, the tiny webs of lines around his eyes made him look nearer to forty, although that trim waistline clearly belonged to a younger man. Dorian's abdomen was tighter than Matthew's had been as a teenager. His wide-set dark-blue eyes were framed by the well-proportioned face. He boasted a strong chin, enhanced by the inevitable designer stubble. Yet – on reflection – that mane was a trifle long for someone his age. He was a surprising choice, to say the least.

If only he could live up to the perfection of his appearance, thought Matthew, as he offered his hand for what he hoped would be a firm, vigorous hand-shake. Taking a closer look, the earrings, the discreet tattoo and his general demeanour suggested "alternative", and it did not take him long to shift from cheap attraction. Sadly, he came to terms with having taken against Dorian in only a few seconds. Was he jealous that Eleanor now found herself with one gorgeous catch? Or was his skin prickling because he felt that he ought to be protecting her?

Dorian ran his eyes over Tom; being dark, he was Tom's type. Matthew tried not to think of James. He flashed his bright, even teeth once more and thrust out his hand towards Tom. 'Welcome! I'm Dorian Manners. Eleanor's told me all about your lovely garden at Langdales. Maybe you could do with a helping hand, or maybe two?'

'That's a very kind offer, Dorian, but Tom has the garden very much under control, thank you,' replied Matthew, in what he hoped was a reserved and dignified manner, just in case Dorian was being a little too forward. Matthew appeared to have no control over his eyes flickering up to the windows. Still no sign of Eleanor, which seemed ominous. Clearly, she was not only holding back to make an entrance, but giving them time to admire Dorian. Meanwhile, Matthew was trying to work out where Dorian came from.

'That's a pity,' said Dorian, continuing in his deep, masculine voice while Matthew caught himself glancing down at those tanned muscular legs.

'That doesn't mean to say that you can't come over and tell us where we're going wrong,' gabbled Matthew.

Tom seemed to have been struck dumb, until now. 'I wasn't aware that I had been doing anything wrong.'

'In that case, perhaps I could come up and have a look. I don't seem to be able to get enough of Lakeland gardens at this time of year, and Eleanor has always spoken so highly of yours. There's often room for a little tweaking I find.'

'Tweaking?' enquired Tom in a rather high voice.

'I can't take any credit, of course,' simpered Matthew. 'Tom is the green-fingered one in our–'

He was on the cusp of saying 'family' or 'household'. Yet Dorian's demeanour was so butch that Matthew was left feeling that he had no desire to disclose more than was necessary; although, surely, Eleanor would have lost no time in filling him in on their domestic arrangements.

Dorian looked Tom up and down and grinned. 'Are you always this quiet, or is it enough to be merely decorative?'

Tom was opening his mouth to reply when Eleanor, as if she had been waiting, came tripping down the front steps in a hat so wide-brimmed that her face was practically invisible, and a yellow summer dress, too tight and too young for her, but looking happier than Matthew had seen her since her divorce.

'You've introduced yourself?' she asked Dorian, whose beauty she seemed to taking in to the full. 'Dorian, this is Matthew's *inamorato*, Tom – and a more decent kind of –'

'No worries, there,' said Dorian, winking at Tom. 'I'm *very* broad-minded.'

Matthew could feel Tom tense beside him.

'You remember the way down to the summer house?'

Matthew thought she was sounding rather shrill as her cheek brushed against his rather too quickly. 'How could I forget?'

She gestured airily towards the lawn and the steps leading down to the lake beyond.

Crossing the lawn, Matthew and Eleanor were soon in step with each other and chatting happily again, as if there had been no rift. Eleanor turned to check that Tom and Dorian were following. She caught Matthew's eye, then took his arm. 'Isn't he a dream?'

He chuckled. 'Delightful, of course. Is that what you wanted me to say?' She smiled. 'But, more to the point, what do you know about him, apart from that he's not local, and he's too young?'

Her face fell. 'You can talk.' She glanced back at a smiling Tom, who was either enjoying Dorian's company, or more likely because he remained skimpily dressed. 'Please don't spoil it for me, Matthew. I've been waiting for something like this to happen for so long, and now that he's finally arrived, you can't begrudge me a little happiness.'

'Of course not, but Tom and I go back ten years. The pair of you go back about ten minutes.' Her lips were trembling and her eyes moistening, so he lowered his voice and made sure that they remained ahead of the other two.

'As far as I'm concerned, he's too good to be true.'

She pouted. 'Jealous?'

'Far from it and don't forget he's something of a stranger.'

'We've been together longer than you might think – '

'That's no excuse. You do realise you're still a very attractive woman, and one look at Spinnakers and he'll have figured out what you're worth practically to the penny.'

'I very much doubt it. Horticulture has never struck me as a particularly worldly occupation.'

'Just be careful. That's all I'm saying. I'll shut up now.'

She stopped as if to consider this and let the others catch up. Seeing the earnest expression on Matthew's face, Eleanor floated off, this time with Dorian, leaving Matthew and Tom to trail behind.

'So, Dorian,' asked Matthew, a couple of minutes later, when they had caught up and stopped to admire a particular planting combination, its complexities of colour and texture quite lost on him, 'how did you find yourself in such a glorious part of the world?'

Gazing at the hump-backed horizon of the Langdale Pikes and the western fells, Dorian hesitated. Windermere shimmered a deep blue beyond the frame of flowering shrubs, Japanese maples and emerald lawn, recently striped by the mower. 'I love rhododendrons and azaleas, and the trees and water make a fantastic backdrop. You're familiar with the term "*borrowed landscape*"?' Matthew was not, but nodded eagerly. 'Working at the garden centre opened up some wonderful introductions for me.'

Eleanor, who had been unusually quiet, added, 'Perhaps your rugged charm helped there, darling?'

Dorian shared a self-satisfied look with Matthew and Tom. 'And I now enjoy helping professional people, who have other preoccupations – like your good selves – to improve and remodel their gardens.'

'Very occasionally,' she laughed, 'he even condescends to do a bit of maintenance.'

'I'm a simple man, just hoping to make my clients' lives easier.' He wrapped his arm around Eleanor's petite, white shoulders. She brushed up against him like a cat desirous of its supper. 'Planning and planting, I can turn my hand to anything.'

'So it would appear,' said Matthew, not daring to catch Tom's eye. 'You never thought of becoming a head gardener?'

'I value my freedom too much.' Dorian pulled away from Eleanor and shuffled his boots. 'You see, I don't like being cooped up in one place for very long. Eleanor is by far and away my best client. I like to think we've found the right balance between work and play, wouldn't you say?' Dorian's eyes came to rest on Eleanor, but she was straightening her dress and looking a trifle overheated.

When she had registered what he was saying she smiled as if it was incumbent on her to add something. 'I'm afraid it's like a private members' club. I know that Felicity is *dying* to pick his brains, but Dorian's got his hands full at this time of year.'

'Quite,' said Matthew, turning to Dorian. 'So, do I take it that this is something of a change of career?'

Dorian fidgeted. 'What makes you say that?'

'Your boyish enthusiasm about a new venture?'

'It's the perfect job. I'm outdoors when it's sunny, and Eleanor keeps me hard at it indoors when it's raining.'

'Plenty of exercise, then?' asked Tom, grinning as he caught Matthew's eye at last.

'I *meant*,' said Dorian, who had noticed, and was quick to narrow his eyes, 'that I'm drawing up a design for a new planting scheme whenever I'm rained off.'

'But, forgive me, you're not from around here, are you?' asked Matthew.

'No, but I needed, or, perhaps...' he pulled back his lips for yet another winsome grin, 'perhaps, should I say, I *felt* like a change of scene.'

'You're not – how can I put it – not what I expected.'

Tom nudged him.

'You should see Dorian's dear little cottage, white and simply drenched in clematis, honeysuckle, and cascades of rose-buds. It's an absolute poem,' said Eleanor, setting off again. *She'll have enough to make an anthology if she goes on like this,* thought Matthew, but merely nodded. They continued to wander round the garden and admire everything to which Eleanor drew their attention, until she asked, 'Do you still have time to join us for a cup of tea?'

Matthew realised she was giving them the opportunity to escape if they were tiring of Dorian, but knowing that the tea things – and probably cake – would be set out in readiness, he accepted.

'In the summer house?'

'Where else?' She was grinning as if she had had a personality transplant.

This was getting altogether too saccharine for Matthew's liking, but he took her arm and pulled her towards him. 'I can't imagine anything nicer.'

'I can,' said Dorian, pulling her back towards him with those great arms of his. This earned him a mischievous tap on the nose from Eleanor. Matthew felt emasculated.

Once the superlatives had begun to die in the warm afternoon air, they made their way down the steps towards the summer house. Matthew could not help noticing that despite some early awkwardness on Tom's side, Tom and Dorian had bonded easily, but Tom was good at being friendly and charming with their guests at Langdales. As long as he liked them. Eleanor plugged in the kettle and once the men had taken their places around the table, she took out a Victoria sponge from a cake tin and sliced it.

To fill the gap in conversation, Matthew admired the deep blue of the lake from the shore-line; there was not a cloud to be seen. When he turned to look at Eleanor, she was passing round plates and letting her arm brush against Dorian's. 'Do you think you could possibly cover up while we eat?' she whispered, putting her head on one side, presumably in what she considered a beguiling manner.

Dorian set his face, but said nothing and rose to fetch his T-shirt. Three pairs of eyes watched his sinewy back, tight shorts and firm calves as he bounded up the steps and out of sight. Matthew mopped his face with his handkerchief.

Eleanor winked. 'The view's good today.'

Tom smirked. 'Especially from where I'm sitting.'

The talk became general until Dorian came swaggering back down the steps, looking as if he owned the place.

Matthew brought the conversation back to gardening. 'But you still have a young man working for you, don't you, Eleanor?'

'You mean Mark?' asked Eleanor, over her shoulder, busy making tea. 'Yes, he takes care of the grass and hedges, and is glad of any digging in the winter that I can give him.'

'I call him Stable-Boy.' Dorian's teeth glinted. 'I point while he digs.'

'You don't get a body like yours merely by pointing,' observed Eleanor.

Dorian glanced down at himself as if to reassure himself that everything was still honed and chiselled beneath his taut T-shirt. 'I've been going to the gym for a number of years now.'

Matthew could leave the question unasked no longer. 'I don't wish to appear rude, but were you actually christened Dorian? It seems such a coincidence.'

'Yes, my mother was a huge fan of the book, although I can't imagine why.'

'The premise is interesting, at any rate,' said Matthew. 'I expect you've heard all about our Oscar Wilde production from Eleanor?'

'I feel as if I had been born into it!' exclaimed Dorian, too vigorously. 'I've been going over her lines with her, and living through every frown, but I've had to sit through that play once too often and I've vowed *never* to see it again.'

Eleanor made a face, but she was clearly enjoying the attention. 'Darling, such a philistine!'

'Far from it,' said Dorian. 'I've never bought into those am-dram ego-trips, not even when I had all the time in the world on my hands.' His eyes searched Eleanor's face in case he had said too much, but she was gazing towards the sapphire blue water, almost within touching distance.

'Things are coming to a head, right now, and we're looking forward to the first night,' murmured Matthew, forgetting to use the fork she had provided and biting into his slice of cake (dry, he noted, but he managed not to cough up any crumbs).

'Talking of festivals,' she remarked brightly, 'Dorian's planning a trip to the opera in Verona towards the end of August, along with the gardens of the Italian lakes.'

This fixation with Dorian was beginning to grate; she seemed to have no curiosity regarding them.

'I should be able to nose my way in easily enough during the final week.'

Dorian had gone up in his estimation. 'Not the best month for gardens, but the opera will be a treat.'

'Well, I tend to look at the bones of a garden, rather than pretty flowers.'

Matthew decided it was safer talking about opera. 'Will you be travelling with some operatic– er, chums?'

'I find it's more of an adventure if I go it alone.' Dorian chuckled. 'You never know who you might bump into.'

Matthew half-smiled. 'Or who you might pick up?'

'Or what one might catch?' asked Tom, with an air of triumph, as he had not spoken for some time, and had seemed content with his view of Dorian.

Dorian's forehead became a mass of lines; no wonder he kept his hair long. No doubt in ten years he would look like a walnut. 'Excuse me?'

'Just one of our little jokes,' muttered Tom.

Dorian leaned back in his chair proprietorially, placed his hands behind his head which allowed his T-shirt to ride up. 'In poor taste, perhaps?'

Matthew glanced at Eleanor to help them out, but she was stirring the pot.

'We never managed it,' she said.

Tom turned to her. 'Managed what, for heaven's sake?'

'Julian and I. That trip to Verona we promised ourselves.'

'You've mentioned plenty of other things, but never that,' said Dorian, subdued now, as if he had been told that her marriage to Julian had been one long list of privations. 'Perhaps you might consider going there with me, if you had nothing better to do?'

'Eleanor never goes anywhere without staying in a suite, and preferably full-board, so that'll set you back a bit,' said Matthew.

Dorian swallowed and grinned nervously.

'*We* have to take our holidays out of season,' declared Tom, 'but I've always liked the idea of opera in that arena.'

'Why didn't you tell me?' asked Matthew. 'Perhaps we might have...'

Tom shrugged, and became more arch than Matthew would have liked. 'Get Archie to *run* Langdales for us while we're soaking up the sun and the culture? I know he's a wizard with eggs, but I think that's asking too much, even of him.'

Eleanor turned the conversation back to gardening and the shadows were lengthening before Matthew realised that they might be outstaying their welcome. From Dorian's body language, it appeared he could not wait to throw Eleanor onto the bed and make love to her, probably for hours. He looked the type.

Matthew thanked her and rose from the table. They departed with insincere assurances from Eleanor that they "really *must* all meet up properly for dinner...soon", ringing in their ears.

They returned to Langdales too full to start dinner, only to find that Rupert had left them a rambling message on their voicemail. Tom stared out of the sitting room window while Matthew shook his head. Rupert, they heard, "could not help but brood over the indignities of the position she had put him in." He was "having venomous thoughts..." The message rambled on, the gist of it being that Rupert had written Eleanor a strongly-worded letter, not only concerning her behaviour, but offering various pointers as to how she should tackle the role of Lady Bracknell. But – he admitted – he had dashed it off hastily in a white-hot rage, and even he realised that it needed modifying before he fired it off. He desired Matthew to take it home and check it after that evening's rehearsal. Knowing Rupert so well, Matthew sensed that it must never be sent.

Chapter Ten

That evening's rehearsal was conducted without incident, and when the others had left, Rupert stuffed the envelope into Matthew's hand so that it shunted against his palm. Fearful of a bad night's sleep, Matthew waited until the following morning before reading it through and then – in the calmest frame of mind possible – telephoned Rupert, so that they could go through it together.

Shortly afterwards, the doorbell rang for a full fifteen seconds. Matthew was reminded of a line in the play: *"Only relatives, or creditors, ever ring in that Wagnerian manner."*

Matthew showed Rupert into the sitting room, while Tom, looking resentful, carried on with the housekeeping. Matthew seated Rupert at the small table in the window and drew up a chair next to him.

Wagging his index finger, he lost no time in observing, 'Before we go any further, Rupert, you do realise that this is wildly inappropriate?'

'Of course it is,' he smiled. 'Isn't that the whole point? But that won't stop me sending it, if that's what you're thinking.'

'Why not email her?'

'You never did have any sense of style, did you, Matthew? No, we must do things properly, or not at all, dear boy.'

Frowning, Matthew found a red pen and turned to the matter in hand. Rupert tightened his fists, but when it became obvious that little of what he had written in anger could be retained, he agreed to Matthew's suggestions. Matthew allowed Rupert to show his displeasure and make his point without being too offensive and left the illuminating guidelines on how to play Lady Bracknell untouched. Ironically, Rupert's knowledge of the role might be useful to Eleanor, but by the time they had finished, Matthew realised that in spite of his best intentions, he could not trust him.

'Best if you rewrite it *here* and *now*, don't you think?'

'The scene: a sitting room that has seen better days in a once gracious home?' Rupert knitted his brows. 'Time: the present. Is that it?'

'You can't expect me to approve it until you've had me check it.'

'That shouldn't take long, seeing as you've butchered it beyond recognition!'

Pretending not to have heard, Matthew handed him some note-paper and left him to it. When he returned, he ran his eyes over the letter while Rupert addressed the envelope. Rupert had seen fit to add one or two rather patronising things, and although they put Eleanor firmly in her place, the potential to give offence had been diminished.

'Are you sure I can't post it for you?' asked Matthew.

Rupert raised his hand. 'Certainly not! Could I bear waiting a couple of days to hear her response? No, nothing less than a hand-delivery will do.'

'A hand-delivery?' asked Matthew, in the stentorian tones of Lady Bracknell asking about that famous handbag.

'I'm going to beard that woman in her den.'

'*No one* calls on Eleanor without arranging something first. The idea of you tackling her at home is preposterous and I forbid you to go.'

'Forbid?' Rupert unnerved him with a stare. 'I have to see her reaction, after what she's done to me.'

'What about the electric gates?'

'Look, Matthew, it's not as if this is *Mission Impossible*. I'm going to hand-deliver this letter even if I have to hire a rowing boat to do so!' His colour high by now, Rupert turned on his heel, and found his own way out. There was so much crunching of gears and spraying of gravel that Tom bounded down the stairs, two at a time, only to find Matthew holding the front door as he watched Rupert's car disappear. He closed the door before the stench of exhaust fumes threatened to overpower the roses on the central table.

'What next?'

For a moment Matthew registered the only course of action possible, allowed Tom to get his breath back and then sniggered. 'Fancy a little ride?'

Tom grinned and went to grab the car key. They then dived into what might have been a high-octane car chase, only with nothing to chase. Astonishingly, Rupert's underpowered little vehicle, with a five-minute head-start, had vanished. To be fair, they would never have seen it on the winding roads anyway. At first, they drove like furies along the track from Langdales until they reached the road, and then slowed down to the usual meander because of the various bends. It was a dull, cloudy day, with no sun to blind them, but they did have to slow down further until a tractor turned off. They arrived, after what seemed like an eternity, to find Rupert's Renault, dusty, abandoned and almost panting, on the wrong side of the Versailles-like gates that guarded Eleanor from the unwelcome realities of the outside world.

They soon found their way in by the unlocked pedestrian gate to the side, just as Rupert must have done. The front door bell was duly leaned on but no one appeared. They then made their way round to the back and noticed that the French windows were gaping. Abandoning Tom on the terrace, Matthew entered the sitting room reluctantly, called upstairs to no avail, and returned.

'You know those steps leading down to the lake?'

'Intimately.'

'Well, what are we waiting for?'

Blind to the view of grey lake, and what now seemed like over-planted borders, they bounded across the sprawling lawn towards the steps down to the water, and got as far as the revolving summer house before seeing any signs of life, Rupert having been way ahead of them. They stopped a few feet away and glanced at each other. Things happened quickly from then on.

Rupert was standing with his back to them, and may not even have been aware of their arrival, for he was staring at the yawning double doors of the summer house. Eleanor and Dorian were caught standing like guilty figures on the set of a doll's house. Eleanor would never do anything like that in the summer house – especially one so open to view – thought Matthew, but Dorian, who had turned away from Rupert's no doubt lascivious gaze, was pulling on pale blue shorts over his firm brown buttocks. Eleanor was in black bra and knickers. Her face was as white as her body.

A throbbing engine noise on the water made Matthew turn and notice one of the large, many-decked lake steamers. Although still a good distance from the shoreline, the absence of thickly wooded slope gave the boat a fine, uninterrupted view of Eleanor's house and garden.

Passengers could not fail to notice Spinnakers, as it was clearly one of the most imposing houses on this stretch of Windermere.

Matthew's mouth opened as Rupert put his shoulder against the summer house, swivelling it far enough round until the doorway faced the lake. It took a lot of pushing to shove it so that Eleanor and Dorian would be in full view of the passing spectators, but Rupert – unfit as he was – succeeded. Everything appeared to go into slow-motion. The steamer seemed to be braking and shuddering, passengers trampled one another for a better view on the starboard side. There were soon so many of them that Matthew's vivid imagination foresaw the vessel listing towards the shore, although that would have been unlikely. A cheer erupted from the crowd, followed by whistling and hand-clapping. For Eleanor, it would be the wrong kind of applause, but Dorian seemed to enjoy the attention.

Matthew and Tom ran forward to accost Rupert, who did not look in the least perturbed. They pushed him away and swiftly shouldered the summer house until the passengers were denied their surprise view. Eleanor's lips were drawn into a thin line. Dorian simply grinned as he made a show of adjusting his equipment in his shorts.

'What the hell's going on?' yelled Matthew.

'It started as a joke,' whined Rupert. 'I wanted to make her feel uncomfortable.'

Matthew suppressed the urge to strike him. By then, the steamer was proceeding northwards up the lake towards Bowness-on-Windermere, when Eleanor laid into Rupert, as only she knew how. Thinking it best to leave the three of them to it, Matthew and Tom crept away silently, like characters at the end of a Coward comedy. No one noticed.

It was warm with a faint hint of sunshine when they reached Langdales, so they decided to recover from their morning's exertions by sitting on the terrace after a light lunch, but Matthew had barely turned a few pages of the dry biography of a tedious actress that had failed to engage him, when he became restless.

'You know, I can't help thinking,' he said, glancing at Tom, 'that we shouldn't have left them to it like we did.'

Tom closed the Rough Guide to Peru that he had been absorbed in. 'What are you suggesting?'

'Do you think we need to check if Rupert is all right?'

'Never mind about him, what about Eleanor?'

They decided to set off again without further ado, leaving their books on the sun-loungers. By the time they reached Spinnakers, Rupert's car had vanished. As before, it was very easy to step through the pedestrian gate and make their way up the long drive on foot. The house retained that deserted air, and Dorian's car had not moved. Feeling slightly robotic, Matthew re-enacted his entry into the sitting room through the open French windows, glancing back through the fluttering voiles to make sure that Tom was following.

The immaculate, snow-white sofas and chairs still looked as though they had never been sat in. The room possessed a chilly serenity which ill-prepared them for the furore that was to haunt them for some time. Having made their way into the hall, Matthew looked up at the landing. Hearing muffled voices, they crept upstairs gingerly. Tom was right behind him. Standing in front of Eleanor's bedroom door, they decided to wait a moment before barging in.

'It's for helping me with the garden.' Eleanor sounded more as if she was pleading than explaining.

'Why are you doing this now, of all times?' asked Dorian.

'I'm sure I've got some cash hidden here, somewhere,' she replied, airily, 'but I can't for the life of me remember where I've put it. Could you be an angel and give me some space?' She was sounding frivolous, not to say light-hearted, so there seemed little cause for concern. Matthew bit his lip. Maybe they had overreacted, and their visit would be seen as prying.

He pressed his ear to the door, and listened to the opening and closing of drawers and banging of wardrobe doors. She must be looking for the cash that Rupert handed over for the property rental, thought Matthew.

'But, Eleanor,' said Dorian, 'you're not really thinking of buying me off and sending me on my way, because if that's the case –'

'You can't really think you can carry on working for me after that dreadful scene? I'm going to be a laughing-stock.'

'Have you really thought this through? Nothing's changed as far as I'm concerned. I love you. You know that?'

'I love you, and I always will,' said Eleanor, too glibly for Matthew's liking. He recalled the younger, kinder Eleanor and wondered what had happened to that carefree creature.

'But I've never met anyone like you, Eleanor, and I'm not prepared to give you up without a fight.'

'I'm sorry, Dorian, but I can't go on. The divorce, the play, and now this. I can't take any more.'

'Why is it always about you?'

She was weeping now, as only she could. There was a scuffle, including what sounded like the clutter on her dressing table crashing to the floor.

'Why did you do that?'

'You drove me to it!' he cried.

'Just leave me to it, Dorian, do you hear me? I'll call you.'

Matthew recognised that it was unworthy to be eavesdropping, especially as he still had every intention of coming to her aid. There was further banging of wardrobe doors, then a scream.

'That hurt!'

'I'm sorry. You moved suddenly.'

'My face!' she wailed. 'What shall I do?'

'Stop this stupid search, for a start,' said Dorian. 'Let me have a look at you. Looks as though the door has caught your cheek – '

'How could you?' There was a pause, during which she must have been scrutinising her face or continuing the search. 'Ah! Here it is, at last!' Matthew took this as the moment to fly into the room to see Eleanor gripping a fat, crumpled envelope while perching on the bed in her dressing gown, her hair wrecked, her eyes smeared. She was breathing heavily.

Chest pumping hard, Dorian was drenched in sweat, his hair was glistening. He wiped his face with the back of a hairy arm and pulled on his shorts.

'I think you've done enough for one day,' said Matthew, determined not to stare.

'But I can't leave her.'

'Please, let us take care of things from now on.'

'Don't forget the money,' said Eleanor, cramming notes back into the envelope.

'I don't want it.'

'*Take it,*' she commanded.

'I'm not leaving you.'

Now lying on the bed, she nodded, and tried to smile, but waved the envelope towards him at arm's length.

Matthew took a step forward. Dorian took it reluctantly, and with tears in his eyes, made for the door. 'Don't think you can get rid of me that easily,' he declared on leaving.

Tom went to fetch any first-aid items that might be lurking in the back of the cupboard in the en-suite, and once he had returned, propped Eleanor up on a raft of pillows. Dabbing her round the eye and the cheek with a pad of cotton wool he then trotted downstairs to make tea. Matthew, who had been replacing everything onto the dressing table in a haphazard manner, decided that Eleanor would never be up to playing Gertrude in *Hamlet*, although she clearly revelled in having a full-scale row with a younger man. He adopted a soothing expression and perched beside her.

She began to calm down. 'I have nobody to blame but myself.'

Smoothing her hair, he murmured, 'Relax, and tell me about it tomorrow.'

'But how can I prepare for the rehearsal?'

'You're not going.'

Her head fell on Matthew's chest; his shirt was soon damp with hot tears. 'This won't go any further?'

He took her hand. 'If you can't rely on me by now...'

She began to ramble, trying to make sense of the confused sequence of events in her mind, until he silenced her. She felt for his hand and pulled him towards her. The colour had returned to her face. 'Do you think I've made a hash of things since Julian abandoned me to my fate?'

'He didn't, did he?' Realising that her remark indicated a sea-change from her usual outlook on life, he hesitated. There was an uncomfortable pause which could only gather weight while he pulled her tightly against himself. 'I'm sorry we have not been seeing eye to eye.'

'And?'

He gave her earlier question a moment's thought. 'You might have handled Rupert better. You can be somewhat high-handed and here you are with a devoted younger lover who – it seems – would carry out anything you asked of him, and you are shoving him away.'

'Just like you with Tom!'

Matthew bit his lip.

'I always knew you'd stand by me,' she said, 'and after what you've done for me today, you know that I'd be happy to do something similar for you. If I *have* to, of course.'

'Let's hope it never has to come to that, although you haven't been as kind to me as you might have been. Remember I knew you in the old days.'

'Ha! You mean when I was lively, enthusiastic and supportive of everybody?'

'I didn't like to say, but – '

'You try going through a costly divorce, coping on a reduced income and I don't know how many other privations and see how *you* feel.'

'Eleanor, you don't do privation, and it wouldn't do you any harm to mellow a little. In spite of my earlier reservations, I was hoping that Dorian was doing you good.'

'All I do is think about myself, and that's not getting me anywhere.' She turned to look for a tissue, so Matthew handed her the box, now lying upside down at the foot of the bed.

'Why the need to get rid of him?'

She looked at him as if for the first time. 'That sounds as if you think I've acted hastily?'

'Frankly, yes, not that I would dare tell you in so many words.'

'That's a relief.'

'All right. You *may* be guilty of being impulsive and irrational –'

'I hope not.'

'From the look in his eyes, I don't think you've lost him.'

'What about my reputation?'

Matthew grinned. 'As chatelaine of Spinnakers?'

She dabbed her eyes. 'It's not even six months since everything was finalised with Julian, and I've been seen cavorting with...'

'He's not going to give you up without a struggle, that's for sure. I was quite struck by his sincerity.'

'Perhaps you were wrong in the first place?'

'I usually am, so let's not say any more about that.'

'Well, if our paths do cross again, I hope he's in a better mood!' She closed her eyes and sank back into the weight of pillows rather ostentatiously, as if playing a big scene in one of those black and white women's films from the 1940s; but rather than some dreadful children rushing in and screaming *"Mother! Mother! Mother!"* in a sickening monotone, Tom returned with the tea tray and some brandy. He waved the bottle at her, but she shook her head, so he busied himself with pouring while she sank deeper into the pillows.

Nodding faintly, she took a couple of sips, grimacing at the sweetness. 'The row began in earnest when Rupert–' She rephrased with, '*After* Rupert scarpered.' There seemed a sudden return to form when she giggled. 'Dorian chased him up the garden steps wielding a fork. That was so funny! Then we began to argue about whose idea it had been to have made the summer house into a tryst.'

'Whose idea was it?' asked Tom, sitting on a bedroom chair.

'Need you ask? I didn't realise that he could be so irritable with me, but the next thing he was kneeling down and begging for forgiveness. Then I made the big mistake of bringing him up here.' She reached for the hand-mirror that must always have remained by her bed, shook her head when she saw her reflection and threw it down. 'How am I going to explain this? It's so close to the opening night.'

'You could get some brandy down you, which might help calm your nerves,' urged Matthew.

'There's nothing wrong with my nerves!'

'We've both told you often enough that you need to take it easy,' said Tom. 'You've done far too much fretting about the play, you're trying to absorb Dorian into your life, and you're nowhere near over the divorce.'

'You're heading for a breakdown, if you ask me,' said Matthew.

'Well, I hate to disappoint you, but I don't need your advice,' she replied tartly.

Tom was pouring out a measure of brandy, regardless, when the doorbell rang. Eleanor froze. Tom stood up, but failed to put the bottle down. 'I'm sure it won't be Dorian,' he stated as calmly as he could, although from his frown, not without misgivings.

'Don't take the bottle with you, *fool*,' said Eleanor. 'What will people think? And I don't care *who* it is, tell them I'm not in.'

Handing it to Matthew with only one raised eyebrow, Tom left the room. For a moment, Matthew visualised her playing Congreve's Lady Wishfort in a few years' time. But now, her lips were trembling, and she had assumed that familiar (intended to be poignant), faraway look that rarely convinced Matthew on stage. This was evidently her "big scene", and she wasn't going to waste it. He gave her the glass of brandy regardless, and she gulped it down, wincing slightly. 'I thought I knew him,' she said, thrusting the glass at him. 'I thought we had something special, the two of us, but thinking about it, I don't know anything about him at all, do I?' She started sobbing again. 'I think the worst of it was that dreadful parting. You see now what I mean to him? I can't tell you how much fun we've had and now it's been spoiled, thanks to that twit.'

'Calm down, Eleanor, while we find the best outcome.' He stroked her arm. 'You need to rest after a shock. If you carry on like this, we're going to take you home and force you to lie down if it's the last thing we do.'

She squeezed his hand and managed a creditable sigh of relief. 'That's the most sensible suggestion I've heard in a long time.'

Tom returned to say that he had been staggering in with a heavy delivery. 'That must be Dorian's new weights,' said Eleanor. 'What if he comes back when I'm on my own here?'

'I don't think he'll show his face tonight. Surely he recognises that you need a few days?'

Even so, they decided that she was vulnerable and should not stay the night at Spinnakers on her own, so she agreed to come to Langdales. Her gates would be locked, but there was nothing to stop him borrowing a boat and making his way up the garden in the dead of night, but Matthew decided not to flag this up.

He glanced at his watch; it was now early afternoon and they had missed lunch. Waiting downstairs while she had a shower and dressed – and not daring to desecrate the chilly splendour of the sitting room – they tried to get comfortable on an unyielding hall sofa for over thirty minutes. Watching her slowly descend, wearing over-scaled sunglasses, her hair and make-up immaculate, and in her favourite navy blue suit, Matthew almost gasped at the transformation. He offered her a lift, but she would have none of it, and insisted on using her own vehicle.

The drive back was uneventful with Eleanor bobbing along in front on her tractor-like tyres. Once they had reached home she seemed happy to acquiesce to anything, so they had no difficulty persuading her to use the spare room, even if it did look a little cheerless with no flowers on the dressing table. Matthew drew the curtains, reflecting on the contrast between her and their last guest in that room.

'I was wondering what I should do about Dorian? Is it too soon to call him?' She was sitting on the bed, turning slowly towards Matthew as if everything ached.

'You must give it time,' said Matthew, sitting down next to her. 'Although, in my opinion—'

'Nobody wants to hear your opinion at a time like this,' said Tom, glancing at her. 'I've been meaning to ask. Did you manage to read it?'

'The letter?' Looking pale, she put her hand to her mouth. 'I almost forgot. It must have fallen on the floor when Dorian was clambering back into his shorts.'

'Well, you can deal with that in the morning. It'll be quite safe there overnight. Then you must destroy it,' said Tom.

Eleanor started. 'Without having the dubious pleasure of reading it first?'

'We won't rest until we know that it's been torn into pieces and is floating on Windermere,' said Matthew, kissing her on the forehead and squeezing her hand before closing the door. He felt that forcing her to lie down in a darkened room would remove her from the usual high level of stimulation she normally craved; he just hoped that she would stay there.

Later, when she reappeared in the kitchen, there was still an hour to spare before the rehearsal, and Matthew could not help giving Tom a sideways look as she slumped in a chair and closed her eyes for a few moments. What were they to do with her? That was the unspoken question. Tom suggested that she might make some scrambled eggs when she felt like it, opened one or two cupboards and pointed. She continued to keep her eyes closed off and on while they tip-toed around the kitchen, the atmosphere remaining strained until she remarked, 'This has to be the worst day of my life.'

'Rupert wouldn't have confronted you if you hadn't snatched Lady Bracknell from him,' said Tom, involuntarily.

'Thanks, Tom,' said Matthew, turning to Eleanor. 'You must put it behind you now.'

'I'd like to put him behind bars.'

'Do you have to be so acidic?' asked Matthew.

Tom put his finger to his lips and shook his head. Matthew nodded. 'We don't have much time.'

'How do I explain what happened?'

'You say you walked into the wardrobe door? That's almost the truth?' suggested Tom. 'I mean, it was an accident?'

'Yes, it jumped out and hit me,' said Eleanor, glibly. 'Although I do sometimes wonder if he knows his own strength.'

Tom nodded. 'Let's hope that Rupert's not got to them first. I can't imagine he'll be discreet.'

'He doesn't know the meaning of the word,' said Matthew.

'What's going to happen to me?' she asked.

Matthew replied before Tom got in. 'That depends on how uncomfortable you are about the summer house. Give it a couple of days, then let the rehearsals take your mind off things, but only when you're fit enough to go back.'

'I'll start the car,' said Tom, winking at Matthew as he headed for the door.

Eleanor smiled. 'How do I look?'

'As good as usual, but that doesn't mean you're joining us this evening. You'd be all over the place.' He checked his watch. 'Can you promise us that you will rest up this evening?'

She eyed him. 'Have *your* passions never spilled over?'

Matthew leaned over and rearranged some hair that had fallen over her eye. 'As a matter of fact, I had to make a decision a long time ago, and – very occasionally – I think that it might have been the wrong one.'

Nodding, she held him in her gaze until he closed the back door.

'This is very unsavoury,' said Tom in the privacy of their car. 'He's shown himself to be completely unsuitable!'

Matthew found himself saying, 'Best not to be too judgemental. More to the point, do you think she'll be able to cope with playing Lady Bracknell, patch things up with Dorian *and* maintain the feud with Rupert?'

Tom laughed. 'Rupert will have no qualms about resurrecting the role if he has to.'

'That's never going to happen!'

Thinking hard, they drove the rest of the way in silence, and were the first cast members to arrive. Matthew marched up to Rupert and told him what he had missed.

'Had you not gone out of your way to expose them to...'

'Public scrutiny? Ridicule?' suggested Tom.

'...that ugly scene might never have happened.' Rupert blinked and retreated a step. Matthew was just about to continue his rant, when Tom put his finger to his lips; the others had begun to trickle in. Rupert gave Eleanor's apologies without going into detail, and once the murmuring had ceased, they launched into the rehearsal.

They had not reached Lady Bracknell's entrance when, much to everyone's surprise, Eleanor floated in.

Matthew marvelled at her strength of character. The bruise was hardly noticeable under those Jackie Onassis-style sunglasses, and that well-made-up face, but Matthew questioned how her mind would be coping. Her row with Dorian – presumably the first major one – must have dented her confidence, damaged her faith in the relationship, and was bound to make her question their future. Eleanor turned her head slowly as if it ached, although she was more likely weighing up the feeling in the room (she would have had no clue as to what they had been told), and began by explaining how she had had an altercation with a cupboard door, but finished by rooting in her handbag for a tissue.

They continued rehearsing, but Matthew was not surprised when she occasionally stumbled over her lines. Whenever she was not required, she sat staring ahead of her, ignoring the book on her lap.

Then came the notes. Loquacious as ever, Rupert cited the importance of listening and reacting, rather than anticipating the other actors' lines with a wide-eyed expression and a marked turn of the head, which had become prevalent. 'And no excess facial twitching, blinking, eyebrow-raising or fidgeting with your hands and feet!' In spite of her accident Eleanor had, apparently, been excellent. Rupert then asked them to remain for a few more moments while he allocated the dressing rooms. This was a task that he had taken over, although it was not strictly in his remit and, to Matthew's way of thinking, extraordinary that he should have decided to meddle with things that did not concern him. The dressing rooms were ground-floor bedrooms located in the hotel wing closest to the ballroom. For this production,

WAFT had hired four of these, on the assumption that people would not mind sharing. Sadly, it was another test to the faith that Matthew had put in Rupert.

'Eleanor and Felicity: dressing room one,' he advised them, speaking slowly and deliberately so that there could be no misunderstanding. 'Jane and Clare: dressing room two.' Rupert paused. 'James and Tom: dressing room three.' The faces of James and Tom registered nothing, but Matthew convinced himself that they would be inwardly rejoicing, and he found himself overflowing with resentment. 'Finally, Matthew and Archie will share dressing room four.' There was a great deal of murmuring until Eleanor, Matthew and Tom were left to swarm around Rupert, like children around their teacher. This was all that Matthew needed. Closing his folder, Rupert's face told them that he still had some unfinished business with her, but before he opened his mouth, Matthew started on him.

'What nasty trick are you playing now?' Rupert merely shrugged at him. 'Why haven't you put me in with Tom?'

'You see so much of each other, as it is,' said Rupert, 'and isn't the festival supposed to be about making new friends?' Matthew grunted. Rupert glanced at Tom, and then back at him. 'Actually, have you ever considered that James and Tom might get heartily sick of joking with each other if they're thrown into a dressing room together?' From the colour of his face, Tom looked as if he was about to erupt, when Rupert turned to glance at Eleanor. 'Clearly, dear lady, I owe you an apology for what's happened.'

'That's all very well, but...' She removed the sunglasses. 'More to the point, do you think this bruise will have gone by the time we open?'

Rupert peered at it. 'If you can turn your back on your many responsibilities for a while, I am sure things will work out.'

Eleanor seemed determined to have the last word, and tore into him. 'This would never have happened if Felicity hadn't offered you Lady Bracknell behind my back; a role I've had my eye on for years. I'd love to know how she got hold of you in the first place.'

'You remember Blake Benedict?'

She gasped. 'I had hoped never to be reminded of him.'

Rupert leered at her. 'Yes, he's an old chum.'

Before she became aerated, Matthew took her by the arm. 'We need to get you back to Langdales.'

She pulled away from him. 'Thank you, Matthew, but I've changed my mind. I need to return home without delay.'

'He's not been texting?' She shook her head. 'You think he might be waiting?'

'I'm not sure, but there's a telepathy – hard to explain – but I refuse to ignore it.'

'Never go to sleep on a row,' observed Tom.

'Well, in that case,' said Matthew, resisting the temptation to thank Tom sarcastically, 'we mustn't leave anything to chance.' He turned to Rupert. 'One last thing, I'm not best pleased about sharing with Archie.'

'I suppose you'd rather watch James changing, but I felt that Tom was not only the more deserving case, but had the stronger claim.'

Tom went scarlet.

'You had no business allocating them,' said Matthew, trying to keep his head.

'Why not?' asked Rupert, wide-eyed. 'My cast needs to be happy backstage, so I've put a lot of thought into this.'

'I, for one, will be very unhappy,' said Matthew, making a move to go.

'I also had to think of James.'

Tom restrained Matthew by his arm. 'Let's forget it.'

'Things have worked out well for you, I must say,' said Matthew, turning on Tom. 'How convenient to have no witnesses.'

'Just because we have a laugh doesn't mean– '

'Play the innocent, why don't you?'

Tom shook his head in disbelief. Eleanor, who by this time had settled into the nearest chair, managed a wan smile when they led her out to the car-park. Following Eleanor's vehicle, Matthew and Tom drove to Spinnakers together in silence.

They hit trouble without warning like a hull splintering on a rock. Matthew's stomach contracted when he saw that the electric gates were wide open, but at least everywhere was lit up. The security lamps over the front porch and garage floodlit the drive and Dorian's pickup was caught in the full beam of Eleanor's headlights. Matthew blamed himself; it would have been so easy for one of them to drive back in her vehicle. Having stopped the car, Eleanor was hopefully fumbling with the garage remote. Meanwhile, Dorian had flung open his car door.

Chapter Eleven

They jumped out of their car – although not as quickly as Dorian – and Matthew tapped on Eleanor's window while the garage door shuddered into action. 'Get inside,' he told her, as if they were in the middle of a storm, 'and we'll sort things out here for you.'

A crease formed between her eyebrows as she jerked the car forward and then glided into the integral garage. Matthew realised he should have told her to close the door, but it was too late for that. A freshly shaved Dorian approached, his hair scraped back into a man bun, looking well scrubbed: designer jeans, what appeared to be a brand new, blue cotton shirt and cream linen jacket. Eyeing him, Matthew also watched the house, while Tom and Dorian stood at right angles with their backs to it.

'Forcing her inside so I can't apologise? Is that your game?'

'You won't be seeing her tonight, I'm afraid,' replied Matthew, his mouth dry, although he was relieved that the garage door was clicking shut.

'She's had more than enough to contend with for one day,' added Tom.

'I think just one of us should deal with this,' urged Matthew, while Tom stared insolently at their foe.

Dorian shifted from one expensive tan leather shoe to the other. 'I've come to return what I owe her.'

'How can we get through to you?' asked Tom, his voice rising. 'We've done our best to make her rest, but that didn't stop her coming to the rehearsal. Now she's deadbeat. Surely this can wait until the morning? Just *leave*, if you know what's good for you.'

'She's had a shock,' said Matthew.

'I'm well aware of that. That's why I'm feeling so guilty. I can't rest 'til this is sorted out.' Dorian took out a crumpled envelope from his inside pocket and handed it to Matthew. 'I really came to apologise for bruising her with the wardrobe door, but I've since realised that she's overpaid me.' He paused. 'Given what's happened, I don't think it would be right to accept any of this.'

'Things will look different in the morning,' Matthew told him, trying not to sound tight-lipped.

'But I don't want to hold onto this any longer than I have to. I would hate her to go to bed thinking I'm a rat because I've taken her money.'

'Why didn't you post it through the letterbox, and make yourself scarce?' asked Tom, stepping forward.

'Tom, *please*,' said Matthew.

'Not with this amount of money,' said Dorian. 'Look, I never meant to strike her.'

'You should have thought of that beforehand,' said Tom. 'What right had you to start rifling through her wardrobes like that?'

Dorian advanced a step or two towards Tom They were about the same middling height, but Dorian had a meatier build. Tom swallowed and retreated a step.

'Listen, both of you,' said Dorian. 'I need to see her in private for just a few moments, and then I *promise* to leave you in peace.'

'She's far too tired to discuss anything now.' Matthew hesitated; he realised that they had not considered Eleanor's feelings in this. She had no idea what they were talking about, and would no doubt be pacing up and down, imagining the worst. 'Besides, I've told her not to let you in until things have calmed down. I'm just trying to do what's best for her.'

Dorian made his way over to his car as if he was leaving, then changed his mind and approached Matthew, his face tense. 'And what about Rupert? He has something over Eleanor and me now.'

Matthew smoothed the back of his head. 'I'll take care of that.'

Dorian scoffed. 'You're very closely involved with each other, aren't you?' A mature Japanese maple on the drive behind him suddenly detonated with small white bulbs that Eleanor must have switched on from the hall, and for a couple of seconds their attention was diverted. 'Fairy lights right on cue?' Dorian folded his arms. Things happened quickly. Tom let out an anguished yell, but although Matthew tried to restrain him, he broke free, squared his shoulders and rushed at Dorian with cannon-ball intent.

He stopped when the door flew open, and Eleanor, reminding Matthew of Mozart's Countess at the end of his opera, *Le Nozze di Figaro*, made an appearance at the top of the steps. The blaze of light behind her in the hall, and the brightly lit maple added to the theatrical intensity. Framed for a moment, she sprang down towards them with her coat flying open.

'Stop!' she cried. 'Stop that at once!'

Dorian, noticing her for the first time, turned to face her. She took him by the hand, started muttering, 'Darling, darling'. Dorian lifted her from the ground in his arms and treated her to a long, hard kiss. Eleanor's hands were all over his back. Matthew became aroused for all the wrong reasons.

'You need to hand over the remote, before you have to rush off,' said Tom, breaking the silence.

'Tom, is that really necessary?' asked Matthew.

Dorian, his mouth still clamped to Eleanor's, threw it on the ground with such force that Matthew thought it must be cracked. Tom muttered something, retrieved it, took out his mobile and glanced at the time. 'Come on, Matthew, it looks as if she can fend for herself.'

They were heading for their car when they heard the regal command. 'Wait!' Eleanor peeled herself away from Dorian. It was like witnessing an amoeba splitting. 'We can't possibly leave things like this, after what you've both done for me today.'

Matthew glanced at Tom anxiously as she turned towards the house and signalled that they should all follow her inside. Once in the kitchen, Matthew surreptitiously placed Dorian's envelope behind a lamp at the end of the breakfast bar.

As the tension evaporated the four of them found themselves grouped together as if nothing had happened, interrupting each other about the funniest moments of Rupert's surprise visit while Eleanor made drinks. 'I shall have to trust him to keep his mouth shut,' said Eleanor over hot chocolate.

'I'll take care of that,' said Matthew, taking in the unusually subdued Dorian and cupping his mug in his hands.

Tom shrugged. 'I'm not so sure. You know how Rupert relishes a good story. And we'll have to hope that the folks on that steamer don't do anything with the pictures on their mobiles.'

'Oh, I doubt I'll hear anything about that again,' said Eleanor with an airy wave of her hand.

Matthew raised an eyebrow. 'Tell me, what is your plan if Felicity and Martin should find out?'

She did not look at him, but she was clearly preparing one of those corny set-pieces she was prone to. 'I'll get over it, won't I? Like I always do. It won't be tomorrow, or the day after that, or even the next day, but I'll get there. The show must go on, and now that I've finally won back Lady Bracknell, I'm not going to lose her again!' Matthew remained unconvinced, but did not respond. They could not help returning to Rupert and the summer house until she cupped her chin in her hand. 'I can never thank you two enough, but now I'm exhausted, and if you'll excuse me...' She stole a look at Dorian, as if to say, *get rid of them.*

Matthew hoped that he had not said too much, but she appeared to have lost interest in him. There was an awkward moment when it became obvious that Dorian would be staying over, but Matthew did not think it was appropriate to question it, or see if Eleanor was happy with the situation. He bowed out with Tom, reflecting that she would have been far from reticent had she had any concerns, and they parted amicably.

Once they had driven onto the road, they waited for the gates to shudder to a standstill; Eleanor was back in her castle, with her handsome (youngish) prince. Silence in the car, at first, as they gathered their thoughts, but when Matthew felt it was safe – for Tom *had* been rather touchy that evening – they found themselves talking over each other. Neither of them could deny that the day's events had become a seemingly inexhaustible topic.

'How do you think *she* handled it?' asked Matthew, when they were nearly home.

'It's all very well playing at being hoity-toity, but not if she's heading for one of her breakdowns.'

'She's positively juggling.'

Tom chuckled. 'She's proved that she's mad keen on *him.*'

'Then she should concentrate on him, and stop scheming.'

'She doesn't have enough to think about, that's her trouble.'

'Maybe she does now.'

Back at Langdales, Tom fell asleep instantly, but Matthew found that he was beyond sleep, and his overcrowded head struggled with the spectre of James. The connection between him and Tom could no longer be ignored.

He could not help thinking that the boys were providing the sort of frisson required on stage between Jack and Gwendolen and Algernon and Cecily, but they had eyes only for each other, and this gave their time together on stage a vigour and sincerity that some of the other scenes lacked. Was Tom too receptive to James, too much in thrall to him?

Adjusting his pillow yet again, Matthew told himself that he could not permit himself to harbour any further suspicions. Rupert was constantly reprimanding them in rehearsal, but in spite of this, James had proceeded to make Tom corpse. On one legendary occasion, they had had no other option but to hug each other and stagger off stage, choking with laughter. Matthew himself had fidgeted, both as an observer and on stage, wondering if they were laughing at him, and could well imagine that Tom was growing frustrated with him as an older man, one who could neither compete with James's looks nor his youth. He finally dropped off, but woke feeling as if he had never been to sleep.

The next incident relating to their growing intimacy in Matthew's eyes came during Thursday's rehearsal, the final one before Sunday's technical rehearsal. During the break, and wanting to think things through, Matthew took himself off to where no one would find him in a hurry. He found himself sitting behind a screen surrounded by a jungle of hired parlour palms of varying sizes (careless of the expense, Rupert had over-ordered) that had arrived earlier than expected. He was still resting his eyes when he became aware of James and Tom chattering, and then sit down in front of the screen. Matthew knew that he should not remain, could have crept away unnoticed, but this was too good to miss. Meanwhile, they remained oblivious of his presence.

'Well, in that case, how about escaping tomorrow?' asked James.

Stationing himself behind that screen like a character in a Restoration comedy, Matthew tried to slow and silence his breathing.

'You make me sound like a prisoner, but it's impossible.'

'Why?' asked James. 'I thought you wanted to be friends.'

A pause. 'Not if it means sloping off behind Matthew's back.'

'Surely you're allowed to do separate things once in a while?'

'Depends what you have in mind.'

'How about lunch out?'

Tom chuckled half-heartedly. 'That's bound to be taken the wrong way.'

'Not if it's a pork pie on a park-bench.'

'Are you serious?'

James laughed. 'Surely you know me, by now?'

Another pause while Tom hesitated, presumably to think it over. 'We only have one departure tomorrow.'

'So what's the problem?'

Tom ignored this. 'Jane's place is out of the question.'

'How about the Birthwaite?'

Standing in its own grounds, the Birthwaite was one of the *grande dame* hotels that had become a household name to many Lake District visitors. A converted Victorian industrialist's villa, it was pricey, a trifle old-fashioned, and had been living somewhat insecurely on its reputation for several years, but it was firmly on the afternoon tea wish-list.

'The Birthwaite?'

'Crisp linen, great food, bouquets of flowers. What's not to enjoy?'

Tom sighed. 'I hate that expression.'

'It was meant well.'

'Look, on the odd occasion I've been, the service is incredibly slow and far too reverential.'

'When did you last go out for a celebration meal?'

'That's not the point.'

'Frowning spoils you.'

'Stop staring then.'

'The Birthwaite is still special,' said James, trying to gain ground.

'You're elevating lunch between friends way beyond ...'

'You like things done properly, and I would like it to be right.'

Tom's voice sounded strained. 'But won't it look like a date?'

'I want to go to a place where we can talk.'

'What's that supposed to mean?'

'Must you be like this?'

'I'm only being loyal to Matthew.'

In spite of finding his chair unyielding, Matthew smiled to himself.

'There'll be next to no one there on a Friday.'

'You lawyers are always so persuasive.'

'Goes with the territory.'

'Perhaps you can explain how you will square going out for longer than your lunch-hour?'

'I've no appointments, and I only have to sign my post.'

'As you're so intent on cementing friendships, why don't we invite Matthew and Rupert along?' asked Tom, adopting a chirpy manner.

'You don't *really* want them there.'

'Why not? You're going way too fast for me.'

James lowered his voice. 'You're happy there?'

'Of course,' replied Tom, too quickly. 'At least I thought I was.'

'Until I took the role you'd wanted so much for yourself?'

'Hardly, but you've thrown me off-balance.'

'Out of kilter, like *"The time is out of joint"*?'

Tom said nothing.

'Don't expect me to believe that you feel really fulfilled at Langdales?' asked James. 'It's a pretty unremarkable B and B.'

Matthew's stomach clenched; he felt like striking him.

'I like the garden ...'

'But what about all the things you don't like?'

'Everything used to be fine before you showed up.'

'You've not enjoyed rehearsing with me?'

Tom did not reply at first. 'My problem is that Matthew, my job, the roof over my head, even the car, are all connected, and I don't want a lunch out to give the impression that I am cooling off in any way.'

James became more insistent. 'You do realise that Matthew has his eye on Rupert?'

'Surely Rupert only has eyes for you?'

'I'm putting up so many obstacles that he can't figure me out.'

'So will you allow him to reach the finishing post?'

'Of course not.'

'Something mischievous – and not quite nice – about you, isn't there?'

'If you say so, but doesn't it strike you that Matthew would be better off with someone nearer his own age?'

'Matthew and I go back ten years,' said Tom, primly.

James scoffed. 'Forget it.'

'Doesn't Matthew have a say in all this?'

'Why can't you relax?'

'Because I don't like where this is leading.'

'You can't trust yourself, is that it?'

'Well, you needn't think I'm up for any funny business.' Tom sighed. 'To be honest, it would make a change to get out. It feels like a long time since we reopened in February. The guests seem to get more demanding, and Matthew's becoming too fond of his home-comforts. Between you and me, there's a lot going on behind the scenes that I'd rather keep to myself.'

'He's too old for you. I *knew* it!'

'You have a genius for reading things wrongly.' The conversation seemed to have dried up, until Tom said, 'But there's no denying that I'm ready for an audience. Come on, we don't want people gossiping.'

'Only because they've got nothing else to do,' muttered James.

Matthew tiptoed away, just as Tom was promising to text James his final decision.

The proposed lunch engagement was not touched upon that evening, but once they had completed the following morning's routine, Tom caught Matthew's eye. 'By the way, did I mention that I won't be in for lunch?'

Inwardly seething, Matthew adopted his curious but jovial face. 'Ah! Anybody we know?'

'James asked me to join him for a bite to eat.'

'I see.'

Tom was heading up to the attic flat, two stairs at a time, but stopped and turned to look at Matthew, who was on his heels. 'He feels he can't go back to La Boutique Fantasque just yet, and...'

'Doesn't he see enough of you during rehearsals?' asked Matthew, slightly breathless. 'It's just the two of you, I take it?'

'We weren't sure whether you'd want to come.' They were standing opposite each other in the bedroom. 'You had so much to say about the Birthwaite last time.'

'*The Birthwaite*? It would have been nice to be asked.'

'To give you the pleasure of turning it down?'

'Not if poster-boy is going to be sitting across the table.'

Tom removed his shirt and Matthew ran his eyes over his chest.

'Well, I'm sure you won't be missing anything.' Tom hesitated. 'Besides, you've been bleating so much lately that you never have enough time to yourself.'

Matthew set his face. '*Bleating?*' Turning his back while selecting a clean shirt, Tom did not reply. 'Of course, I've no objection to you going anywhere, Tom, but if you'd have let me know sooner, I could have organised something for myself. That never entered your head, I suppose?'

'I wasn't invited until the last minute.'

'Even so...'

Tom looked up from buttoning his shirt. 'Why don't you phone Rupert? He's *bound* to be free.'

His mocking tone rankled. Matthew struck his forehead. 'How stupid of me. Rupert's trying to make friends too, isn't he?'

'Well, who better than you to cosy up to?'

Matthew said nothing, but smiled to himself watching Tom making such a performance of combing his hair over his bald patch. Reaching for his jacket, Tom muttered a hasty goodbye.

As soon as the car engine grew fainter, Matthew called Rupert. Naturally, he was available. In the ten minutes or so it would take him to drive over, Matthew prepared some sandwiches to have at the kitchen table. If they went into another room, or out onto the terrace, Rupert might get the impression that he could stay all afternoon, and on this occasion Matthew favoured a quick fix, rather than an overdose. Rupert arrived sooner than expected, and soon had a glass of white burgundy in his hand while Matthew explained Tom's absence.

'You astonish me, dear boy,' said Rupert, theatrically wide-eyed, as he sat down at the table. 'Can James really be turning his attentions to Tom?'

Matthew shook his head. 'Tom's sudden yen for fine dining is beyond me.'

Rupert plunged his nose into the wine glass. 'Well, he's in the business, I suppose...'

'You should have seen him racing to get out, *and* wearing a jacket!'

Sniffing appreciatively, Rupert took a sip and ran the wine around his mouth. 'Well, it *is* one of the finest hotels in the area so they tell me.'

'He couldn't escape quickly enough.'

'Would *you* be late for a date with James?'

'Who said anything about it being a date?' asked Matthew, sitting down on Rupert's side of the table in an attempt to be pally.

'Not that you're in denial?'

'I'm not sure Tom actually *likes* him, although James does seem to have some sort of hold over him.'

Rupert smiled to himself as he lifted the glass to his lips again. 'He would not wish to be late for lunch *there*, so I wouldn't read too much into it. What have *I* been doing, did I hear you say?'

'Easy for you to be glib, but–'

'Listen, Matthew, do you really think that Tom would put you two under unnecessary strain right now?'

Matthew shrugged. 'There's a big difference between *wanting* to do something and being compelled to do it, because he's...'

Rupert raised his glass, as if for a delayed toast. 'In love?'

Matthew looked down. 'Smitten. Possibly.'

'Here's to youth! Wait until you've seen Tom's eyes crackle after seeing James. Then you'll know if he's in love.'

The back of Matthew's neck prickled as he glanced up. '*Crackle*?' he scoffed. 'It's as simple as that?'

'Like yours when you follow me around the room.'

Matthew gritted his teeth. 'I do *not*–'

'Joke, Matthew. But back to James and Tom. Apart from the incessant horsing around, which is *extremely* tiresome, they make life easier for me. In fact, they don't need me much now.'

'I've got the feeling that I might be made redundant, too.'

'Spare me the self-pity.'

'I'm convinced he's getting restless,' argued Matthew, 'and James is encouraging him. I'm no fool.'

Rupert grinned. 'Never mind – you've always got *me*.' With a sideways movement that almost knocked Matthew off his chair, Rupert lunged at him. Matthew recoiled instinctively. Rupert tried not to look put out as he straightened his clothes. 'You wouldn't have done that twenty-five years ago.'

'That was in another life. Please don't try that on again. Perhaps I've not made myself clear, but I'm worried.'

Rupert savoured another mouthful of wine. 'It sounds as if you have every right to be.'

'Thanks. James could break anyone's heart.'

Rupert pursed his lips. 'I wish he wasn't so attractive, young, and hot-blooded.'

'You wouldn't have him any other way. And to think that I was almost growing to tolerate him...'

Rupert chuckled. 'Nothing's actually happened between him and Tom, that's one thing I am sure of.'

'Until today?'

'I half-expected that James might be flirting with me by now.'

'You wouldn't find the age-gap easy, day in day out.'

'On the contrary, I would welcome it. He's so anxious to please.'

Matthew shook his head while topping up Rupert's glass. 'However nice he may be, it won't stop me lying awake half the night.'

Rupert seemed to be thinking this over while sipping his wine and nodding appreciatively. 'As Lady Bracknell puts it, *"the number of engagements that go on seems to be considerably above the proper average that statistics have laid down for our guidance."* Of course, we have not had any engagements yet, but it appears that James is unlikely to be defeated in his pursuit of pleasure.'

'Is that what you really believe will happen?'

'Yes and no, but if I were you, I'd be tempted to let it run its course.'

'Not sure I'm brave enough. I lack your experience.'

Rupert narrowed his eyes but managed a smile. *'Relax!* If there is something beyond a mild flirtation on James's side, I can't see it lasting.'

Matthew drew his brows together. 'How do you work that out?'

'These affairs during a production have a habit of tapering off.'

'Ah! And you of all people must know what you're talking about there.'

'I'm afraid so, but meanwhile, make a fuss of him.'

'What if – Heaven forbid – Tom takes the bait?'

'Hidden in the main course? Sure, he'll be feeling flattered – who wouldn't if James *is* sniffing round? But it'll burn itself out after a week on-stage. Familiarity so often breeds contempt.' Rupert glanced at Matthew's spacious, well-appointed kitchen. 'Besides, where else is he going to find someone like you, and Langdales, where he can live in comfort?'

Matthew was quick to question this. 'James looks set to do well in life, don't you think?'

'I'm not sure that Tom's very materialistic.'

'I think you'll find he is.'

Rupert steepled his hands. 'Let's look at the facts, shall we? Tom is thirty-five?'

'Correct.'

'It would appear he owes you everything? Not only are you his partner, but provide his livelihood, even the roof over his head.'

'That thought's keeping me going.' Matthew's stomach turned over. 'If he leaves, he risks losing everything. Who would jeopardise that?'

'On the other hand, you would not want him to feel trapped?' Matthew made no reply. 'If you insist on pursuing this line of thought, you must observe them in rehearsal.'

'I'm so busy watching that I'm frightened of missing an entrance!'

'I find you very difficult to deal with. Everything I suggest, you twist, but then you always have done.'

After that rebuff Matthew was ready to eat the sandwiches, and desirous of a change of subject, he steered the conversation towards other things until it was time for Rupert to leave.

After clearing the dishes, Matthew returned to the terrace and sat brooding. Recalling that lunge of Rupert's, it crossed his mind that Rupert might have told him that things would probably die off between Tom and James for a reason. It would influence Matthew to do as little as possible, and then if the situation between Tom and James did develop, Matthew would be available for Rupert to step back into his life. This remained his worst fear, if things with Tom did actually disintegrate.

His mobile rang; it was Eleanor. He braced himself.

'If I don't get out of this house soon,' she told him, 'I shall scream. Dorian's working somewhere else today, and I'm going mad with boredom.'

He found himself inviting her round for tea, if only for a second opinion about Tom. He was also half-hoping for some juicy development with Dorian. Determined to make the most of his time with her, he laid out what remained of their "Royal Gardens" china, but he had hardly finished when he heard her car door slam, as if she had been parked nearby. He hurried to open the front door; Eleanor disliked being kept waiting.

Sunglasses still in place, he noted, but the lines scoring between her nose and her mouth were deeper than yesterday, and her clothes hung loosely. She hadn't been eating enough, probably to keep herself trim for Dorian, and combined with her recent anxieties, she was looking gaunt rather than super-slim. To complete the picture, new shoes forced her to walk awkwardly, her hair had recently been restyled rather stiffly by the hairdresser, and her partially bruised face glowed with too much make-up.

The garden was looking impressive in the afternoon sunshine and the conditions for sitting out were unusually good. Tom had planted up the containers on the terrace in early May, and, when brushed against, there was the scent of lavender edging the terrace. Having shown her to a sun-lounger, Matthew returned to the kitchen, and seeing that she needed feeding up, he cut into a fruitcake that Tom had been allowing to mature. Returning, he placed the tray on a low table between them.

She dithered over the narrowest slice. 'Is Tom not joining us?' Matthew explained while easing himself onto his sun-lounger. She leaned back. 'He should be in the garden on a day like this.'

Matthew rubbed his forehead as he looked up at the leaves on the trees under a cloudless blue sky. 'As a matter of fact, he's been wondering whether we should offer light lunches *here*, so we're putting it down to research.'

'Really?' She eyed him. 'Then why didn't you both go?'

Feeling that they were getting off to a poor start, and that her curiosity might get the better of him, he longed to change the subject. 'We felt that there was more to be gained if just one of us went and really concentrated. He's reporting back with his findings, so hopefully you'll catch him then.'

'Lunch for one isn't much fun.' She nibbled her cake. 'What's going on, Matthew?' She stared insolently over the top of her sunglasses, waiting for an answer, while he poured the tea.

'Please don't tell a soul, Eleanor, but until a few days ago I'd have said that everything was normal, until –'

'Between you and me, I noticed *them* earlier, but didn't think anything of it.'

He swallowed. 'Who?'

'You know.' She removed her sunglasses. The bruise was hardly visible. 'I thought they must have bumped into each other. Although, I have to say, it did strike me as somewhat odd at the time.'

He held out the cup and saucer for her. 'What are you implying?'

'They looked radiantly happy.'

'Radiantly? Not like you to exaggerate? If you must know, Tom is having a bite to eat with James, but where's the harm in that?'

Eleanor shrugged. 'As long as they're not taking a bite out of each other.'

'Tact never was your strong point.'

'Didn't you say at first that Tom was doing research on his own?'

He found himself cringing under her stare. 'If you must know, they're having a sandwich.'

'No one goes there for a sandwich, Matthew. Besides, you'd never serve lunches on that scale. They have a different clientele.' She stared at him expectantly.

'The truth is, I didn't feel like going.'

'Ah, now we're getting somewhere.'

'Don't read too much into it. I still haven't recovered from that business with Dorian.' He glanced over to see if she found this unsettling. She did not. 'Why couldn't they have gone to a pub, where no one would be any the wiser?'

'But in the unlikely event that they *were* seen, no one would think twice about them lunching there.'

'Nonsense. It has first date written all over it.'

'I beg to differ. Lunch at the Birthwaite shrieks business, not romance.'

'You mean a cunning plan to avoid suspicion?' He mulled this over while sipping his tea.

'It's usually deserted at lunch-time in the summer, and probably the quietest place for miles. If they needed to be discreet, they couldn't have chosen better.'

Matthew would not let it go. 'You blew their cover quickly enough! Anyway, it was James's choice. Tom was invited.'

'You're joking?'

'That's something I am sure of. You see, I accidentally overheard them.'

She raised an eyebrow. 'Eavesdropping? Has it really come to that? James was setting out to impress, no doubt, and Tom was too polite to turn him down?'

'I don't think politeness comes into it.'

'You think James really is fooling around with Tom?' Still holding him in her gaze, she became conspiratorial. 'You realise the cast has noticed?'

He tried to ignore the dull ache within. 'Oh, don't think you can hurt me with that, because it gets worse. I caught Tom doing press-ups – or sit-ups, whatever you call them – and if that isn't the behaviour of someone trying to impress James, I don't know what is.'

'You jump to the oddest conclusions!'

'But he's never bothered before.'

'From the look of him, he doesn't need to.' She sipped her tea. 'You do realise that James is likely to be a partner in that firm? He has everything going for him.' Matthew could only respond with a sullen look. 'Would it put your mind at rest if I tackle Tom about James when he comes back?'

He groaned inwardly. 'Tactfully, of course?'

She grinned. 'Tactfully tackle? You can observe how he reacts, and it'll save you the embarrassment of having to enquire point-blank.'

Matthew leapt at this. 'Try not to register any emotion?'

She laughed. 'Just pretend you're on stage.'

'Like you with Dorian I expect, in the early days, not that one was privy to that?'

'He always smelt very manly, with overtones of spice.'

'Sounds like a bottle of Shiraz.'

'You don't seem to have much time for him.'

He closed his eyes for a moment. 'No one could say that he isn't presentable, but I never felt that he was *good* enough for you. It's not that I don't have time for him, it's just that I can't fathom him out.' She looked away. The silence was unnerving. 'For me, the summer house was his undoing.' Her (unusual) reluctance to respond was becoming unnerving. 'More to the point, what have you learned about him?'

A shadow crossed her face while she finished her cake. 'He did come with glowing references –'

'Which you failed to take up?'

Eleanor clattered her cup onto its saucer, placed it on the table and crushed the nearby lavender with her finger-tips. The scent wafted towards him. 'I took them for granted.' She rubbed her temples. 'Why would he go to the trouble of boning up on plants? If you had so many misgivings, you shouldn't have kept them to yourself.'

'I wasn't aware that I had. Besides, do you think you'd have listened?'

She thought for a moment. 'I try not to be influenced by others, as you know. What a pity that in your haste to put him down, you've conveniently omitted to remember he's returned that money.'

'Having seduced you first.'

Her face hardened as she struck the rickety garden table. The china wobbled, and Matthew grabbed his. Recalling the scenes they had played as husband and wife, he should have been better prepared. Eleanor had not moved since she had arrived, but now she rose, walked a few steps and turned to look down on him. 'Not that it's any of your business, but he didn't seduce me.' Feeling that she might be feeling his stare unnerving, he looked away. 'You don't have any idea what it's been like, do you? Dorian has triggered something within me that's hard to put into words. If only that meddling *fool* had not come snooping.'

'You're telling me that nothing has changed?'

'Before you continue to wield the hatchet, I'm well aware that it doesn't reflect well on me.'

'You mean seducing him or throwing him out?'

She shot him a look. 'Both, possibly.'

He could not resist wagging his finger at her. 'I did warn you about being impetuous.'

'Perhaps I *may* have acted hastily, but I've learned a lot.'

234

'Now I've heard everything.'

'Having thought it over, I don't want to get rid of him, and how could I, without exciting comment? It's May, and the gardening season is at its height. People will think I'm deranged.'

'That's just a cover. We all know that. They'd come to their own conclusion if they knew the full story.' Something about the set of Eleanor's face prevented him from elaborating further.

She raised her finger to her lips. 'Perhaps I should have mentioned this earlier.'

Matthew rolled his eyes. 'Not another development?'

'Two dozen red roses arrived this morning.'

'You actually counted them?'

'There's nothing quite like receiving flowers. It was usually a sensible houseplant from Julian.'

'Julian was too busy making money to succeed in all the niceties, whereas on the strength of a few flowers, Dorian has convinced you that you're the one?'

She folded her arms. 'Having had a husband who knew how to make money, maybe it's time for one who probably won't?'

His eyes widened. 'Or cannot? But surely you're not seriously considering marrying him?'

'Who knows? But I resent the way you have to undermine *everything*. When did you last send Tom any flowers, or a sensible houseplant for that matter?'

'We're not talking about Tom.'

'Only because, *my dear*, you steered us onto Dorian. Perhaps we should have been, seeing as things are clearly reaching critical pitch with James.' She glanced at him, as if registering how far she dare go. 'I never thought Tom would have the nerve to go on a date with James, right under your nose.'

Knowing that she had the better of him, his mouth tightened. 'I think that deserves an apology.'

'Have it your own way, but I'm seldom wrong.'

'Never wrong, in fact. But seriously, I'm frightened.'

Eleanor rarely wanted to have a meaningful conversation about anyone other than herself, and this had the immediate effect of pulling down the curtain. Her face had become a blank, she seemed to have no advice to impart, and this led him to believe that he had said enough. Yet the unspoken link between them was always there, even if it was sometimes hard to tap into. Although she had riled him, he rose and took her in his arms as if to indicate the subject was closed. Remembering a frisson of their old passion, he pressed her slight frame to his chest. They stayed locked together, until her lips began seeking his. He pulled away as if he had been electrocuted.

'Am I so ugly?' she enquired, over-reacting as usual.

'No, but there's a time and a place. Don't tell me you're still attracted?'

'Some things never leave you.'

'But you have Dorian now.'

'Quite.' Pause, while she glanced round, uncertainly. 'He's very inventive in bed – '

'Unlike me?'

She sighed. 'Sometimes I could live without him being so pleased with himself.'

'Hard to believe we meant so much to each other once.'

'For a singularly brief space of time.'

'Complete and utter infatuation. But we can never go back.'

'It's held us together though.'

'If you say so.'

'How can I put it? You've been a stable presence in my life.'

'Glad to hear it.'

She edged forward and gently touched her head against his. 'We mustn't ever lose that.'

'I have no intention – ' His stomach clenched when he heard a car on the drive. Matthew pushed Eleanor away as if she was contagious, and tried not to look errant.

A young and care-free Tom approached from around the corner of the house with a tread lighter than usual, and within moments they found themselves standing awkwardly and not knowing where to look. A gaudy bouquet of their least favourite flowers dangled by his side; it *was* late in the day, and perhaps there had not been a lot of choice. Struck by the brightness, if not the "crackling" in his eyes, Matthew stole a look at his watch in disbelief. It was almost four. Had they really lunched out, or downed a quick drink, before racing off to James's flat for an afternoon of uninhibited sexual gratification?

Still clutching the limply hanging flowers, Tom seemed to be sniffing out the frisson of wrongdoing. 'Have I missed something?'

'It's Dorian,' smiled Eleanor.

Tom appeared to be more confrontational than usual. 'Funny, but I don't see him here, so this confirms everything.'

'What on earth are you babbling about?' asked Matthew.

'I am *not* babbling. But I must tell you what a relief it's been escaping the intrigue for a couple of hours.'

'*Four*, to be exact.' Tom hesitated in case Matthew might divulge something juicy about Dorian, then handed over the flowers while pecking him on the cheek. 'Thank you. What have I done to deserve these?'

'An impulse buy. There was I, imagining you spending the afternoon practically in solitary confinement, but I couldn't have been more wrong.'

His tone was way too belligerent for Matthew's liking.

'You made your way back via Windermere, then? I hope you weren't *tempted* to pop into his place for a coffee?' Not wishing for a reply, Matthew turned his head and studied the kaleidoscope of colour in the garden.

'You're not to blame for having deserted him.' Eleanor sat down again and began checking her lipstick and hair in her hand-mirror.

Tom frowned.

'Can we tempt you with a morsel of your delicious cake?' asked Matthew to break the silence, while resuming his place next to her.

Tom waved away the idea dismissively. 'I don't suppose there's any tea left?'

'I'm afraid it's stewed.'

Eyes narrowing, Tom turned to her. 'So you've been here for some time?'

'Not long enough, it seems.' She glanced up from her reflection. 'How was it?'

'The Birthwaite?'

'So it *was* you,' she replied, as if it had been bothering her. 'I almost pulled over.'

His expression was hard to read. 'So it *was* your car I saw gliding past? Very slow service. I can't believe how long they took.'

'Although the time must have flown with James,' observed Matthew, drily.

'And how was he?' asked Eleanor.

Tom slid onto the lounger on the other side of her. 'He's the same as ever, thanks.'

She gave a throaty laugh. 'He looks very handsome without that beard.' Tom failed to respond. 'You persuaded him to shave it off?'

'He was going to anyway. For the play.'

'I hate it when Dorian has stubble. So rough when he kisses me, not that you would know anything about that.' Tom blushed and looked down, but then he would at that sort of remark. She pressed her fingers to her forehead. 'I ought to think about going. I can feel one of my bad heads coming on.'

'Can I get you anything?' asked Tom, rising, but she shook her head, as if this was something only she could remedy.

'Rest when you get home,' urged Matthew, hoping this might dislodge her, for he wanted to interrogate Tom on his own.

Eleanor smiled patiently, as if only she had the distinction of knowing how to ease it. 'I'll do my best. Thank you for the tea and such delicious cake.'

'Now, if there is anything that we can do, call us, even if it's in the middle of the night,' urged Matthew, while Tom smiled uncertainly.

She picked up her bag and hugged them. It was a tearful farewell on her part – she was still tired – but having seen her off via the side path they hurried back to the terrace, each eager to know what the other had been up to.

'So what was all that about?' asked Tom, palpably more relaxed now that they were alone.

'I was going to ask you the same,' said Matthew, collecting the tea things together on a tray.

Tom took in the adjacent border in the afternoon sunshine – the aquilegias had just started to go over, but the peonies were budding up – before turning to Matthew. 'Please don't spoil what's been a nice occasion for me.'

'Eleanor couldn't wait to announce that she had caught you unawares, looking *radiant*,' said Matthew, struggling to be diplomatic. Tom tried to laugh in disbelief, but fumbled it. 'I'm sorry, Tom, but I can't help thinking that this recent little performance with James has

238

been very ill-considered.' Tom crossed his arms. 'And, what's more, now that you've been spotted, she'll waste no time in broadcasting it.' Wary of saying too much, he stared at Tom.

'You're asking me to believe that Eleanor, anxious about Dorian, and stressed about the opening night – who isn't – will have the time or the inclination?' Tom floundered as if he was battling with the reality of the situation. 'Are you really suggesting she will be spreading tittle-tattle about *me*?'

Matthew tried to keep his tone measured. 'Surely even you must admit that it looks a trifle odd?'

Tom considered this. 'How long have we been together? You're the one who is behaving curiously.'

Matthew closed his eyes for a moment as if being very patient. 'Apparently, it's common knowledge, and has been for some time.'

'You don't really set any store by their gossip?'

Matthew eyed him. 'Not out of choice.'

'Didn't you once say that the cast needed to work as a team?'

'There *are* limits!'

'You seem to be implying that James and I shouldn't have made it up?'

'There must be a middle course between first detesting him and then falling head over heels.'

Tom's eyes darkened. 'That's a grave charge.'

'I only speak as I find.'

'You owe me an apology.'

Matthew, choked, and not recognising his own voice, struggled to make amends. 'You owe it to me to tell the truth.'

'Is this really about one lunch out?'

'You've seen how easy it was for Eleanor to melt under Dorian's influence?'

Tom tossed back his head. 'Please don't bracket me with *her*.' Then he tore into him. 'What exactly have I done? Have I ever lied to you?' Silence. 'You're implying I can't even go out for *lunch* with someone nearer my own age?' Matthew flinched. 'How do you think I felt when I saw you two together?'

'I was merely consoling her.'

Tom laughed, mirthlessly. 'Really? I thought it was bad enough witnessing the spectacle of you and Rupert, but this time you have excelled yourself.'

'I don't see how.'

'You now seem to be taking more interest than is appropriate in *that woman.*'

'If you've quite finished?' asked Matthew, hoarsely.

'How you have the audacity to accuse me of anything is beyond me. For all I know you're not only carrying on with Rupert, but Eleanor as well. Or has he been dropped?'

'Look, Tom, how can I get through to you? It's what most people would call comforting a friend.' Tom smiled insincerely back at him. Matthew continued, 'I suppose you've adopted this way of thinking because she's still agonising over whether Dorian is in fact the right man for her?'

'Eleanor's never *agonised* over anything in her life – apart from a leading role – but I don't mind telling you that it looked as if there was more to it than that,' said Tom, becoming louder and breathing hard. 'So stop giving me a hard time about James, because I *will* be seeing him again, if only to get some respite from *you* and *this place.*' He swept up the tray and headed for the back door, head held high.

'*Tom!*' Matthew called after him, but he did not even slow down. Bruised though he was, Matthew could not help but admire his exit. However, he was left in danger of throwing up as he anticipated the prospect of James and Tom laughing, joking and making eyes at each other during the forthcoming technical rehearsals.

Act Three

Chapter Twelve

Not surprisingly, nothing more was said on the subject of Tom's lunch out. Later, faced with the unwanted dregs of a bottle of red (not as silky as Matthew had hoped) after dinner on the Saturday evening, Matthew was tormenting himself about the dressing rooms. In the end, rather than let the latest silence of many gather weight, he decided to broach the subject.

'I think this making jokes whenever you're with James has gone far enough, don't you?'

'No, because I haven't laughed so much in years.'

'I had hoped that the dressing rooms might have been allocated differently.'

Tom stopped fidgeting with his place-mat and looked up. 'Remarkable how you refuse to leave me alone, isn't it? If you remember it wasn't *my* choice.' Matthew made no comment. 'I'd be interested to hear what exactly is wrong with sharing a dressing room with James, except for the obvious one?'

'Which is?'

'You're clearly put out that I was chosen over you.'

Matthew's eyes met Tom's. 'Can I say something without you getting defensive?'

'Depends.'

'Your body language on stage leaves a lot to be desired.'

Tom glanced sideways as he ran his hand through his hair. 'Have you never heard of on-stage chemistry?'

'But your eyes follow him around the whole time.'

'They do not, but yours do with Rupert. Presumably you're oblivious to the whispering?'

Matthew felt his stomach turn over. 'All I'm trying to say is that things seem to be getting out of control with you and James.'

'I've been subjected,' said Tom, slightly pompously, 'not only to seeing you and Rupert holding hands, but witnessing you and Eleanor pulling away after an embrace, but I'm supposed to let those minor details pass?'

'Never mind that. I don't want you to get hurt.'

'Hurt? When James and I get on so well?'

'You know what I'm talking about. Besides, you weren't exactly keen at first.'

Tom sipped his wine a little too quickly and his eyes flickered over Matthew's face as he put down his glass. 'We're just having fun.'

'You expect me to believe that?'

Tom's tone changed. 'Are you calling me a liar?'

He heard himself becoming louder. 'Have you any idea what you're doing to me?'

'No,' replied Tom, spacing out his words, as if addressing a child, 'because – nothing – *is* – happening. He may be good-looking, but he's trouble, and I would not touch him.'

Feeling that he was losing ground, Matthew leaned forward. 'How do you explain that you're different when you're around him?'

Tom's head jerked towards him. 'In what way?'

'More attentive, for one thing. Anxious to please. Often getting a little too close. Smiling more. Need I go on?'

'What's wrong with being livelier than usual, in company? We all do it.' He paused. 'Wasn't it you who originally suggested that I join the festival to make friends?'

'Friends not lovers.'

'Take that back.'

'I don't see why I should, do you? Not only will you have to get changed in front of each other, there's the shower in the en-suite to consider.'

Tom laughed in his face. ' *"The shower to consider..."* How would you feel if I made a fuss about you sharing with Archie?'

'Never mind about Archie,' said Matthew, slowly and patiently, although feeing he was losing even more control. 'Archie is sixty, bald, and inclined to corpulence. James is – well, you don't need me to tell you that.'

'He's probably the most beautiful man I've ever set eyes on, but that doesn't mean to say I've fallen in love.' Tom raised his voice. 'Thank goodness *you're* not sharing with James.'

'What's that supposed to mean?'

Looking him straight in the eye, Tom smirked. 'It's no secret you're fond of younger men. Isn't that where I came in? But let's get back back to you and Rupert. It's pretty obvious that he's been occupying your thoughts for some time.'

Matthew recoiled. 'I suppose that's James talking?'

There was a pause, during which neither would look at the other. 'Would it help if I switched dressing rooms?' asked Tom. 'Because – believe me – I'd do anything to keep the peace, although that's a forlorn hope these days.'

'It will only give rise to *more* speculation...' Matthew stopped. 'And it won't make me any the less furious with Rupert.'

'I bet he still fancies James, and can't bear the idea of *you* sharing a dressing room with him, so he chose me. He couldn't very well put the leading man in with Archie, could he?'

'I hadn't thought of that.' Matthew pondered this. 'But you agree you do have a connection with him?'

Tom stood up as if the subject was closed. 'Please don't push me any further, Matthew.'

Matthew started. 'What do you mean by that?'

Tom left the room without replying, while Matthew reflected that he'd probably said enough, and the atmosphere remained strained for the rest of the evening.

Apart from Rupert, who had told Matthew that he still harboured ambitions to play Lady Bracknell, those involved were optimistic about the festival, especially as everything indicated that they would have a good show on their hands. The week before the opening night on the Saturday was traditionally the hardest. It was the first time that the cast would play on stage, and everyone was steeling themselves. The plan was to hold the technical rehearsals on the Monday and Tuesday evenings. Technical rehearsals were invariably slow, and they were boring for the cast, who had little to do but stand in various positions and be lit, or work in tandem with sound-cues. These would be followed by three dress rehearsals on Wednesday, Thursday and Friday.

It was uncharacteristically warm for the time of year, and the Monday of the first technical rehearsal was humid; the air stiffened as the day progressed. Both Matthew and Tom would flare up without provocation, and it was soon apparent that the week of rehearsals could not be over quickly enough. Weary after an unfulfilling day, and impatient to get it over with, they set off, with Matthew's stomach continuing to turn over at the thought of Tom and James not only alone together, but out of sight.

James, Tom, Eleanor, Jane and Archie had been called for the opening scenes. They disappeared into their separate dressing rooms, those four ground-floor bedrooms in the wing closest to the ballroom, with Tom's next door to Matthew's. Hearing the occasional burst of laughter did not help, and when Matthew picked up on their muffled voices, his mind began to wander, and not in a particularly good direction. At some point, James would be strutting into the en-suite shower and when he emerged – flesh beaded – Tom would be shooting him admiring glances.

When Matthew knocked on their dressing room door, he was startled to find that it swung open to the touch. Nothing to hide, then. Tom was dressed, but James – towel draped on bare shoulders – was still putting on his make-up in front of the mirror. Disappointed at not having caught them doing anything, Matthew found himself gazing at James's eyes in the reflection. They were cold and expressionless, and he realised how swiftly he had become unwelcome. The tense, hostile atmosphere and their blank faces made it clear – to Matthew, at any rate – that they had no wish to be intruded upon.

In time, James condescended to take a good look at Matthew. 'Please don't expect us to entertain you. We'll be needed on-stage soon.'

Disappointed that James could not find it in him to be a little less ungracious, Matthew turned away, his eyes searching the room, but the bed was pristine and served as a reminder that his suspicions appeared groundless. A fraction – which he tried to suppress – of him realised that a crumpled bed was no proof of anything, but his anxieties and fears were conspiring to rob him of reason. He glanced at his watch.

'I think I'll see if I can watch the first act from the back.'

James turned to Tom. 'Didn't Rupert say he did not want anyone to show their faces out front tonight?'

Matthew stood with his arms dangling in the silence. Attempting to make a dignified exit, he made his way to the door with as much nonchalance as he could muster, but brightened when he turned round and noticed that Tom was smiling. Their eyes sought each other fleetingly, and for a moment it appeared as if nothing had altered between them. It astonished him how even a small shard of encouragement could be uplifting.

Yet once he was back in his own dressing room he felt sick. Unable to ignore the guffaws coming from behind the wall, he could not get out of his dressing room fast enough and walked briskly to the ballroom with a renewed sense of purpose. Slipping into the darkened auditorium with its drawn curtains, an Anglepoise lamp shone on Rupert at his table, five rows back, highlighting his golden hair. Matthew slid into the chair beside him. He liked what he saw: the set was lavish. Rupert had clearly had his own way on this as well. Still smarting about the dressing rooms, he could not resist whispering, 'I don't think I've been able to thank you properly for putting Tom and James in the same room.'

'Listen, I have enough to think about without your heavy sarcasm, so don't start,' hissed Rupert.

Matthew refused to let it go. 'If you did it to spite me, you've succeeded.'

Rupert looked put out. 'It wouldn't have been appropriate for someone older to share with James.'

'He's not a minor.'

'No, but he's temptation on a stick. Look, I'm in no mood for this, Matthew, so if you wouldn't mind shutting up, I'd be grateful. Besides, no one in the cast is supposed to be out front tonight.'

Determined to stay, Matthew quietened down and remained seated, for spying on James and Tom had become something of an obsession. As he had anticipated, it was a long, repetitive evening and Matthew was more than ready to go home by the end, especially as they had run late. Archie was soon washed and changed to be in time for his night shift at the Queens. Matthew was also quick to get changed and waited for Tom to come to him as they had arranged, but all he could hear was someone thumping the wall intermittently. It was insistent enough to make it impossible to ignore. When he could contain himself no longer he gathered his things together, and rapped his knuckles on their door. Gripping the door-handle, he hesitated when he heard James laughing so much that he could hardly say come in.

They were practically naked. Brandishing rolled-up towels, they were hitting each other – seemingly in jest – and must have struck the wall by accident from time to time, if one of them missed. The provocative undertow prevented Matthew from edging into the room. Tom, wearing the guilty expression that so often follows delirious and illicit enjoyment, was looking ashen. To cover his embarrassment, he reached for his shirt. James – his heaving chest spangled with sweat – pulled on his trousers out of decency. Matthew told Tom he would wait for him in the car, but having closed the door he heard James howling with laughter.

While Matthew was driving them home, Tom apologised.

'It's not what you think.'

'Not again! Please don't carry on as if I'm some kind of fool. I certainly saw more than I needed to of James preparing for his so-called fun.'

Tom chuckled. 'Yes, he has nothing to be ashamed of, does he?'

'I didn't look,' lied Matthew, struggling to concentrate on the driving. 'I'd like to see how long you'd survive on your own.'

Tom turned to peer at him in the fading light. 'No, you wouldn't. But I shan't *be* on my own, according to you.'

'The fact remains that I dread to think what might have happened if I had not come blundering in. He was patently aroused.'

'You realise that you're over-reacting to a game?'

'Is that what you call it? Well, we'll see about that.'

'What's that supposed to mean?'

'Forget it.'

Matthew would live to regret this discussion. At the time, however, he realised there was no point in pursuing the conversation so soon after he had discovered them. Back at Langdales, they were forced to talk to each other while doing the nightly check. They were in the habit of making sure that everything was in place for the following morning's breakfast, but once that was over, they kept to themselves while turning in for the night, and there was none of the usual cheerful chatter about the day's events.

Things continued to unravel next day. They only spoke when they had to, and spent most of the time avoiding each other. It was another humid day – difficult for making beds and hoovering – and it sucked the life out of them both. Once they had finished their morning's work, Tom fled outside and dragged one of the sun-loungers under an oak tree, while Matthew retired to bed, still stinging about what he had witnessed, and firmly of the belief that the attraction between them was mutual.

Unable to stop brooding, he eventually got up and stumbled out into the white, hazy afternoon light, found Tom had dozed off and muttered something about needing to make one or two errands. Tom sat up and blinked, but Matthew was making his way to the car before he could respond. He spent the short journey mapping out what he was going to say and by the time he drew up outside Rupert's cottage, he had calmed down.

Rubbing his eyes, Rupert looked as if he, too, had just woken up. 'Your timing's a bit out,' he grumbled, but showed Matthew into the kitchen.

Matthew put his elbows on the table and cradled his head in his hands. 'I don't suppose this will take long.'

'Tea?' asked Rupert in his artificially bright voice. Matthew shook his head while Rupert peered into the empty biscuit barrel. 'What seems to be the trouble?'

'It's them again.'

'Oh, that. I don't suppose you've any proof?'

'Only horsing around in the dressing room.'

Rupert raised an eyebrow and threw him a cheeky look. 'Like stallions, I presume? My dear, that positively brims with innuendo.'

Matthew went on to describe the full horror of the incident. Sitting down opposite and leaning forward, Rupert remained silent throughout, so Matthew finished by asking, 'What made you do it?'

'What difference does sharing a dressing room make? It's a bit much if actors of the same sex can't share–'

'Shut up will you – because I'm not sure whether to bring matters to a head.'

Rupert stared open-mouthed. 'Not in the week before we open, *please*.'

'Tom has a strange look about him, as if he has almost reached flash-point. He could up sticks at any moment.'

'We all say things we don't mean from time to time.'

'But what's to become of *me*?' asked Matthew, his voice thickening.

Rupert searched his face and smiled suggestively. 'I'm sure it won't come to that, but have you never thought about looking for someone your own age?'

Matthew was in no mood for this and ignited quickly. 'Never! Since we split up, I don't *want* someone my age.'

'I still think that we could have made a go of it,' said Rupert, wistfully. Matthew shook his head; he could not imagine living under the same roof with him. 'Will you promise me something, Matthew? Please wait until we've got the festival out of the way before you do *anything*. Try and let it blow over.'

'*Blow over?* It's already *spiralling* out of control.'

'Calm down, Matthew.'

'How can I when he's become so exceedingly touchy that we're unable to talk anything through?'

'You're probably reading far too much into it.'

'This is torture.' To alight on a new topic Matthew wondered if this was the moment to ask a question that had long been bothering him, although whatever answer he received would no doubt fail to put his mind at rest. 'Can I ask you something?'

Rupert was rising from the table, and sat down again. 'Yes? What is it?'

'I haven't liked to mention it, but...' He faltered for a moment. 'I was interested to hear that you had become a father.'

'What's your drift?'

'You have a son. I don't.'

'You have Tom, which is practically the same thing.'

'If only. I'm sorry, but it intrigues me, that's all.'

Rupert stared at him as if he was off his head. 'Why?'

Matthew grinned. 'Well, I did wonder how you had the time.'

'Procreation doesn't take long, in case you didn't know,' said Rupert, airily.

'It really isn't any of my business...'

'No.'

Matthew waited to see if he volunteered anything. 'But when did you last see him?'

Rupert withdrew instantly, and instead of being his usual loquacious self, became tight-lipped. 'Some time ago. Why?'

'Have you a photograph?'

Rupert half-smiled. 'Caroline was sent some pictures on his twenty-first, but he's not as good-looking as I was in my heyday.'

Matthew decided to humour him. 'So you said, but how could he be?' There was a pause. 'How would you feel if you found him again?'

'*Found!*' cried Rupert. 'I love that line! Well, I'd welcome him back, naturally.'

He glanced at his watch. 'That's good to hear. Any news from France?'

'I've not had much time to think about my father, or that potentially sinister carer. My dear, it's all so macabre.'

'Listen, I'd better go,' said Matthew, making for the door. 'I've said too much as it is.'

Rupert made a wry face. Driving home, Matthew had plenty of opportunity to think and he gained some equilibrium on finding that Tom appeared thoroughly refreshed after his afternoon rest, and more his usual self. So much so, that he was almost convinced that things were better between them. Perhaps he had been overthinking things. Maybe it would burn itself out and all be over sooner than he could have wished. After an early dinner they left for the second technical.

During the break, Matthew followed James and Tom backstage with the intention of having a positive discussion, and was about to knock when he overheard the muffled sound of James talking seriously but quietly to Tom. There was none of the high-spirited but irritating laughter. Occasionally, there was a silence. Although their door was never locked, Matthew tried not to visualise them squeezed together in an embrace. It did not occur to him that they could have finished a topic of conversation, or were changing. Heart thumping, he thought it best to creep away. He trembled to think that he may overhear something *not* to his advantage, or worse still, be caught by them, or Eleanor, who might suddenly appear when he least expected it. Concerned, in case he should be further rattled by their antics, he pressed himself against the back of his door and found he was breathing heavily.

Archie looked up from his detective story. 'That's rather a good pose. Why don't you save it for when you're on?'

Matthew could not bring himself to reply, only smiled and half-listened to him while he got ready for the third act. It went well, although he could hardly bear to look at James and Tom whenever they were on stage together. Once the rehearsal had staggered to its conclusion, and Rupert had finished giving out notes, Matthew disappeared into his dressing room to change and waited impatiently for Tom to join him and go home.

In the dusky anonymity of the vehicle, he stole a look at Tom, who was driving. Why could he not leave things alone?

'You and James seemed in excellent spirits,' he found himself saying.

Tom gripped the wheel, concentrated on the road and looked steely. 'Is that something else that is wrong?'

'No, unless you had set out to achieve the distinction of flirting openly with each other, both on and off-stage.'

Tom changed colour but did not respond. They spent the rest of the journey in silence.

Once they were back home, they made a hot drink and sat down opposite each other at the kitchen table. There seemed to be an unspoken mutual understanding that it was time to talk things over, rather than aim to bring one another down with inflammatory and caustic remarks. Matthew's mind was made up, but he remained unsure as to how to pitch what he needed to say without upsetting Tom more than he had done already.

'I'm sorry to harp on, but you and James seem to be getting closer and closer.'

'I hope you've not been taken in by common gossip,' said Tom, too glibly for Matthew's liking.

'It's just that I feel left out.'

'I hate to hear you say things like that because there's no foundation for it. You wanted me to forgive James for taking the lead, which I *have* done–'

'Over-zealously, if you ask me.'

'I wasn't,' said Tom. 'It seems that although we're good friends and playing well together on stage, that's not right either.'

'I'm not the only person who has noticed.' Matthew struggled for the appropriate words. 'You know how much I care about you, but if you insist on brazening it out, I cannot go on.'

'Brazening what out? I don't know what you're talking about.'

'It seems that you can hardly bear to look at me.'

Tom gave him a quick sideways look. 'Is that better?' Trying not to look fazed, Matthew said nothing. 'I think the time has come to settle this, once and for all.'

'Sounds ominous. Did *he* put you up to this?' asked Matthew.

'I cannot, and will not defend myself against your unjust allegations.'

'And why not, I wonder?'

'Because you're being perfectly idiotic.'

'Don't hold back whatever you do.'

'I have no intention of doing, because I may have come up with a solution that might help us.'

'You think I need *help*, do you? What on earth are you going on about?'

'Good question, but that's not for me to say, but it's something that might keep the peace.'

Feeling a weight lifting, Matthew continued in a calmer vein, 'Sorry. I shouldn't have snapped. What did you have in mind?'

'I was thinking about a few nights apart,' said Tom, calmly.

'*What?*'

'It might be the only way, at least until we've got through the dress rehearsals, and possibly the first night.'

'Are you out of your mind? Leave me at home on my own?'

'It's not such a daft idea,' persisted Tom, in a quieter tone. 'It won't be forever.'

'But to stalk off now, when things are so delicate between us?'

'I'd like to get to the first night in *one* piece.'

Matthew flared up again. 'If your mind's made up, why not remain apart through the *entire* festival?'

Tom looked away. 'Because we might have become strangers by then.'

'Why come back then? I suppose you've cooked this up under *his* influence?'

'Far from it. I'm merely reacting to you.'

'I've heard him working on you. I know what he's like.'

Tom looked him in the eye. 'When exactly?'

Matthew's cheeks burned. 'Never mind, but with all due respect, a hasty departure conveniently leaves the way open for you to stay with him, or hadn't that occurred to you?'

'With all that's going on with the play?'

'What other reason could you have for leaving now?'

'It's quite simple.' Tom puffed out his cheeks, and placed his hands behind his head. The atmosphere calmed further. 'I can't prance about on stage, remember my lines, even make a stab at acting convincingly, with all this going on.'

'It's not the National Theatre,' grumbled Matthew. Slowly and deliberately, even though his voice was shaky, he added, 'I'm sorry, but I'm not going to play into your hands.'

Tom grabbed his mobile, as if that was the end of it. 'If that's the support I'm getting, I'll go tonight.'

'You'll do no such thing,' said Matthew, fearful that the situation was escalating out of control. Putting on as much charm as he could muster, he tried to retract. 'On the other hand, a couple of days apart may not be a bad idea, as long as it doesn't go on too long.'

'In case you can't cope with all the menial work?'

'I shall ignore that. Any idea where you might be staying?'

'Is that likely?' asked Tom. 'When I've just come up with the idea? A B&B I suppose.'

'Why not the Birthwaite?' Matthew set his face. 'You must have been turning it over in your mind.' Tom shook his head. 'Look, it will kill me to do it, but I don't mind phoning Eleanor for you. She and I go back such a long way, she's sure to want to help out – '

'I've noticed. And Spinnakers does have five bedrooms, not that I could care less.'

'Alternatively, there's that spare room at Rupert's?'

'Thanks all the same, but I have no desire to fall into his clutches.'

Determined to bring things to a head, Matthew reached for his phone, but couldn't get hold of it. Shaking his head, Tom handed it to him. Eleanor picked up immediately, and Matthew began to babble.

Looking murderous, and without a word, Tom left the room, closing the door behind him.

'This is very sudden?' was not quite the response he had been hoping for.

'It's been building up for some time and he needs a bed–'

'What, in our house?'

The last thing he needed was her sounding like Lady Macbeth. 'It isn't as if you don't have a room.'

'Not when I'm trying to take my relationship with Dorian onto another level, surely?'

'You don't mean you're going to marry that self-satisfied creep?'

'That, my dear Matthew, was unnecessary.'

Knowing he would pay for that, he tried to find a fresh angle. 'We put Rupert and his sister up for the night, or have you forgotten?'

'Normally, I'd have been glad to help.'

'I'm worried that he'll beat a path to James's door, and I'm offering him a way out.'

She held the pause long enough for him to feel uncomfortable before making it clear she refused to help. 'But you – of all people – know what it would entail having another person around. Besides, I'm not sure I feel well enough yet.'

He thanked her as sincerely as he was able to, and rang off. Ignoring Tom's negative response to staying with Rupert, he contacted him. 'Listen, I'm having a spot of bother with Tom, and he was wondering–' He swallowed. 'Your spare room is still vacant?'

'Oh, no! You're not catching me out like that,' replied Rupert. 'Much as I like Tom, do you think I'm going to leave myself open to the inevitable gossip?'

Matthew tried to remonstrate, but ended up thanking him for nothing, and ended the call. He thought hard before calling Tom back into the room.

When Tom was finally enticed to return to the kitchen, Matthew felt his heart flutter. From the look in his eyes, he might be having second thoughts.

'Neither Eleanor nor Rupert show any desire to help, so you'll need to look for a B and B, after all. I can help you with that, but I do wish you hadn't got us into this mess. Now they have it confirmed that we've reached crisis pitch, tongues will be wagging even more than they are already.'

Tom bowed his head, and then raised his eyes. 'When did we have the time? I've either been working or rehearsing.'

'Something happened when you were changing. Your eyes were shining too much.'

Tom bit his lip. 'I still don't understand how my so-called behaviour with James is any different from yours with Rupert?'

'Let's leave Rupert out of this for now, shall we?' Matthew paused. 'If the decision has been made, do you agree that it would be best if you left in the morning?'

Tom hesitated, as if registering this new predicament for the first time. 'But there's so much at stake. Not only would I be losing you–'

Matthew still had an urge to hug him. 'I know. This is your home and workplace, too.'

'Not only that, I've no vehicle.' Tom's eyes darted from side to side. 'But never mind me, have you given any thought as to how you'll cope?'

Matthew's voice became unsteady. 'I'm sure – if asked – that Archie will be happy to pick up where he left off.' (Up to this point, the day-to-day running of Langdales had not been discussed.)

Tom's eyes grew rounder. 'You have it all worked out, obviously? I feel as though I'm unwittingly playing into *your* hands. You're not *really* expecting me to come back, are you? Well, I can assure you that I won't be going anywhere *near* James.' He chuckled. 'So, as well as having Archie lined up to work, you haven't got Rupert waiting in the wings, as well?'

Matthew was in no mood for this. 'Look, it might be better if you sleep in the spare room tonight. I, for one, don't want to lie awake half the night discussing it. We both have a long day tomorrow.'

Tom opened his mouth, seemed to think better of it and headed upstairs in order to transfer what he needed to the spare room. Matthew lay awake half the night.

It was already warm and sunny at seven o'clock, when Matthew crept into the spare room to rouse Tom. Matthew's tender feelings for him surged when he paused to stare at his handsome face in repose. Tom, however, was clearly in no mood for a reconciliation, and did not take long to be up and dressed. The two men were soon padding about the kitchen in silence.

Matthew could not wait for the torment to be over, and it showed, for he was irritable with everything. Tom, however, must have decided that he might as well start the first day of his new life on a sure footing, and grilled himself a hearty breakfast. Out of politeness, he asked Matthew if he would also like a grill. Unable to concentrate with his head full of Tom's feelings and needs, Matthew turned down the offer. He sat down, nibbled on his toast and marmalade and contented himself with the occasional glance at Tom.

Tom must have grown aware of this for it did not take him long to ask, 'Have you thought about how we're going to behave to each other in front of the cast?'

'Mutual indifference?' He smiled, anxiously. 'No, just carry on as normal.'

Tom's brow furrowed. 'What's normal?'

Anxious that he might say too much, for his take on the situation had altered since their talk the night before, Matthew made coffee and pretended not to notice the look in Tom's eyes. He was now congratulating himself on how he was handling the situation, with no insight as to whether he may have overreacted to what might or might not have happened with James.

With nothing further to occupy him before the guests descended, Matthew disappeared into the sitting room, ostensibly to read the paper, but the minutes of waiting seemed interminable. While listening out for Tom, he was unable to concentrate, repeatedly staring at the same paragraph until he heard him carting his bag downstairs, as if simply visiting his parents. When Tom came in and stood next to him, he glanced up from the front page.

'I'm ready.' He half-smiled, although it looked more like a gash across his face.

Matthew shifted his position. 'I hope things work out for you today.'

'What about tomorrow?' Tom's voice was thin and sounded far away.

It was at this point that Matthew almost broke down. 'I'll be thinking of you every day until I die, you fool.'

'Remember it's just for a few days.'

'So you keep saying.'

'No hard feelings?'

'Of course not,' replied Matthew, his voice quivering while he tried to ignore the lump in his throat. 'I think it might be better if you see yourself out, don't you? We wouldn't want our guests witnessing an emotional scene.'

'I'll be back soon enough, so let's not get too heavy about it.' Tom shifted his weight from one leg to another. He kept glancing out of the window.

'That depends on whether you really want to or not.'

'I can't just *disappear*.'

Matthew's face lengthened, but he felt they had to go through with it, before either of them cracked. 'Who knows? Some time apart might do us good.' His assumed breeziness struck a false note probably because he was about to lose control. They found themselves smiling at each other uneasily so it came as something of a relief when Tom started to head for the door. Matthew half-rose from his chair.

'Do you remember that time we had the power cut?' asked Tom, stopping in the middle of the room and making a valiant effort to sound cheerful.

Matthew sat down heavily. 'And you had the dining room looking like an altar?'

Eyes glistening, Tom nodded. 'And what about that time you were photographing me with no shirt on, scything the bank, and that couple showed up early?'

'They couldn't work out the relationship.' Matthew could not trust himself to speak for much longer. 'The garden's looking better than it did ten years ago, at any rate.' Tom swallowed and nodded. 'I appreciate everything you've done.'

Tom was blinking. 'And I'll always be grateful for what you've done for me.' He edged closer, and rested a hand on his shoulder. His voice sounded strangulated. 'If it's all the same to you, I don't think I'm ready for this. I can't leave you with a house full of guests.'

'Nonsense. The decision has been made. You've heard of that phrase: when it's time to leave the stage, get off?' Matthew leaned back in the armchair and placed his hand on Tom's. 'We've both agreed that it would be wise to keep our heads clear for the play.' He tried to smile. 'Can you imagine trying to act in this state?'

'Although our present worries will only be replaced by a raft of new ones if I do go.'

'You may have a point.'

'But I *will* be coming back.'

'To collect the rest of your stuff?'

Tom looked heavenwards, but in a nice way, like in the old days. 'No, to live here, you idiot!'

'Of course,' said Matthew, swallowing. 'Foolish of me, but I still have no idea how long you're going for, and neither do you I expect. What with the rehearsals and – I suppose the run will have to be included, after all – the next ten days or so will be over before we know it.'

'This still feels unreal.'

Matthew felt the tears welling up. 'And now all we're fit for is a good cry.' His voice dwindled as he choked them back. 'I think you'd better get yourself off, don't you? You have a busy day ahead.'

Tom removed his hand. 'I know you'll be turning it over in your mind, so I want you to remember that I've been telling the truth about James.'

'I'm sorry.'

'Don't tell me you're apologising?'

'Not exactly. I meant to say that – so far – everything points to him having designs on you, and – as we all know – you're not averse to the attention,' said Matthew in a voice not his own.

'I have to disagree with you there. Flattered maybe, but he's not a very lovable person.'

'Perhaps we'll see things more clearly once we've got the play out of the way?'

'We?'

By now, Matthew had lost any ability to elaborate further and looked away. His head was pounding. Tom gave him one last look, swung round and bolted. Matthew listened for the front door closing and resisted the temptation to look out of the window. The front door was never locked when they were in residence, so Matthew waited for Tom to make a sudden reappearance, as surely he must. With not a floorboard creaking from their guests upstairs, he found the silence hard to bear.

Listening out for sounds of a vehicle, Matthew was wondering if he had overreacted, when Tom burst back in and stood by his chair. Spirits soaring, Matthew's heart seemed to miss a beat. Tom's voice was husky. 'I'm afraid I haven't come back to insist you have a proper breakfast. I don't suppose there's any chance of a lift?'

Matthew had to be firm, but was in danger of breaking down again. 'Who's going to take over breakfast? Why don't you just ring for a taxi? Here, let me give you some money for the fare.'

'That won't be necessary. It's just that – with so much on my mind – I forgot to ring, and I don't have the number on my phone.'

'Do you even know where you're going yet?'

'Not exactly.'

'And you're sure you're all right for money?'

'Of course.'

'Because if there's anything I can do – '

'Don't.' Tom glanced at him quickly, and then looked away again. 'You know you were my future, don't you?'

'I could say that you were mine.'

Matthew could no longer speak, had great difficulty keeping his stomach under control, and was grateful that he hadn't eaten a full grill.

Tom nodded briskly, closed the door quietly, and went to make what might well be his final telephone call from Langdales. This time he disappeared outside without popping his head around the door. Minutes later, Matthew heard the taxi pull up on the gravel. The front door finally clicked shut, a car door slammed. He sprang out of his armchair and watched the car drive away slowly, until he dissolved and reached for his handkerchief. It was not even eight o'clock. In less than an hour, they had wiped away a decade.

The blood seemed to drain out of him. He began to question their relationship more thoroughly, but trying to think things through was not easy. If it was not right now, would it ever be so again? A remembrance of things past with Rupert interrupted his fractured thoughts. He wished that they did not, but he had to face reality. If life with Tom was over, might anything be salvaged with Rupert? It would not be easy; they were too opposite for that. Yet if the spark they once had could be re-ignited, Matthew wondered if he would have the strength of mind to turn his back on Rupert should he be available?

His mind was so disassociated from Langdales that when he heard a guest on the stairs it gave him a start. He struggled out of his chair and rearranged his face.

Matthew had taken an instant dislike to these guests from the moment he saw the huge vehicles come pounding along the track, all black paint and tinted windows: a group of friends, with three loud husbands showing off to their bored wives. There had been some ill-suppressed sniggering when Matthew and Tom greeted them, no doubt coming over strongly as the "perfect" gay hosts, and no one appeared convinced when Matthew apologised for Tom's sudden absence due to his parents' ill health.

Breakfast was something of a nightmare. Not only was he out of practice, but all six wanted their eggs done in different ways. Matthew hoped that they could not smell the burnt toast and opened the windows. Co-ordination had never been his strong point and he did not get any of the orders correct; he must have looked so flustered that nothing was said – to his face at any rate – although he was aware of muffled giggles on leaving the room. As breakfast proceeded they delighted in sending him back for manuka honey, more berries, croissants and wholemeal rolls, unsalted butter, no doubt with the intention of catching him out.

Once they had left the dining room even more rowdily than they had entered it, he laboriously cleared the table, hung around for them to go out, and went up to tidy the rooms. He took his time: lingering over the manual labour for its potential therapeutic effect. When he could no longer spin this out, Langdales felt subdued, not to say desolate, and he returned to his favourite armchair in the window. Yet all he could visualise was the spectre of Tom, stripped to the waist, working in the adjacent border.

Matthew switched his gaze to the Beatrix Potter figurines, but they soon became a blur. Letting his mind wander back to earlier partings of the ways with previous partners, hadn't he just dusted himself off, and wasn't he going to do exactly that all over again? Only this time, he realised that it was going to take a great deal longer.

Once more, his thoughts reverted to Rupert; he came to think of him more seriously as a possible lifeline, an escape route from the loneliness that was staring at him. He knew only too well that

Cumbria, with its sparse population, was never going to be an easy county in which to stumble upon a life-partner. Frowning, as he crushed this unwelcome prospect, he began to find the room claustrophobic, undid a shirt button and shot out into the fresh air.

Not exactly day-dreaming, he lingered on the terrace for too long, gradually noticing how long the shoots from the climbers had grown. It was as if Langdales was being strangled. He glanced at the lawn, and looked away just as quickly. It had needed mowing for some time, but he had simply ignored it. How he had imagined that he could survive without extra help was beyond him.

Emotionally, it was too soon to venture into the garden without wanting to weep, for every other plant had a connection with Tom. He returned inside and sank into the same armchair. And then the tears began to spill down his cheeks again. After several minutes of this, he finally pulled himself together, and on the basis that the fresh air might do him some good, forced himself to go for a stroll to see if he could make it towards the end of the garden without breaking down again.

Filling his lungs, and slowly feeling brighter, he caught the scent of a honeysuckle. There was nothing to say that his future was not loaded with possibilities; after all, he was only fifty. At least he had some time left, should he have to start a new life without Tom. He was quite a way down the garden and lost in thought, when he became dimly aware that his phone was ringing, as if in another room. He had not expected Tom to be begging to return so soon, but it was Rupert. Although this was the last thing Matthew needed, he decided to take the call.

'Good morning, dear boy,' drawled Rupert. 'Just a courtesy call to check that you've managed to sort things out with Tom?'

Matthew could not speak for at least half a minute, and he used the time to make his way back to the terrace and rest his legs, before they gave way. 'As it happens, there was no need,' he replied in a constrained voice.

Rupert's tone took on a honeyed quality. 'You're sounding very evasive. I hope you mean you've patched things up?'

'Not quite.'

'But you were under strict instructions not to – '

'He's left me.'

'Why didn't you stand in his way?' There was no answer to this. 'Did he go of his own free will?'

'One question at a time, please. Let me put it this way: I didn't have to force him to go.'

'But you can be quite persuasive, so why weren't you? I can't believe you've let Squirrel fend for himself in the outside world. Well, I just hope it's some sort of mid-life crisis on your part. But what about *my* festival?'

Matthew wished that he were not so insistent. 'It's to help us to *get through* the damned festival that we're doing this.'

Rupert turned to sarcasm. 'You mean ending a perfectly good relationship will keep your heads clear?'

'He's only gone for a few days, so don't make too much of it.'

'He'll be back soon enough,' said Rupert, with conviction. 'If only for his ornaments.'

Despite Rupert's flippancy, Matthew's mind-set shifted again and he found himself mentally changing the sheets and placing some garden flowers on Tom's side of the bed.

Rupert tutted. 'So where's he gone, or daren't I ask?'

'I have no idea, but hopefully to a B and B. There *are* plenty.'

'You allowed him to go just like that?'

'It was his idea.'

'And it's been your fanciful notion that James has been bedding him?'

'This isn't very helpful, Rupert.'

'I can't help that. You need to face facts. Hasn't his life been totally bound up with yours?'

Matthew did not like the way this was going. 'Your point being?'

'Langdales is in your name, I take it?'

'Yes – at least that's safe.'

Rupert harrumphed. 'You have been paying him a proper wage?'

Matthew kept the emotion out of his voice. 'We were a couple. He ate here; he slept under my roof; he had free use of the car.'

Rupert was relentless. 'Holidays? Meals out?'

'I paid for those, naturally. Frankly, I think I've been pretty generous.'

Rupert continued in terrier mode. 'Did you consider that when you banished him?'

'I did *not* banish him! He left of his own free will, I tell you, and it's only supposed to be for a couple of weeks at most. Maybe not even that.'

'You've blown it, Matthew. Would *you* lose face and slink back after the way you've treated him?'

'So when did I get to play the villain? He was the one making eyes at James.'

'Excuse me,' said Rupert, 'but wasn't it the other way round? James is nothing but a flirt, and should not be taken seriously.'

'That's not how I see it, and that uncharitable little thought doesn't seem to have prevented you from ogling him.' He was not going to be bullied by the likes of Rupert. 'Have you finished now, because I'm not sure what business this is of yours.'

Rupert did not spare him. 'You're damned right it's not, but I'm going to make it my business, because I happen to like Tom.'

'Not you, as well?'

'Not in that way, silly. Look, I want him to succeed in my play.'

'Which is why you refused to allow him to play Jack?'

'If you'll let me finish? He is no longer young, and we both know how that feels. He is even showing the odd grey hair. You can't let him wander off and airbrush a dozen years away.'

'Ten.'

Rupert let him have it. 'He has every right to go for half! You're in too deep this time, Matthew. You can't dissolve things as quickly as you did with me. Nothing's that simple any longer.'

'Whatever happened to "possession is nine-tenths of the law"?' bleated Matthew, wishing he was anywhere but on that terrace.

'Totally irrelevant, dear boy.'

This time Matthew snapped; he had heard enough. 'Please don't start that "dear boy" nonsense again, you patronising little prick.'

Silence, and then an edge to Rupert's voice. 'You *owe* him, Matthew, and the law is on his side. I'll be only too happy to check the facts with James, if you'd like me to.'

'*Are you mad?* We don't want *him* knowing what has to remain private. But I was already occupying the house, and it's not like I've asked him to put up any money of his own.'

'Perhaps because he doesn't *have* any money of his own?'

'And, therefore, Langdales will always remain mine.'

'You mean *half of it.*'

Ignoring the insidious creep of unease, Matthew asked sharply, 'How do you work that out?'

'You once had the cheek to ask Caroline and I if we had a power of attorney for father.'

'I fail to see the relevance?'

'Did you two never think to get a cohabitation agreement?'

This hit home. 'What do you think?'

'The simple answer to that is if the law wasn't on his side, you owe it to him anyway, Matthew. And there's no way you can run that place without Tom's...'

'Well?'

'I was going to say Tom's little touches, but that sounds a trifle mean-spirited.'

'Never stopped you before.'

'In that case, left to your own devices,' said Rupert, 'don't you think that Langdales would be even stuffier?' Matthew focussed on the nearest border. 'One last time – do you have enough to buy him out?' Matthew remained silent. 'Presumably you can't or *won't* answer that?'

Matthew could hear the doorbell so he wound up the call and dashed through the French windows. Checking that he was presentable in the hall mirror, but startled at how drawn he looked, he peered through the front door's stained glass and cringed. He had not fully opened it, when a forest of flowers and greenery supported by a apir of shapely legs, practically knocked him off-balance and sped past him.

Chapter Thirteen

'I thought *these* might *divert* you from feeling sorry for yourself,' Eleanor informed him on her way to the kitchen. Matthew nodded and sidled in behind her. 'Dorian's idea, so I can't take any credit!'

While selecting a vase from the cupboard, he was ashamed that he was welling up. Not only was he touched by Dorian's thoughtfulness, he began to experience a sea-change in his feelings towards him. Here was someone exhibiting few signs of the self-absorption that not only he himself was guilty of, but surrounded by; a potential friend who existed outside the circle of cast members more than likely to blame him and not Tom.

'Isn't it too early for long-stemmed roses?' he asked, having bitten back the tears, but admiring the tasteful combination of creamy white flowers among the greenery.

'I had to buy those.'

Matthew grinned. 'With *"ready money"*?'

Eleanor seemed in no mood to start sharing jokes and said, peremptorily, 'Dorian has a lot of sympathy with you two, although I can't imagine why.' She smiled and winked at him. 'And so have I, to a certain extent, although I could do with shaking the pair of you.' Silence. 'So, how long do you propose to continue with this state of affairs?'

Deciding to ignore that, Matthew half-filled the vase with water, covered the granite with old newspaper and began to separate the flowers from the foliage. 'Do I take it that you and Dorian are fully back together?' From her slight fidgeting, he sensed that she might not be. 'In that case, have you given any thought as to what kind of life is in store for you?' Eleanor seemed overly curious to see through the kitchen window and peered out. 'Dorian must be at least ten years younger.'

'He's thirty-nine.'

'That probably means forty-three. Whatever, it's still quite an age difference.'

'What about you two?'

Matthew was using his measuring eye on the flowering stems, especially the rose blooms; it seemed a shame to slice off the bases. He decided to venture a difficult question. 'Dare I ask what plans you have for him once the festival is over?'

'I know you want to talk about Dorian, but I'm going to head you off. I came over here with the express intention of talking some sense into you.'

Matthew's voice thickened. 'Tom would have loved these, and known exactly what to do with them.'

She edged closer. 'You've not heard?'

A pit formed in the base of his stomach. 'Don't tell me he's done anything foolish?'

Looking him in the eye her voice became constrained, as if she was wary of saying too much. 'No, but he's in a state. Feels as if he has no one to turn to.'

'You have a thorough grasp of the situation, no doubt?' he asked, loftily.

Her expression altered, and not for the better. 'Well, tell me, just who the hell else is there, Matthew? I've had it up to here. To hear him grousing about you makes me realise he's little more than a kid. You have a lot to answer for.'

Foxed by the change in tone, Matthew sighed, especially as Rupert had remarked that Tom was no longer young. 'Why is that my fault? No, don't answer that.' Not daring to look at her, he discovered some florists' scissors in a drawer and tentatively re-cut the stems, muttering, 'His idea of a few days apart suggests a collision course. To me, at any rate.'

'I'm surprised that he was the instigator. Is he testing you?'

'What am I going to do? I need him.' His face was contorted.

Eleanor clutched his arm tightly. 'You need to stop this nonsense at once.'

Just when he was hoping she would desist, she gripped him harder; he pulled away and raised his hand to his forehead with a mocking gesture. 'Why didn't I think of that? Anyway, it was his idea, as I'm tired of repeating.'

'You excel at shifting the blame, but have you ever considered why it came from him first?'

Anxious to draw her visit to a close, he was thrusting all the foliage into the vase, but the stems refused to stand up and flopped in different directions. 'You do know they were practically showering together?'

She laughed out loud. 'Come off it.'

Tutting, Matthew tried to jab in a rose. 'Hate to ask you of all people, but I don't suppose you know where he got to?'

She looked askance at him. 'You've allowed him to wander off without knowing where?'

He shrugged. 'Only because you refused to help. Anyway, he's a grown man. I can't very well keep him here under duress.'

'So you've let him slip away. You're not going to like this, but the last I heard he was plucking up courage to sound out James.'

'I knew it!' he cried. 'If he stays there just one hour, I'm through with him. And – this time – he needn't think there will be any second chances–'

'Oh, do shut up and calm down. I explained why I wasn't up to taking him in as a lodger, so give him a chance. From what I could gather, he wants nothing more than for it to be two blokes flat-sharing.'

'*Blokes flat-sharing?*' Matthew spluttered.

'Until he finds somewhere to rent.'

'James won't be able to keep his hands off Tom in that set-up.'

'But presumably not vice-versa?'

'It's all fitting into place, just as I expected.' He snatched up another rose, but seemed at a loss what to do with it.

She went a trifle pale. 'I hope you're not suggesting that Tom's testing out James as a potential partner?'

He turned to face her. 'Lover? You *are* aware that it's a one-bedroom flat?' He was struggling to squeeze any rose into a plethora of greenery, and began talking to himself more than to Eleanor. 'Although where he gets the idea that trying to stay at James's will be less stressful than remaining here, I cannot imagine.'

'Don't let your thoughts run away. He's not stayed the night yet. Are you aware there's also a bed-settee in the living room? And where else could Tom go? While the festival's on, his parents are too far away.' She smirked. 'Or perhaps you might have preferred him to have fallen into Rupert's comforting clutches?'

'That's not funny, or even likely. I called him after I called you, *actually*, but he wouldn't hear of it.' He accidentally cut the choicest flowering rose stem in half, and started to break down.

'He may have more sense than I've given him credit for. Here, let me do that,' said Eleanor, pushing him out of the way and starting again with her usual well-honed flair.

Unable to extract it at first, Matthew finally yanked his handkerchief from his pocket, and retreated to the table, where he sat and watched.

'I don't think James was quite ready for this dramatic turn of events, so I feel a little leeway from you is required,' she declared after a few moments, while stepping back to admire her handiwork. Satisfied, she proceeded to march into the hall holding out the vase well in front, as if various bugs were planning to descend on her.

'You don't think it would benefit from a lightness of touch that some gypsophila or fern might lend it?' he asked.

This was met with a steely glance. So close to the front door, Matthew prayed that she would take herself off, but as there seemed to be no sign of budging her, he felt obliged to throw open the door to the sitting room instead.

'Coffee?' he found himself asking in a rather high voice.

She glanced at her watch before settling in his favourite armchair, and shook her head. 'I've promised Tom I'd treat him to lunch. We're going to the Birthwaite! And I'm going to tell him *exactly* what I think.'

His mouth felt as if it was filling with sand. 'As someone who is never wrong, what *do* you think?'

'That he should return. Sooner, rather than later. You don't want him out of here for long; you may never get him back. No, I'm sorry, Matthew, but I really must be going.' Yet she made no move, merely clutched the chair by its arms.

Stomach still rioting, he perched on the sofa and went into his familiar head-in-hands position. 'Who says I want him back if he's been living with James?'

The famous eye-brow arched. 'Soiled goods? He hasn't done anything and I doubt that he will, but he's biting his nails over whether he's acted wisely leaving your beautiful home.' She glanced around the room approvingly.

'Leaving *me* might sound nicer?'

'In some ways, it's helped him not to be under the same roof as *you*.'

Matthew could hardly believe it, and squinted at her through his fingers. 'You've cast me as the villain?'

'Not entirely, but it always takes two to fall out.'

'Not necessarily.'

She evidently did not care for the way this was going. 'At any rate, you both deserve full marks for putting the festival first.'

'Didn't get us far, did it?' He hated any mention of the festival now. 'Seeing as you know so much, what's he going to do?'

'None of us is going to let him starve,' she replied. 'Each and every one of us can find him some work for a few hours in the week, which will tide him over until he returns here.'

'Us?'

'You know: the gang. Me, Jane, Clare, Felicity, perhaps even Dorian.' She checked her watch. 'There was one other thing.'

'Yes?'

'What's the situation with Rupert?'

'The situation?'

'I thought–'

'Perhaps you ought to stop overthinking.'

'Surely he's been playing Tom's understudy for too long?'

'I'm not with you.'

'Unspoken longing for you?'

'Tom only left this morning, and I'm pleased to announce that Rupert shows no indication of moving in, and I doubt if he ever will.'

'That was hours ago. I wouldn't want you to get any funny ideas, because if you *do*, that really will finish things with Tom.'

Matthew's mouth tightened, and he stood up. 'I don't want to beg, but can you see your way to putting Tom up?'

Eleanor shifted her position and glanced out at the garden. 'Those peonies ought to have been staked by now. It's not that I don't *want* to help...'

'Sorry to labour the point again but I'm desperate. We did put Rupert up in January for *you*.'

'How could I forget?'

'It was much against our better judgement, but we did come to your rescue.'

'Yes, all right.' She smiled nervously, glancing at her watch. 'But how many times do I have to stress that I'm feverishly trying to establish a new *modus operandi* with Dorian? I'm practically hoarse.'

'*Please*, Eleanor.'

'A third person will alter the dynamics, even someone as noble as Tom.' From her frown lines, she seemed to be determining on the best course of action. She stood up and faced him. 'Very well. I *will* check with Dorian. If he's agreeable, I'll sound Tom out. Sorry, but I must fly. It's not every day I can treat a handsome man fifteen years my junior to lunch.'

'I would have thought you were quite well-practised by now?' Jovially, she put her finger to her lips. 'Please don't let me keep you, Eleanor, but don't forget that I can't bear the idea of James taking in Tom.'

'You should have thought of that.'

He managed to edge her to the front door, and she climbed into her vehicle in a flutter of air kisses. With little inclination to do anything else, Matthew laboured up the stairs and threw himself on their bed, which seemed to have grown so much that he felt dwarfed. Soon curled into a ball, he accustomed himself to the idea that he might have been irrational.

His friends had been right; he had acted both ignorantly and idiotically, and if he was not careful he would lose face. After turning the matter over for longer than necessary, he was left with a single aim: to atone. After all, he had not only let Rupert down all those years ago, he was guilty of wrecking another young man's life. Determined to carry out this newly forged ambition before he changed his mind, he fixed his eyes on a particular corner of the roof-space. A low door opened onto an area of flat leaded roof suspended above the master bedroom's turret window.

It was windy and he took a moment to steady himself. Leaning over the parapet, he peered down. The terrace swam beneath him. Recognising that his new resolve was the best course of action, he was tempted to go through with it. Swallowing hard, and fighting the tears, he wasted several minutes struggling to establish some kind of closure in his head. Finally, determined to see things through to their natural conclusion, and gripping the stone until his fingers ached, he gingerly eased one leg over the parapet. Feeling his foot dangling, he let it sway; it was exhilarating to feel no resistance. Feeling partially weightless, his troubles seemed to drift away in the wind. Closing his eyes, he took a couple of breaths, and was set to tumble, when common sense prevailed.

All he could think of was a confused jumble of Tom, Rupert and maybe James reacting wildly to the news, and slowly he retracted his leg. Enjoying the wind on his cheeks, he opened his eyes – as if his sight had been returned – to enjoy the vista beyond the tree tops. He pulled back, and having regained some self-control, missed his footing, but ducked under the doorway in time and stumbled back inside. No matter how much they tried to bring him down, he would not end it this way.

The Wednesday dress rehearsal began shakily, primarily because it appeared that the camaraderie between James and Tom had finally disintegrated. Moreover, Tom's eyes were red. James's mind was clearly elsewhere. Eleanor compensated by increasing the volume, and the number of mannerisms she could squeeze into a scene multiplied. She was clearly struggling and Matthew watched her seeking out Rupert in the darkness and playing all her lines to him. Much to the amusement of anybody watching, except Rupert, Archie tried to exit through a window rather than through the double doors. Only Jane seemed to be her normal self.

When it came to the second act, the strain between Matthew, Tom and James became evident when they were together, and by the time they had completed it, Rupert had his eyes firmly closed. He gave a few desultory notes – irritably – before storming into Matthew's dressing room, and asking Archie if he wouldn't mind leaving them together for a few moments.

'You've *ruined* my hard work,' he began. 'Torn apart my rehearsal with black looks, and I won't have it. *Demand* that they sort themselves out, will you?'

'Why is it always me?'

'Because I'll probably say *far* too much.'

Once Rupert had banged the door behind him, Matthew tore into the neighbouring dressing room. Facing away from each other, James was scowling at his reflection, Tom was sitting on the bed studying the vile patterned carpet. He glanced up, but looked away again swiftly.

'Rupert is furious with you both,' Matthew began. 'But he's too beside himself to tell you himself.'

This did not create the stir that Matthew had intended.

'You mean he's scared and he has to send his boyfriend in?' enquired James, smiling wryly.

Matthew was about to erupt but Tom got in first. 'That's enough, James.' Tom glanced at Matthew. 'Could I have a word afterwards?'

James neither spoke nor looked at him again, so having agreed to Tom's request, Matthew closed the door gently behind him. The third act was marginally better. Even so, it was something of a relief when the curtains jerked across the stage. Seeing that everyone's eyelids were sagging, Rupert gave out his notes quickly, finishing with, 'I don't believe that any of you can feel deservedly proud of your efforts.'

The cast slunk back to their dressing rooms. Archie was removing his make-up in the en-suite, and Matthew was removing his in the bedroom when there was a knock, so quiet that he almost did not hear it.

Tom crept in, his head bowed. 'I must say something before I go home.'

'Home? Where's that exactly?' asked Matthew.

'Don't mind me,' chirped Archie, from the en-suite.

Matthew smiled as if nothing was untoward, closed the door and returned to his chair. 'Well, what is it?'

'I'm not sure that this has been the best idea I've ever had,' replied Tom. Matthew waited. Standing behind him, Tom gazed at Matthew's reflection. 'I've been looking for work, but there's nothing that grabs me.'

'You can hardly blame me for that.'

'Who said anything about blame? The point is, I used to get so tired – the early starts, the late finishes – and I've got out of the habit.' Tom hesitated. 'I sometimes wonder if I'm too old.'

'Nonsense,' said Matthew, folding his arms. 'Maybe you're out of practice, after such an easy time of it at Langdales?'

Tom half-smiled. 'I'd work in one of the better hotels, but they keep their staff.'

'Why not have a shot at the Birthwaite, regardless?' Had he become work-shy regarding hotel work, and was he accepting Matthew as a meal-ticket? He stared at Tom's reflection, could feel the anger building inside him, and decided to take the upper hand. 'I'm perplexed. Are you indicating that you wish to return because you can't find suitable alternative employment?' This did not come out quite as he had planned however, and he bit his lip.

'Not exactly.'

'I thought this was a temporary situation to save the production, but here you are, going on about long-term career prospects?'

'I just don't know any more, Matthew. Maybe I've been subjected to too much.'

The sharp, distinctive rap on the door spared Tom from being subjected to any more tactless observations.

'Ah! You're decent,' observed Eleanor, throwing open the door.

Tom glanced at her despondently. 'Matthew used to be.'

'Hurry up, my boy.' She ran her eyes over Matthew. 'He's coming back with me.'

'What happened?' asked Matthew, trying to thank her with his eyes.

'I felt I had to pitch in, so I had a long discussion with Dorian. He *is* happy for Tom to stay, as long as he doesn't make a nuisance of himself and it's not for long.'

'Oh well, if Dorian's happy...' said Matthew, stung.

'Makes me sound like a dog,' muttered Tom.

Tom said goodbye before padding out behind Eleanor and leaving Matthew dreading the night ahead as he drove home. He spent most of it tossing and turning, rose sullenly to prepare breakfast and sat glowering in the kitchen, waiting for his guests to descend. Fortunately, he had no departures in the middle of the week. Yet, *unfortunately*, Archie had no availability to help out at Langdales, which convinced Matthew that he was being boycotted.

Should he have discussed the situation with Tom more thoroughly? He pondered the situation they had allowed themselves to fall into. Maybe James *had* been leading Tom on, after all, just as he had done with Jane, and had simply been looking for another conquest.

This form of self-indulgence, to anyone else, perhaps older and lacking his sex drive, would have come over as meaningless.

It troubled him to think how Tom would be able to cope financially, and where he would end up living. Slowly, Matthew began to feel that he had neither given Tom a fair trial, nor allowed him enough time to defend himself. His head bursting with conflicting thoughts, he resolved to visit Tom before he cooled off the idea, accepting that it might prove hard to get him on his own with Eleanor – and no doubt Dorian – lurking in the background. Inevitably, they would both be overflowing with hindsight. At a more basic level, he would be curious to discover how things were turning out under Eleanor's no doubt quickly assumed beatific gaze, and Dorian's presumably newfound paternalistic qualities.

By the time Matthew drew up outside Spinnakers, he had fully convinced himself that he had acted hastily and was feeling so upbeat that he was prepared to make things up. He leaned out of the window to press the buzzer to alert Eleanor. The gates swung back slowly, in the grand manner, while Matthew drummed on the steering wheel. Dorian's pickup was parked on the other side of the double garage. He was in two minds as to whether this was a good sign or not.

Eleanor came to the front door in person – it was something of a relief that Dorian had not yet been cast in the role of manservant – and showed him into the kitchen where a cosy scene awaited. Tom seemed already very much at home, enthusing – of all things, at this time of crisis – to Dorian, about the short stories of Oscar Wilde. Matthew made a mental note to re-read them. The customary greetings over, it seemed clear that Dorian was not intending to budge, so Matthew joined them. Although his insides were shrivelling, he came to the point quickly.

'I'd like to apologise for not helping you out last night Tom, but Eleanor seems to have stepped in very competently.'

Tom glanced up. 'I'm very grateful, but I still have no immediate future worth discussing.'

'That's why I've come. The door is still very much open. Why not come back with me now, while we still have the day ahead of us?'

'About time,' chorused Eleanor and Dorian, as if in performance.

'After what I've been through, I'm nowhere near ready, but thanks.'

Feeling uneasy with Eleanor and Dorian goggling at him, Matthew searched for a change of subject, but it was Dorian who came to the rescue by turning his attention back to Tom. 'Eleanor tells me you're at something of a loose end?'

Tom switched his gaze from Matthew to Dorian. 'Yes, this is the second day of the rest of my life.'

'Looks as if there's some explaining to do, Matthew?' asked Eleanor, clearly giving him the opportunity to develop his argument.

'That's what I came to see you about, Tom,' said Matthew, feeling as if he needed to steady himself. 'I've been thinking...'

'Isn't it a bit late?'

Matthew cleared his throat. 'I may have overreacted.'

'That wasn't the impression you gave yesterday.'

'That was yesterday.'

Tom's eyes widened. 'Very mercurial all of a sudden, aren't we? Well, let me tell you that you're not the only one who's been thinking. I know you'll be having trouble running the B&B on your own, but I have no intention of returning yet. I'm sorry, but I need to get through the festival.'

'It's too soon, if you ask me,' said Dorian.

'I wasn't,' said Matthew, feeling outnumbered.

'As I was saying,' said Dorian, 'I know you've got plenty of gardening experience and...'

Seeming to take pleasure in ignoring Matthew, Tom smiled and placed his hands on the table. 'What did you have in mind?'

'There are always more lawns and hedges than I can cope with, and you seem to know what you're doing.'

'Perhaps I could discuss this with you in more detail later on? I could be interested, although I'd like to finish by four, and I don't do winters.'

'I'll take myself off then,' said Matthew, feeling unsteady as he rose from the table. When Tom stood up, Matthew grabbed him by the arm and hugged him, no doubt for the last time. Although Eleanor had been watching his every move, she did not come running after him as he had expected.

Back at Langdales, Matthew was tidying the bedrooms, and wishing he would never have to do it again as long as he lived. His aim not to have permanent housekeeping staff had been misguided, especially at times like this, but his goal had always been to save so as to enjoy early retirement with Tom. Denied the pleasure of having Tom at his side – or Archie, for that matter – meant that he could not delegate the tasks he most disliked. Relief from the tedium came when his mobile rang.

'I wonder if you can help out?' asked Rupert, in familiar wheedling tones. 'Tom has requested to go in with Archie, as he thinks sharing with James isn't appropriate.'

'What brought that on?' asked Matthew, intrigued and almost thrilled to have a diversion.

'Actually, he can't *bear* the idea of sharing with James for a moment longer than he has to.'

'Because?'

'There's been a falling out. James is not keen on your scheme for a trial separation.'

'It wasn't my idea in the first place.'

'I thought you'd be pleased they've cooled off?'

Matthew merely sighed.

'Tom obviously can't share a dressing room with *you*, and I can't ask the leading man to move, so *you'll* have to go in with James. You've really made a mess of this, haven't you?'

'*Me?*' roared Matthew. 'What a pity you meddled with the dressing room allocations, when it was none of your business.'

'But I made it my business, didn't I?' With that, he ended the call.

Partly because of being manipulated, Matthew was out of sorts for the rest of the day. He arrived at the rehearsal earlier than usual to switch dressing rooms – for it seemed that he had been presented with a fait accompli – as did Tom, but when they passed each other in the corridor carrying armfuls of clothes Tom stopped.

'You and me...'

Matthew's heart raced. 'Yes?'

'We're the ones who should be sharing,' he whispered. Matthew smiled. There was hope; Tom was speaking. 'I'm glad you came round.'

'How did it go?'

'With Dorian? The job's mine, if I want it, but I've reiterated I can't do winters.'

'Too old for that as well? But what will you do?'

'Something more congenial is bound to turn up, especially in the run up to Christmas, then maybe I'll go abroad...'

'Not with *James*?'

Out of the corner of his eye, Matthew noticed Eleanor approaching. Feeling that she was about to wave her index finger at him, he fled. Glancing around the dressing room that had been thrust upon him, he prayed that the rehearsal would be an improvement on last night's mess. James, of course, was already ensconced at the mirror, and they nodded curtly. Hanging up his clothes until he could no longer avoid sitting down on the bed, for there was only one chair, he rued the day that James had joined WAFT.

Meanwhile, James had made a point of telling anyone who would listen that he had been unfairly misjudged, and did not want anyone to *imagine* that he would have shied away from giving Tom a roof over his head, had he been asked. Ill at ease with the silence, Matthew went into the en-suite and closed the door. Staring into the mirror, he risked a look at his drawn face, and no longer liked what he saw.

During this new sharing regime – whenever James was out of the way – Archie flitted in and out of Matthew's dressing room with the latest gossip, of which there was more than enough to be going on with. Inevitably, word of Tom's predicament had spread quickly among the cast, but Dorian's job offer had not yet filtered into their collective conscience.

First, Jane and Clare had come up with a sensible offer. They could offer him a part-time weekend supervisory post in the café with immediate effect, until a full-time position became available. Secondly, Felicity had mentioned that she would be glad of a few hours' extra part-time help around her house and garden. Matthew was now well into introspection mode. He could not help reflecting that – apart from the flowers from Eleanor and Dorian – he had not been bombarded with help, yet everybody was trying to encourage Tom, who was probably coping better than he was, even though he was luxuriating at Spinnakers.

Once the next dress rehearsal had begun, Matthew slipped into the wings to see how James and Tom were getting on. It was clear that the atmosphere between them was still strained. Kicking back his chair, Rupert stopped the proceedings and gathered everybody together.

'I am not sure if there's a conspiracy afoot, but you're in danger of undermining everything that we've worked for.' He called James and Tom over and searched their faces. 'What's happened to you both? I feel like reaching out for an ice axe. You cannot allow your personal troubles to drift in here. Tom, you seem to have transferred all your charm to Eleanor, but you have to charm *everyone*. Please, buck up. It's supposed to be a soufflé, not a blancmange.'

Galumphing to the end of the act, they made little headway, and the second act deteriorated further. Although Matthew had only a few lines, he found that he could not bring himself to look at either James or Tom, which meant that all three barely made eye contact. Rupert told Matthew to behave, and although he tried – begrudgingly – the pace had slowed irrevocably. The second interval began with another pep-talk, and when they had finished the final act, Rupert stood up and made a point of singling out Matthew, James and Tom with one of his cold stares.

'I know it's my job to support and encourage you, but that was nothing short of abysmal. Notes will have to wait until tomorrow.' Matthew slunk back to his dressing room and went into the en-suite to remove his make-up. He now had a desire to escape not only from Langdales but from the festival altogether; he was on the verge of paying Archie to run the B and B on his own for the next couple of weeks, and slope away without telling anyone. (He automatically assumed that Rupert could easily cover his small role.) After all, there was nothing to stop him walking out. He could go at once, or at least after breakfast tomorrow, but – ultimately – he had no idea where to go, or what good it would do. This mental turmoil was leading nowhere. He was roused from his thoughts when he heard Eleanor laughing and joking with Tom on the corridor.

Emerging from the en-suite, Matthew heard her exclaiming in the corridor, 'I'm so excited at the prospect of having a house full of men!'

Friday morning did not find Matthew at his best. Housekeeping kept him busy with three changeovers, but he brightened when he realised that he was relishing the final dress rehearsal for the wrong reason; no doubt Archie would reprise trotting in with any gossip whenever James was on stage, and he was grateful for any information that might lead to enticing Tom back. He wolfed down a scratch dinner, and arrived at the rehearsal early.

Up to now, Matthew and James had only been speaking when they had to, but when Matthew entered their dressing room this time, James actually smiled. Bewildered, Matthew returned it and while he was in the en-suite putting on his make-up and changing, it struck him that only the other day Tom's and Matthew's separation had been on everybody's lips. Since then, it had become stale. Did that smile signify that a similar thing had happened over the brouhaha surrounding himself and Tom, and that the gossip was now on the turn? Matthew knew from experience that the cast was insatiable for fresh tittle-tattle, and would be seeking new gossip until they became bloated with it. Still cogitating along these lines, he heard a rap on the door. He opened it without thinking, only to find Tom. His well-fitting costume was flattering and he was looking very handsome.

Matthew signalled for him to sit on the bed, while he remained standing.

'This may be the only chance we all get to talk this through together,' began Tom, perching uneasily on the edge of the mattress.

'Before you go any further, can I ask if this visit is for my benefit or James's?' asked Matthew. So isolated had he been, that it seemed an age since he had last spoken to Tom seriously.

'Whoever will listen, I suppose?'

At this, the half-naked James stood up, strutted past them and selected a shirt from the rail. Matthew could not help noticing Tom's level gaze falling on James's navel hair.

'I can leave you two together if you like, but you won't have long,' said James, sticking out his chest as he shouldered into his shirt.

'You're not going anywhere. You're a part of this,' murmured Tom.

'Can't you listen to what Tom has to say?' asked Matthew. 'You *did* get us into this mess.'

'That's news to me.' James glanced down while his fingers fastened his buttons. 'Did you two plan this as an ambush?'

'Don't be absurd,' replied Tom. 'Listen, I no longer have a roof over my head, no job, no vehicle...'

'No *partner*?' asked Matthew. Tom made a face. 'Tom, you haven't left yourself long for whatever you've come to say.'

Tom stood up and moved over to James. 'It's fair to say that you've been leading me on. You know this has proved disastrous as far as

278

Matthew and I are concerned, so I would like Matthew to hear – from us both – that nothing happened.'

James, who was shooting his cuffs in front of the mirror, spoke languidly and with complete disregard. 'I was searching for a connection, but it seems I misjudged you.'

'I *liked* you, of course – ' ventured Tom.

'Yet you were clearly frustrated at Langdales?' James sounded as if he were cross-examining him.

'I may have been a bit glum from time to time – '

'Best to get it over with now.' James glanced at Tom. 'I grew fond – perhaps over-fond – of you. It's a pity – but seeing as we're being so honest – I think the moment might have passed.'

'Excuse me?' asked Tom, looking ashen. 'When did I become a *moment*?'

James eyed Tom. 'It seems I owe you an apology as well, Tom. I should have known better than to look at a married man.'

Tom stammered, 'Who... who said anything about being married?'

'You might as well have been. However, you enjoyed the attention – and I don't think you were averse to flirting with me a little – but that was as far as it went. I'm sorry for any anxiety I might have caused.'

Matthew frowned. 'Is that it?'

They were still staring at him open-mouthed when James returned Matthew's gaze. 'Far from it. Don't you think that Tom deserves more respect than he's been given?' Matthew felt the blood rushing to his face. 'Look, I may as well be honest...' They continued to stare. 'I can't help flirting with someone I like the look of.'

Tom looked ready to knock him down.

'Not the most desirable of traits,' remarked Matthew.

'That's why I came here. I went further than intended with someone.'

'Male or female?' asked Matthew, stonily.

James half-smiled. 'That would be telling, but there's never any shortage of people willing to throw themselves at me.'

'Modesty never having been your strong point,' observed Matthew.

Tom, glaring at James, said huskily, 'I never flirted with you, or anyone else for that matter, let alone threw myself at you.'

James was admiring his reflection before going on. 'Sorry, I must have read the situation wrongly, but I got the impression that you were unhappy at Langdales and ready for a change?'

Tom glanced at Matthew. 'I never said that.'

'You're playing with peoples' lives here, James,' said Matthew. 'I can only hope that it doesn't backfire on you.'

Tom was shaking his head. 'The fallout seems to have no limit.'

Matthew ran his mind over various incidents. 'So what did you mean by that horseplay?'

'What have you latched on to now?' asked James, wearily.

'Let's call it by its proper name, shall we? Foreplay.'

James chuckled. 'You have a vivid imagination.'

'Don't tell me that when you were hitting each other with your towels, that it wasn't sexually stimulating?' asked Matthew.

'Simply a release of nervous tension,' said Tom, as if he had rehearsed it.

James turned to reply. 'Will it help if I explain? Rupert had got into the habit of popping in and out – ostensibly to give further notes – but in the hope of catching a glimpse of me half-naked, so we were wondering what reaction we'd get if he saw us fooling around.'

'I find that a tad disingenuous.'

Tom caught Matthew's eye. 'And then *you* had to appear.'

'So I'm to blame?'

'Your timing wasn't the greatest.'

'From what I've seen on stage it still isn't,' said James, drily.

Matthew could hardly bear to look at him. 'You're really asking me to believe this?'

Tom glanced at his watch. 'We need to be on stage.'

Matthew found it hard not to chase after him, but waited to see if James had anything further to add, although Tom was heading for the door. Searching their faces, he closed it gently.

'I was astonished – not to say, alarmed – to hear that you had kicked him out,' said James, sitting down and steepling his hands, as if he had been relishing speaking his mind in the absence of Tom.

Provoked, Matthew spelled out the situation. 'I did nothing of the kind. It was his idea to have a few days apart. Whatever he says, I think he's still interested in you.'

'Haven't I done my best to put him off?'

'Did Tom ask you to put a roof over his head?'

James shook his head wearily. 'He might have been thinking of it when he realised that he had nowhere else to turn, but Eleanor got in first.'

'She happens to be my best friend.'

James smirked. 'Yes, I've heard all about your sorry little intrigues with her.'

'One day, I'll make *you* sorry you said that.'

'Ooh! Is that a threat?'

'The fact remains that your antics and self-regard may have blown our relationship apart.'

'I've apologised, haven't I? What more do you want?'

'Sort of. Nonetheless, the dynamics have altered, both for him and for me. I've seen a change in him, and not for the better.'

'Perhaps you both needed this, to bring you to your senses.'

'Nonsense. You were hoping that he would fall for you with what seems now like...' Matthew struggled. '...some Olympian disregard for the consequences because, like it or not, lunch at the Birthwaite had "date" written all over it.'

'To your small and addled brain, maybe.'

'But not to a compulsively sexual area of your anatomy? You must admit that inviting him for lunch there was nothing short of inflammatory?'

James had turned scarlet under his make-up. 'I never expected things to get out of hand. Sure, I was aware of a connection, but I hadn't realised where it might be headed.'

'Don't give me that.' James made for the door, while Matthew plucked up courage to ask, 'What really happened at the Birthwaite?'

James turned sharply and raised his eyes to the ceiling. 'When did we have time, Matthew? I wish you could lay things to rest.'

'Impossible! How do I *know* you didn't whisk him back to your flat afterwards?'

'Has anybody ever accused you of overthinking? Because it's high time they did.'

'What about in the dressing room?'

'Oh, *please*, Matthew. You know we're either in practically every scene or waiting in the wings to go on, and I don't suffer from premature ejaculation. I can't speak for Tom, of course.'

Raging inside, Matthew was hoping he would come out with the right words. 'You're saying that you've never had any *serious* intentions?' James bowed his head. 'In that case, how could Tom misconstrue...'

'I'm struggling to understand how *you* could get it so wrong.'

'Don't you mean spectacularly wrong?' asked Matthew, his fists clenched. 'It baffles me, too. At one point everything about Tom became almost too vivid. Unhappiness? Discontent? A certain restlessness? It doesn't take long when you live with someone, believe me.'

'Which is why you should be holding on to him, instead of making life easier for him. If I may be so bold, you have a *genius* for mistrust.' James allowed himself a smile.

'I'm trying, aren't I?'

'But hardly succeeding. I'm equally perplexed, seeing as it's common knowledge that you fancy Rupert.' James's smile was becoming more reptilian by the second. 'It's been needling Tom for some time now.'

Matthew, feeling as if he was falling into an abyss, tried to collect his thoughts. 'Why weren't you ready when he might have needed you?'

'You would have hated it, had he moved in.' James thought a moment. 'Because I soon realised that if I *didn't* make him welcome, he might see sense.'

'Cleverly concealing that you were abandoning him to his fate?'

He shrugged. 'As we know, Eleanor got to him first.'

'Only because I begged her to.'

James stood up. 'Whatever. I wouldn't be surprised if a queue didn't form.'

'Your idea of friendship seemed to involve breaking up his relationship with me, or will you be arguing your way out of that?'

'I dispute that. One minute we were laughing, and the next he was gazing soulfully into my eyes.'

'But you must confess that you led him on in the first place?'

Edging for the door, he shifted from one foot to the other. 'I might have encouraged him a little, but that was part of the fun.'

'*Fun?* You have a singular way of putting things.'

'I was very relieved that Eleanor got to him before he got to me.' James scrutinised his face. 'Before it spiralled out of control?'

'You under-estimate that he appears to be leaving me?'

'You're sure he never complained of feeling hemmed in at Langdales?'

Matthew cleared his throat. 'I was aware of the inevitable frustration of living over the shop, as it were– '

'But you did nothing about it. He, meanwhile, was experiencing some form of claustrophobia.'

Matthew folded his arms. 'He loved the garden, appreciated the house and struck up a genuine rapport with several of our visitors, but I suppose that counts for nothing?'

'He does have his enthusiasms.'

'He's too nice, and perhaps rather naïve.' He looked James up and down; he could not help but admire him in his costume. 'But there's a big difference between feeling hemmed in and walking out.'

James reached for the door handle. 'You made a big mistake letting him go. See if you can't patch it up.'

'Patching things up has never been my style,' muttered Matthew to the back of James's disappearing head, before sitting down and questioning whether Tom had been content. It seemed bizarre – seeing himself wearing clerical garb – that he should have to be so judgemental. Wondering how best to encourage Tom to return, he was still ruminating when Archie entered conspiratorially.

'Ready for the latest?' Wearily, Matthew lifted his eyes to Archie's shiny domed head reflected in the mirror. 'What do you think about Tom staying on at Eleanor's until after the run?'

'A pity.' Archie's face fell. 'But it's no more than I expected.' He removed the clutch of banknotes he had placed in his wallet and passed them to Archie. 'Do me a favour? Slide these into his jacket?'

Nodding vigorously, Archie pocketed the notes and hurried off. Matthew spent the first act stretched on the bed, still turning things over in his mind, before making his way to the auditorium to hear Rupert's notes and gauge how the rehearsal was going.

'I'm concerned that it's dragging a little in places, so you needn't be afraid of picking up those cues as fast as you can. But you've all worked very hard. Well done.'

Matthew determined to confront James in the interval, only to find him admiring his reflection from different angles. With his strong features enhanced with make-up, and his glistening black hair,

Matthew recalled only too clearly why so many fell for him. They spent the interval in silence and he only stopped glancing at James's profile when Felicity knocked, and told him that she was ready.

Everything went smoothly. Rupert's constant drilling had paid off. Doors were opened and closed without a murmur; tea poured and drunk with ease; food manipulated correctly. Once the middle act was over, he congratulated them on their return to form, but reminded them not to become complacent. Feeling that he and James should have a break from each other, Matthew sat out the next interval – uncomfortably – lurking in the wings.

They launched into the final act with brio, especially as Lady Bracknell's entrance saw Eleanor brimming with renewed vigour. She and James were at their most brittle, and the sparks flew effortlessly between them. Even so, as the final revelations of the play unravelled, Matthew wondered if anyone else recognised that she remained firmly on Tom's side.

During the final notes, Rupert went over the odd bit of business that was still eluding them. He pleaded with them not to look at the floor when they went off-stage, but to keep their heads up, not to glance in the direction of the prompt, and to stop fidgeting with their costume if they were not speaking. However, knowing that they were tired, he wound things up quickly. As the other players began to leave the stage, Matthew timed his walk to the dressing room so as to coincide with Tom's.

'How are you coping?' he enquired.

To his surprise, Tom grinned. 'Eleanor has been extremely kind.'

This was not a description that Matthew normally associated with her. When they reached the corridor, Matthew – noticing that his eyes were moist – looked at him as if for the first time. This might be the moment to get him back on his side. 'Tom?'

'Yes?' he replied, turning eagerly.

He reached out for his arm. 'Are you doing anything tomorrow?'

Tom shuffled his feet. 'It's Dorian's birthday.'

'Well, they can't celebrate both lunch and dinner, surely?'

'What did you have in mind?'

'To do *nothing*. Just to enjoy *you* again. I love you, Tom, and I'm sorry for any upset I've caused.'

Tom smiled non-committally, slipped back into his dressing room and closed the door. Was this an unspoken admission that they could get back together? Entering his room, he found the door to the en-suite was open, and when he caught sight of James's silhouette behind the shower screen, he recognised the torment that Tom must have endured.

He sat down heavily and removed his make-up. The time had come to pull himself together. How could things have spiralled out of control? One problem, as he saw it, was that he had no one to turn to with this particular predicament. Rupert – who would be scornful and unsympathetic – was out of the question. Having come to Tom's aid, Eleanor had demonstrated where her allegiance lay, so she was equally unapproachable.

Matthew tried not to run his eyes over James's beaded chest when he emerged, but it was difficult, and the silence grew painful. Empathising more with Tom's quandary over James in the role of heartthrob, Matthew dressed quickly, wished him as civil a good night as he could muster, and escaped.

It felt peculiar driving home, when he would normally have been chattering to Tom about the day's events. An owl flapped in front of the car and was last seen gliding into the lush growth of the nearest tree. As he closed the front door, Matthew could not decide whether it was worse being surrounded by the cast, or being left alone.

Although, as he saw it, he had forced himself to put on an agreeable front, he was not enjoying the festival; his role was minuscule, there was too much sitting around, and it irked him whenever James cosied up to Tom. In short, this was a far from satisfactory arrangement. Unable to face the bedroom on his own just yet, he opened the sitting room door and flicked on a couple of lamps.

Without Tom, he decided that life was not worth living, and running the B and B single-handedly was gnawing away at him. Something had to be done. He curled up on the sofa, wondered how long he could go on, felt he could not contact either Rupert or Eleanor because he might break down in tears. He was well past the point of contacting anyone: he did not want his friends to see him so far gone. Had anyone enquired that evening – which they had not – Matthew would have told them that he was managing, when in fact he was barely existing. When he had had his fill of brooding, he struggled to his feet. Realising that he had not only misjudged Tom, but had made a fool of himself, he dragged himself upstairs to bed.

Waking on that Saturday morning before the first night, Matthew wished that he was anywhere but at Langdales, and could not help remembering the first night of the previous year, when – in spite of the inevitable nerves – they had enjoyed acting together. As if this was not a depressing enough start to the sunless day, it was freakishly humid for the time of year. Possibly a storm was brewing, keying in with his defiant mood.

Once the tedium of knocking breakfast together was over, he became acutely aware that his guests' departure for the day could not come soon enough. Quite simply, he was bored. Emptying his mind, he braced himself to make the beds and hoover like an automaton, with only the prospect of the first night giving him a focus. Even that was shadowed by a negative undertow. The best he could hope for was that the inevitable menial work might take his mind off Tom, but as he climbed the stairs it seemed as if the gradient had been altered. He found himself playing a game to see how quickly he could finish a room, but soon tired of that and had to resume his normal pace, which was slow at the best of times. As the morning wore on, the reality of the first night continued to dog him. Matthew's role was well within his range, but he was as susceptible to first-night nerves as the next man.

Still feeling restless – not having seen a soul apart from his breakfast guests, and barely passing the time of day with them – early afternoon saw him relaxing on the terrace. The sun had tried to break through, but vanished just as quickly, and although the sky was overcast, it was warm enough to sit out. He stretched out on one of the sun-loungers and promptly dozed off.

He had not been comatose for long when the first spots began to splash on the terrace with enough force to rudely awaken him. He had been dreaming that something was pin-pricking his bare arms. Clutching the cushions, he made a run for it and stared out of the kitchen window. The sky flashed white, followed by the grumble of distant thunder. A few spats railed against the glass before becoming an unforgiving tumult, and it became so dark that he had to switch on the lights. The down-spouts gurgled; puddles formed quickly on the terrace. Even the lawn was temporarily water-logged in places.

He had woken feeling groggy, but the abrupt change from inertia to bustle helped him to come round. Even so, anticipation of the first night now weighed heavily on him, and as it was only mid-afternoon the hours stretched interminably ahead. He climbed up to the attic to lie down, and soon began to doze. When he woke up, it was still raining – although more steadily – and he had a bite to eat before making a dash for the car.

First-night nerves and anxiety about the condition of the roads had prompted the others to arrive early. Already in costume, James was preening in front of the mirror. Not long after Matthew's arrival, everyone grouped on stage for notes and Rupert oozed positivity. Matthew still regretted that Rupert was not playing Lady Bracknell, and could not help glancing at Eleanor, but her face was mask-like in its concentration. Cast members showed their nerves by remaining solemn and preoccupied, or babbling, or – like Matthew – trying to hide their irritability.

As the audience trickled in at a leisurely pace, it became clear that there was no question of commencing on time. Seven thirty was fast approaching, and there were still plenty of vacant booked seats. Feeling tense and in pursuit of any kind of occupation, Matthew hovered in the wings to get a feeling of the audience's mood before he went to change. He had often played characters who opened the play, and once he was made up and dressed, his heart quickened with the adrenalin rush of first-night tension before the curtain "went up". (WAFT audiences had become blasé regarding wobbly curtains jerking, usually a few seconds late.) With the sense of anticipation heightening the moment, the audience ceased their chatter – and as soon as he heard the odd, inevitable cough – he recognised that the house lights would be dimming. Only half-listening to the final instructions from the assistant stage manager, he basked in the expectant hush on the other side of the curtain. This was the moment he treasured most, and it was best savoured from the wings.

The curtains were pulled back in fits and starts that he found inexcusable, and like over-drilled puppets the actors were hurled into the dramatic action. Within seconds Archie won an unexpected laugh and round of applause when he tripped over with a tray, performing the little bit of business that Rupert had given him while Algernon was playing the piano off-stage. Tom squeezed Matthew's arm as he went on. This was a moment to treasure, but was it merely camaraderie, or was it intended to be inspirational and forgiving? A few moments later and it was clear from the concerted murmuring that James was alluring. His sex appeal wafted across the stage into the auditorium, but for Matthew it was slime, sticking firmly to the stage. From Tom's demeanour, and from the way he was standing slightly too close to him, relations seemed more cordial, or could they have been following Rupert's instructions to be more professional and less immature?

Rupert had consistently emphasised the importance of a sense of pace. First-night nerves helped them to maintain this, and it was soon obvious that the audience was with them, especially in the famous scene between Lady Bracknell and Jack. Eleanor had the audience just where she wanted them, but she always did love showing off.

"To lose one parent may be regarded as a misfortune; to lose both seems like carelessness..." had the response it deserved, and Eleanor built well on the laugh she had when Jack described how he had been found as a baby. *"Found!"* reverberated through the auditorium. She delivered one of the best lines with the required hammer-blows. *"You can hardly imagine that I and Lord Bracknell would dream of allowing our only daughter – a girl brought up with the utmost care – to marry into a cloakroom and form an alliance with a parcel."* This was rightly capped by the most famous line in the play, and there were mutterings of recognition; *"A handbag?"* was bellowed with exaggerated astonishment.

By the interval, there was a sense of relief on both sides of the curtains. A beaming Rupert bounded backstage and told them that they were a success. Archie apologised for tripping up, but Rupert merely shrugged it off. He then gave the occasional note to individuals before heading off to rub shoulders with anyone who would listen to him in the bar.

Having watched most of the first act from the wings, Matthew was more than ready to prove himself. He, Felicity and Clare romped through their scenes and by the second interval the applause was impressive. They all appeared to enjoy the revelations of the third act, and it was clear that the first night of *The Importance of Being Earnest* had been a triumph.

Once back in the dressing room, he and James were, as usual, forced to change together; making light conversation seemed to be up to Matthew.

'We don't appear to have done so badly...' he began.

'Yes, Rupert seems to know what he's doing, even though he was denied the opportunity of acting,' observed James.

Matthew turned to him. 'I never imagined that you gave him much thought.'

James threw him an enigmatic smile. 'People change.'

Not having enjoying the first night party as it often degenerated into mean-spirited cackling, Matthew had long shied away from it. His feelings were more profound this year, but he had come to realise that it would look peculiar if he did not put in an appearance, however fleeting. Never missing the opportunity to sneer about the acting members, if not the production in general, those sour-faced members who had failed their auditions always made a point of turning up. As Matthew knew from previous bitter encounters, if people failed to mention your performance, you knew the worst; if they gushed, you feared they were being disingenuous.

James had changed in record time, and such was his haste that he had left the door swinging open. Matthew wanted to take his time, and when he was satisfied with his appearance, he made his way to the hotel's smallest (and cheapest) function suite. Intimate groups had already formed and the din was indescribable. Not wishing to prise his way into a sea of backs, Matthew's eyes were ranging the room when he overheard Eleanor (amid what sounded like artificial peals of laughter) shouting into an elderly listener's ear that she had every confidence in Rupert. Groaning to himself, he also noticed James making Rupert double up with laughter, before he finally noticed Tom seated in the furthest corner away from him. He made his way over.

'I found some money in my pocket. Thank you for being so thoughtful,' said Tom, half-smiling.

'I was worried that you might not approve.'

'You don't have to worry on that score. I want for nothing, and in return I've been making myself useful.'

'If I seem to have overreacted, I take it back.'

Tom's face fell. '*Seem?*' One or two members turned outwards from their cliques to glanced over and face away again, muttering.

Tom lowered his voice. 'Will you believe me when I tell you that nothing – happened – between – James – and – me?'

'I feel as though I've made a fool of myself, and I'm sorry.'

'The problem as I see it,' said Tom, lowering his voice, 'is that I no longer have a future here.'

'At L-Langdales, or the L-Lakes?' stammered Matthew, his gravelly voice betraying his desperation.

'My parents have suggested that I go back home as soon as this is over. Look about me.'

'Not Northamptonshire? But you hated it there.'

Tom chuckled half-heartedly. 'You never know, I might benefit from a rest.'

Matthew was almost in tears. 'We'll close Langdales for a week – ten days. I'll take you away. Verona?'

'With no opera?'

'Then let's wait a few weeks. I'll do anything.'

Tom shrugged. 'I don't think you realise how bruised I feel? I'm still trying to work things out in my head, but this is something I *have* to come to terms with.' He looked at Matthew. 'I need to get away.'

'That's really what you're planning?'

'Not out of choice, but you know how it is.'

'I don't, actually.'

Tom cleared his throat. 'This situation is quite claustrophobic, and I don't just mean the play. Everybody's been so kind with their offers, but I have no intention of spending my life doing umpteen part-time jobs.'

'The last thing I heard, you were planning on gardening under Dorian's watchful eye?'

'The hourly rate is not brilliant, and I'll need to top it up with some part-time work if I'm ever going to buy a small place of my own. I want to do the decent thing by Eleanor too. You realise that she won't accept a penny from me?'

Matthew swallowed; he had ignored the basic integrity of the man fro too long. 'You don't appear to have that many options.' Glancing at the uproarious crowd knocking back their drinks, he was thankful they were not interrupted by some garrulous member. 'I know you've wanted to pay your way with Eleanor. There will always be odd jobs to do there, I suppose?'

'Tasks no one else wants to do, especially Dorian. I've come to realise that although he enjoys working out, he's quite lazy when it comes to actual work.'

'Come to think of it, his nails are always fastidiously clean.'

He glanced at Matthew. 'By the way, I'm not expecting to walk out of Langdales with anything.'

'That's very decent, but...' He could not finish his sentence.

'No wish to fleece you,' muttered Tom. 'Remember, getting a mortgage at my age will be a stretch, whatever I'm earning, and this is not a cheap area to live in. I *have* to go.'

'Have you mentioned this to the others?'

'Not yet. But I'm determined to.'

Matthew squeezed his hand. 'I see, but I'm begging you not to be hasty.'

Tom had suddenly become absorbed in the floor. 'It's been pointed out that I need a career. back in management.'

'But you loathed management.' Final realisation clicked. 'You won't be gone for a while? This will be forever. That's a tough one.'

Tom blinked a few times. 'Let's not make this harder than it is already.'

Matthew was desperate to take the weight off his feet, but the few chairs that had been scattered around had been occupied for some time. 'I implore you to do nothing drastic. If only you would agree to sitting down together, and talking this through. I need you to know I still love you.'

Tom spoke slowly. 'Not here. You see, it hasn't always felt like that, and no amount of talk seems to get us anywhere. I feel gutted.' Matthew felt there was little he could add to this, and stood lamely, eyes darting around the crowded room in the hope of making his escape. Tom began a new thread. 'I couldn't resist a Pembroke table from Bainbridge and Mounsey, the other day.'

'Have you come into some money?' asked Matthew, suspiciously.

Tom looked put out. 'Hardly. Beautiful condition and a fair price at auction. And a crystal vase for practically nothing. Eleanor said it was important to – '

'I could give you some bits and pieces from Langdales, if you weren't hell-bent on being so hasty.'

'Don't.'

Tom's glistening eyes and the sight of their esteemed director bustling towards them – wearing the inevitable complacent grin – deprived them of any further discussion. Tom dug in his pocket for a tissue.

Fixing Rupert with a smile, Matthew mourned the fact that someone who had once meant everything to him and who had been a part of his life for weeks, would be leaving tomorrow. He prayed for some last-minute information that would prove otherwise, imagining a hot-footed messenger darting in from the wings gabbling news of a stay of execution. Try as he might, he could not ignore the lump in his throat.

Rupert was first to speak. 'Well, dear boy, almost time for me to say toodle pip.' From the carefully measured drawl it was clear he was well oiled.

Matthew could not meet his eye. 'Indeed.'

'No need to look glum, dear.' Assuming a mysterious tone of voice, he pretended to be a fortune-teller. 'I see a strikingly handsome visitor, blond not dark...'

'Really?'

'Who will not only be visiting the Lakeland retreat that has become so dear to you, but fetching some delicacies to make an occasion of it.'

Matthew brightened. He was still shaking his old friend's hand when Rupert turned suddenly, only to be swallowed up in the throng.

By that time, Tom was also looking askance at Rupert's disappearing golden head, and with no attempt to keep his voice down, he remarked disparagingly, ' *"Toodle pip?"* Where does he think he is? For what it's worth, I see a lot of fun on the horizon for you.'

'That's never going to happen.'

'You're quite sure?'

'Why don't you forget all this and come back, Pembroke table and all?'

'You just don't get it, do you?'

'We can help each other when we most need it.'

'It's not just you Matthew, it's everything. We were in a rut. The routine was getting to me. One of my problems is you're so bound up with Langdales that you'll never leave it, so I don't see that there's any hope for us.'

'I'll put it on the market at once.'

Tom smiled knowingly. 'To borrow your immortal phrase: *"That's never going to happen."*'

'What else is bothering you?'

'I despair that you couldn't trust me.'

'Oh.'

'If you've lost faith in me, there seems no point in carrying on.'

'You appear to think that you have thought it through well enough,' said Matthew, stiffly. 'Don't forget that you're in no position to see anything clearly while you're living it up at Eleanor's. The real world is going to look very different.'

'Not for long.'

'Has she put you up to this?'

'Of course not.'

'James, then?'

'No. This is *my* take on the situation.'

Matthew thought quickly. 'You're clearly not yourself. Let's wait a while.'

'I'm really not sure that would be good for either of us.'

'Have I missed something?' he demanded, testily. 'When did we leap from so-called trial separation to full-blown walkout?'

'My mind is made up.'

'An admission of defeat?'

Tom thought for a moment. 'I prefer painful acceptance.'

'You're sure you haven't rehearsed this?'

Matthew took exception to the shrug, and they parted coolly. In the mood he was in, it did not take long to extricate himself from the bash while it was still propped up by alcohol. He swept out to little effect, but at least he had been seen. On the drive home, he could not believe how far they had drifted apart in such a brief space of time. With not even an overblown dramatic scene, it had been more like a snuffing out. It was a relief to get into bed.

Anxiety regarding the prospect of saying farewell to Rupert only served to illustrate that Matthew would also be seeing his best friend vanish.

Chapter Fourteen

The following morning, when Matthew was working in Jemima
Puddleduck – the room he liked least – and immersed in thoughts of
both Tom and Rupert disappearing from his life, his mobile rang. He
emerged, over-heated, from the bathroom with his nostrils full of the
smell of cleaning fluid.

'We never managed to finish our conversation,' said Tom,
supplying no other greeting.

'Maybe because it's a conversation that never can be finished.'

'Look, I don't wish to hurt you, but I have to tell you that I've felt
a lot happier since leaving Langdales.'

'You're implying the place is a problem, and not me?'

'I've been thinking.' Tom hesitated. 'Wouldn't you rather be
spending more time with someone your own age?'

'What are you saying?' Matthew swallowed. 'And where on earth
did you get that idea?'

Tom said in a monotone, 'He could not wait to invite himself over
today, could he?'

'Merely a courtesy farewell.'

'Although you *were* holding hands that time.'

'That was all on his side, as you well know.'

'How do I know? Look, I'll be coming round later to collect the
rest of my stuff, if that's okay?'

'You're dissolving ten years? *On the phone?*'

'Eleanor says it's imperative to have familiar things around me at
times like this. Dorian's been very supportive, too.'

Matthew shook his head. 'Oh! Bugger Dorian!'

There was a long silence.

'Matthew, I think you need to *calm down*. Let's see where this
journey takes us.'

'*Journey?* Oh, please!'

'I won't be long,' said Tom.

Mindful that he was expecting Rupert, Matthew began to panic. 'In coming, or taking your stuff?'

'Both, so that you can get on with your life. Goodbye, Matthew, and thanks for everything.'

'Have you thought this through properly?' asked Matthew, but Tom had hung up.

Having absorbed this bombshell as best he could he devoted the morning to wondering whether he should affect being moody and rejected, or flashily upbeat with a dash of devil-may-care insouciance, when the doorbell rang. Rupert's farewell visit was bound to look awkward, seeing that Tom would be coming round to remove his possessions at any moment. Opening the door to find Rupert clutching a cool-bag confirmed his fears, and he found himself listening out for another car on the track.

Matthew did not like to think that Rupert – and probably Tom – would be walking out of his life in little over an hour. Dare he reveal Tom's most recent plans? Should he quietly imply – at the very least – that he could always be contacted by Rupert? Thinking this over, he showed Rupert into the kitchen and watched him pull out a half-bottle of champagne, ready-made poached salmon salad and his favourite luxury ice-cream.

'Now, *you* are very welcome to enjoy a glass of champagne, but I have to live up to my usual state of denial and deprivation,' Rupert told him, sounding as if he had prepared this.

'Thank you, but there's been a development.'

Rupert winced. 'To quote Lady Bracknell, your life is clearly *"crowded with incident."*'

Matthew was placing the half-bottle and the salad in the fridge, and the ice-cream in the freezer, 'Tom's on his way.'

Rupert raised an eyebrow. 'I don't like the sound of that one bit.'

'There won't be any unpleasantness.'

'I was more concerned that there may not be enough food to go round.'

'I didn't have it in me to enquire whether he was hungry.'

He half-smiled. 'Because you're getting back together again?'

Matthew lowered his head. 'I'm afraid not.'

Rupert's face fell. 'He's going to take a dim view of me being here. Talk about *in flagrante*!'

'I somehow doubt it, but perhaps it would be tactful to keep the champagne hidden? You see, he's coming to clear his stuff.'

'He has *time*, with so much going on?' Rupert hesitated. 'In light of this, your feelings haven't changed towards me?'

'It's out of the question, I'm afraid,' said Matthew, unable to look him in the eye.

'Just thought I'd ask. Lovely place you've got here.'

'I'll let you know if it goes on the market.'

'Now that I'm no longer young, you have no use for me.' Rupert stuck out his bottom lip, perhaps in jest.

'Even if I were interested, this is neither the – '

'Does that mean you've not ruled it out?'

Matthew hoped that he was joking. 'We're no longer compatible. Perhaps we never were.'

'So you're not going to beg him to return?'

Matthew gritted his teeth. 'My big scene? How does that go? *Remind me.*'

'I shall miss trying to knock some sense into you, dear boy.'

The doorbell rang and – intent on escape – he almost ran into the hall. Matthew had put on a special smile to greet Tom, but all the muscles in his face seemed to collapse when he saw Eleanor. He reeled back from their over-zealous grinning and showed them in, hoping that his face did not betray his mixed feelings about Tom. They were never far from the surface.

Glancing over her shoulder in the direction of Rupert's car, Eleanor iced over the minute she stepped inside. 'You might have waited.'

'He's still only a friend.'

'That remains to be seen. How could you, and with almost indecent haste?' She rolled her eyes. 'Probably because you have *no* insight, and never will have.'

'He's saying goodbye, seeing as he's superfluous to the production, remember?'

'You expect us to believe that? And Tom is bidding *his* farewell for the last time, if he's got any sense!'

'I hope you don't mean that,' said Matthew.

She began to fiddle with her hair.

'It didn't seem right to let myself in,' said Tom, holding out his keys at arm's length so that Matthew was forced to step forward to relieve him of them. Having placed them on the hall table, he directed them into the kitchen, where Rupert was busy with the champagne, clearly having paid no heed to Matthew's suggestion. Tom's eyes dulled. Their self-styled sommelier gave Tom and Eleanor his most radiant smile.

'It's not what you think,' said Matthew.

'"*Is that not somewhat premature?*"' asked Tom, quoting Lady Bracknell.

Rupert gently waved a half-filled glass at Eleanor, but she shook her head. 'It would choke me.' But having narrowed her eyes at the label, which was a good one, she changed her mind. 'On reflection, as it's Dorian's birthday, I'd like to propose a toast.' They raised their glasses. 'We're not interrupting your little celebration, I hope?'

Rupert smirked. 'Matthew's glad to be rid of me, I think.'

'Yes, the moment we've all been waiting for,' muttered Eleanor. No one could see Rupert's face as he was pouring himself a glass of water from the tap. They toasted Dorian, so quickly that it might have been missed. Rifling his hair and realising that he had seldom played host to a more ill-assorted gathering, Matthew decided that things might be less claustrophobic on the terrace. He ushered them out, noticing Tom wincing at the unkempt lawn as he did so. They stood stiffly under the sun-shade, glancing everywhere but at each other.

'I suppose we ought to have a toast to the festival, too,' mumbled Matthew, enjoying the biscuity aroma rising from his glass.

'And to getting through the run in one piece,' said Eleanor.

They clinked glasses. Then, taking his glass with him, Tom excused himself. Eleanor challenged Matthew the moment he was gone. 'It's none of my business, but–'

Rupert caught her eye. 'It's never stopped you before.'

Eleanor threw Matthew a sideways look for him to get rid of Rupert. 'I'm *very* concerned, if anyone will listen.'

He needed to hear what Eleanor might have to say. 'Can you give us a moment?' Looking rather deflated, his old love made his way into the garden, and was soon safely out of earshot.

'I've had a long chat with Tom,' said Eleanor, taking him by the arm in conspiratorial mode. 'He swears that nothing has happened, but he doesn't think he's convinced you.'

'So you think I should forget everything, insist he stays here and stop him packing?'

'Better than *sending* him packing...'

'So we continue as if nothing happened? If you think I'm going to beg–'

She tightened her grip. 'Have you considered how much hurt you're causing by not climbing down?'

'I have apologised,' replied Matthew, grandly, gently easing his arm away. 'Even so, he appears mistrustful, both of me and of returning to the dull routine. Do you think I was right offering to sell up so that we could start a new life?'

'I can't see that happening for one minute. There's too much at stake.'

'Don't forget,' said Matthew, losing ground, 'it was *his* idea to part company, and all I've done is agree, so why is it me who's at fault?'

'You don't seem to have accepted that Tom has done nothing that he shouldn't, but you *do* know that James had designs on him. If you let him go now, you might regret it for the rest of your life. After all, what's the alternative? *Him?*' She grimaced at Rupert's back; he was still sauntering along the border.

'There's been far too much speculation if you ask me. You saw this; he heard that; someone overheard something. I've lived through it.'

'Haven't we *all*?' Eleanor's expression unnerved him. 'Keep calm. We're not on stage. Just because everyone has been gossiping about James and Tom, you take it as gospel?' She clasped his wrist. 'Look, I've always been a fan of Tom's. It seems such a waste. Is there no chance of patching things up?'

'Patch? At this stage? You *are* joking?'

'You're probably right. He's had enough, and I can see why.'

Sensing Tom emerging through the French windows behind her, Eleanor dropped Matthew's arm as if she had been scalded, but Tom pretended not to notice. 'I'm sorry to intrude, but would you mind if I wrapped my ornaments now?'

Seeing Tom dwarfed by the house, Matthew wanted to get rid of her and Rupert, and hold on to whatever he might have left with him. Having listened but not having agreed with her, it struck him that this might be the moment to win back Tom. Rupert returned from his wanderings, full of extravagant praise for the flowering shrubs, but this went unheeded.

Matthew turned to Tom. 'They're yours to take whenever you like, surely?'

'I thought it was polite to ask.'

'Why don't we all help?' asked Rupert, assuming his artificially bright voice.

Eleanor glanced at her watch. 'But there's so much stuff, and we haven't got long. I promised Dorian we'd be back for lunch.'

'But if we all do a bit, I need never come back,' said Tom, catching Matthew's eye and then looking away just as quickly.

'Surely there's no rush?' Matthew was hoping to keep Tom as long as possible, but by now the herd instinct was funnelling them back into the sitting room. Eleanor gave Dorian a quick call to reassure him that they were almost on their way. Tom began to remove the Beatrix Potter figurines from the glazed cabinet and handed them over to Matthew and Eleanor – who wrapped them individually on their knees while remaining seated on the sofa – followed by Rupert who packed them into one of Tom's boxes. Intent on their joint enterprise, they worked in silence until Rupert broke the peace.

'Oh! I have some news, although Matthew knows something about it already.'

'Knows what?' enquired Eleanor, carefully wrapping a ceramic bunny in some tissue paper.

'I feel that a reunion is about to be thrust on me,' he replied.

'There are two types of reunion. Pleasant and unpleasant. How do you class yours?' asked Matthew, while recollecting his own rapprochement with Rupert.

Rupert ignored this, but smiled. 'You remember when we talked about my long-lost son?'

Tom arched an eyebrow. 'Your *son*?'

'It's like something out of *Le Nozze di Figaro*,' said Eleanor.

'Only less fun. Well, thanks to my sister, he's been found.'

'Found!' enquired Eleanor, in her Lady Bracknell voice.

Rupert smiled. 'Isn't it incredible?'

Matthew stiffened while Tom absent-mindedly handed Eleanor a ceramic squirrel.

'So why did your sister choose this moment?' she asked.

'I'm not sure choice came into it, dear. Caroline and I haven't seen much of each other since I began to dedicate myself to *your* festival. Since she's had more time on her hands, she's become something of a private investigator.' Rupert beamed. 'My sister is nothing if not persistent.'

'And where is he now?'

'Yorkshire.'

'He might only be a few miles away,' observed Tom, forgetting to hand over any further ornaments and sitting down in the nearest armchair.

'Don't forget it's a huge county,' said Matthew, nervously.

'Caroline has the details,' said Rupert, airily. 'He might even come to see our play.'

'Midweek is slack, so I do hope so,' said Eleanor.

'Is there a photograph?' asked Tom.

Matthew looked ashen while Rupert reached for his wallet. Eleanor glanced at the photograph before passing it to the others. 'I feel as though I know that face.'

Tom looked for resemblances between the photograph and Rupert, and shook his head.

'I think we can safely agree that he's reasonably good-looking. Of course, he's always taken after his mother rather than me,' said Rupert, as if some explanation was in order.

'I see what you mean, Eleanor. His face *is* vaguely familiar,' observed Tom, handing it to Matthew, 'but I can't place it. He looks absurdly young compared to the rest of us.'

Matthew ran his eyes over it quickly, before returning it.

'Well, the main thing is you've found him,' yawned Eleanor, quickly losing interest when the conversation did not relate to her. 'Dare I ask, how many more?'

Rupert sat down. 'Long-lost children?'

'Figurines, my dear...'

There was a long silence which no one seemed in a hurry to fill. Eleanor, Matthew and Tom had no progeny and possibly their thoughts meandered towards what might have been. But their few remaining moments together were measured out. This snippet of information concerning Rupert's son, emboldened Tom to seek out the facts regarding Matthew's former infatuation with the father.

'As we may not meet so informally again,' said Tom, as if opening a village fête, before going in with a dagger thrust, 'I was wondering if you could bear to tell me what *really* happened between you two?'

Wishing he had turned down the champagne, Matthew fingered the back of his collar long enough for Rupert to leap in.

'Oh! I've been *dying* for someone to ask me that! Let's start with me asking Matthew to be my best man, shall we?'

Tom stared. 'Sounds as if that wasn't a smart move?'

'It certainly was not,' said Rupert, enjoying himself. 'I'm sure you're familiar with that part of the ceremony where the vicar asks anyone present if they know of *"a reason why these persons may not lawfully marry?"'* He placed his hands behind his head. 'Perhaps *Matthew* should explain further.'

'I couldn't tell it with the same panache as you intend to,' he replied, not meeting his eye.

'You flatter me,' said Rupert, checking that he still had Tom's attention. 'Let me see. A few days beforehand, he informed me that he was planning to declare that I was not the marrying kind.'

A smirking Eleanor caught Matthew's eye, but he looked away. 'At the actual ceremony?' she enquired. 'But was that a sufficient reason to prevent someone from marrying? It wasn't as if it was unlawful.'

'You're missing the point. It hardly inspired confidence in *me*, as the bridegroom.'

'I was not afraid to speak the truth, and feelings were running high,' said Matthew, studying the rug at his feet while picking off some imaginary thread from his shirt sleeve.

'You feel strongly about many things,' said Tom.

Matthew let that one go.

Rupert gazed heavenwards. 'The whiff of self-righteousness.'

Matthew's jaw tightened. 'Rupert had worked his way through every man his own age – or preferably younger – in whatever film he happened to be in.'

'You see, Tom, he was jealous,' said Rupert. 'And he was *furious*. Because I was going off with a woman. You see, he liked the look of her as well as me.' Rupert tittered, nodded at Eleanor and Tom. From their expectant faces, it was clear that they were more than ready to appreciate new revelations. 'Although interest in the opposite sex was only a phase. Anyway, a huge row began to erupt.'

'With good reason,' muttered Matthew, feeling he was in for a pummelling.

'Can you imagine how *I* felt, having Matthew's threat hanging over my wedding day?'

Emboldened by the alcohol, Matthew glanced up. 'I was doing you a favour.'

'Take that look out of your eyes,' said Rupert. 'Everything had been paid for. The wedding day is just as important to the groom as to the bride.'

'Really?' asked Eleanor, glancing at her watch. 'Let's get to the point, shall we?'

'I'm not going to rush it, not even for you. Naturally, my nerves were in *tatters*, and I was in two minds about what action to take.' He widened his eyes. 'I decided to risk it, and pray that it would be *"all right on the night"*, so to speak. But I hadn't bargained for what happened on the day.' He tapped the side of his nose with one finger.

'Do tell,' said Eleanor.

'Matthew actually went through with it.'

'No!' cried Eleanor, while Tom glowered at him.

'I'm afraid so,' grinned Rupert. Matthew wanted to hit him.

'So what happened?' asked Tom, tilting his head to one side.

'Well, my intended got cold feet. Of course, she *knew* about me, but we hadn't really found time to discuss it in depth. But facing the truth in front of the guests was going to be challenging to say the least. He left us both looking like idiots.'

'Not such a stretch in your case,' observed Eleanor.

Matthew said wearily, 'You would have turned out less than an ideal husband.'

Shutting his eyes on him, Rupert turned to the others and said, 'Hardly surprising, but I did not set eyes on *that man* again until early this year.'

'So it wasn't a teenage crush on Rupert's side?' enquired Tom.

Matthew hoped his face did not reveal too much. 'Not exactly.'

'That's really what he led you to believe?' asked Rupert. 'You astound me.' A crimson-faced Matthew had difficulty restraining himself from slamming every door in his wake. 'Please note that he's not denying it.'

Tom leaned forward. 'So what happened?'

'We were forced to call it off. It was only later, when I discovered that she was pregnant, that I realised–'

Tom shook his head; Eleanor rolled her eyes. 'Achieved on the basis of Immaculate Conception, presumably?'

'Neither of us was a virgin on our proposed wedding day, so I didn't think too deeply about it. The problem, as I saw it, was that my child was going to be brought up in a single parent family, but she wouldn't have me by then.'

The other three glanced at each other but said nothing. Tom resumed passing ornaments to Matthew and Eleanor, who speeded up as if energised. Meanwhile, the atmosphere reeked of distrust.

Once Rupert was closing the lid on the second and final box, Eleanor declared that she could not stay a moment longer. Their departure was swift. Matthew helped carry out the boxes and suitcases, placed them in the boot of Eleanor's vehicle and promised to put any forgotten items on one side. It had not been the hysterical group farewell he had been dreading, perhaps because they would be bumping into each other during the week to come. His stomach rumbled, and much as though he was aching to show Rupert the door he did not have the heart, especially as he had been drinking his champagne and was preparing to devour his poached salmon.

Having waved them off he determined to have it out with him, but Rupert got in first. 'Not only did you ruin my– '

'You realise there's no chance of any rapprochement with Tom now?'

'Isn't it time to make a fresh start, Matthew?' Too full of loathing to reply, he shrugged. 'An old, high-maintenance house that's way too big for one person, with you *suffocated* by paying guests you don't much care for?'

There was no answer to this, so they went to fetch the salad, and laid the table on the terrace in silence. When they had sat down, Rupert ran his eyes over Matthew.

'I'm familiar with that look, and I know you won't be content with this scenario for long.'

'What *"scenario"*, as you put it?'

'Existing as a single man?'

'Oh, that.'

'Have you considered that there might be a better and simpler way out of the predicament you find yourself in?'

Matthew's stomach fluttered. He spilled the water he was pouring. 'I know this is probably yet another illustration of your sense of humour, so I hope you're not suggesting we join forces?'

'You know only too well that you could stay here,' said Rupert, watching him, 'and enjoy the company of someone your own age, if you weren't so stubborn.'

'What about your flat in Manchester?' he asked, guardedly.

'Allow me to explain.' Rupert sounded uncharacteristically business-like. 'So much has changed since we last spoke on the subject.' Trying not to bite his lip, Matthew waited. 'My father has been failing for a while, and I think this might be it.'

Matthew raised an eyebrow. 'I know that face. You mean he's passed away?'

'I didn't want *them* to know. It's been very distressing.'

'I fail to see how. You didn't exactly do much to help in his final months, apart from fretting over your inheritance.'

'I could not have played Lady Bracknell very easily this week, being so grief-stricken. Perhaps things turned out – '

'Let's get to the point, shall we?' He would regret that.

'We were never that close, so I mustn't pretend to be too devastated, but according to Caroline, the will has not been meddled with.' His tone became more self-congratulatory. 'As Lady Bracknell put it, there is *"a large accumulation of property"*, and under the terms of the will, it will be fairly divided between the two of us.'

Matthew took a second or two to focus on this. Was Rupert implying that Matthew was included? ' *"The two of us?"* What are you saying?'

'My sister.'

'Of course.'

'We can both look forward to retirement with impunity,' beamed Rupert. 'It's too early to clutch at figures, but she has given me a ball-park figure, and if I'm sensible...'

'You've never been that.'

'Caroline will make sure that I don't fritter it away. She's already told me what I ought to be investing in.'

'In property, of course, if you have any sense.'

Rupert nodded. 'There might be something in it for you, too?'

'I hardly knew your father, so I very much doubt it.'

'Something that will ease you out of your present dilemma?'

'Thoughtfulness is not something I usually ascribe to you,' said Matthew, uneasily. He reached for his water.

'Perhaps you should start?' Then came the wide smile. 'You see, I've been told that I will not only have enough to provide me with an income, but I'd be able to buy out Tom.'

'That's rather a leap, isn't it?' Appetite vanished, Matthew leaned forward in his chair and tried to ignore his stomach. 'You're suggesting that you'd own half of Langdales?'

'Effectively.'

'But this seems to indicate that Tom won't be returning?'

Rupert flashed a broader smile. 'He's grabbed what he could, but let's not read too much into that.'

Matthew poured himself another glass of water and asked huskily, 'You realise I need time to think?'

'*Think?* What is there to think about? You'll be able to stay here and live happily ever after. Don't forget that this is the most generous proposition you'll get.'

Matthew's scalp prickled. 'But wouldn't that make me beholden to you?'

'Is that a problem?'

'But you could lord it over me, in *my* house.'

'That's a bit strong, although perhaps not too wide of the mark. Yes, I could stay here any time, but that is not the point. *You* need to rethink your...' He chuckled. '...Rather fixed ideas about ownership. You've never been all that bright have you, dear boy?' Visibly wilting, Matthew appeared to have been struck dumb. 'Let me explain.'

Compelled to hear what he had to say, Matthew recognised that Rupert was working towards a denouement. Dreading that whatever Rupert had over him would come to light, he listened hard.

'You are solitary, maybe forever, but inhabit a house that is far too grand for a single person. You need to make it pay, but you lack the bonhomie to shine as a natural hotelier.' Here Matthew attempted to protest, but Rupert held up a hand, and continued as if he had memorised a set speech. 'The common touch with guests eludes you, and – delusional though you are – you cannot help but find the work uninspiring. Moreover, you have insufficient funds to fulfil your dream of early retirement.'

Matthew had heard enough. 'Just because you've known me a long time doesn't permit you to be rude.'

'Known *of* you, dear boy, remember? However, with me on board, you *could* carry on with the B and B without having to borrow. I suppose you *might* sell up, but you hold the place dear, and I presume you are not averse to the prestige it lends you.' A wry grin made him look younger. 'Don't worry, you wouldn't have to share the flat with me. I'd be quite happy in the spare room – once it's been redecorated and is devoid of squirrels, hedgehogs and bunnies – although I would never refuse an upgrade.' Then the stabbing look. 'I still haven't worked out where your true feelings lie?'

'I can't imagine why not.' Matthew, head aching, pushed away the remains of his lunch. 'I couldn't have made them clearer if I tried.'

'No one could say that you haven't tried, and you have always excelled at denial.' Rupert looked at him beadily, but there was nothing that Matthew could add. 'Incidentally, I would think carefully before chucking me.'

'I have my pride.'

Rupert laughed out loud. 'You've just confirmed that we couldn't *possibly* have made a go of it.'

'That's a relief.'

'But there's no reason why we couldn't remain friends?'

Matthew did not try to hide the look of distaste. 'More like business associates, you mean?'

Rupert chuckled. 'Perhaps you're right, because I've long felt that Langdales looks more like a Victorian bank than a house. By the way,

306

my beloved sister is also looking for a weekend retreat in the Lakes. You wouldn't mind her using the spare room in my absence?'

'Caroline?' Head spinning, Matthew's patience almost snapped. 'You're implying that *she* would be here as well?'

Rupert winked. 'It seems that she would like to see more of Archie. She was quite distraught when she bade him farewell.'

Anticipating that he could not endure Caroline's pursed lips for long, he wondered whether Archie would resume his duties as paid help, or be reinvented as her ageing houseboy?

'Do I have a choice in the matter?'

Rupert outlined Matthew's options; they were not extensive.

When he was not forced to listen, Matthew was mulling over how he could ever hope to find another partner with Rupert descending on the place whenever he was resting – which would no doubt be frequent – given his new-found security?

For such a life-changing course of action there were too many unanswered questions, and as Matthew had been feeling that they had chewed over more than enough for some time, he brought matters to a close. Besides, perhaps because he had found Matthew less of a pushover than anticipated, and mindful of his journey, Rupert seemed determined to stay no longer than was necessary. There was no courtesy call later on to announce that he had arrived safely at his flat in Manchester.

Alone once more, Matthew carried the dishes inside. His spirits plummeted. Langdales began to feel desolate, but he soon had time to think while puffing behind the lawnmower.

It was too easy to visualise Rupert ensconced at Langdales for weeks on end, hogging the fire with his hands behind his back, opining for hours at a stretch. Then there would be Caroline's baleful expressions whenever she came to stay. Matthew wished to retain control of Langdales, but he did not relish adding to his mortgage to buy out Tom; if so, those thoughts of early retirement would need re-thinking. Having the Hammonds as benefactors forced upon him was not without menace, and would threaten to override his existence in ways he had never conceived. Although he was mowing the lawn, he shivered.

Meanwhile, he had little to do with the rest of that Sunday afternoon but fret, until Caroline, of all people, appeared. She must be using his cottage for the final days of the letting agreement. This, surely, was no coincidence? Even so, the shock value was immense; noticing her driving up while mowing at the side of the house, he tried to appear happy.

As he watched her extricate herself from her green sports car (hood down) and glance upwards, he imagined she must be weighing up the size of the attic. She looked conspicuously cool in a becoming cream outfit. Matthew, however, had not finished mowing, was overheated and dishevelled. He would have benefited from a shower.

Flinty eyes notwithstanding, she smiled while pulling off her driving gloves, and waited. 'Good afternoon, Matthew.'

Quickly removing his gardening gloves he shook hands, dutifully offered her his condolences regarding her father, and apologised for looking unsightly.

She winked at him, which boded well. 'Fortunately, I have not come to see you in your summer finery.'

'May I offer you some tea?'

'Not just at present, thank you. I really came to talk to you about the attic flat. What is the situation with it?'

'The situation?'

'You realise that Langdales has brought me here?' He nodded. 'No doubt you have heard a lot of nonsense from Rupert regarding my search for a second home?'

He glanced down. 'Indeed.'

'The plan is as follows – I *am* looking to invest – and the possibility of your attic apartment has been wafted in front of me. There is only one problem.' She searched his face.

'You've never actually seen it?'

'Therefore my aim this afternoon, or what's left of it,' she told him, glancing at her watch, 'is to make some sort of reasoned assessment.'

'But the bed? What if it's unmade?' he asked, remembering its dishevelled state.

'That is irrelevant, and I won't be fobbed off. I am here to view the layout, and gauge the light levels, but if this is not a good time?'

'No problem, but I must bathe and eat after I've finished the grass.'

She smiled. 'Surely that does not take precedence over a prospective purchaser?'

He showed her inside, and they walked briskly up two flights of stairs with their heads down, he bare-footed.

Throwing open the door to the flat, he dreaded to think how hideous it might look, and headed for the bed, while she poked about – stooping occasionally – and finally fanning the tiny kitchen by opening various cupboard doors.

'Everything seems to be in order,' she told him, gravitating towards the centre of the living area, just as her brother would have done. 'As you may also have guessed, I am not visiting merely to view what's available.'

He offered her a chair. 'I prefer standing, but thank you. Rupert has disclosed a great deal of late, not least his plans regarding this place, which now appear to have become mine, too.' All Matthew wanted was to shower and get rid of her. 'What are *your* feelings in all this?'

'From what I've experienced, I realise that we could not have succeeded as a match.'

'Just as I thought, although it's good to have it confirmed.'

'Quite.'

She coughed. 'However, I feel I must emphasise that the embers of his feelings – for *you* – have not been extinguished, no matter what he may have led you to believe.'

'And there was I, hoping that I'd be allowed to live in peace.'

Knitting her brows, she paced up and down, desirous of completing her inspection. 'If you recall, we touched on Rupert's recent past when we were reunited, and I have no wish to digress on the horrors of that sordid episode. I'm afraid I must warn you against trusting him.'

'But *you* seem happy enough to?'

Chancing a smile, she replied, 'I am his sister, for my sins, and therefore have little choice in the matter.'

He nodded. 'Tell me, did you mean trust him as a potential partner or a business partner?'

She stood still and looked him in the eye. 'Both. If he does move in, you must be firm with him from the outset, so that he understands the boundaries. I have no desire to arrive for a relaxing break to find myself encircled by a throng of squabbling homosexuals.'

The back of his neck prickled. Not for the first time did he think that she would have made a better job of Lady Bracknell than either Eleanor or her brother. 'Is that the collective noun?' No reply. 'Why do you imagine that we would be squabbling?'

'No doubt Rupert would be putting it about that you are not prepared to share your favours with him. Forgive me, I'm not explaining myself well.'

'Far from it. You've made yourself perfectly clear.'

'If he becomes a business partner, with a half-share in this property, make sure everything is water-tight.'

'I have no idea what happens if I come to sell, and I need both your permission and his?'

'That's enough to give anyone a headache. However, his plans may never come to fruition.'

She had lost him, but his spirits rose. 'You're suggesting that – ?'

'Depending on your position with Tom, of course.'

He blinked. 'You don't mean sexual?'

She pursed her lips. 'Of course not! The situation as it seems to me, is to forget Rupert's elaborate scheme and recover whatever you can of that relationship. From the little I witnessed, you appeared to be a lively and interesting couple. What happened?'

'My instincts told me that Tom had fallen for someone younger.'

'Which begs the question as to whether they were reliable?' She met his gaze. 'I'm afraid I have had more than my fair share of that with my brother. He is oscillating between at least two younger men just at present, and it's not a habit I seem to be able to break him of.'

'What a pity.'

'For him, or the young men?'

'Both?'

'Touché,' she replied, smiling. 'But we digress. You must not only apologise, you must do everything possible to start a new life with Tom.'

'I would have liked to, although if I did? I mean, that really would prevent Rupert, and presumably your good self, from buying out Tom's half-share?'

'A new life may not necessarily involve Langdales for any of us,' she observed, mysteriously. 'You never know, you might even have an idea of your own about this?'

'If you say so.'

Although she was now peering out of the largest window, she turned to see if he was listening. 'As you can imagine, I had to test Rupert on his lines before he came up here. So many of them resonate with your predicament. Tom is thirty-five, I hear?' Matthew agreed. 'A very attractive age, as the play has it, in which to settle down. With his fresh-faced appeal and charm, few impediments – it would seem – prevent him from settling into a new relationship?'

'I can't argue with that.'

'From what you've just indicated, he may have achieved that happy state already?'

'The two things rarely go together,' he replied testily, beginning to sound like the play and ape Caroline's measured way of speaking. 'Surely you're not implying that as I am older, I am therefore at a disadvantage?'

'You will certainly find it more difficult than him. Of course, his new relationship, such as it is, may not prosper, which brings me to my next point. Are his parents living?'

'I believe so.'

'I advise you to be careful.' He tried to cover a swallow. 'If his future with you continues to look bleak, his most obvious exit is to flee to them, and disappear for good.'

'I'm afraid that particular escape route is already in the planning stages, Caroline.'

'Then you are in danger of saying farewell to him for good. What is his income?'

'Without me, very little.'

'He seems indebted to you for a great deal?'

'I shared everything with him.'

'Except understanding, perhaps? And since that time, no occupation, no income, no dwelling-place?'

'You appear to be relieving him of that.'

She eyed him sternly. 'I must urge you to consider a volte-face with him. You have probably overreacted to his wrongdoing – whether or not it existed is a case in point – but we can blame that on your dramatic bent.'

'*Excuse me*, but I'm afraid everything pointed to a liaison under my very nose.'

'Then you must make time to reflect.' She stood up straight. 'Undoubtedly, a whole raft of problems will come surging your way, if he makes his final exit? It would, undoubtedly, leave you lonely and isolated. Just get him back is my advice, before it's too late. My plans for a second home are still fluid, and Rupert might just have to put himself out and look elsewhere.'

'I intend to.'

'Intentions are no use!' she exclaimed. 'Get weaving. And whatever happens, don't give Rupert any quarter. Hopefully, you shouldn't find that too difficult?'

'I shall make it a priority.'

'No, your priority involves making a fuss of your handsome young friend.'

'You have given me renewed hope – '

'Wine and dine him then. You will be more in tune with the niceties than I am, unless you've forgotten?'

'If I can't win him back, the house will be densely populated with Hammonds, so I will block you both if I can.'

She forced a smile. 'You don't relish our being on hand?'

He was not sure how far he dared go with her, but as this could be their final meeting he plunged in with, 'To be brutally frank – and without wishing to upset you – not in the least. But your advice is more than I deserve. Thank you for coming.'

He was hoping this would prompt her to leave when her eyes fell on the low door in the corner. She was soon ducking beneath it. He squeezed next to her, could sense that she was impressed by the early summer view of wood and meadow, and convinced himself that she might well be on her way to becoming a part-owner of a place that had become so dear to him.

Chapter Fifteen

A renewal of nerves notwithstanding, the Monday evening's performance passed off straightforwardly, as did the second, but the third night was eminently unforgettable, for reasons he had least expected. The first interval was in progress and he was happily dozing in the dressing room when he was rudely awakened by a familiar sharp rap on the door. It was Eleanor, and she was looking her age. Matthew's shoulders drooped but he tried to appear nonchalant. Knowing they did not have long, he offered her James's chair in front of the mirror, while he perched on the edge of the bed. Furtive beyond belief, she opened her mouth but appeared to think better of it. Then she looked away, and then back at him quickly. 'I'm not sure if you noticed, but I don't think that my big scene could be regarded as an undisputed triumph.'

He did his level best to appear non-committal. 'What's the problem?'

'I can't possibly go on stage again with all this whirring around in my head.'

'With all what whirring around?'

Her voice was flat and expressionless. 'I can't go on.'

Half-smiling, he asked, 'Do you mean you can't go on stage or you can't go on with life?'

She gave him a sideways look. 'Things have altered since I met Dorian.'

Seizing upon this, he was unable to conceal the note of triumph in his voice. 'Didn't I tell you he would be a problem?'

'Living with Dorian is not without its difficulties.'

'He's behaving himself, I hope?'

'Exemplary, but we can attribute the latest upset to Felicity. She's been asking him about replacing her winter casualties and claims that he is ignorant of sub-tropical-looking plants.'

'That would either need a specialist or an enthusiast? Which is he?'

She shrugged. 'She's undermining him, and she may well be spreading it.'

'Like manure? She probably covets him.'

'Maybe. But worse than that, do you remember telling me that Rupert was making a far better job of Lady Bracknell than I ever could?' Matthew could only offer her a lame expression. 'That really dented my confidence.' Shame-faced, he made no comment. 'But, knowing I'll never be as good as Rupert has been gnawing away at me.'

'You do take things to heart.'

She narrowed her eyes. 'And you don't?' He let that one pass. 'Can you keep a secret?' He nodded. 'I don't mind telling you that I've had an attack of stage fright this afternoon. Imagine! I didn't want to go on.'

He began concentrating more intently. 'You've clearly been over-doing it, but how can I help?'

'I'm coming to that.' She hesitated. 'I'm not exaggerating when I say I'm falling apart. I need an excuse to escape before the end of the run.'

'*Escape?* It's not as dire as all that, surely?'

'I don't suppose you have ever felt as drained of all confidence? I'm worried I'm not going to make it.' She heaved a sigh and reached for a tissue in front of her.

'We did warn you that you were taking a lot on.'

'I can't help being so much in demand, can I?' Deep breath. 'This is going to sound very peculiar, but you wouldn't happen to know if Rupert is still available?'

He stood up, mainly because sitting on the bed was making his back ache, and placed his hand on her shoulder. 'To perform Lady Bracknell? I never thought I'd hear those words.'

'I mean it.'

'You're timing is rotten, as usual. He left on Sunday.' Seeing that she had dried her eyes, Matthew hoped they were over the worst. 'Correct me if I'm wrong, but surely you can't be thinking of begging him?'

Noticing her reflection in the mirror, she started taking an interest in her appearance. 'I do not *beg*, but he'd come scurrying back soon enough if I requested him to. I suppose he's been *longing* for something like this to happen, but with diminishing options and all that– '

'I suppose there's no harm in sounding him out,' said Matthew, struggling to think straight. 'But not for tonight, surely?'

'Just the last three nights,' she said quietly, as if realising how much she was giving up.

'Hold on. Are you really proposing that Rupert replaces you for the rest of the run?'

Her fists were clenched in her lap. 'I know when I'm beaten. How I've just dragged myself through that big scene I'll never know, and the thought of continuing is torture.'

Matthew stroked his chin for a moment and returned to the bed. 'I've never seen you this flattened. Is there something else you haven't shared with me?'

She lowered her eyes. 'Actually, something *has* happened.'

Secretly delighted that she was now in his confidence, he resumed his perch on the bed. 'From the look on your face, presumably not for the better?'

'Dorian has taken me on one side for a long chat.'

'About the garden?'

'Of course not!' She looked away. 'Thinks I should be less mean-spirited in my dealings with Rupert. Tap into my chivalrous side.'

Matthew stared. 'Is there one when it comes to WAFT?'

'If there is, it's gossamer thin.' She grinned. 'But I've had to promise Dorian – and you've no idea how it galls me to tell you this – that I need to forgive Rupert. It seems the least I can do.'

'To atone? You *have* been unstable for some time now.'

'And you haven't?' She examined his face. 'Can I share something else with you?' He leaned forward. 'I really do believe he is the one.'

He stretched out his arm and offered her his hand. 'I've been thinking along similar lines myself.'

'Not about Dorian, surely?'

He shook his head. The room felt airless, and he moved further back on the bed. 'Tom. There's no denying I've made a hash of things. I'd go so far as to say that I may well have lost him for good.'

'I'm worn out with hinting that you need to get him back.'

'How can I, when he's planning on leaving the Lakes?'

'You don't think there's been a change of direction?'

Matthew felt his stomach tighten. 'Not with James? I haven't got long before I have to go on, you know.'

She rose from the chair. 'But I've nowhere near finished.' She took a step towards him. '*I* may not be giving of my finest, but surely you've noticed that they're playing opposite each other better than ever?' Her words followed in a rush. 'They can't take their eyes off each other, and I get the impression that it might have re-ignited.'

Matthew could not bear to think that their rapprochement would inevitably spell out the end for him. 'It might just be that they've decided to give the production everything they've got? Have you thought of that?'

'Well, I've just been on stage with them, and you haven't. I can assure you that they were electrifying. So much so, that I felt up-staged. What's more, from the look on his face, James is cosying up to Tom during the interval in a big way. That's how I knew you'd be sulking in here.'

'I was *not* – '

The door flew open. As smug as ever, despite his hair being tousled and his clothes rumpled, James stalked in. Eleanor greeted him coolly, and left. Matthew could ignore his own entrance no longer and followed.

Once the performance was over, and Matthew was watching James out of the corner of his eye, he began to ponder Eleanor's latest angle on the leading man and Tom. Yet he remained uncertain as to how he could bring himself to ask James directly, because he dreaded the reply.

James had almost finished undressing, when he glanced over. 'What's this I've been hearing about Eleanor?'

'A private matter so I can't help you there, except that she's planning to step down.'

'So it *is* true.' James chuckled, while admiring himself in the mirror. 'We assume that Rupert will be ecstatic, and fully able to reappear at a moment's notice? Funnily enough, I'm missing him.'

'I'm sure he's aching for you, too.'

'I *meant* not having him out front.' He prodded Matthew in the chest. 'But what uplifting news for *you*.'

'And what is that supposed to mean?' enquired Matthew, recoiling slightly.

'Oh, *come on*, Matthew. It's common knowledge that you're pining for him.'

Matthew set his face. 'I don't know how you work that out.'

'He would be much better company for you in here than I could ever be.'

'So that you can go back to sharing with Tom?'

James pulled on his jeans and went on to button them slowly, clearly enjoying the audience of one. 'We're over-familiar with your defence, but it's been obvious that you two are biding your time.'

Matthew gasped. 'Tom doesn't believe that?'

'He had convinced himself that it would be a matter of weeks.'

'Why didn't he speak up?'

'When you were doing more than enough to unravel things?'

'What do you really think of Rupert, as the instigator of so many of our problems?'

James was combing his hair with the utmost care. 'So droll, especially about you.'

'What a pity that you two share the same vicious sense of humour. Why don't *you* share this room with Rupert?'

'And have him look me up and down, like you do? No thanks.'

Matthew blushed. 'I thought you enjoyed the attention. Well, there isn't time to sort out the dressing rooms now, and we're both tired. Just between ourselves, I don't think Tom could have played Jack quite as well as you have.'

'That's very gracious of you in the circumstances.' He replaced his comb in his pocket just as Tom entered.

Tom nodded cautiously at Matthew and looked at James. 'Ready?'

James turned and smiled at Matthew from the doorway before finally disappearing. Matthew refused to look at him, and covered his ears when he heard muffled laughter wafting down the corridor. He was numb with tiredness when he got back to Langdales, and could remember nothing about that journey the next day. Still, work had to be done and he was stripping a bed the next morning when his ringing mobile became a welcome distraction.

'I suppose you've heard the latest?' enquired Rupert.

In teasing mood, Matthew asked, 'But where will you stay?'

'You can't have forgotten our arrangement so quickly?' responded Rupert, in familiar tones. 'I have some other news, but that will have to wait. See you before the performance.' With that, he rang off.

Matthew spent the rest of the day wondering what the news might be and feeling tired; tired of Eleanor, Tom, James, and especially the play.

It was after four o'clock by the time Rupert showed up. 'There's somebody in the car I'd like to introduce you to.'

In no mood for sudden surprises a nonplussed Matthew followed in Rupert's wake, and greeted the well-dressed young stranger emerging from the front seat. He, in turn, seemed intrigued by Matthew. Seeing as he was young and well-put-together, Matthew assumed that Rupert could not resist showing off a new conquest, but a gnawing doubt made him uneasy.

Matthew was encouraged to retreat a little, while Rupert whispered something private in the young man's ear. Incensed by Rupert's rudeness, but watching the man resume his place in the front passenger seat, Matthew smiled and walked the few paces to the house with Rupert. From Rupert's expression and brisk pace, Matthew felt as if he had landed up in the wrong scene. Sensing discord, he braced himself.

Once the front door was firmly shut Rupert made for the sitting room, bade Matthew to take an armchair and slammed the door with such force that the nearest pictures shook.

'Sorry for the impromptu visit, but there *is* something *vital* I need to share with you. Sadly, I wasn't in a position to raise it before.'

'Let me guess. Festival fund-raisers such as "*Selected Readings from William and Dorothy Wordsworth*", with Eleanor during the winter?'

Rupert scoffed. 'No, but ever mindful of your acute sensitivity, I decided to wait until we were alone. You won't have forgotten the conversation earlier because it – fortunately or unfortunately – impacts on you?' Matthew shifted his position. 'Sorry to inflict this on you, old boy, but even you – dim as you are – must have registered that I became a father several months after she called off the wedding?'

Matthew made no reply, and the silence persisted.

'There's no use looking at me,' he told Rupert, finding his voice at last.

'But I *am* looking at you.' Rupert sat on the sofa. Drumming on the side-table with his finger-tips, he allowed another silence to gather weight. 'And never more intently.'

'What does he think?'

'Let's hope he doesn't take the same dim view– '

'You're not suggesting..?' Matthew pushed back his chair, struggled to get up.

'Now you've seen him, doesn't it seem a coincidence that he has your nose and dimpled chin?' Rupert's smile was more than he could bear.

He sat down again with a thump. 'But your fiancée had dark hair.' Rupert sighed. It had become clear that there was no point in lying. 'You were always on some assignment or another, and we were both missing you.' Rupert snorted. 'Let me finish. We both needed a part of you. We felt impelled to get closer to you–'

'By getting closer to *each other*?'

'I know this won't sound good, but she grew very fond of me while you were away.'

'So one evening, when you'd both had too much to drink..?'

'You, of all people, know how quickly things can spiral out of control.'

'You got your revenge three times.'

Matthew widened his eyes. 'How do you mean?'

Rupert stared back. 'You not only bedded my fiancée, but sabotaged the wedding, and fathered my son.'

'I was jealous of you with her, and of her with you, I won't deny it. But you can't begin to understand how frustrated I had become with you.'

'You've always been that.'

'When it came to the wedding day, I was fuming.'

'Nothing new there, and as you'd been jealous enough to bed her–
'

'I'd grown fond of her, *actually*.'

'So it happened more than once?'

Matthew looked down. 'You cast a long shadow for too long.'

319

'The fact remains that, because of *you*, my son was brought up pretty much single-handed by his mother. I was responsible for him, of course, and I paid up.' Rupert chuckled sarcastically. 'Oh, yes, I paid up all right. But thanks to you, Matthew, who deceived me all those years ago, he's been denied the family life he deserved. Have you anything to say?'

'I'm sorry, but I had no idea that she was pregnant.' (True, he had suspected something, had feared recriminations, exacerbated when Rupert bounced back into his life, had gone as far as bracing himself to bear them, but he had not imagined this confrontation.)

Experiencing feelings of both shame and pride, Matthew eyed him. 'This won't upset your plans?'

A flash of teeth. 'Buying half? Far from it. I had drawn my own conclusions long before I made my decision to bail you out.' He pondered this for a moment. 'I may as well continue to rescue you, but on one condition.'

'Go on.'

'As long as you promise to leave my share of Langdales – or the equivalent held in any other property you may have at the time – to our son in your will.'

'*Our* son? I rather like that.'

'There's no need to be flippant.'

'How will he react to having two fathers?'

'I haven't the faintest idea, and I care even less.'

'What's he like?'

'Surprisingly placid,' replied Rupert, 'given his parentage. Although I could have lived without him going off to *find* himself.'

'Perhaps he sensed something wasn't right? That you might not be – '

'I can't see how, seeing as I lavished every possible luxury on the boy.'

'I trust you haven't spoiled him.' Matthew hesitated. 'You don't think she might have hinted at something to him?'

'I doubt it. In general, whenever I showed up, she had enough of a challenge being a peacemaker.' He paused to reflect. 'Although she could be vengeful if trifled with.'

'You're not far wrong there. But back to our son, I wonder if he found what he was seeking?'

'So many of them go through that restlessness and unease, but I didn't have time.' Rupert smiled. 'I've never done angst. If my family didn't like what they heard, that was their problem.'

'Best not to dwell on that for too long,' observed Matthew. 'From what you've said, I'll agree to anything to atone for what I've done in my will.' Rupert nodded. Mindful of the visitor waiting patiently outside, and hoping to round things off, Matthew asked, 'It looks as if you're the master of the situation once again, but where does this leave Tom?'

'Don't be so obtuse. I'm buying him out, aren't I? I think you can safely forget about Tom once he's secured his – may I say, munificent – financial settlement.'

'Remind me, what was Wilde's definition of a cynic?' Matthew could feel his cheeks burning. 'I can never forget Tom.'

'Just as you purported never to have forgotten *me*, during your initial phone-call?' Matthew refused to rise to this, and a somewhat deflated Rupert appeared to soften. 'Time to crack open the champagne?' Matthew nodded distractedly, and Rupert went to fetch the young man.

Seth wore a slightly bemused – but not hostile – expression. Matthew liked what he saw. Tall, with even features, he appeared to be wearing his best clothes, as if desirous of making a good impression. Matthew's emotions could hardly have been described as creaking from lack of use, but seeing this manifestation of his own flesh and blood made him catch his breath. The more Matthew took him in, he began to recognise himself. Seth was a copy of himself in his mid-twenties. He felt his eyes pricking with tears, and he had to swallow hard.

'What about our celebratory drink?' demanded Rupert.

'Don't spoil this for me,' Matthew replied absent-mindedly. Shaking his son's hand, he discerned a genuine warmth, and attempted to clasp Seth in his arms, but it turned into a clumsy hug.

Seth sounded thoroughly masculine with his deep voice, deeper than Matthew's. 'I am so pleased to meet you at last.'

At least, he's presentable, thought Matthew, reflecting on the days when he had missed Rupert, how he had been attracted to his fiancée, and the occasions when he had succumbed to her charms. They had a dream-like quality as if never having taken place. A quarter of a century later, he was forcing himself to come to terms with reality. Here was the result; something he had never imagined as a remote possibility. Not only did he have a son, he was smiling. Yet his main concern was whether he would be accepted.

Having believed that Rupert had been his parent for twenty-five years, only to have him replaced by his biological father might lead Seth to reject him. To have one gay dad *"may be considered a misfortune"*, although looking at Seth's calm face he somehow doubted it, but what would his take be on having *two*? From what Matthew knew of Rupert, he would not be content to be airbrushed out of the picture.

Not having come to terms with fatherhood yet, Matthew failed to share the jollity of comic-opera librettists in creating funny situations. He allowed himself another fond look at Seth, and as there did happen to be a bottle of champagne in the fridge, reserved for Tom in case he had shown up after the first night, he went to fetch it. Rupert was on his heels.

Having closed the kitchen door firmly, Matthew lowered his voice. It would be easy to ask questions while he had something to do, even putting ice in the champagne bucket. 'How much have you told him?'

Rupert smiled. 'He must have been curious, or he wouldn't have joined me.'

'And his reaction?'

'Surprisingly – given the circumstances and your antics – he didn't seem unduly put out, but right now he's being polite to cover his surprise.'

'You don't think young people today have as many hang-ups?'

'Although you did put him in an unusual situation – '

'As long as it's not a predicament. Can I ask where he might be staying?' asked Matthew, anxious to deflect the attention from himself.

'I imagined you'd be full, so he's staying with Caroline at the cottage. He's promised to come to the show tomorrow night.'

'That's a relief,' said Matthew. 'I would have been running out of rooms.' He grabbed three flutes and gestured to Rupert to bring the champagne bucket. Once their glasses were bubbling, Matthew glanced at the better-looking version of himself.

'I'm sorry if this has come as something of a shock,' he said, handing Seth his glass and signalling that he should sit down. Rupert continued to stand, as if directing the proceedings.

Seth smiled. 'It sounds as though the situation has been out of your hands.'

'That's been the trouble. I was in a difficult place for so long. I'm also sorry for not being there for you as a father.' Matthew sat down on the edge of the sofa nearest Seth's chair. The reality of this new state of affairs was getting to be more than he could cope with. 'Owing to the peculiar situation we found ourselves in, I was never told that I'd made your mother pregnant, and we went our separate ways.' Seth nodded. 'I have never seen her again, and I only met Rupert – quite by chance – in January.'

'If it puts your mind at rest,' replied Seth, acknowledging Rupert. 'I've had a very good upbringing. Yes, it would have been nice to know the truth about my circumstances earlier, but I'm not here to take anyone to task.'

'I was worried you might have been upset that I never came forward, as if I had been abdicating my responsibility, but I remained ignorant. I am sorry, but more to the point, can you cope with two fathers?'

'As long as you don't compete with each other in getting over-protective! But who should I take fatherly advice from?'

Rupert joined Matthew on the sofa. 'And you mustn't play one of us off against the other.'

Seth grinned.

'But you're fine with us both?'

'I wouldn't be here now if I wasn't.'

'He is too much in the sun,' said Rupert.

'Isn't that from *Hamlet*?' asked Matthew.

Rupert looked from one to the other. 'I'd forgotten how handsome you used to be, Matthew.' They drank a toast to Seth. 'Now I insist that you have some time together.' Rupert rose and let himself out through the French windows, refilling his glass as he went.

Seth smiled at Matthew nervously. 'I've not seen him to talk to – or should I say, listen to – properly for so long now.'

Matthew eyed Seth over the top of his flute. 'You can put your disappearing act behind you now and see more of him, but I hope you used to meet up – even if only occasionally – as part of an established routine?'

Seth laughed. 'Rupert doesn't *have* an established routine. It was haphazard – to say the least – when I was small, when he still had lots of work. But I don't want to spoil today by complaining.'

Matthew took another sip or two while he absorbed this. 'I'm sorry for not giving you the childhood you deserved.'

'How were you to know? Besides, Dad – Rupert – always spoiled me dreadfully, did his best for me, and I'm now a management trainee.'

Matthew smiled. 'To think I never knew of your existence. This may sound odd, but I loved both your parents.'

'You were head-over-heels with Dad, from what he told me.'

'Tapping into his inexhaustible need for adulation? Whether we like it or not, that's all in the past.'

Seth was staring at him. 'I wouldn't be too sure of that on his side.' Matthew tried not to fidget. 'He was telling me how much you meant to each other aged from seventeen to twenty-four, was it? That's a long time.'

'A very long time ago now,' said Matthew, feeling a warm glow as he thought back to those days.

'And now that your past does seem to have caught up with you, you should embrace it.'

Matthew looked away for a moment. 'Maybe I should, but I even messed up their wedding. There is a lot I would do differently.'

'There's no point in torturing yourself.'

Matthew wondered how he could be so mature. 'I excel at it, as you'll find out.'

The young man sprang up from his armchair and moved around the room, pausing at the occasional painting. 'A daft question, but do you think Dad might benefit from some stability in his life?'

Matthew chuckled. 'Your father and stability seem diametrically opposed.'

'Seriously though, is it not something you've contemplated?'

'Is that what he favours?'

'For what it's worth, he's indicated that you're still the one.'

'That's not always how it comes over,' said Matthew, coolly.

'Don't you feel anything for him these days?'

'Hard to say. Even back then, I felt it was more on my side. Perhaps I was burnt out with him at the end, and I've not totally recovered.'

Seth smiled. 'He just wanted me to put in a word, nothing too heavy.'

'You are very uncomplicated, and it's very noble of you, but before you have us living happily ever after...' Matthew hesitated. 'Has Rupert mentioned that he's planning to buy a half-share of this property?' Seth nodded. 'I'm interested in whether you can see yourself visiting from time to time?'

'I could visit you both, assuming things work out.'

'Please don't bank on us getting back together.'

'But you *have* to, especially now. You realise that Rupert adores this place?'

'You may be missing the point. If he's intent on forging a new relationship, he should adore *me*, but I am not sure that he does.' He searched Seth's face. 'Besides, I was under the impression that he considered it rather ugly.'

Seth winked. 'More like, he was envious.'

Rupert wafted back in, placed his empty glass on the table and gave his Seth a knowing look. 'I suppose you're complaining that I wasn't around enough?'

'I wasn't there for you, either, because I didn't know you existed, but I intend to be in future.' Matthew glanced first at Seth and then at Rupert. 'So what happens next?'

'We try and act normally?' replied Rupert.

'Life without Tom can never be the same for me to do that.' Rupert groaned while Matthew studied Seth's face. 'You've heard about my problems, I take it?' He agreed that he had.

Rupert smiled at Seth. 'You will always be welcome here.' He included Matthew in his gaze. 'Won't he?'

The difficulties of the last few weeks began to recede; Matthew murmured in agreement.

'I'd like that,' said Seth.

Matthew gave Seth his full attention. 'Yes, of course, you must visit as often as you like.'

Rupert checked his watch. 'Oh, my word, I feel we should make a move, grab something to eat and get ready for the performance, without delay.'

Chapter Sixteen

No one would have thought it possible, least of all Matthew, but it took place: Rupert performed the role of Lady Bracknell, and carried it off superbly. Much to the ire of the stage-hands, who kept bumping into him, Matthew made sure he had the best view from the wings to observe his performance. Although he had enjoyed Eleanor's portrayal of Lady Bracknell, she was indisputably arch and often mannered beyond belief. Rupert's would always be the more fully realised performance. He could transform himself into Lady Bracknell, and – although his overplaying towards the end tended to grate – his crisp intonations and expressions of bewilderment were savoured by the majority.

The cast responded, too; they usually managed to give more of themselves whenever Rupert appeared. There was little doubt that his presence lifted the action to a higher plane, and in turn, they responded by giving more credible performances. A desire to please prevailed, especially after the way Eleanor had stolen what they had come to accept as *his* role. It was as if they needed to salvage something positive from the altered change of events, and those scenes involving Rupert soon became the highlights of the play. Rupert had returned to take his rightful place, and James made sure that their scenes together crackled; he was instrumental in easing the transition from Eleanor to Rupert.

James had certainly improved immeasurably since the first rehearsals, both in his command of the role, and with his stage presence. Eleanor had been correct; he and Tom were still gazing into each other's eyes and playing so well together that they were a joy to watch. In spite of the ongoing exhibitionism between "the boys", Matthew found it difficult to ignore the charged atmosphere emanating from Rupert and James in their scenes together, even taking in to account their innate sense of mischief. He was slightly perplexed.

Not only were they working in harmony as actors, there appeared to be a growing personal attraction. Was it Matthew's imagination, or were they brushing against each other on purpose? It was easy for Rupert to hold James in his gaze when Lady Bracknell interviews Jack in the handbag scene. Knowing Rupert so intimately, Matthew had an inkling that there was more to it than that. Could it be a repeat of James and Tom? Interestingly, James was quite distant with Rupert when they were not in a scene together, as if he was carefully diverting the cast from sly murmurs and innuendoes. Matthew, however, convinced himself that something was afoot.

He was also missing Eleanor. She had *"not felt up to watching"* the play that evening, and Matthew imagined Dorian attempting to console her in probably the only way he knew how. Sadly, she had become, in Matthew's eyes, a woman of no importance, but he hoped that feeling would pass.

The remaining two nights went off without incident, but the glowing review in The Westmorland Gazette, which, naturally, had caught Eleanor's first night performance, would be retained in the festival archives long after Rupert's performances had been forgotten.

There was the usual after-show party at the end of the run, but Matthew did not attend. Quite simply, he was exhausted.

The following Sunday morning was warm and sunny, and after the paying guests had breakfasted and heard quite enough about Rupert's film career, he remained alone in the dining room. It would soon be time for Matthew to repeat his farewells; wearisome, when they had uttered whatever they had to say a few days prior to this. Still, it had to be done, so once Matthew had tidied the kitchen, he joined Rupert with a fresh pot of coffee and sat down opposite.

Rupert glanced up from the newspaper and Matthew felt himself trapped in a scene that showed every appearance of becoming scarily domesticated. 'So, do you think you'll be happy with the new arrangement when it takes place?' asked Rupert.

'I wouldn't go that far.' Matthew busied himself with the coffee and wondered how much domestic bliss he could have coped with had things been different. The newspaper was folded and placed to one side. 'But there again, why would I be happy?'

'Don't forget that with my money, you'll soon be able to buy out Tom.'

'I'm hardly in the mood for thinking about that.'

'Even though your troubles would be over?'

'Some of them, perhaps, but I wouldn't like to put you to more bother than I have already.'

'No trouble, when you think what I'm gaining.'

'Meanwhile, my options seem to be diminishing rapidly,' sighed Matthew, wishing that he could get rid of him before too much was said.

'So, am I right in thinking that Tom is planning to live with his parents?' asked Rupert, making himself more comfortable. This question floated between them like a toxic stench, while Rupert sipped his coffee and contented himself with eyeing his host for a few moments.

At length, and trying to look imperturbable, Matthew replied, 'I had hoped for a change of heart; not that anything matters now.'

Rupert, lingering over the last of the coffee in his cup, became expansive. 'No doubt he'll find it a wrench, although his loss is my gain. Poor Tom. He's bound to miss living in not one, but two spacious properties? I'm sure he's wanted for nothing at Spinnakers – '

'Talking of Spinnakers – '

'You haven't heard?' asked Rupert, gravely.

Matthew swallowed, wondering what he had last said to her. 'Nothing serious, I hope?'

'She was looking very wan, and – quite out of character for her – was almost contrite.'

'You charged in? Uninvited?'

'More like crept inside a mausoleum. You see, I felt I ought to do the decent thing —'

'In that case, that was kind, considering how she's treated you.'

'My dear, she was looking an absolute *ruin*.'

'I've known her a long time,' said Matthew. 'She'll get over it.'

'I'm not so sure, but – there again – I've never been as intimately acquainted as you have.' Matthew let that one go, watching in relief as he finally downed the last drop, and glanced at his watch. 'Dorian does seem genuinely fond of her, and that's bound to help. Well, I'd better be going. I have to collect Seth.'

Matthew turned his head slowly. 'Is this it?' He nodded. 'I'll wait to hear from James, then?'

Rupert looked at him sharply. 'You mean as my solicitor?'

'What did you think I meant?'

'Doesn't it feel strange?' Rupert fiddled with the newspaper, while Matthew did not trust himself to speak, and kept his face blank. 'The end of life at Langdales, as you once knew it?'

'I'm hoping it won't change *that* much,' said Matthew, testily, for he hated the mention of a prospect that was becoming increasingly inevitable. 'Although the *occasional* visit from you will make a change, I shall always relish a visit from Seth.'

'Oh, more often than that, I hope,' laughed Rupert. 'I'm *so* looking forward to us getting to know each other again properly, aren't you? Just think, with no rehearsals and no play hanging over us, you might guide me through some of that glorious countryside.' He waved vaguely in the direction of the French windows. 'Although, without Tom fetching and carrying for you, won't you be more tied down out there?'

'I wish I didn't dislike it so much without him.'

Rupert wagged his finger. 'You should never have agreed to that trial separation.'

'That was his suggestion, I tell you! Not mine.'

Rupert threw up his hands theatrically. 'Whatever, you've blown it. Even if Tom did want to return, which I doubt, he'd lose face, because you've allowed him to remove his belongings.'

'Do you require anything else before you have to leave?' asked Matthew.

Rupert turned to gaze out of the window more fully; he seemed in no hurry to make a move. 'I do hope I'm not getting to you? So glorious here, when the sun is shining. I'll be in touch. Don't you worry.'

Impatient to be rid of him, Matthew shook hands frostily, but once he had waved him off, it was time to reflect. Running Langdales with paid help during busy periods was just about viable, but recent days had confirmed that what Langdales really needed was a couple who were equally committed. He held out little hope that Rupert would exert himself to be anything more than a talkative sleeping partner with a predilection for rich food and white Burgundy. It was clear that Matthew would no doubt remain disenchanted with the B and B, but without Rupert's financial intrusion, there seemed to be no other solution.

For the rest of June, Matthew enjoyed something of a reprieve from Rupert. Fortunately, Tom, in the safety-net provided by his parents, and conveniently distant in Northamptonshire, was not pestering him for his half-share. Matthew remained stalled, merely going through the motions with his paying guests, while waiting for something to happen. Finally, the news broke.

In early July he received a rather formally worded letter advising him that Rupert had a purchaser for his father's villa. A couple of afternoons later, and again without warning, he landed on the front doorstep in person. They were settled over tea in no time, side by side on the sitting room sofa, just like old times. Yet once once the preliminaries were over, Rupert dropped his next bombshell, for which Matthew was totally unprepared.

'Caroline and I have been thinking,' he announced slyly, after a couple of dainty sips of tea.

'Please get to the point.'

'We were wondering if you could ever see yourself selling the old place?'

Trying not to blink, he tittered. 'Not to you two?'

'Who else is going to come forward?'

Matthew's voice rose by several octaves. 'In its entirety?'

'There's no need to sound quite so enthusiastic, when I'm doing you a favour.'

'Now let's not carried away.'

'Caroline, you already know about,' continued Rupert, airily. 'And once you and I have agreed on a price, I will be in a position to purchase.'

'What's brought this on?'

'Help from a backer.' Rupert rested his chin on his palm.

Matthew's eyes widened, as he looked around the sitting room as if for the last time, for this new take on his predicament had never seeped into his consciousness. Thinking quickly, certain aspects of this new scheme were not without merit. Not only to be released from Langdales, but to see it go to what he considered "the right sort of people" gave him satisfaction, but who had become the mysterious "backer"? Was Rupert really offering him an escape route? Having never warmed to the idea of Rupert owning a half-share in Langdales, he mellowed slightly.

Even so, he would need time for the idea to germinate. To be free of Rupert at the same time as Langdales – and all the work it entailed – lifted his spirits no end. Since Tom appeared to have left the area for good, Matthew now tried to envisage what a new life without both him and Langdales might involve, but failed.

Although the house meant so much to him, living there was a trial without like-minded help, and this summer only served to prove that the B and B did not run itself. Snapping out of these thoughts with a start, he registered that Rupert was addressing him.

'You realise you're in danger of overthinking this?'

'In all fairness, you will need to give me some time.'

'I fail to see why, when it couldn't be simpler. You pay off your mortgage, downsize to something more manageable, and invest what's left or put it in a rental property to provide you with an income. You will just have to curb your expensive tastes.'

'I don't really have any.'

'In that case,' said Rupert, 'a modest home and car should be adequate for your self-imposed bachelor status.'

'I appreciate your common sense, although the fun factor eludes me.'

'How *are* things with Squirrel, by the way? Made any progress?'

'I have no idea what you're talking about.'

'You know you can do better than that.'

'Even if there had been any developments you'd be the last to hear.'

Rupert smiled to himself. 'Touchy today, aren't we? Perhaps surrendering the old place is getting to you more than you care to admit?'

'All right, I do have news. He's had enough, given in his notice. Jane and Clare will be upgrading the café at La Boutique Fantasque and have offered him the position of manager.'

'When did you soak up all this if you're not speaking?' asked Rupert, not looking happy to hear this news one bit.

'I have to rely on Eleanor to keep me posted,' replied Matthew, unable to look him in the eye.

'So, he might creep back here, after all?'

'I don't see how, when he's staying with her and Dorian for the remainder of the summer but you can go through the finer points with him yourself soon. He plans to be back within the fortnight.' Rupert did not respond. Matthew rubbed his chin. 'Meanwhile, I'm struggling with what to do for the best.'

'This is your *cue*, Matthew. How can you just mope about?'

Matthew sipped his tea slowly: this needed careful consideration. 'I am *not* moping! James is still knocking around, of course. That worries me.'

'I wouldn't worry too much about *him*, if I were you,' replied Rupert, breezily.

'What's that supposed to mean?'

'James has more in common with Tom than you might think.'

Matthew put down his cup. 'I knew it! They *are* thinking of making a go of it, then?'

'Not exactly,' purred Rupert. 'He likes mature men, too, although I can't for the life of me imagine why.'

Feeling a weight lifting, he murmured, 'So you're saying those two are *not* compatible, after all?' Then, with dawning realisation, Matthew looked at Rupert more closely. 'You're not suggesting that you and he are making a go of it?' His voice trailed off. 'I hadn't realised it was reciprocal.'

Rupert covered his mouth coyly with his hand. 'Love at first sight. For me, at any rate.'

Registering who the mystery backer was, Matthew asked, 'But can you be sure he feels the same about you?'

'Let's say it's been gestating for some time. He's been visiting, and I've been popping up here occasionally, but I've kept it very hush-hush.' He put his finger to his lips. 'He's told me that Tom was his final flirtation — he was very upset about what he'd done to you both — and now he wants to settle down.'

'You're asking me to believe it's that simple?' Matthew raised an eyebrow. 'But could you cope with a surfeit of domestic bliss?'

'To think that someone might want to be cared for and loved by *me* gives me goose pimples.' Rupert shivered slightly.

'Speaking from memory, it's normally the opposite, but it has a chance of working if you both genuinely care for each other.'

'It's not just you and Eleanor who need a man. I'm in *dire* need of some stability, and I'm determined to make it work this time.'

'As long as neither of you misbehaves,' observed Matthew, in as even a tone as he could muster. 'Personally, I think you're congenitally incapable of existing in a monogamous relationship, and although James may be highly decorative, you know the pit-falls.'

Rupert blinked in mock surprise. 'You make him sound like an object in the V & A. Thinking about my new abode, I like the idea of seeing more of Seth.'

'In what way?'

'Providing a family home for him,' replied Rupert. 'Until he gets himself sorted. And you'll be able to visit him as much as you like. Having mentioned La Boutique Fantasque to him, I've been putting out feelers.'

'The shop you took an instant dislike to?'

'You're so out of touch! Haven't you heard that Jane and Clare want him to apply as trainee manager on the retail side? The girls are there most of the time, and I can't imagine he wouldn't fit in with all those up-scale goods, *"constantly being sourced in Siena."'*

Matthew smiled. 'Young Seth could well be working alongside Tom?'

'No reason why not. And as for his living arrangements, he could stay in the attic flat when Caroline's not there, and go into one of the bedrooms when she is. Until he finds his own place, that is.'

Matthew took a moment to reflect. 'Your plans suggest the B&B will be nothing more than a memory.'

'Our aim is to return Langdales to being a private house. Surely, that's what it deserves?'

'With you or James as chatelaine?'

Rupert grinned. 'That remains to be seen.'

'And you think you can trust James, in the event that you'll be working away from home?'

'Funny you should ask that. *Jubilee Way* has renewed my contract. Time will tell with James, but if Seth is working at La Boutique Fantasque, he can keep an eye on him for me. Don't forget that Caroline will often be here, too.' Rupert stood up. He was not long in going, and had timed his meeting with Matthew so that he could be waiting in James's flat for when he came home from work.

In spite of his dry mouth, Matthew had to concede that Rupert had been correct; he did indeed "want out", and he might not get as good an offer again for some time. They managed to agree on a price relatively quickly, but nothing could match up to the relief that James had been diverted from his interest in Tom. As planned, Tom returned to Spinnakers around the third week of July, in time for the summer holidays. For the time being, Matthew felt that any overtures on his part might not be considered welcome.

Without further ado, he began to wind up the B and B, packing discreetly, and accepting no further bookings after the middle of September. Any deposited bookings thereafter, or for the following season were refunded owing to an "unforeseen sale due to ill health". As there was no chain, the sale went through smoothly.

Knowing that James would be at work, Matthew had come up with the notion that he wanted to personally hand over the keys to Rupert. The first day of October began chilly, but bright. The place was looking almost as forlorn as on the morning when Matthew had arrived; the removal men had taken away most of the furniture the day before. The bulkiest items and most of the beds had been included in the sale, some of his remaining furniture was in store, and Matthew had over-filled the flat he was renting with what he deemed as essentials.

Having decided to rent on a temporary basis, he aimed to be in a strong position as a cash buyer and pounce on a desirable property as soon as it came on the market.

On that crisp autumn morning, having only just moved out, Matthew returned to Langdales with mixed emotions. While waiting for Rupert, who was several minutes late, he did not wander mournfully – like Madame Ranyevskaya in *The Cherry Orchard* – as he had intended; now that Langdales had ceased to be his property, his mind-set had altered. He had no desire to stay in it for longer than he had to, and anxious to disassociate himself from the over-familiar interior, he took himself off into the garden.

Hearing Rupert's car pull up at the front at last, he walked briskly to the porch and was quick to beckon him inside. He pretended not to notice the left-hand drive Bentley. What a pity it was white; it smacked too much of wedding limousine. Neither its size nor its colour were suited to the narrow lanes and the ample rainfall.

Looking slightly disappointed, because the car had not been remarked upon, Rupert greeted Matthew in the echoing entrance hall, glanced around like an actor demonstrating he is in new surroundings, and shivered. The house was chilling down fast. It was warmer on the terrace, so they perched on a couple of rickety garden chairs rejected as too flimsy to take, and gazed at the last fiery yellows and blues in the border.

Although the electricity had not been disconnected, Rupert had brought a flask with him, and they were soon cupping foul-tasting instant coffees in their hands. Matthew tossed the keys to Rupert with a nonchalant air. (The spare sets remained in the key cupboard.)

'I hope that you'll be very happy,' said Matthew, not without a struggle.

'I'm looking forward to starting again.'

Matthew wondered how many times this had happened, but kept it to himself. 'In *some* ways, James is a desirable catch.'

'Implying that in others he falls short of the mark? But he is far more than just his face and figure.'

'Which, unless he becomes like Dorian Gray, will wither and age.'

Unheeding, Rupert rattled on. 'Great career prospects.'

'If a trifle hard-edged?'

'Large family, teeming with nephews and nieces.'

'Hopefully not too energetic for you? I'm sure you'll enjoy getting to know each and every one of them. In due course.'

'Stop undermining me, because you won't succeed.'

An uncomfortable silence followed, during which they lifted their faces to enjoy the sun; Matthew was reluctant to break it. A breeze wafted across the back of the house, and clouds were building up. He would make his visit short, but before he finally drove off, he wanted to clarify things.

Matthew had long felt that men did not excel at sharing their feelings, and said quickly, 'You've added an extra dimension to my life, and I'm so grateful for that.' Easy with each other once more, they both said nothing for a while, until he found himself murmuring huskily, 'You won't drop me in a hurry again, will you?'

Rupert's eyes were unnaturally moist. 'I wasn't the one who disappeared last time, remember?'

'Will I never be allowed to forget that?'

Closer than they had been for half their lives, he plucked up courage to rest his hand on Rupert's. He had intended a gesture of friendship, but there was little doubt that Rupert experienced a frisson of excitement, even if he did recoil in mock horror. The atmosphere changed when Rupert sneaked a look out of the corner of his eye that could only mean one thing. Matthew withdrew his hand and shuddered.

'A moment ago,' said Rupert, rather too casually, 'you were resting your hand on mine.'

'What of it?'

Rupert smiled condescendingly, and shook his head. 'You realise you are in denial?'

'I don't know what you're talking about.'

'I think you do, dear boy.' He smiled lecherously. 'One little action betrays the fact that you've never got over me.'

'Isn't it the other way round?'

'Eh?' Rupert mulled this over. 'You flatter yourself.'

'No more than you.'

Rupert became less superficial, and, perhaps for the first time, was being honest with Matthew. 'All right, I grant you that some, er, affection on my side persists, but for me, it's more than that.'

'In what way?'

'Because it's proving to be a bond that is not easily broken.'

This was stirring news, and he was at a loss to know how to deflect him. 'Young and foolish perhaps, but we went through a great deal at an impressionable age...' Matthew's coffee was still warm, but he longed to escape.

'You know how keen I am on seizing the moment?' Tensing slightly at the salacious grin, Matthew did not reply. 'As we're all alone, with not the remotest possibility of being interrupted.' Closing his eyes, Matthew hoped that it would soon be over. 'I'm sure we still like, maybe – deep down – even *love* each other, although we're too scared to admit it.'

'You've foxed me. A moment ago you indicated that James was the one.'

Rupert winked lasciviously. 'I haven't ruled him out by any means, but how about it?'

Matthew looked askance at him. 'In *my* house?'

'*My* house now. It will no doubt be chilly but I could soon warm you up. Does your mean-spirited expression imply you would be up for it in less austere surroundings?'

He stood up. 'I wish I knew what went on in that goatish mind of yours. Incidentally, were you lewdly planning a one-off, or do you see yourself two-timing James over a prolonged period?' Rupert blushed. 'You won't live so licentiously with James, surely? Make no mistake. Whatever debauchery it is you're counting on, I'm having none of it.'

'You need to save yourself for Squirrel, I suppose.'

'What is there left, without trust?'

Rupert covered a yawn with the back of his hand. 'You have said quite enough for one morning, dear boy. I'm not sure I can cope with any more lectures.'

'Could you do me a favour, Rupert?' He nodded, but his eyes were glazed. 'Seeing as you're making a fresh start here, will you agree never to speak of this conversation to anyone? It would only get twisted in the telling.' Rupert drew his lips into a thin line. 'And may

I perhaps be permitted to ask *you* a question, an echo of something you once asked me?' Rupert replied with an insolent nod. 'What will you do when James is bald and toothless?'

'Matthew! The gleam in your eyes implies we won't make it that far? If he loses his looks, he should at least remain distinguished.' The wind had more of an edge to it now, and he shivered. 'But what if the question were reversed? If James gets beyond seventy, I'll be over ninety, or no longer here.' He covered his face with his hands. 'Something I dare not contemplate.'

Deeming that it would be unwise to prolong this further, Matthew went inside to fetch the maintenance folder. Having proffered practical information about the house and its idiosyncrasies, and knowing full well that Rupert would remember very little of it, Matthew was now intent on a speedy final exit.

When it came to parting, he was surprised by the strength in Rupert's hug, but it sustained him during those difficult seconds hurrying to the car. Gathering himself together, he blew his nose, but made a point of not looking back at the house, already shadowed by a forbidding cloud. In spite of his best intentions, he spotted Rupert in the rear-view mirror. Framed by the porch, he was waving frantically, while Matthew set off with funereal caution. Struggling to see straight did not prevent him from noticing the gaping tear in the oak tree as he passed it.

Matthew had still not been in touch with Tom, until something catapulted him out of his inertia. (His hands were full with the B and B up to then, and he had been packing during any free time.) The trigger involved a property newly on the market that he had driven past countless times, located a couple of miles or so from La Boutique Fantasque: a traditional white cottage seemingly sagging under the weight of clematis and honeysuckle.

Following in the wake of the burbling estate agent, he liked most of what he saw. Granted, it could do with a new kitchen and bathroom, but the garden had been planted up by Dorian and would no doubt be a huge draw for Tom. Hadn't Eleanor called it *"a poem"*? Dorian had just put it up for sale, and Matthew planned to put in an immediate offer, safe in the knowledge that if he ended up there alone, it would not overwhelm him.

As soon as he could escape Matthew hurried back home, made himself some tea, and after an hour or so of self-torture plucked up the courage to phone Tom. He had to endure a slightly strained conversation to begin with. Tom was guarded, but listened patiently to all the virtues that Matthew pointed out regarding the cottage. However, Matthew could sense him squirming over his invitation to dinner at the Birthwaite the following Saturday.

Yet he was clearly intrigued to hear the full story; there was the promise of having plenty to catch up on, including Rupert's possibly ill-starred liaison with James. And there would be more good news: during their chat, Matthew gleaned that Tom was enjoying working for Jane and Clare. It was only when he had finished the call that Matthew realised that the Birthwaite might not have been the most appropriate choice of venue.

Feeling the responsibilities of the host, Matthew arrived in plenty of time and headed straight for the bar. Finding a table by a window, he was soon agonising over whether Tom would turn up. Just as he was beginning to feel that he had been stood up, he saw Tom waving as he approached the entrance. He watched him tense, waver slightly, and pick up his pace again. Tom was picking his way around various cumbersome sofas and armchairs in the cavernous lobby – panelling, baronial wrought-iron chandeliers, hunting scene canvases too vast for a domestic setting, and far too many antlers – when Matthew greeted him.

Standing beside each other in the double doorway to the dining room while waiting to be seated, and relieved not to be picking up on any awkwardness, Matthew nudged Tom, who was also cringing. The room was over-bright with overhead lighting, wall lamps, yellow chrysanthemums and candles. However, they were soon shielded from the glare by the shadow of the tall, cadaverous head waiter who had seated them at a corner table secreted in an alcove. The cruet was dusty, he noticed. It was soon apparent that Matthew's timing was out. The middle-aged or elderly diners were either chewing deliberately or had moved onto puddings. Matthew could not remember the last time he had seen a dessert trolley being wheeled between the tables.

When they had made their safe, unimaginative choices from the menu, Matthew went into humorous – although potentially tactless – detail about the burgeoning entanglement between Rupert and James, and finished by looking at Tom expectantly.

A shadow crossed his face. 'I'm not really surprised.'

'I haven't given it a huge amount of thought, but Rupert is convinced it will work, and — you never know — James may have found whatever it was he was seeking.'

'You believe me now?' asked Tom, his fair hair golden in the candle-light.

Matthew looked him in the eye. 'Yes, but not only do I believe you — I trust you. In my defence, the steamy hot-house atmosphere of the production did not help. James chasing you was more believable than the play. At the time, it seemed so vividly real, with everything falling so swiftly into place – the hero-worship of him – '

Tom grinned. 'And the showers we were supposed to have shared?' It sounded as if he might be thawing.

'I have so many questions. Why did you leave?'

'I had to bring you to your senses.'

'And did it work?'

'Shall we politely describe this as a work in progress? After all, would I be sitting here now if I felt the situation was hopeless?'

'I weep when I look back at what I put you through. I'm so sorry, but please, Tom, can you forgive me?' Tom smiled tentatively, glanced at the other couples hunched in silence over their plates, and located Matthew's hand under the table. He was glad of it. 'Looking back on it, if we had not met James, we could never have reached this new stage in our relationship.'

'It seems a roundabout way of going about things, if ever there was one?' asked Tom.

Mindful that some of the guests may be straining to hear, he lowered his voice. 'A circuitous route, I admit, and not one I would wish to dwell on —' He felt himself welling up. 'I'm so glad you've struck out on your own with Jane and Clare, but what made you come back?'

'For the record, my parents warned me against it, and told me I should have nothing whatever to do with you. Just at this moment, I feel guilty.'

Perhaps he had read too much into Tom's having returned of his own free will. Wanting to stroke his cheek, Matthew searched his face. 'Dare I ask if it was because of me that you returned?'

'It's early days, so let's not "chase rainbows". You know I've lived up here most of my adult life. I was missing it. And the *peace*, compared to living with my parents.'

He tried to sound casual. 'So, sitting here as we are, do you think I might be in with a chance?' (This did not come out as Matthew had intended.)

Tom was playing with his napkin, and murmured, 'This is not a game of chance. You don't get it, do you? Before we could even think of getting back together, some changes would have to be outlined. Things would be different, and you'd need to accept that. I'm afraid I can't promise you that big reunion scene tonight, if that's what you're banking on.'

'Forgive me, that was the last – '

'You know you put me through way too much?' Matthew struggled to ignore the dull thud within. 'I'm ashamed of how immature I was. I had actually come to believe I was totally dependent on you, but life has since proved otherwise.'

Feeling anything but, Matthew affected joviality. (Where was that champagne he had pre-ordered? He had planned to be proposing a toast to them both by now, but felt they were in danger of capsizing.) He looked directly at Tom. 'So where do we go next?'

'Eleanor has offered me Rupert's cottage until Easter. She is happy just to have the place aired.'

'Perfect.' Matthew saw Dorian's cottage sliding out of his reach as a home for them both.

'She's told me that I ought to be setting up on my own.' Mouth dry, Matthew was concentrating on the chrysanthemums jammed into the vase. 'Looking back, Langdales was like a dream, and I was lucky to share it with you, but it was so isolated. I'm now thinking Kendal might be less…'

'Rarefied?'

'People more my own age, perhaps.'

'Have you considered Lancaster?' asked Matthew, regretting this instantly.

'Possibly, but I've not finished yet, and this is important. You know what we both meant to each other, but there are things I've witnessed that I wish I hadn't.'

He dared not look at Tom. 'I see. Tell me, why did you have to leave so suddenly?'

'You can't have forgotten how fraught things were? I'd had enough.'

'If only you had not been so impetuous.'

'Weren't we were both guilty of that?'

They had to break off when the deferential head waiter returned with the champagne. While presenting the half-bottle of "house", he caught Matthew's eye with the well-honed icy look that signified that he had been too cheap. Having reduced them to an uncomfortable silence, and with white napkin to hand, he made a big deal of popping the cork, over-filled their glasses and stalked off with the utmost gravity. When he was out of ear-shot they dissolved, and proposed a toast to each other before getting down to practicalities. Meanwhile, their fellow diners had either smiled or grimaced at the disruption.

'It wasn't very decent of you to…'

'I'm sorry, Tom,' said Matthew, hoping no one could overhear them.

'I meant, what you did to Rupert, all those years ago.'

Matthew raised a hand to his brow. 'I wonder if the day will come when I'm not to be tormented by my ancient misdemeanours?'

'And that ill-founded jealousy and mistrust?'

'Yes, all right.'

'I feel quite sick when I look back on it.'

'Well, don't spoil your appetite. I'm sorry.'

Tom looked at him fondly. 'I still think about you.'

'That means a great deal to me, you must know that.'

'Although I don't feel quite the same as I once did.'

'Best to be under no illusions.'

'I'm not sure I'm ready for total forgiveness yet. It's too soon.'

'I'm sure you're right, but you do realise how much I've missed you? The luxuriousness of you stretched out next to me…although I'm beginning to forget even that.'

'And who knows, we might have reached a point where we're incapable of getting back to where we once were?'

'That frightens me, too.'

Tom placed his hands neatly on the table in front of him 'We need a trial period.'

'Not another one?'

'One approach might be to work at getting to know each other again, but in our separate homes? Maybe another festival might do the trick?'

'That seems a long time to wait.' He drained his glass.

'Have you heard what the next production is, by any chance?' asked Tom, sipping delicately.

'It's too early for them to have decided. You know that. Besides, I've distanced myself from that particular circus for the present. Talking of WAFT, one thing still haunts me. The night Eleanor announced she was dropping out, the Wednesday, I think it was, James returned towards the end of the interval, with his hair ruffled and his shirt buttoned up unevenly. Eleanor was convinced you had spent the interval with him.' He knew he had said too much, but found himself staring at Tom's stony face. He wished he had not mentioned it.

'How can we move forward if you are constantly looking back? I don't know what you're talking about. Now, tell me, where are you living?'

'James's flat became available.'

Tom sat up. 'No bad vibes, I hope?'

'Not really. It's all I need, until…*if* anything happens, and it's convenient.'

'Have you been in touch with Eleanor?'

A handsome young minion breezed across the room and over-filled Matthew's glass; fast-popping bubbles winked and popped on the white damask. Shaking his head, Matthew waved the waiter away and dabbed the cloth with his napkin.

Tom looked down. 'That's probably because I'm there.'

'Don't worry about that, Tom. It doesn't affect me as much as you'd think. You see, I've only been there three or four days. The intention was to unpack before I lost my momentum, but I've taken to people-watching.'

'That's not like you.'

'Such a lot going on. I can happily lose an hour gazing out of the window. And the radio is permanently on. Even though it means going alone, I can always drive down to the cinema. If I plump for that cottage – you never know – I *might* get a little dog.'

When Tom started to laugh, the hushed atmosphere intensified. 'I hadn't realised that things were that desperate. I hope it likes Callas. They have very acute hearing.' Now that he was smiling to himself, the atmosphere between them lifted. 'When did you become so mad about Windermere?'

'To be honest, I'm not as wild about it as I used to be, compared to what we had at Langdales, but those days have gone. I had to make a decision.'

It was galling to think that Tom was presently basking at Spinnakers and would soon be tucked up for the winter in Eleanor's well-appointed holiday let.

'By the way, I looked up that cottage you mentioned,' said Tom.

'Impressive, don't you think?'

'The garden will be even better next year, I imagine.'

'No doubt over-filled with plants from the garden centre he worked in?'

'You must invite me over in the spring.' Tom looked at him coyly.

'You mean I have to wait?'

'Have you managed to forgive Eleanor for spoiling Rupert's time here, or is that out of the question?'

'Despite my best intentions, I can never fall out with Eleanor for long.' Matthew chuckled. 'Even though she's not in touch as often, we're bound together for the long haul. It's still going well with Dorian?'

'From what I hear.' Tom winked, and lowered his voice. 'Their bedroom is two doors from mine.'

Before Matthew could think of a suitable response, their twice-baked soufflés appeared, which kick-started a change of subject. The service remained slower than ever, but each course — when it eventually arrived — was a study in perfection. Tom drank sparingly; Matthew, knowing he would need a few drinks to get him through dinner, had booked a taxi back to Windermere. The conversation began to run on familiar lines, but in some ways it was something of a relief by the time it was over. Even so, Matthew concluded that it had been a promising new beginning. He had tried not to wince at the bill; they were soon shaking hands rather formally, yet there was no promise of a repeat performance from either side.

Next day (day five in Windermere for Matthew, although it seemed longer) was typically autumnal; rain and gusty winds. Without a routine, he was struggling to adjust; it felt peculiar not having to rise at a set hour to make breakfast. How had he found himself renting a one-bedroom flat? He went over his finances; there would be enough to provide him with an investment income after he had put in an offer on that cottage. After a few hours of feeling cramped and unfulfilled, and noticing a gap in the rain, he could bear it no longer. He must take the air. Springing up from the sofa, he shouldered into his coat and attempted a walk, in spite of the slippery pavements and soggy leaves. Feeling as though he had aged since Tom had left, he was taking extra care.

Although the rain had eased, the wind threw him against the street front door before he had his gloves on. He extricated his glove from a puddle and clung to the drain-pipe for a moment to steady himself. Making for the most sheltered side road, he was not sure why he had come out with no errands, but turned up his collar and set himself a brisk pace. After a minute or two his breathing slowed and although lacking a destination, he just kept on walking.

A couple of streets later, Rupert popped up in his head. Goose-pimples pricked his skin. The thought of the once adored golden-haired prodigy prostituting himself in *Jubilee Way* was not to be borne, and his head soon became crowded with thoughts of what might have been. A sudden gust took him off-guard – almost knocked him over – and forced him to turn around. He slunk back in the direction of the flat.

Yet his mind continued to chase after *Jubilee Way*. That evening, with more time on his hands than he knew what to do with, he could resist no longer. (As he had still not unpacked properly, or tidied up, it took a while to locate the remote.) It felt peculiar watching Rupert on television, but the few minutes he endured told him more than enough. Masquerading as a mean-spirited camp hairdresser, unhappy in his own skin, Rupert's rather seedy role was typically one-dimensional and required little more than camp eye-rolling, spitting out acid remarks and shrivelling the cast with malevolent glares. Although the role was beneath him, Matthew had noticed that Rupert had been flagged up by the television pages as giving a creditable comic turn.

So soporific was the soap when not enlivened by Rupert, that he had nodded off within minutes, and only came to when the sound of his mobile ringing bit into his nap: *Eleanor*. He flicked off the yakking television.

'Matthew, I need to ask you a favour.' No preliminaries, he noted, but she was often like that, so he let her wait. 'You're very quiet?'

'Don't I have good reason to be? Not heard from you for a while. Come on, then. Out with it.' He pressed the phone closer to his ear.

'It's been brought to my attention,' she said, grandly, 'that you've not renewed your WAFT sub.'

'Haven't I earned a year off?'

'Nonsense! Does the name Andrew Crocker-Harris mean anything to you?'

Despite remaining drowsy, he concentrated hard. 'Don't tell me. Rattigan? Not *The Winslow Boy*? No, it's *The Browning Version*, isn't it?'

'Well done! We were wondering whether you would like to play Andrew?'

He groaned inwardly. 'We?'

Her words came tumbling out. 'Tom and I. As it happens, we've been requested to head a new plays selection and casting committee. Look, if you play Andrew – which, to remind you, is the lead – we could play Millie and Frank. Strong play. I've just re-read it.'

'Yes, bits of it stay with you.'

'The love triangle works well, and – '

Matthew already knew his decision. 'Spare me the detail.'

'Millie's well within my range. And, as if by some miracle, our ages would fit!'

'For a change. And how does James fit in? I seem to recall a minor role of a young schoolmaster replacing...'

She chuckled, and then burbled on. 'He has resigned. Apparently, James has big plans for Langdales, putting it on a commercial footing again, but giving the whole place an executive overhaul – and goodness knows it needed it – to make it *far* more deluxe.'

'I feel crushed.'

'He is planning select weddings for next year in the house, with perhaps the occasional marquee. Honeymoon suite, superior guest rooms, and all that goes with it, but no guests without a wedding, so they won't be on a treadmill like you were.'

'And they can press that ancient Bentley into service,' said Matthew absent-mindedly, for he was swiftly coming round to the idea of rejoining WAFT, and winning Tom back. 'Don't tell me they are crowding into our old flat if they have a wedding?'

She chose to ignore that. 'He's going to play Stanley.'

'Who is?'

'James, of course.'

'Dorian has the better shoulders.'

'Sadly he has no truck with acting, but next spring James will be playing opposite Felicity's Blanche Dubois in *Streetcar* for the Woodside Players.'

Matthew smiled to himself. 'That sounds like an excess of timber. What was that old catch-phrase? "Wood" by name and wooden by nature?'

'We must sit on the front row and put them off. Listen to her mangle the southern accent.'

'Try and be magnanimous, for once.'

'A bit more of the what was it? *"The kindness of strangers"*? Perhaps you're right.'

'Just to be clear, I wouldn't...I would have no intention of turning down Crocker-Harris, as long as you think—'

'Tom's very keen. Rehearsals might just bring you two back

together.'

'He's still on his own?'

'And still here. As you know, I'm not one to gossip, but I know for a fact he hasn't found anybody. After all, I'd soon find out if he had.'

Matthew had no intention of seeking a partner elsewhere, and remained uncertain as to how he would cope if Tom was dating someone his own age. 'You say he's all right?'

'*Eating* heartily, at any rate. You've helped him grow up. Even so...'

'Yes?'

'I've been observing him. From what he told me the other day, he's beginning to take stock of his new life, and I can already see cracks.'

'Do you think I might be – ?'

'He may come to value what he's surrendered, and start remembering the good times with you. As I maintained.'

'Did you? *The Browning Version* is his brainwave I take it?'

'You know me, always happy to fall in with the ideas of others.'

Matthew allowed her to rattle on, while he enjoyed the glow running through him, and a sense of longed-for peace. To be wanted, even by WAFT, meant a great deal.

'But you didn't ring me just to discuss WAFT?' he enquired.

'You're being unusually perspicacious.'

'Let's get it over with.'

'I need to ask you that favour, and as a thank you, I wish to give you credit for something, or rather *about* a particular person.'

He sat up straight. 'Unusual, but not unknown.'

'It concerns Dorian.'

'You don't say.'

'He does have something of a past.'

'Didn't I keep telling you?'

'Yes, you were irritatingly insistent on that score, but you needn't sound quite so censorious.'

He chuckled. 'Usually your domain.'

'It's as if we were back on stage.'

He smiled to himself. 'If only.'

'Dorian felt that – before he and I go any further – '

'He's not proposing *marriage*?'

'Your habit of constantly interrupting me is beginning to grate.' She waited. 'Do you want me to finish the story or not?'

'Sorry.'

'His conscience, for want of a better word, told him he ought to tidy up a few loose ends.'

'You mean he has one?'

'I don't mind telling *you* that he had one or two debts to pay, but not a word to anyone.'

'Large or small?'

'I'm not prepared to say.'

'Which no doubt you have settled for him?'

'That's what I'm here for.'

'How did he come to have that cottage?'

'A loan from his parents – '

'Thrilled to get him off their hands, I suppose?'

'And with a steady job supervising at the garden centre, he had managed to talk his way into a mortgage – '

'Before he changed his mind *again* and stuck his claws into you.'

'Stop it, Matthew.'

'You must agree that he's plotted all this from the outset?'

'I agree to nothing of the sort. True, he doesn't have a great deal behind him.'

'You realise that he won't be able to contribute anything like what it costs to run your place?'

'He doesn't need to.'

'That's something you might have to come to terms with.'

She hesitated. 'I have more than enough to keep us both.'

'Surely you don't want a kept man?'

'Isn't that what Tom was in danger of becoming?' Stunned for a moment, Matthew did not feel up to making an adequate response. 'After a season of freelance work, Dorian is more than ready to chuck it in, and make a fresh – '

'Do be careful, Eleanor.'

'If you'll let me finish, Jane and Clare are going all out for extending their business.'

'No doubt once they've flogged everybody senseless, they'll retire early with a handsome profit.'

'I think you're being a trifle unfair, especially as they're still far too young to think of retiring.'

'I wouldn't put it past them.'

'Try and be a little more charitable,' she said, in the same unwavering tone. 'As you may recall, Dorian had more than enough experience at the garden centre. And other centres, down south, he tells me.'

'If he's to be believed.'

'I'm convinced that only good can come of this.'

'Clearly I need to be more attentive.'

'And less flippant,' she told him, sternly. 'In short, they want to branch out with a garden centre on that land attached to La Boutique Fantasque. They assume that Dorian will be sufficiently enterprising to take over.'

'All very laudable, but won't it be getting a tad overcrowded with people we know?'

'You might do worse than think about joining them. Becoming a meeter and greeter could never be your forté, but perhaps pushing trolleys might do?'

'Please don't tell me that they already have permission to expand, and will be throwing open the doors next spring?'

'More than likely, but Dorian will be employed before then.'

'Naturally. As long as he doesn't order any *spiky* plants, he should be fine. Or perhaps that could be *your* domain?'

'I have every confidence in him.'

'Even though nothing seems to have worked out for him so far?'

'Unless you include his meeting me?' she asked.

'That certainly made job security somewhat academic.'

'I wish you could lose that edge to your voice.'

'Well, on a more positive note, when can we look forward to you becoming Mrs Dorian Manners – or should I say – Mrs Eleanor Manners?'

'I was just coming to that. Father's no longer up to it, and although I know you've had difficulty with weddings in the past, would it be desperately ageing for you to give me away?'

'Your parents are struggling to approve?'

'You really have become incredibly tiresome since Tom left.'

'So that's the favour you're phoning up about? I'd rather be the best man.'

'That position is already spoken for.'

He tutted. 'I might have known.'

'I can't help it that Dorian and Tom are mingling so satisfactorily.'

'In spite of your initial misgivings?'

'They've become the best of friends.'

Matthew cleared his throat. 'It was obvious that Dorian had a soft spot for him.'

She came out with a whinnying laugh that he did not like the sound of. 'What can you be implying?'

'Forget it. So, Tom will be playing best man, will he? Tell me, do you think he and I will ever be able to claw back what we've chucked away?'

'I don't see why not. After all, I've seen how keen he is to act with you again. Give Tom time. I'm sure he'd love to make a go of it.'

'As long as I don't mind waiting, is that it? Before you go, don't forget I'll always be there for you. And Dorian, too.'

'I won't. So, is that everything settled?' she enquired. He could sense that she was warming to this renewal of friendship.

'Have it soon, don't you think?' He could not cope with Langdales next summer, and hoped for any location rather than that. 'In case he becomes over-familiar with your less easily assimilated personality traits?'

He could feel the temperature plummet. 'I'm not quite sure how to take that, Matthew.'

'Merely an observation.'

'I see. You're indicating a Christmas wedding?'

'Yes, before Dorian gets too involved with his career in the spring.' He paused. 'I can visualise you in scarlet and gold more easily than I can in white.'

She laughed. 'Like a bauble? Perhaps I could have my hair spangled with silver?'

'Isn't it already?'

'I may surprise you and go blonder than our mutual friend.'

'And if you could bear it, they might hire you the Bentley.'

'That's all very well, but it's not really *me*.'

They chirruped away happily about potential wedding breakfast venues, mentioning the *Birthwaite* so frequently that it felt like old times.

Next morning he rose at first light, hastily prepared a packed lunch, and drove the short distance to Ambleside. Some goal that Tom had mentioned – but never managed to achieve – had swelled in his memory. It promised to be a crisp, autumnal day, and therefore appropriate for walking the Fairfield Horseshoe. He might see life in perspective from almost three thousand feet above sea level.